continued . . .

"An adrenaline-pumping science fiction thriller that keeps readers' interest from the onset and never decelerates until the final confrontation . . . Jeff Carlson proves he is a magnificent world builder and destroyer as he writes a mesmerizing tale of science and technology going astray. Riveting and frightening, the future is very dark in Carlson's world, but a few lights give hope that humanity will survive this ordeal with a new harmony."

—*SFRevu*

"Intense. Carlson has reinforced what I admired about him in *Plague Year*, conveying his story and themes with as much authenticity and emotional truth as possible. Just consider yourself warned. This one is a literary level-four hot zone."

—*SF Reviews.net*

"Carlson knows what he's doing, making us feel the terror, pain, exhaustion, frustration, and triumph of his characters . . . It's a good book, telling a good story, and the speculation is excellent."

—*SFScope*

"Carlson's nightmarish landscape presents a chilling albeit believable picture of a postapocalyptic world devastated by a nanotech plague. *Plague War* is the second of his trilogy, but it can still be enjoyed as a stand-alone. The carefully crafted plot is a mix of sci-fi, military adventure, and political intrigue. Strong, dynamic characters bring the story to a conclusion you won't see coming."

—*Romantic Times*

Praise for
PLAGUE YEAR

"An epic of apocalyptic fiction: harrowing, heartfelt, and rock-hard realistic. A cautionary tale. Not to be missed."

—James Rollins, *New York Times* bestselling author of *Altar of Eden*

"A grim and fascinating new twist on the postholocaust story, unlike anything I've read before."

—Kevin J. Anderson, *New York Times* bestselling coauthor of *The Winds of Dune continued . . .*

"Jeff Carlson is a terrific writer, and *Plague Year* is a marvelous book, full of memorable characters, white-knuckle scenes, and big ideas."   —Robert J. Sawyer, Hugo Award–winning author of *WWW: Wake*

"Carlson has crafted an exceptional, gripping debut that exposes the worst and best of humanity while maintaining a constant tension level that will keep the pages turning to the very end. The personal and political machinations are credible, the characters are well developed, and the climax satisfying. This apocalyptic view of nanotechnology provides plenty to think about."
—*Monsters and Critics*

"*Plague Year* is a masterful debut novel that has me putting Jeff Carlson on my must-read list without a second thought . . . Carlson's character development is meticulous, with believable characters alert to all the nuances of human behavior. Please, sir, send more!"
—*SFRevu*

"The fascination with *Plague Year* is how fast humanity becomes beasts with survival all that matters . . . exciting."
—*Midwest Book Review*

"Carlson's debut grips the reader from its opening sentence. A strong, character-driven tale . . . This book is both chilling and timely."
—*Romantic Times*

"Characters never stand still, political intrigue abounds, and the characters face almost-certain death every time they turn around. The story is good, even garnering Carlson a nomination for this year's John W. Campbell Award. *Plague Year* is a unique take on the old apocalyptic-fiction trope, full of the hard science of nanotech, and it will appeal to a broad audience. Highly entertaining."
—*Grasping for the Wind*

"One of the best postapocalyptic novels I've read. Part Michael Crichton, a little Stephen King, and a lot of good writing . . . The complexity of the plot, the full development of the characters, the science behind the nanotechnology—Carlson makes it all seem plausible and thrilling. This is a master at work, and I can't wait to read the sequel."   —Jamie Thornton, *Quiet Earth*

The Plague Year Series

And for Coach Derek —
Get into the Zone!

PLAGUE ZONE

JEFF CARLSON

John Jeff

give Ben

ACE BOOKS, NEW YORK

THE BERKLEY PUBLISHING GROUP
Published by the Penguin Group
Penguin Group (USA) Inc.
375 Hudson Street, New York, New York 10014, USA

Penguin Group (Canada), 90 Eglinton Avenue East, Suite 700, Toronto, Ontario M4P 2Y3, Canada
(a division of Pearson Penguin Canada Inc.)
Penguin Books Ltd., 80 Strand, London WC2R 0RL, England
Penguin Group Ireland, 25 St. Stephen's Green, Dublin 2, Ireland (a division of Penguin Books Ltd.)
Penguin Group (Australia), 250 Camberwell Road, Camberwell, Victoria 3124, Australia
(a division of Pearson Australia Group Pty. Ltd.)
Penguin Books India Pvt. Ltd., 11 Community Centre, Panchsheel Park, New Delhi—110 017, India
Penguin Group (NZ), 67 Apollo Drive, Rosedale, North Shore 0632, New Zealand
(a division of Pearson New Zealand Ltd.)
Penguin Books (South Africa) (Pty.) Ltd., 24 Sturdee Avenue, Rosebank, Johannesburg 2196,
South Africa

Penguin Books Ltd., Registered Offices: 80 Strand, London WC2R 0RL, England

This is a work of fiction. Names, characters, places, and incidents either are the product of the author's imagination or are used fictitiously, and any resemblance to actual persons, living or dead, business establishments, events, or locales is entirely coincidental. The publisher does not have any control over and does not assume any responsibility for author or third-party websites or their content.

PLAGUE ZONE

An Ace Book / published by arrangement with the author

PRINTING HISTORY
Ace mass-market edition / December 2009

Copyright © 2009 by Jeff Carlson.
Maps by Meghan Mahler.
Cover art by Eric Williams.
Cover design by Judith Lagerman.
Interior text design by Laura K. Corless.

ISBN: 978-0-441-01799-7

ACE
Ace Books are published by The Berkley Publishing Group,
a division of Penguin Group (USA) Inc.,
375 Hudson Street, New York, New York 10014.
ACE and the "A" design are trademarks of Penguin Group (USA) Inc.

PRINTED IN THE UNITED STATES OF AMERICA

10 9 8 7 6 5 4 3 2 1

This book is for my father,
Gus Carlson,
who taught me to read.

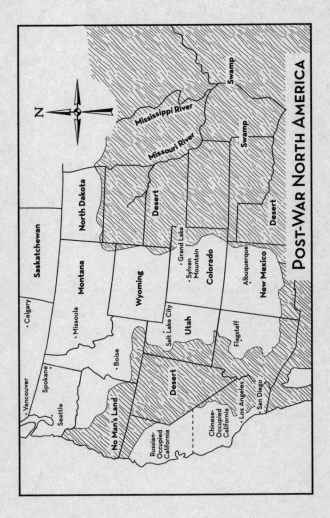

Post-War North America

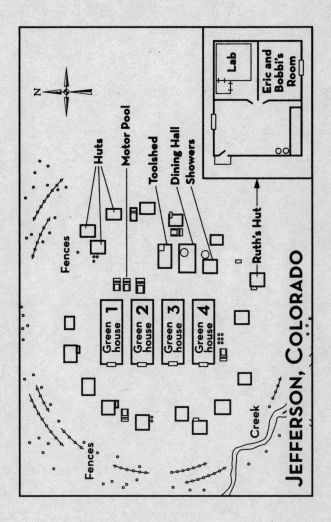

Huts

Motor Pool

Toolshed

Dining Hall

Showers

Lab

Eric and Bobbi's Room

Ruth's Hut

Fences

Green house 1

Green house 2

Green house 3

Green house 4

Fences

Creek

JEFFERSON, COLORADO

1

Cam Najarro pushed into the fallen greenhouse with one arm, struggling through the torn sheets of plastic. In his other hand he held his flamethrower down against his leg, the blue fire in its muzzle guttering near the back of his knee. He didn't want to start a blaze if he could avoid it, so he used his body like a shield, hiding the weapon as he waded into the tangled, slumping mess.

The fuel tanks on his back snagged in the plastic. Then he encountered a broken two-by-four and had to duck, awkwardly protecting the nozzle of the gun against his belly.

The plastic was clear in single layers—but when the greenhouse collapsed, its roof and walls had twisted into knots. Worse, the sunset was fading. Cam wore a flashlight on his belt, but he'd found that the light only reflected in the plastic, blinding him. He could see better in the shadows.

The greenhouse smelled like fresh earth and a dank, more humid scent. Everywhere the concrete floor was speckled with ants and locusts. Some were dead. Others jittered and flexed, trapped in the folds of plastic all around him.

His headset crackled in his ear. "What's it look like?" Allison asked.

"It's quiet," he said.

"I've got a bad feeling, Cam."

He smiled. "Don't you always?"

"Get out. Please."

"No. Eric might still be alive. What if he's unconscious?" Cam reached into another curtain of plastic, but he could barely move its weight. He knelt and tried to squeeze past. On his right, the way was blocked by a long wooden planter, its soil blasted over the floor. Cam pushed left instead, crawling on one hand and both knees.

He stopped. There was a red-colored drift on the floor where the crushed ants were particularly dense. Cam brought up his weapon before he continued forward, wanting to be sure these ants were casualties, not a new invasion. He saw immature queens and winged males mixed with worker drones. By necessity, every man and woman on the planet had become a practicing entomologist, and Cam had a very healthy fear of these insects. The ants were both delicate and powerful. Their fragile legs and mandibles were capable of incredible force, as witnessed by the destruction around him.

He put his boot down, crunching the red bodies. "I think I know where they came in," he said. Each word echoed in the silence. Beyond the greenhouse, he could hear the wind and people shouting, and he heard those voices more clearly when Allison answered on the radio.

"Just leave it alone," she said. "It doesn't matter."

But it mattered to him. He'd built Greenhouse 3 with his own hands, and now one of his friends was missing inside.

Cam brushed at the ants with his glove, trying to make sense of the swarm's direction. He found his clue against another ravaged planter. There was a hairline crack in the floor where they'd bolted the planter's sides to the concrete pad, which was only inches thick. That hadn't been enough. One end of the crack was now a ragged hole. The ant colony had scratched through with inhuman patience and strength.

Less than an hour ago, ten thousand fire ants had billowed into the greenhouse, surging through the protected area like a cyclone. The weight of the frantic people inside was enough to topple one wall. Then someone crashed against a support beam. The ants were more interested in the corn and tomato plants, but still they stung and bit. Three people made it out.

Eric Goodrich was the only one who hadn't emerged through the two doors that served as an airlock, sealing off the sweet, moist plants inside from the world of the machine plague.

The locusts came after the plastic had ripped. Like the fire ants, the black-spotted desert locusts were nonnative to Colorado, but they were adaptable and opportunistic, filling the gaps in the ecology like so many other species. The locusts were also suicidally ravenous, expending at least as much energy as they gained. They suffered huge losses just to attack the crops and their rival insects, allowing their own numbers to be decimated even as their dead provided more food for the surviving ants.

Cam would have burned them all if he could. "The ants came from underneath," he said.

"It doesn't matter!" Allison was impatient now, even rude. She could be combative when she was worried. "Just get out of there," she said. "We can salvage things in the morning."

Eric might still be alive, Cam thought, but he didn't want to argue. He simply rose into a clear space and kept walking through the dark maze of lumber and plastic.

He moved with a limp. His hands were bad, too, already cramping on the nozzle of his weapon. Old injuries. There were few people who didn't bear some mark of the machine plague or the wars that followed, but Cam Najarro had faced any number of hard choices. Sometimes he marveled that he was alive at all. He wanted to share his good fortune.

"Eric?" he called, forgetting to turn off his headset.

"Goddamn it," Allison said. "He's dead. We would have heard something."

"What if it was me, Ally? You'd come in after me."

"Get out. Idiot."

Cam smiled again. Allison had softened now that she was four months pregnant, although she would have denied any change in her outlook. She was more selfish of him, more protective, which made her a better wife but not such an excellent leader. She no longer put everyone else first. *And she's probably right,* he thought, peering into the shadows. There was a shape on the floor like two bags of fertilizer . . . or was it a man?

Suddenly he clapped his hand against his cheek, killing an

ant before it could bite. Then he discovered more of the red bugs on his arm. Cam repressed a shudder, scraping his glove over his hood and his jacket sleeves. His hip was spotted with ants, too. Their stragglers and their wounded were beginning to focus on him in the swift, disturbing way of a hive mind that communicated solely through motion and scent.

"Okay, you're right," he said, looking for a way out. Unfortunately, the nearest wall of the greenhouse had rolled, creating a heavy barrier. "I'm on the north side," he said. "Can you guys cut through?"

"Turn on your light so we can see you." Allison's voice was sharp with relief, and then he heard her yelling faintly outside the greenhouse. "Over here!"

The ants were unpredictable. They were always breeding now, and they became more vicious with each short-lived generation. Cam and Eric had led "smoke" teams to poison four colonies just last week. Obviously that hadn't been enough. Maybe the area around their village would always be infested, no matter how careful they were with their garbage and other waste—but the ants' metabolism was dependent on the heat of the sun. In the cold nights of the Rockies, especially in early September, the ants went to ground until morning. Cam knew it would be safe to look for Eric's body in another hour if he could only convince himself to abandon his friend.

No, he thought. They'd served together in the Army Rangers, and dying here was a stupid way to go for a man who'd helped bring an end to World War III. It made Cam angry, so he turned back into the ruins of the greenhouse with his flashlight.

"Cam?" Allison asked. "Cam, you're moving away from us."

He was twenty-six years old. He could still be impulsive even though he was physically worn as if twice his age. Like the ants, Cam hated the cold. In the Colorado nights, his hands ached with arthritis. A badly healed knife wound rippled across his left palm, and his fingers were thick with burned tissue. His face was equally blistered, although he could hide most of this scarring with his beard. He wore his coarse black hair at shoulder-length to cover a disfigured ear.

But the bugs were here, too.

"Jesus!" Cam staggered back from the lump on the floor. The irregular shape seemed to leap up, startled by his approach. Winged ants pattered against the plastic overhead. Then they flew toward him.

Before the cloud obscured the body, Cam saw that Eric was gone. Hundreds of red worker drones crawled from the wet cavities of Eric's face, exhuming his insides through his mouth and eyes. They filled his clothes, too, writhing and bustling.

There were other cracks in the floor where columns of ants marched through eroded gray concrete and dirt. Somehow the insects had torn through. The colony was still expanding. They were insulated from the night by the greenhouse itself, glorying in their find despite the oncoming cold.

Cam destroyed them, screaming, *"Yaaaaaah!"*

The gun roared. Burning streams of fuel splashed between the low ceiling and the floor. The heat turned the plastic into melting runners. The carpet of ants shriveled and disappeared, blown away by the fire. Even the bugs at the edges of the inferno curled into dry cinders, whirling up through the air like a blizzard. The smoke was intense. Coughing, Cam reared back from the fire. Eric's body reacted, too, its muscles contracting. The corpse twisted within the blaze, arching its hips and neck as the empty gap of its mouth pulled impossibly wide.

Cam tried to shut off his weapon but the flamethrower was a clumsy thing they'd built themselves. It shot gasoline in fat, deafening blasts that weren't easily contained. He was forced to expend another two seconds of fuel, clearing the gun, and he kept the blaze on Eric's corpse rather than turning the fire away. Cremating his friend was better than hurting anyone outside.

I'm sorry, he thought. *Oh, Christ, Eric, I'm sorry . . . What am I going to tell Bobbi?*

A section of the roof fell in. As the plastic burned, it separated. A wide heap of plastic slammed into the concrete. The fiery tongues covered Eric. Another hunk of it lashed down on Cam's right, splashing his arm with drizzles of hot liquid.

The smoke was more dangerous. It was toxic. Cam was lucky that when the roof collapsed, the haze was taken away by the wind. Suddenly his breath came easier. He barely noticed, sick with adrenaline and grief.

He'd lost his flashlight in the confusion. Now it was dark except for the bubbling fire and several lights beyond the greenhouse. Cam stalked through the mess, punching his weapon against a slick hill of plastic when he couldn't get past. The night overhead had a gorgeous blue quality he'd never seen anywhere except in the Rockies, but he winced and turned his eyes down.

Then there were arms reaching for him. Four people pulled him out. Bobbi and Allison were among them, a contrast in colors. Cam's wife was blond, her long ponytail bleached almost white by the sun, whereas Bobbi Goodrich was black, with a tight, dark cap of hair.

"Are you okay?" Bobbi asked, her face gleaming with tears. Both women held knives. Their jacket sleeves were coated with strange dust from cutting at the plastic, and Cam could see that Bobbi had transferred her emotions to saving him. She knew Eric was dead.

He couldn't meet the urgent heartache in her eyes.

"Poison," he said roughly. "We're going to poison the whole fucking colony tonight."

Allison leaned into his chest and pulled Bobbi after her. Cam embraced both women. Behind them, the greenhouse smoldered. Then another man spoke up. "I'm sorry, I don't think we have enough insecticide to—"

"We'll do it with gasoline," Cam said. "I don't care. We'll pour ten gallons into every hole we can find and light 'em up."

"Let's put a team together," Allison said, moving away from him. She tugged at Bobbi and the other woman nodded, even though she was still crying. Long ago, they had all learned there was never any time to waste, and yet Cam saw the doubt in Allison's gaze.

We might not have twenty gallons in the entire village, Cam realized, walking into the night with her, but Allison didn't say it and neither did he.

They were losing the battle for the environment.

* * *

Most of the survivors called it Plague Year, restarting the calendar and forgetting everything else in human history. The machine plague killed more than five billion people and left thousands of animal species extinct. Now it was Year Three. In many ways, Earth had become a different planet. The microscopic nanotech disintegrated all warm-blooded life below ten thousand feet, where it self-destructed. What remained of the ecosystem was beyond repair. There were only reptiles, amphibians, and fish left to whittle down the exploding insect populations. Entire forests had been devoured by beetles and ants. Lakes and riverways were forever changed by erosion.

The wars that followed caused another level of damage. The plague left few habitable zones anywhere on Earth, and mammals and birds could only dip into the invisible sea for hours at a time. Without a host, the nanotech was inert. But as soon as anyone crossed below the barrier, the plague got into their lungs or their eyes or the slightest breaks in their skin, where it began to multiply.

The nearest cities and towns beneath the barrier were immediately picked clean by the survivors. After that, there was nowhere to turn except on each other. North America was lucky in that it had the massive Rockies and the smaller range of the Sierras to hold just three nations. Nevertheless, civil war divided the U.S., with Canada and Mexico ultimately siding with the rebels.

On every other continent, the fighting was far more savage and mixed. India, Pakistan, and China battled for the Himalayas. Everyone in Europe fought for the Alps. Russia took Afghanistan—but during the second winter, they lost their struggle against the Arab world. The Russians looked for any escape, offering their veteran armies to both India and China. They planned to reinforce either side in exchange for a sliver of real estate to call their own, but there was one problem. They no longer had enough aircraft or fuel to move their population.

At the same time, the American civil war began to heat up. Scientists everywhere had made great strides in nanotechnology, especially in the consolidated labs in Leadville, Colorado, where they used the plague itself to learn and experiment. Originally designed to attack malignant tissue, the *archos* tech was a versatile prototype—the cure for cancer and more.

First their science teams created a new bioweapon. Next they developed a vaccine that would protect people from the plague, but the Leadville government intended to keep this discovery for themselves. They saw an opportunity to control the only way down from the mountains, ensuring loyalty, establishing new states, leaving every enemy and undesirable to succumb to famine and war unless perhaps they agreed to come down as slaves. The prize was too great, after too much hardship.

Three of their top researchers betrayed them, stealing the only samples of the vaccine. These heroes wanted to spread the new technology freely and end the fighting. That proved to be a mistake in several ways. The vaccine became a flashpoint in the American civil war. Worse, as the vaccine spread among the pockets of survivors in California, the inoculated people became a target for a new enemy.

On the other side of the world, the Indians and the Russians had reached an agreement that also benefited the Leadville government. Leadville would help ferry the Russian Army into the Himalayas in exchange for India's research teams and equipment. Leadville was eager to stay ahead of the Chinese in the sprint for nanotech supremacy. As part of the deal, Leadville agreed to bring the wives and children of Russia's highest leaders safely into Colorado along with the Russian treasury, deepening the bond between the two nations. But there was a double cross. The Russians smuggled a doomsday bomb among their gold and museum pieces. They murdered their own families for the chance to destroy the world's only superpower, erasing Leadville from the mountains with a fifty-megaton nuclear strike. U.S. and Canadian forces across North America were blinded by the electromagnetic pulse. Hours later, the Russians flew into California, supplementing their few aircraft with the rest of the planes sent by Leadville, which they'd commandeered.

They captured most of the scattered Americans who carried the vaccine in their blood. Then they spread the immunity among their own pilots and ground troops, not only in California but on the far side of the world. The Russians became the first organized military to own the vaccine. It gave them an insurmountable advantage. They raided below the barrier everywhere, not only restocking from their motherland but also using Arab and U.S. planes, armor, fuel, and food to turn the tide against their enemies.

Even then, the Russians barely had the strength to mount an invasion, but they were committed. After bombing Leadville, their safest course was to defeat the entirety of the United States rather than retreating home, where they might have been vulnerable to reprisal missile strikes.

The Russians also shared the vaccine with the Chinese. Their new allies brought naval fleets into Los Angeles and San Diego, accelerating the push for control of North America.

Beneath the air war, Cam became instrumental in spreading the vaccine. He was one of the very few Americans who escaped California. Later, he also had a hand in developing a third new generation of nanotech. More importantly, he also joined the conspiracy that betrayed the U.S. leadership again. Their generals wanted to unleash a new contagion against the Russians and the Chinese. Instead, Cam and the other traitors forced a cease-fire. None of them wanted to see any more killing, no matter what the enemy had done.

The peace they created was an uneasy one, yet the Russians and the Chinese pulled back to the coast. Some of the invaders had already left for Europe and Asia. Presumably the rest were preparing to go, too. The war had ended fifteen months ago, but the combatants on all sides were exhausted. There were shortages of fuel, medicine, and tools. They had to deal with the bugs and widespread crop death.

America had become a frontier again. Outside of its military bases and the few civilian populations of any size, there was no law. The government was a loosely tied conglomeration of territories and city-states led by generals, farmers, engineers, and the occasional religious messiah. Many people were seasonal nomads, forever trying to stay ahead of the insects. They retreated up into the Rockies each summer and moved down again in wintertime, which made the foothills a perfect place to hide.

Among the military, Cam and Allison were still wanted criminals for their role in ending the war.

2

"We're going to starve if this keeps up," Cam said bitterly. For the moment, he was alone with Allison at the short metal doors of their toolshed. Otherwise he never would have said what he was thinking. That was the price of leadership. He was never allowed to falter, and he worried that becoming a father would only increase that pressure. A small son or daughter would need unerring guidance to survive.

Cam knelt and set his flamethrower beside a fuel can. "I don't know what else to do," he said.

"It'll be okay," Allison said, handing him a funnel.

He stared out across the dark blocks of their homes and greenhouses. Beyond the village, the vast, pyramid shapes of the Rockies were still distinct against the night. Much closer, flashlights cut and swayed through the buildings, as restless as the wind. Batteries were priceless, and only four of their lights were rechargeable—but in an emergency, all rationing efforts were forgotten despite the fact that they had no industrial base whatsoever. This village was barely more than a collection of huts, like so many other towns, most of them with patriotic names like Freedom or Defiance or Washington, celebrating their lost heritage. There were probably ten villages called Independence in Colorado alone. At least these people had been more original, naming their home Jefferson after one of America's slightly less popular founding fathers.

"We were going to have a tough winter even with all that corn," he said. "There's no way to tighten rations any more."

Allison shook her head. "We can trade with Morristown if we have to. The other greenhouses are fine, right? We'll inspect the floors, and we can rebuild the third one. We'll make the concrete thicker this time."

Cam opened the flamethrower's tanks but stopped there. Then he stood and kissed her. Allison grinned and pressed against him. Cam slipped his hands on either side of her waist. Inside her jacket, Allison was strong and lean except for her rounding belly. She smelled like soap, a good, healthy, feminine smell.

They'd reversed their normal attitudes while Cam was inside the greenhouse—her pessimistic, him upbeat—when Allison was usually more positive, even bold. They handled danger differently. Cam tended to be clearheaded in the face of a threat. It was only afterward that he sometimes invented new problems, as if, deep down, he'd long since become more comfortable with stress than with calm.

He knew he would never have been a successful voice in Jefferson without her support. She steadied him. Allison had a huge grin that could be aggressive but she also used it to make friends, like a beacon, drawing everyone to her. It didn't hurt that her willingness to work was unparalleled even now that she was in her second trimester. Allison just naturally found her way to the front of any group. She had no trouble riding herd on a township of forty-four souls, whereas Cam preferred to work in small groups on short missions like burning out the ants.

He lacked her easy calm—and he was always proud of her. He cupped his hand on her stomach. "You know you can't build a whole city by yourself," he said, teasing.

Allison flashed her teeth in the dark, obviously pleased by the joke. "We don't need a city," she said. Then she squeezed his hand and turned away, ready to get back to work.

Cam tried to share her optimism. He didn't like it that he was always angry. Allison was right. Their village was more than he'd ever expected to have, and he clung to his sense of gratitude. But he knew he would miss Eric. Worse, they could no longer trust the ground under their feet.

Their homes were built on concrete pads like the greenhouses, with few windows, because every board and nail had to be pried out of the old cities, where the bug infestations were unimaginable. Every scavenging mission was a risk, but fabricating things such as glass, hinges, or doorknobs was beyond them. They were limited to what they could find, and they were always desperate for cement, paint, and caulking. Every seam needed to be sealed. Ants, termites, spiders, and beetles were all attracted by one appetite or another. Everything was a target, even electrical lines or simple items like motor oil or tea or clothing.

It was true that the machine plague had done some good. Pests like mosquitoes and ticks were practically extinct. Even the common cold seemed to have been wiped out because there hadn't been enough people left to sustain it.

The flip side of this one benefit was that some of the long-isolated survivors were Typhoid Marys who'd developed immunities to their own nasty strains of spotted fever or herpes or a seeping black nail fungus called finger rot. Some of them had also harbored lice or fleas all this time, both of which were making a comeback. As the population mingled again, they made each other sick. Cam had heard of a measles outbreak in Wyoming, and people said most of the Idaho panhandle was under quarantine for some kind of dysentery that was killing babies.

So far, it was only insects that had been a problem in Jefferson. The fire ants had migrated up from Texas last year, while the desert locusts were thought to have spread out of the Middle East with the Russian invasion.

They lived almost like astronauts, locking away every speck of food in airtight containers such as ammunition boxes and Tupperware. Their urine, excrement, and garbage all needed to be canned until they brought it to the greenhouses, where they sun-baked their waste into safe, rich fertilizer. It was a difficult way to live. Maybe it was pointless. Cam worried that the ants might surge through someone's home, burying them in tiny, stinging bodies—and suddenly the images in his head became very personal. What if a colony erupted over Allison and their newborn child?

He finished reloading the flamethrower, then slung its tanks onto his back and looked at his wife, who'd lifted two more five-gallon cans herself. That was the extent of the gasoline in the village, except whatever was in the tanks of their few jeeps and trucks. *Thirty gallons if we're lucky,* he thought, reaching for her. "Let me carry those."

"I got it."

"You can't help us with the ants."

"I'm going to tell you how much gasoline you can use," Allison said, "and you're going to listen."

"We need to make sure we burn them all."

"Tomorrow we'll drive out to the highway and look for more fuel, but we need to be able to get there, Cam. So we save most of what we have."

If we leave any part of the colony alive, they'll tunnel somewhere else in a frenzy, he thought. The image of her disappearing beneath the ants . . . *It won't happen,* he told himself, feeling anxious and grim, and yet those same emotions were bound up in the tenderness he felt for Allison and their baby. He would die to protect them, which is why he yelled at her. "Give me the cans, Ally! There's plenty of fuel in the trucks. We'll probably siphon some of that, too."

"Goddammit," she said.

Then several people hurried toward them in the night. In addition to their flashlights, everyone carried ski goggles, masks, and canteens. Greg Estey wore another flamethrower and the rest of the group bristled with crowbars and shovels, ready to dig open the colony. One of them was Ruth.

Cam and Allison hesitated, trying to shift gears from their private argument to assuming command of the group. "You guys ready?" Cam asked, looking only at Ruth, as Allison said, "You shouldn't be here."

"I'm so sorry about Eric," Ruth said.

She was careful to keep her distance, but Cam would have recognized her silhouette even if he hadn't memorized her voice. Ruth's curly brown hair was longer than it had been during their run from California, and he knew her long nose and the slender lines of her shoulders and neck all too well. They had been lovers briefly. Ruth had also been the ring-leader in their conspiracy to end the war, using the threat of a new plague against the United States as well as the invaders.

Ruth Goldman was the last of the top nanotech researchers in America. She was the reason why Cam and Allison had invested themselves in Jefferson, making what had been a shantytown into a more permanent outpost.

"You shouldn't be here," Allison said again. "You can't be on the smoke team."

"Eric was my friend, too," Ruth said.

"We can't put you at risk," Allison said, but the undercurrent of mistrust between the two women was achingly clear. Allison protected Ruth, accepting Cam's friend for her own reasons, but the awkwardness of their triangle had never faded. If anything, Allison's pregnancy heightened that tension, introducing a new kind of jealousy to their dynamic.

Ruth was thirteen years older than Cam. He thought the age difference was partly why things hadn't worked out between them. It was also part of the allure. Ruth had not been shy at all with her body or his.

The two women were similar in many ways, not physically, but in character. Like all of the best survivors, they were both active, tough, and smart, and yet Ruth's maturity gave her an edge over the younger woman. She could usually anticipate what Allison would do and say. On the other hand, that self-possession also worked against Ruth. She'd kept her heart from Cam, wanting time to understand her feelings, whereas Allison hadn't hesitated.

Cam and Ruth had never fully consummated their interest in each other. Allison thought otherwise, because Cam had lied to his wife by implying it was over and done with. The truth was that he and Ruth were unfinished business.

"Ally's right," Cam said, emphasizing his wife's nickname as he pointed for Ruth to leave. "You can't help us."

"I knew Eric better than you." There was a dangerous tone in Ruth's voice. She backed it up by stepping closer to them.

"I just don't want you to get hurt," Cam said, but he regretted his honesty. *That was the wrong thing to say,* he thought. "Go. You're not on the team."

"Fuck you," Ruth said. "I'm staying."

"We don't have time for this," Allison said, and Greg Estey nodded with obvious relief.

"Yeah, let's get started." Greg gestured at his flamethrower and said, "This gun's full, Cam. You want to drain some of it off?"

"Absolutely. We'll soak the ground as deep as we can."

"How big is the colony?" another man asked.

"Twenty feet across, maybe more," Cam said.

Ruth scowled at them, clenching her hands on her shovel. Cam thought she might throw it down, but Ruth wasn't given to melodrama. "Fine," she said, thrusting the shovel into another woman's hands.

Cam watched her walk away.

In the darkness, Greenhouse 3 continued to burn weakly. Some of the framework was exposed now, smoldering in the melted plastic. Cam knew they would be crazy to bring gasoline into the fire, but the longer they waited, the farther the ants might burrow from the heat. *Okay, you're off the team, too,* he thought at Allison, preparing for another argument.

He got lucky. One of their scouts ran out of the night, a sixteen-year-old boy with an assault rifle. "Wait!" the boy said. "Hey!"

Tony Dominguez was the youngest person in the village except for three infants. He was also one of Allison's most ardent supporters. The boy had a crush on her about the size of the moon, for which Cam forgave him. For one thing, he approved of Tony's taste in women. The poor kid didn't have anyone his own age to lust after in Jefferson and his mom never let him join their trips to Morristown, probably because she was afraid he'd stay there. With a population of twelve hundred people, Morristown was practically a city. It was also a religious enclave and worked like a shield for Jefferson, deterring most travelers even as it provided a welcome source of crops and wealth in the area.

"Someone's coming!" Tony said. "I heard someone in the fences on my side!"

Allison said, "You're at Station Five?"

"Yes, ma'am."

Cam glanced at the southern perimeter, impressed that Tony hadn't abandoned his post despite the ant swarm. He knew for a fact that other lookouts had left their stations, because he was one of them.

The village was supposed to have three people on patrol during the day and twice that many at night. The best time to travel was in the cold and in the dark, when most of the bugs were dormant. That made it tough to see people coming, but they'd surrounded their home with irregular rings of early warning fences. In some places, they'd actually strung barbed wire. Mostly these "fences" were just fenders, hoods, and hubcaps stripped from the dead traffic on Highway 14, which they'd scattered on the ground like bells and gongs. Not everyone who walked out of the hills was friendly. Sometimes there were bandits, and they were constantly afraid the military would learn where Ruth was hiding.

"It's just one person?" Allison asked, tipping her head at Tony's weapon. The M16 was equipped with a big infrared sniper scope, and Tony said, "Yeah. I think he's either shit-faced or hurt. He's making a lot of noise in the fences."

"Great." Allison's tone was sarcastic.

Their village was one of the smallest in northern Colorado, but they did business with Morristown and New Jackson. Word got around. Sometimes their permanence made them a target for people who hadn't worked so hard, like the weed-heads, drunks, or other troublemakers who weren't welcome elsewhere.

Cam seized the opportunity. "See what this guy wants," he said to Allison. "We'll take care of the ants."

His wife met his gaze in the dark. She knew what he was doing, but she grinned like a cat. "Fine," she said, almost daring him. It was precisely what Ruth had said. Cam didn't know what to make of that, although Allison could be playful about the weirdest things.

She was very pretty. A few blond strands had pulled free of her ponytail and framed her steady eyes, flagging in the wind. Then she set down her gas cans and left. Tony hurried after her, toting his rifle.

Cam glanced at a couple named Michael and Denise Stone, who both wore pistols. "Go with them, okay?"

"No problem," Michael said, dropping his shovel and ski mask. Denise added a pry bar and her own makeshift body armor.

Now we've got more tools than people, Cam thought. He considered going after Allison himself, but he was in no mood to be diplomatic to some lost, hungry loser. "Let's throw some dirt on the fire," he said. "I want to get Eric out of there."

"Yeah." Greg winced. In a different life, Greg had been Eric's squad leader. Cam could barely imagine what he must be feeling. With Eric's death, the best link to Greg's days as an Army Ranger was gone.

They heard Allison call out at the edge of the village, challenging the newcomer. Her voice was strong in the wind. A moment later, she repeated herself. Cam and Greg began to suit up with the other three people on their smoke team, donning goggles and masks.

"I'll go in first," Cam said.

Then somebody screamed from Allison's direction, a high, boyish shriek. It was Tony. Cam whirled, trying to place the sound beyond the blocky silhouettes of homes and greenhouses. He saw flashlights and human shapes. One was familiar, fair-haired and lean, yet round in the middle. The others were only shadows. They seemed to dance spastically.

Jefferson was under attack.

3

Ruth was standing at her door when Tony and Allison hurried past. She almost said something, but what? Allison didn't even like to hear *thank you* from her, much less complaints, so Ruth stood quietly against her home as their flashlights rocked by, followed by Michael and Denise. There was someone in the fences. Ruth could hear him banging through the car parts, and Allison called, "Hey there! What's your name?"

Her mild tone was an odd counterpoint to Tony's M16, which the boy seated against his shoulder with the barrel pointed skyward. It was a position that made the weapon more visible in the glinting white beams of their flashlights. Ruth nearly went to add herself to the guns beside Allison. The girl was a force to be reckoned with, but she was pregnant, and that increased her importance in more ways than Ruth could put into words.

They should have been friends. They owed each other their lives, but it wasn't only Cam who stood between them. Allison excelled at being mayor and she had always been very watchful of Ruth, seeing her as a potential rival for this role as well. Ruth's nanotech skills were a brand of authority that Allison could not match. The girl had never believed

Ruth when she said she wished she could give it up. Allison was always thirsty for more control over their lives, whereas Ruth's decisions had led to thousands of deaths during the course of the war. Given the choice, Ruth would have become just a regular person again, anonymous and ignored—and yet she felt that old conflict of responsibility now.

I should back her up, Ruth worried, watching Allison. Then her gaze shifted. Michael's flashlight had picked out the stranger in the fences.

It was a woman about fifty years old. She was short and thin and dirty. Ruth thought there was blood on the woman's elbow, staining her jacket sleeve. She was unarmed. She wasn't even wearing a backpack. Had she been robbed? She looked skittish as hell, turning away from them when Michael's light traced over her pale face.

Even so, Allison was cautious, holding her ground instead of going to help. "It's okay," Allison called. "We have food and water and a place where you can sleep."

Michael aimed his flashlight into the dirt. Tony lowered his rifle, and, and, well behind them, Ruth lifted her hand from the 9mm Beretta on her hip.

There was no question that she and Cam would have been a better fit cosmetically. He was black-haired and black-eyed and Ruth's coloring was dusky, whereas the darkest thing about Allison was her sunburn. Ruth often wondered what their baby would look like, but it had been the same with Bobbi and Eric. Bobbi was black, Eric was white, and neither of the mismatched couples turned many heads. They were *alive.* Nothing else was important.

The only exceptions were people of Chinese or Russian descent. There was still widespread hatred since the war, which made things tough on anyone with Asian heritage. Some idiots didn't bother to differentiate between Japanese, Koreans, or Chinese—or even Filipinos or Malaysians—not even those who'd lived in the U.S. for generations.

Racism had become a very different thing after the plague. Yes, there were some communities where people were trying to preserve ethnic purities, breeding only with fellow whites or Hispanics or blacks. Once a runner came through their village with marriage offers for anyone who was at least 50 percent Jewish. Ruth hadn't been tempted, but it did make her wonder. Had the Israelis reestablished themselves on the other side of the world? Were there enough Jews alive to sustain their culture? For nearly everyone, though, race was trivial, and Ruth knew she was grasping at straws comparing her skin to Allison's.

She was jealous of the younger woman. She was afraid for Allison, too. They had all been exposed to high levels of insecticide and other chemicals, not just in their village but during the plague year. Many of the pathetic refugee shelters had been slapped together with welding torches or made of vinyl or rotting carpet or cardboard, exposing the inhabitants to heavy metals, mold, or toxic compounds like vinyl chloride. Everyone had burned furniture, tires, plastic, and dung for warmth and cookfires, filling their homes with poisonous smoke.

Ruth had missed most of that. She'd spent the first thirteen months of the plague aboard the International Space Station as the centerpiece of a crash nanotech program, but the ISS was its own hostile environment, like a submarine. The recycled air became foul with human smells and bacteria. They were exposed to solar radiation and the more subtle damages of zero gravity, losing bone and muscle mass. Later, Ruth had also spent weeks on the outskirts of the Leadville crater, absorbing fallout. Perhaps worse, her body had been a war zone for different kinds of nanotech.

The next generation faced all the same problems as their parents and more. Babies required not only nourishment and warmth. First they needed a healthy start. The human body was capable of extraordinary resilience, but the most sinister wounds were those that went unseen, inside, at the cellular level or even deeper within their DNA.

So far, the women in Jefferson had suffered only four stillbirths and one toddler who showed every sign of being autistic. The other two children were okay. From what Ruth heard, however, the infant mortality rates were even more severe in Morristown. She hoped that was only because Morristown was thirty times larger, thus allowing for more data. It surely didn't help that most of the people there were New Evangelicals, who pushed for as many babies as possible, no matter if the women were in their teens or in their forties or worn out from earlier pregnancies. Either way, the statistical curves were alarming. If the numbers continued to play out so poorly, the human race was no more than a hundred years from extinction.

There was a more personal insult. Ruth was thirty-eight. Her best years of fertility were already behind her, with few prospects in sight. She knew Cam tried to avoid her, which was impossible. They didn't have enough firewood to make hot meals individually or to provide warm water in every home, nor were there enough pipes to install central plumbing throughout the village. It wasn't safe to eat alone, either, so they ate in shifts and they bathed in the same hut beneath sun-warmed tanks, always with guards on duty. She saw Cam every day.

Who could blame her if she lived a bit vicariously through Allison? The girl should have been a sister to her, even if they were sisters who mistrusted each other.

Is it my fault we never got along? Her thoughts boiling, Ruth turned her eyes from Allison and the stranger and opened the door into her home at last. *I'll try harder,* she thought.

Then the screaming began. Ruth jerked backward, staring, just in time to see someone drop to the ground with her spine bucking in the grip of a violent seizure.

The stranger killed Allison first.

The flashlights added to the confusion. One of the white beams spun into the ground, rocking up through the human shapes. The other two briefly pinned the old woman. Then another flashlight fell away. The sight paralyzed Ruth. She lost crucial seconds trying to understand what she was witnessing.

Allison had touched the old woman, reaching for her shoulder. In fact, Allison's left arm was still thrown sideways from her body and clawed at the earth with a short, ripping motion. It peeled her fingers to the bone. Then her cheeks ran dark with blood as she chewed through her tongue.

There was one thing more that struck Ruth despite her wrenching shock. The old woman's expression never changed. The wide look in her eyes was nervous, even rattled, but she didn't even glance down at Allison as the others reacted. *She's contagious,* Ruth thought before she added her voice to the yells rising across the village. "Get back, get back!" she screamed, running toward them.

Tony's M16 fired a three-round burst. The shots were ineffective, aimed into the sky. Ruth saw him stagger as Allison continued to hammer herself against the ground. Then the boy fumbled his assault rifle and went to one knee, trembling. It was only a spasm that pulled the trigger.

Michael should have known better. He tried to drag Tony away from the old woman and suddenly he swooned, affected by the same shambling movements.

Nanotech, Ruth thought. Nothing else spread so fast.

"Michael!" Denise yelled, but her instincts were stronger. Instead of charging after her husband, she hesitated. "Michael! Oh Jesus, no!"

Allison had stopped moving, bloody and limp. Ruth was aware of more flashlights and yelling behind her. A small crowd was hurrying toward them, and her neighbors had emerged from their home with a lantern—but there was an enormous danger in bringing reinforcements, because they would go to their friends. Cam would run to his wife.

Ruth pulled her sidearm and shot the old woman dead, firing twice over Allison's body.

"No!" Denise screamed.

The old woman toppled, knocking Michael down, too. Her blood must have been contagious, but they were partially upwind. If there was nanotech in the explosions across the woman's chest, the microscopic disease was swept away from them.

Ruth shoved Denise farther into the slow current of the breeze. It was critical to keep their distance. Then she turned her pistol on Michael and Tony.

Denise drove Ruth to the ground, punching at her chest and gun hand. The worst part was that Ruth understood. Denise still had some frantic hope for her husband, but Ruth struck her in the head with two quick panicky blows.

Denise fell sideways and Ruth leapt up. "Stop!" she yelled in a flurry of lights. The other villagers had arrived while she was down, blazing with lanterns and flashlights.

Cam shoved through the crowd. His face was hidden in his goggles and mask. "Allison!" he yelled, as another man shouted, "What are you—"

"They're contagious! Get back!"

"Oh my God, *Allison*." His voice was raw with agony. Ruth didn't think he'd even heard what she was saying.

He must have been thinking of his baby. She was, too, but she struggled for control of herself. "Stop! It's some kind of nanotech! Cam, if the wind changes—"

Behind her, there was a distinct gritting noise as Tony rose to his feet.

Ruth swung around.

Tony was already advancing in a clumsy, looping path. He stumbled on Allison's hand but kept coming. Something was wrong with his eyes. They were like holes. In the many beams of light, his brown irises looked black, as if his eyes consisted only of the whites and giant, hyper-dilated pupils.

"Stop him!" she yelled.

Cam hurled his flashlight. Someone else threw a spare clip for a rifle. The clip bounced off of Tony's arm, but Cam's flashlight banged into his shoulder. It knocked him back. Suddenly everyone was bobbing up and down, scratching at the ground for dirt and rocks, pelting the boy and shouting as if their voices might also drive him off. Their flashlights stabbed and winked. Tony staggered in the onslaught. Then he lost his balance, stepping on Allison again and falling down.

Michael came at them next. His eyes were lopsided. Only one pupil was distorted. The other had shrunk to a pinpoint, and his body hunched to that side as if to compensate.

The brain, Ruth thought. *It's something in the brain.*

"Oh, fuck, shoot them!" a man yelled, but Denise drew her own pistol and thrust it at the nearest person who was also armed, a woman with a rifle.

"Don't you touch him!" Denise cried.

"No, wait!" Ruth yelled. There were too many voices. The crowd hurled rocks and gear at Michael, a knife, a belt, even stripping off their jackets just to have something to throw. In the madness, two people fled. Ruth saw another man stagger. He wasn't running away. He simply let his head slump. Was he infected? The man dropped to the ground as someone else began to jerk beside him, shaking all over.

It jumped the gap, Ruth thought. She meant to shout a warning but she couldn't breathe. The reflex was too powerful. *Don't breathe.* The nanotech was multiplying, swirling unseen from everyone it touched, and she wondered if she would be next.

Michael continued to wade toward them through the barrage. Unfortunately, the hail of rocks and equipment was slowing as they cleaned the ground and emptied their pockets. Ruth heard a woman swearing desperately as she scratched at the dirt. Someone else turned and ran. Then a flashlight pegged Michael in the face, its white beam spinning. He collapsed. But the other two men who'd been infected would rise in seconds.

"Give me your shovel," Cam said to Greg. Both of them still wore their makeshift armor. Their goggles, hoods, and gloves would offer the slightest protection.

"Stay upwind!" Ruth yelled. "Cam!"

Otherwise they were helpless. Every survivor knew how easily the invisible machines could penetrate their lungs. A new plague was their most intimate and public nightmare, shared by everyone. They would have been less unnerved by another distant nuclear exchange. Panic took over.

Someone fired in the dark, then someone else. Orange muzzle flashes tore the crowd apart, because not all of the shots were directed outward. Tony died in a burst of rifle fire, flailing into the ground. Denise fired, too, driving one man to his knees before a third gun popped at the base of Denise's skull, silencing her high-pitched screams.

It had been less than five minutes since the old woman transferred the nanotech to Allison.

Cam and Greg took the front line in the fight, clubbing three infected men as Ruth turned and ran. She pinballed through a jumble of silhouettes. "Wait!" someone yelled. Let them think she was a coward. Ruth crashed through her cabin door and slammed it shut, throwing the lock behind her.

* * *

Someone was pounding at the door when she yanked it
open again, holding a sawed-off shotgun in one hand. Outside, the storm of lights and voices continued. Ruth had
thought maybe Cam was trying to reach her, but it was Bobbi
Goodrich.

Bobbi's face was a grimace of terror, her fist raised to
strike again. "You—" she said.

"Take this." Ruth's voice echoed in her helmet. She handed
Bobbi the shotgun. "Don't let anyone grab me."

"I can't—Just watch out," Bobbi said.

The two women moved into the darkness together. Ruth
walked ponderously in her bright yellow gear, a Level A
microbiological containment suit with two SCBA tanks on
its back. One of the air tanks was only half full. Even so, the
aluminum cylinders weighed thirty pounds. Both the Nomex
jumpsuit underneath and the suit itself were too big. The chest
piece billowed around her small breasts like a giant bag. The
sleeves rubbed against her torso, filling her ears with the *rsssh
rsssh* of the loose, heavy rubber.

Despite the suit, she knew immediately that a lot of the
noise had moved away from them. Ruth barely recognized
Jefferson anymore. The buildings were the same, except for
the fallen greenhouse, but she'd never heard screaming in this
place before. Their community had become a riot.

She turned into the sound of hoarse voices. "We can't just
kill everyone!" Cam said, pleading with an array of other villagers. Everyone kept their distance from each other. They
had also been smart enough to throw their tools away after
beating down the infected people, although doing so only left
them with guns if there was another outbreak. Worse, now
they faced each other with pistols and carbines.

Greg had sided with the larger contingent of the group.
"There's no other way," Greg said. "We can't tie them up."
He meant because they were afraid to touch their sick friends.
Prolonged contact would be even more dangerous than jump-
ing into range with a club.

Ruth shouted inside her helmet. "I can do it!"

The villagers didn't notice, locked on each other.

"You could be next," Cam said. "Don't you get it? What if the nanotech hits you next?"

Ruth saw they'd lost more people. There were six men and women on the ground between the huts, plus, farther out, Michael and the sprawled corpses of Tony, Allison, and the old woman. She didn't see the man who'd been shot by Denise. They must have carried him away along with any other uninfected casualties. Were more people hurt? At least 20 percent of the village had been incapacitated or killed and Ruth moved slower than she wanted, devastated by the scene.

Some of the figures closest to her were probably dead, too. Even in the sporadic light, she could see head wounds where they'd been beaten. One of them was Denise, her skull blasted open beneath her dark hair. Another of the crumpled figures was still alive, straining for air through a throat obstructed by blood or dirt. His breath came in hoarse gasps.

Was it possible Allison was also alive? Cam must have been clinging to the belief that she could be saved—but if she was, she'd sustained horrible injuries to her mouth and one hand. Ruth would be surprised if Allison hadn't also experienced a massive stroke, and their medical abilities were limited to setting broken bones or helping women through childbirth. Even the doctors in Morristown might not be able to perform the surgeries Allison would require.

Please be dead, Ruth thought, closing her eyes against her grief. But she couldn't ignore the doubt she also felt. *Do I want her to be dead?*

"There has to be something we can do!" Cam shouted.

"We can't let them get up again," Greg said as another man drew his pistol and a third turned away from Cam.

"Enough," the third man said. "Let's do it."

Cam grabbed his arm. "No."

The debate might have been harder because most of their faces were wrapped in goggles and masks. They were friends, but their armor was another layer between them, like the darkness, their guilt, and their fear.

"Wait!" Bobbi said. "Wait. Look!"

Some of the flashlights came around, playing on Ruth's suit. "I can do it," she called through her brightly lit faceplate. "I can take care of them."

"Ruth," Cam said, desperate with relief.

She was glad, faintly, but she couldn't forget that she had been the first to start shooting. What if there had been another way? Could they have subdued Tony and the old woman without killing them? Denise would still be alive, too.

Ruth was afraid of walking into the field of bodies alone. What if they woke up? She might tear her gloves or her sleeves when she tried to carry them. The suit wasn't designed for heavy labor, much less for combat—but she couldn't leave those people to die.

"We'll use my cabin to hold them," she said, "but I need help. Rope. Water." Her windows and doors were bug-proofed, but those seals wouldn't hold nanotech. "Get me as much plastic sheeting as we have."

"Tear down Greenhouse 4," Cam said, shoving at the man who'd drawn his gun. "Go."

Maybe they still could save most of their friends.

Ruth went to Allison first, sidestepping Linda and Doug. She should have tied some of the unconscious men and women before doing anything else—she had a bit of duct tape left after sealing her gloves to her sleeves—but she was drawn to her longtime foe. She told herself it was because Allison was pregnant, but the girl was dead, her crimson eyes bulging from the pressure of some intracranial rupture.

Whatever the nanotech is doing, the process doesn't always work, she thought, taking the only lesson she could from Allison's death.

Somewhere in her sadness, Ruth was also comforted. It was a backward sort of feeling, as if she'd lost a burden she would have preferred to keep, but she couldn't imagine this bright young woman living with her hideously chewed mouth, especially if her mind was gone.

Ruth had wanted to hold Cam's baby even more than she'd realized, and her hand paused above Allison's belly. But no. No. *Stay with your mother,* she thought, weeping inside her helmet. They lacked the technology to care for a premature birth. Even before the machine plague, saving a fetus early in its second trimester would have been remarkable. Today, it was impossible—so they'd lost the child, too.

I can't let Cam see her like this, she realized, pressing her glove to Allison's swollen face. She turned the girl's head and hid her partly in her jacket hood. Now her tears were hot and thick and she tried to wipe her eyes, which was stupid. It would have infected her if she got inside her helmet. Instead, she only smeared blood and dust across her faceplate.

Her voice broke when she called back to the stabbing flashlights. "Allison's dead. So is Tony. And the stranger. Michael's alive."

"You better hurry," Greg yelled back. "Linda's starting to move her arms."

Ruth walked toward the lights again. Greg, Cam, and another man had stayed to hold three beams on her. Deeper in the village, other flashlights and lanterns swarmed. Then she knelt beside Linda Greene, who was weakly stretching her arms as if dreaming. Ruth pulled Linda's wrists together and secured them with duct tape, binding the other woman like a criminal.

What's happening to you? she wondered.

4

Doug Tillman quit breathing before Ruth got to him, and Martha Shemitz had a broken neck. The other four were still alive. Michael had lost some teeth and Ruth tried to staunch the gash on his chin, tying Doug's shirt around Michael's head as a crude bandage. Andrew also seemed unlikely to recover, his scalp split in two places where he'd been beaten.

Meanwhile, both Linda and Patrick woke up. Linda was agitated, grunting and shuffling on the ground as she fought her bonds. In contrast, Patrick nearly seemed lucid. He trembled, but he was silent, blinking his distorted eyes. Ruth also noticed a recurrent tic in his cheek. What did he see? Was he *feeling* nonexistent stimuli like cold or heat? Itching?

"You need to get out of here," she called to Cam. "Leave everything inside my place. I'll seal the doors and windows."

"Ruth," he said distantly.

"Get out of here."

"Ruth, how long can you breathe in that suit?"

That was the least of her worries. She should be able to swap out her air tanks without contaminating herself, so dehydration became the greater threat. Even though it was made for a much larger man, her suit was like wearing an individually sized sauna. Already she could smell her own sweat, and she'd forgotten to drink her fill before she suited up. In the short term, that was fine. The suit had no sanitary features, so if she had to go to the bathroom, it would run down into her boots, but ultimately the water problem meant that Ruth only had hours, when she might need days to take care of these people and to study them.

She wanted to go to him. She knew she couldn't.

"Leave me a walkie-talkie and a pistol," she said. "Make sure I have lots of tape." *I love you,* she added to herself. *Be careful.*

She was stunned when Cam echoed the thought exactly.

"Be careful," he said.

"Yes."

He set his weapon beside his flashlight, near her door, where the others had stacked plastic sheeting, rope, tape, batteries, a med kit, and jugs of water. Someone had lit two kerosene lanterns for Ruth, leaving one in the open, the other inside her hut. The bandages and the water were for the people she hoped to save, but already her mouth was dry. *Stop crying,* she thought, summoning a grim resolve from within. She was alone. That was the truth.

Ruth dragged Linda inside first, cracking the woman's head against the doorframe when she jerked and spasmed. "Oh shit," Ruth said, but Linda didn't seem to associate the pain with her. She reacted to things Ruth couldn't see, groaning and straining.

Ruth left her in the corner, tied to the only piece of furniture, a low, heavy table. There were only three rooms in the hut—two thin bedrooms in back and this bigger space by the door. Ruth had normally eaten breakfast here with Bobbi and Eric, sitting on the floor, and she regretted the mood of all those mornings together. She was often envious of the couple, happy to be included but edgy because of what she couldn't share. She hated to see herself as the old maid. Now she was the lucky one. Bobbi was a widow, Eric lay dead in Greenhouse 3, and this house was already saturated with nanotech.

She dragged Patrick in next, then Michael and Andrew. Then she returned outside and began to wrap the dead bodies in plastic sheaths, sealing them as best she could. More than once, she stuck her gloves to the tape. Every time, her heart leapt with adrenaline. But the suit held.

She paused over Denise. The woman had died uninfected, hadn't she? Ruth was very tired, but she had never been one to cut corners. She rolled Denise in plastic, too. Then she dragged each of the six corpses inside, turning her home into a prison and a morgue.

The gruesome feeling in Ruth's chest grew louder as Linda squirmed against the table, moaning. She ran back outside. She knew she had to go in again, but there was another job to do first. Maybe she was more meticulous about it than necessary. Ruth dug in the earth until she had enough dirt to cover the bloodstains. In the shallow pits, she buried the tools and the gear they'd used to subdue their friends. She even gathered as many of the rocks they'd thrown as she could find, even though she could never completely sterilize this place. *Poisoned ground,* she thought. A lot of the nanotech would remain on the surface, exposed to the breeze or lifting away in the morning heat when the sun rose tomorrow.

If they survived the night, even if they sealed this place in concrete and built a heavy fortress to contain her home, Ruth knew they could never stay. The village needed to be permanently abandoned. Still, her best efforts might buy them some extra time. Ruth continued to work despite her exhaustion.

Her mind wandered.

She glanced at the stars, remembering better times. She knew she was trying to get away from herself, but at last she turned and walked back into her small, crowded home. Then she began to tape the door shut from the inside.

Originally, Cam and Allison led their party east from the Rockies down into the plains beyond Boulder and Greeley, where they were sure the summers were hot enough to destroy the insects. In sufficient heat, even bloodless or cold-blooded organisms became vulnerable to the machine plague. Their guess proved to be true, but the absence of bugs also turned those areas into deserts. The insect swarms were the only pollinators available. Every species that required hives or cocoons had been destroyed by the ants. There were no bees, butterflies, or moths left of any kind. In their greenhouses, they'd manually brushed pollen from one plant to another. Outside in the world, however, it was only the clumsy, brutal movements of the swarms that continued this process, spreading the delicate powder even as they obliterated forests and meadows everywhere.

Ruth could only guess what the Midwest had become. She'd seen the edges of it herself, and there were rumors supposedly passed on from pilots and scouts and the specialists who controlled the remaining U.S. spy satellites. Without grass, the prairies had been peeled down to the bedrock, sluffing away in the rain and ever-more frequent windstorms. Megatons of silt had displaced the Mississippi and Missouri Rivers into a continent-wide swamp, filling low places like Arkansas and Louisiana with stagnant, creeping bogs of mud.

Ruth and her friends quickly abandoned the plains. At the time, she'd still hoped to lure Cam from Allison, but there were other problems besides her wounded heart. They would always be regarded as criminals by some. They'd planned to keep their heads down, but they were recognized and betrayed in the second town where they made their home. In the third, there was an outbreak of some respiratory disease—a normal disease, not nanotech—and Cam ran a fever of 104° for two days, frightening both women badly.

As always, it was Allison who was the boldest. She led them into the heart of the Rockies again, where they hid almost directly under the noses of Grand Lake. Jefferson lay just forty miles west of that mountain peak. Grand Lake was no longer home to the president and Congress—those people had been relocated to Missoula, Montana, far, far away from occupied California—but the Air Force maintained Grand Lake as a fortress, and Allison believed the military would never think to look for Ruth so close within reach.

Mostly Ruth was happy. Certainly she was never bored. They'd spent seven of the past fifteen months on the move, hiking and scouting, negotiating with other survivors. Most of their energy went into the basic necessities. Food. Shelter. Ruth was even glad to forget her research, contributing instead to their day-to-day struggles. It was selfish, she knew. More critical than any other challenge was the next-generation nanotech that must be designed as quickly as possible. A second invasion wasn't impossible. The Russians and the Chinese had dragged their feet as they prepared to leave, bickering with each other and haggling with the disunited American government, even constructing new bases to house their airmen and soldiers in the meantime, playing for every advantage as they developed their own nanotech.

Ruth had no illusions about what had finally happened.

Her hands shook as she double-sealed the windows of her home. She thought her tremors were only bad nerves and exhaustion, but what if it was something else? *Would I know if I was infected?* she worried. *What if it's possible to absorb a low-level dose of the contagion that's breeding in me right now?*

Another thought occurred her, and it was even more awful. What if their village had been specifically targeted because of her? They knew Colorado was under intensive electronic surveillance. What if the invaders had heard something or if a facial recognition program had finally made a match? The nanotech could be meant for *her*, infecting Allison and the others only because they were in the way.

Michael woke up behind her. He thrashed against his bonds and huffed for air in guttural, rhythmic grunts. *"Haaah. Haaah. Haaah."*

Ruth turned only to make sure he wasn't pulling free of the tape. But her gaze lingered. Michael's eyes were half closed and roamed endlessly behind his eyelids, almost as if he was in REM sleep. His mouth hung open like a cave.

"Haaah. Haaah."

He was ugly, wrapped in the flopping bandage of the shirt. Ruth fought down an urge to smash his head with the lantern. The infection wasn't his fault, but she couldn't look at him anymore. She was embarrassed by the sounds he made.

"Haaah. Haaah."

Her claustrophobia was like a tidal wave inside her, swelling and hurting. Her pulse didn't make it any easier to be careful with the knife, slicing another big square of plastic. Every minute, she was sealing herself deeper in plastic and tape. Would she ever get out?

"Listen," Cam said to Bobbi, gesturing for her to join him by the radio. They crouched together in a busy hut as other people hammered plastic sheeting over the windows. "We need to find somebody," he said, but Bobbi was distracted.

"I don't hear anything," she said.

"Listen to *me*." He showed Bobbi the frequency control, trying a second band and then a third. Each time, he clicked twice at his SEND button and waited to hear something in return. "We're going to have to walk through as many channels as possible," he said. "One at a time. Like this."

"Why can't you just call?"

"It's more complicated than that."

The hut stank of marijuana, which was their only anesthetic except for alcohol. Brett had been gutshot. They were afraid to let him drink, although Susan had used a jar of 150 proof moonshine to sterilize his torso as best she could. The alcohol was expensive. Marijuana was not. The plant was called "weed" for good reason. It had survived in the wild only to be recultivated in Morristown, where it was grown for its fibrous stalks for cloth and rope and as an easy cash crop as a drug.

Cam breathed clean air as people continued to hurry in and out of the door, piling backpacks, canteens, and other gear in the corner. Jefferson was consuming itself. They'd torn down Greenhouse 2 as well as 4, intending to use the plastic and the last of their tape, staples, and nails to seal most of the villagers inside.

They had to assume the worst. No one had responded to his calls on the civilian channels. Morristown, Steamboat, New Jackson, Freedom—every town within reach was off the grid, so he'd abandoned the CB for their Harris AN/PRC-117 instead. Cam wanted a helicopter for Ruth and he was prepared to face a jail sentence if necessary. Let the U.S. leadership punish him if there was ever time for it. The important thing was to get her to safety, but first they needed a bit of luck.

Like most of their military hardware, the Harris was something that had been abandoned by American troops whose positions were overrun. Cam regarded it with a mix of old pride and pain. His time in the Rangers had been short but intense, full of the quick, meaningful friendships that were born of relying on each other, and Eric and Greg had continued his training after they went into hiding. Bobbi was still a newlywed or she might have known more herself. Eric had focused more on her weapons training during their courtship. Guns were exciting, so she'd learned to shoot instead of other basics.

"This radio was Z'ed out," he said. "That means the encryption software was dumped to keep it from the Chinese, so we can't hear or talk on the secure net. That's why it's so quiet. I guarantee you there are people talking right now. We just can't hear their transmissions."

Bobbi pointed at the handset. "But you can still call."

"No. This radio is only capable of open broadcasts. We can only reach people who are monitoring or broadcasting in the open."

The Harris was a sixteen-pound chunk of metal intended for use in a vehicle or as a field pack. It didn't have the strength to contact Grand Lake or Sylvan Mountain directly. It was meant to be deployed as a part of a larger net—and they were in friendly territory. There were signals corpsmen and retransmission stations scattered across the Rockies. He might even be relayed through a plane if U.S. forces had put the right equipment in the air, trying to find stragglers like himself.

Or to kill them.

Cam was paranoid enough to believe that the new plague might have its origins on the American side. The U.S. weapons programs wouldn't have stopped after Ruth went AWOL, and it wasn't impossible that the plague zone was limited to this valley. What if, through sheer bad luck, this place had been chosen as a test area? He needed to make it clear who was at risk. They would come for Ruth. He was certain of that.

"The best we can do is stumble onto a frequency that's being monitored or find two units talking in the unsecure and step on their transmission," he said. "That's why this could take awhile. There'll be units who don't have any better equipment than we do, but there are hundreds of frequencies. So you need to do this for me."

"Hey!" Owen called from across the room, hefting a staple gun and a roll of tape. "We're done except for the door. Are you coming out?"

"One minute."

"We gotta seal up!" Owen shouted. He was a tall man and among the most visible in the crowd, which included his wife. The village gossip was that she'd miscarried twice, which was why Owen doted on her like nothing else. Cam didn't want to argue with him.

"Close it," he said. "I'll come out as soon as I can."

The air wouldn't last. Sealing two huts in plastic was a temporary fix. Ripping down the greenhouses had also left more of their late-year crops unprotected, increasing the likelihood of more insect swarms tomorrow. Meanwhile, the fire ants were still expanding beneath Jefferson. Even if the colony stayed in the ground tonight, Cam knew they could count on dealing with the bugs again after sunrise. The vicious goddamned ants would be excited by the blood they'd spilled.

He switched to another frequency as hammers sounded on the outside of the door. He tried another and another, and suddenly the radio came to life:

"—through Medicine Bow and we need extraction off a hot LZ, over," a man said very fast before another voice answered, "Roger, Cougar Six Two."

Jesus, Cam thought. *What if the nanotech isn't just in this valley? Where do we go?*

There were large sections of National Forest called Medicine Bow nearby in Wyoming, and he knew those mountains were peppered with civilian and military camps. Cam didn't recognize the call sign—Cougar Six Two might have been anyone—but they were American and that was all that mattered.

"Break break break," he said. "Any station this net, this is Two Echo Two, any station this net, over."

The first man responded. "Two Echo Two, Two Echo Two, this is Cougar Six Two. Over."

"Roger, Cougar Six Two, I need you to pass along an emergency message, break. Flash code Revere. I say again, flash code Revere, over."

Silence. The other man obviously had his own problems. He had been calling for some sort of evacuation himself, but his discipline held. The man said, "I need you to authenticate, Two Echo Two. Over."

"I say again, flash code Revere. This is Corporal Najarro with the Seventy-Fifth. I need to speak with Major Thrun or the current operations officer in Grand Lake, over."

His flash code was ancient by military standards. Call signs, encryptions, and communications windows were changed every thirty days. Cam had been out of contact for a year and a half, but Grand Lake would have archives that contained the OPORD mission profile from his last assignment. Grand Lake should know his name, and, knowing him, they should realize who might be with him.

"Roger that, Two Echo—" The background exploded with small arms fire and the man's voice rose into a shout. "What is your current location, over?"

Cougar Six Two was under attack. Who were they fighting? Could there be enemy forces inside the plague zone or was Cougar defending himself from infected people? Cam spoke with icy control, trying to make himself more significant to Cougar Six Two than the disaster surrounding the other man. "I say again, Revere. Revere. I need you to pass that message ASAP, Cougar Six Two. I'll monitor this frequency for the next thirty minutes and will come up on this station every hour on the hour for ten minutes thereafter, over."

The man yelled just to be heard over the gunfire and screaming. "Understood, Two Echo Two! Godspeed. Out."

"Do you think they'll do it?" Bobbi asked, and Cam said, "Yes." He'd seen nothing but self-sacrifice from the troops he'd served with. *The only thing that'll stop him from relaying our call is the plague,* he thought.

All they could do was wait. They couldn't even scan for more transmissions because they had to sit on 925.25. Cam left Bobbi by the radio to help Susan with Brett, who was unconscious now. Maybe that was for the best. She'd done a good job of applying a pressure bandage to their friend's mid-section, and Cam tried to assess the damage. The bullet must have missed the aorta—Brett would be dead already—but it couldn't have missed his intestines. The bacteria released from his digestive tract was a problem. They didn't have anti-biotics, which meant peritonitis would probably kill him even if he survived the wound itself. Cam nearly forgot everything else. He was among the best medics in the village, but they weren't equipped for surgery, and opening Brett up would create at least as many complications as Cam could fix. He was still weighing their options when a smooth female voice filled the hut.

"Two Echo Two, this is Arapaho Five, over," she said.

Cam jumped on it, pushing Bobbi aside with a hand slick with Brett's blood. "I read you. Over."

"Authenticate, Two Echo Two."

"This is Corporal Najarro from Second Platoon, Echo Company, Second Battalion, Seventy-Fifth Ranger Regiment. Over."

"Roger, Two Echo Two. Send your traffic, over."

It was enough that Cam was elated. He glanced at Bobbi with his mouth bent in a thin line like a smile. The woman in Grand Lake must have run his ID on a computer. He and Ruth were probably flagged on a dozen programs along with Eric and Greg and other suspected collaborators like Allison.

He still couldn't believe she was gone. He blurted out, "People are sick, ma'am. I need a medevac now. Over."

"Roger, Two Echo Two. Flash code Streak."

That one simple word sent a chill up the back of his neck. *Streak.* It meant to change frequencies to avoid being trian-gulated by the enemy. If she was concerned about enemy surveillance on the unsecured net, it could mean there really were hostile forces moving in behind the plague . . . *We'd bet-ter hope they miss us,* Cam thought, shifting his eyes from Bobbi to the other men and women in the hut. They couldn't hold the town against enemy infantry.

He went up two bands as he'd been taught. "Arapaho Five, Two Echo Two," he said on the new channel.

The woman in Grand Lake didn't waste a moment, either,

resuming their conversation in knifelike bursts. "What is your current location? Over."

"We're eighteen clicks southwest of Wackyville." That was Morristown's unfortunate nickname because so many of the people there were cultists, and Cam said, "Are you familiar with this area? Over."

"Affirmative. Over," the woman said, as Cam heard a snatch of a man's voice behind her.

"—they get so close?" the man said.

"Ma'am, I'm not alone," Cam said urgently. "Two Echo Two is still together. Do you understand me? The gang's all here and I need that chopper now. Tonight."

"Can you maintain your position? Over."

"Ma'am, we have wounded and a lot of people sick. Over."

"You need to hunker down, Two Echo Two, because everybody's in the soup right now. All air assets are committed. Sit tight. I'm going to get you that helicopter, but I need a little time. Over."

"Are you"—he almost couldn't say it—"Are there people sick there, too?"

"Monitor the radio, Two Echo Two. We'll patch you into our pilots as soon as we have an asset available. Over."

"Oh, shit." Cam stared at the handset without hitting his SEND button.

"Two Echo Two?" the woman asked. "What are you using for far and near recognition signs, Two Echo Two?" she asked, but Cam had already stood up and turned away from the radio with a cold, fresh sense of rising dread.

Bobbi touched his jacket. "Cameron?"

He couldn't meet his friend's eyes. What could he possibly say? He knew a Black Hawk would need most of an hour to cross the distance between Grand Lake and Jefferson—much longer, if Grand Lake was in chaos itself. He'd hoped to get them into the underground bunkers in Grand Lake, but that might be impossible if the surface of the mountain was crawling with infected people.

"Two Echo Two!" the radio said. "Two Echo Two, do you copy?"

Cam knelt and picked up the handset again as if it weighed a hundred pounds, uncertain it was worth the effort. Whoever had launched the plague, whatever the nanotech did, she wouldn't tell him on an unsecured transmission. She might not even know.

"Just get here as fast as you can," he said.

5

In the blue light of the display screen, the colonel's face was ghastly pale. The effect was supernatural. The light transformed his round features into something lean and monstrous, creating shadows like a mask. He used it well, turning to grin at the four technicians beside him. He knew his teeth shone like fangs because Dongmei's pretty mouth glowed in the same way when she matched his expression.

They were all afraid. He wanted to harness that energy. As a senior officer, Colonel Jia Yuanjun had been trained to browbeat his troops if necessary, driving out weakness, but not every situation called for blunt force. These four were among his select. More importantly, they were right to be nervous, so he'd planned to redirect that adrenaline, binding them to him with aggression and pride. Everyone in the blue light of the flatscreens was very young for this task. They were so lost, too, here on the other side of the world from their home. Colonel Jia was only thirty-two, less than ten years older than any of his technicians—but like their fear, their youth could also be an advantage. Their hormones ran healthy and strong. That was another reason why Lieutenant Cheng Dongmei was present. Dongmei was the only female in the room, and, in fact, one of just eleven women in the entire battalion.

She was smooth-skinned and elegant even in her tan jumper and with her black hair cropped as short as the men's. The red Elite Forces patch on her chest curved along the top of her breast. Her gun belt flared from her hips, accentuating the hourglass of her waist. Colonel Jia did not want Dongmei for himself, for reasons that he could never tell anyone, but he was not above using her to drive the others.

He spoke in Mandarin, the dialect of the ruling Han. "If these signals are correct, it's spreading even more quickly than we'd hoped," he said.

"They are correct, sir," Huojin said.

Jia swung on him. "Your sector shows the most gaps! Why?"

"The wind is not as strong in northern Colorado as it is elsewhere tonight, sir," Huojin said. "Perhaps the weather predictions could have been better."

Jia nodded, concealing his pleasure behind a stone face. Huojin was the only one in his team who was not Han. Huojin was nearly full-blooded Yao, one of China's many ethnic minorities, a distinction that had become even more significant since the loss of three-quarters of their nation's populace. Jia often put him on the defensive even though Huojin was his second best data/comm technician. That constant tension, like the presence of Dongmei, helped everyone in the group as they strove to outperform each other.

"The weather is ideal," Jia said, rebuking Huojin. There would never be a time when the wind carried evenly from British Columbia to New Mexico. Then he relented. "Your dispersal patterns are adequate given local conditions."

"Sir," Dongmei said, "I still have one fighter southbound from Idaho with two bomblets onboard. Shall I route him toward Colorado?"

"Hold your fire," Jia said.

Their attack had been painstaking, because they'd possessed only ninety-three capsules of nanotech to spread up the entire length of North America. Jia wanted to keep any reserves as long as possible. In truth, Huojin's sector appeared to be no less saturated than the others', especially given the innumerable valleys and basins hidden within the Rockies.

Huojin was operating with another handicap. The military

installations in Utah had prevented overflights farther east, shielding Colorado from the border patrols they'd used to seed the mind plague elsewhere. Reaching into Montana and Wyoming had been equally problematic, so hours ago they'd detonated thirty-four of their capsules high in the atmosphere, allowing the nanotech to sift down toward the areas where the Americans maintained the core of their Air Force and government.

Jia turned his gaze to the screens again as if looking for those invisible streams. The bunker where he stood was on the outskirts of Los Angeles, but Jia had almost forgotten. This room transcended that distance. The quiet that held these young soldiers in the eerie blue light was a place of its own, and Jia reveled in it. Together they hung poised above America through a distant constellation of satellites and planes, watching as the plague zone grew and consumed the enemy.

It was a humble scene from which to conquer a superpower. They had only a few pieces of expensive equipment mounted on desks made from crates, with so few chairs that Huojin and Yi sat on crates themselves, buried deep within a hurriedly built complex of naked concrete. A single air-conditioning vent rattled above them. The cables to and from their electronics lay banded together on the raw floor, twisting away toward data and power jacks set in the wall by the only door. The room was cold. The sole, overwhelming smell was the dusty rock stink of the concrete.

Jia couldn't think of anywhere else he wanted to be, not even his parents' apartment in Changsha—not even if some magic could have resurrected them.

"There," he said, pointing at Gui's third screen. VANCOUVER. The tangled coastline of British Columbia was still lightly populated, which left few breeding grounds for the nanotech, and Jia had been reluctant to send his fighters inland from the Pacific. The Chinese and the Russians both regularly patrolled the coast, and they had every reason to send their jets into eastern Oregon, contesting their borders with the Americans, but until the initial strike they'd tried not to act out of character. The aircraft Jia sent from L.A. were no different than their usual patrols except that these fighters dropped tiny, explosive-free bomblets into enemy lines.

The wind was unfavorable in Vancouver, blowing south,

not east. "Begin our next wave now," Jia said. "All of you. Secondary targets."

His team murmured to faraway pilots, their fingers clacking through several keystrokes and preset commands. Jia was struck again by Dongmei's elegance, not her physical perfection but the fine clarity of her voice. In their own way, the men were even more graceful, like dancers. Jia was cautious to watch Dongmei instead, pretending the same habit as everyone else. For once, he didn't resent her. The first-wave fighter she'd preserved went dark on her screens, then realigned itself—a red triangle now moving east instead of homeward. Other fighters rocketed inland from the coast. Jia hoped to see strikes deep within British Columbia, Montana, and Wyoming within minutes.

"Sir, we have contact over Arizona," Yi reported.

"There are also American fighters scrambling out of Cheyenne," Huojin said.

"Advise your crews," Jia said calmly.

The enemy knew something was very wrong. More aircraft would get off the ground, but their options were limited. When the American planes ran low on fuel or ammunition, or if they were hit, where could they go to? They might touch down in no-man's-land west of the plague zone, where they would be useless, unable to rearm—or they could take their chances in the deepest stretches east of the Rockies.

Either way, a few aircraft made no difference. Jia had every advantage of surprise and position. He was up-weather.

He allowed himself another measure of satisfaction as he studied his team again, taking in their display screens, their voices, and their rapt young faces. The American West lay before them like the pieces of a puzzle. Dongmei's three screens each held slightly more than half of Idaho or northern Utah, with the state borders digitally superimposed along with major landmarks such as GREAT SALT LAKE and BOISE.

Most of the terrain was captured in low-res satellite video. Even more resolution was lost because the displays were nearly colorless. Still, these maps were sufficient. Freeways and old cities marred the land like dark veins and clusters, and, in many places, those features were closely tied to the data that most interested Jia.

The People's Republic of China did not possess the same presence in space as the United States, not even after the Americans' losses during their civil war. In fact, the Zi Yaun series were also known as CBERS, the jointly developed China–Brazil Earth Research Satellites. The Brazilian Space Agency had provided a significant percentage of the technology and also funded much of the launch costs, sharing in the satellites' operating time until China took full control during the plague year.

Nominally, the Zi Yuan satellites were for weather and geological studies. Of course they also contained military grade optics and communications systems. First launched in 1999, the satellites were the result of a not-unlikely alliance between two developing nations who hoped to close the gap with the United States. Bringing those eyes to bear on the American West had been the easiest part of Jia's preparations, because China had long since realigned its orbital assets. After the near-total destruction of traditional enemies like Japan, Vietnam, and South Korea, all four of China's Zi Yuan satellites were aimed solely at India and the U.S. The same was done with most of China's other, far less precise weather and communications satellites. Jia had simply patched into several eyes that were already perfectly arranged, supplementing his surveillance grid with ASN-104 unmanned aerial vehicles. The UAVs provided the best video, yet those feeds were limited to small areas, less than a square mile, whereas the satellites saw everything.

There was no way to track the mind plague itself. In many places, the disorder it created was easily visible, but for the most part Jia's team was only able to track the spread of the mind plague via computer projections. They combined wind and atmospheric models with military intelligence on American population centers and eyes-only data on the nanotech's parameters and replication speed.

The projections were conservative. Even so, Jia worried about missing some pockets of enemy territory. The nanotech was shown on his screens as swirls and clouds of darker blue. The mind plague blossomed as it touched American populations, especially the larger military bases that had grown alongside the old cities. In some places, there were also pathetic evacuation attempts. Vehicles and pedestrians lunged in chaotic stampedes for the highways, which were the clearest routes into the mountains.

Nearly all of them ran for elevation. That instinct was strong even in Jia. Every survivor would always think of the highest mountaintops as safe, although none of the enemy made it that far. The clumps of people and trucks all darkened with the same unstoppable blue shapes. Then the wind carried the plague deeper into American and Canadian lines.

Together, we win, Jia realized with certainty. It was the one thing of which he had no second thoughts.

There was a deafening crash behind him. The door was only reinforced wood, the weak point in the box. It splintered open as a trooper in black assault gear fell to the floor, thrown off-balance by the steel ramming cylinder in his grip. Light slashed into the room—the yellow, searing brilliance of floodlamps. The light was as much of a shock as the assault itself, although it rippled as other men rushed the door.

They were Second Department troops. A dozen of them burst into the room, pinning Jia's team with short-barreled Type 5 submachine guns. "Down!" they yelled. "Get down!"

Dongmei leapt up with her pistol drawn, still tied to her equipment by her headset.

"No!" Jia shouted. "Don't fight!"

The other men continued to yell. "Get down! Get down! On your knees! Down!"

But it was Jia's command that Dongmei answered. She lowered herself to the floor, placing her weapon as far from herself as possible. Her teammates obeyed, too, kneeling with their hands lifted high. Huojin and Gui winced in the dazzling light. Jia also saw Yi react to a voice in his headset, wanting to respond but stopping himself.

Was there a problem with Yi's planes? Were the pilots receiving new orders on the same frequency? Jia's thoughts surged with frustration, but he was far more unsettled when he saw Sergeant Bu Xiaowen among the Second Department troops. The black-uniformed men had spread out, encircling his team. Bu stood to Jia's right. He must have been among the first soldiers into the room. Their eyes met for a single, startled instant until Jia wrenched his gaze away.

"I said get down!" another sergeant yelled.

Jia remained standing, looking for their commander. The Second Department was the electronic counterintelligence division of the Ministry of State Security, the top intelligence wing of the Communist Party, and Jia was hardly unfamiliar with the MSS officers in Los Angeles. Obviously someone had traced his signals to this room. But who had given the order to shut him down?

Two of the troopers stepped closer, patting at Jia's uniform. "Don't move," the first one said, taking Jia's sidearm and his combat knife. Then they relieved the rest of his team of their pistols, too.

Jia heard Yi's headset mumble again and it was only with great discipline that he kept his back to their electronics. What was happening above Colorado and Wyoming? Did they need to concentrate their aircraft in other places?

We don't have time for this! he thought.

More black uniforms paced into the room, creating an ever-greater obstacle for him to deal with before his team could return to their work, yet it wasn't until one of the Second Department troops moved to disconnect the data jacks by the door that Jia spoke.

"Don't touch those," Jia said.

"Be quiet," a different man snapped.

Jia immediately turned to direct his words at him. "This is a sanctioned operation," he said. The officer might have frowned. Jia couldn't be sure, because his face was obscured in the shadows of the floodlights behind him.

"You're under arrest," the officer said.

The governor himself hurried into the room once a signal was given that Jia's people had been secured. He was followed by a Ministry of State Security general. Jia snapped to attention, saluting General Zheng. All of the Second Department troops did the same, except two who continued to aim their submachine guns at Jia's team.

"Are you mad!?" the governor asked, blustering. Shao Quan was an older man who wore his authority in traditional ways. At seventy-five, Shao was twice as old as anyone else in the room, and his hair was thin and gray on a round head like a nut, browned by the California sun. His business suit was conservative and dark, blue jacket, blue tie.

Jia kept his eyes straight ahead, holding his salute to General Zheng. He knew he could not let his agitation show. He noticed, however, that four of Governor Shao's personal bodyguards had also entered the room, their assault rifles pointed at the floor.

"You've cost us years of work!" Shao yelled. "And for what? Bravado and revenge? You idiot!" He sneered at the insignia on Jia's collar, perhaps amazed that a colonel could be so ambitious.

Every second you delay us is a chance for something to go wrong, Jia thought.

"Are you killing them!? What are you shooting at the Americans!?" Shao jabbed his finger at Jia's display screens and then swung his arm toward General Zheng as if incriminating him as well. "Our forces are unready! Do you realize what another war would do to us now?"

"Sir," Jia said, addressing the general.

Governor Shao continued to yell. "Shut it down!" he ordered the Second Department troops. They hesitated, glancing at Zheng for instructions. Shao's voice became shrill. "Go! Move! Turn off their computers and take these men to interrogation."

Shao emphasized the word *men* in his last sentence, staring at Dongmei. She was the only female in the crowded room. The young woman was still on her knees, like all of Jia's team except Jia himself, which left her even more helpless. She was shaking, although she hid it well. Dongmei's face was expressionless and her back was rigid, but her short bangs trembled above her dark eyes.

Shao's old face was alive with power, and Jia felt revulsion and anger that one of his technicians might be singled out for any reason. He wouldn't let them abuse her. "Sir!" he said, looking for General Zheng's eyes.

"It might not be too late to stop the Americans from retaliating," Shao said. Shao was also speaking to Zheng now, although he sounded as if he was rehearsing for a public statement. "This was a rogue operation that we shut down immediately," he said. "The perpetrators have already been dealt with harshly."

General Zheng was in his forties, heavier than Governor Shao and not as sunburnt. His face was equally lined, however, especially around the eyes, which gave him a shrewd, skeptical appearance. He wasn't interested in Jia or Shao at the moment. He squinted past them at the bank of electronics, his gaze ricocheting from one display screen to another. He was curious. Jia concealed a smile. Governor Shao was the top civilian in the Western Hemisphere, but California was a military state and General Zheng could overrule Shao if he so chose . . .

Shao pressured him with one word. "General," he said.

Zheng glanced up and nodded.

"We must be swift," Shao said, "before there are repercussions. I do not mean only from the Americans, but also from home."

"Yes," Zheng said.

The general's decision was made. He gestured to his troops and several of them rushed toward the computers and display screens. Yi was foolish enough to lean into their path, blocking the first soldier, who struck him in the cheek with the butt of his submachine gun. It drove Yi to the floor. Another man yanked Dongmei to her feet and grabbed her belt buckle, cinching his fist in the top of her pants. The man grunted, not from the effort of pushing at her slim body but from something much heavier inside himself. Lust. There would be no mercy shown to Jia's team.

Shao and Zheng believed they could somehow make amends for the attack, honoring their nonaggression pact with the U.S. and Canada, in part by making an example of Jia and his technicians.

Too late, Jia thought.

6

The new Cold War was unsustainable. The politicians could posture all they wanted. The reality was that neither side had the resources to maintain their standoff indefinitely. Someone would stumble, and Colonel Jia was among those who believed it might be their own side.

Yes, the Americans had been on the verge of defeat before the cease-fire. Their losses were staggering. But with the end of the fighting, the People's Liberation Army suffered one of its greatest military defeats. The cease-fire was not a stalemate. It was a horrendous beating because of the price they'd paid just to reach that detente. Their wars had left them with countless veterans and the new Elite Forces like Jia's Striking Falcons—but every day that passed, their strength bled away a little more.

Even though the two places were seven hundred miles apart, California had been demolished by the nuclear strike on Leadville, Colorado. Every fault line on the West Coast let go. The vast metropolitan areas of San Francisco and Los Angeles were ripped apart. Undersea shock waves brought the ocean over the land. Adding to the struggle, most of California consisted of arid, dry grasslands or outright desert, especially

in the south where the Chinese forces were gathered. Before
the plague, the Golden State had only been able to sustain its
population by an elaborate system of reservoirs and canals
that stretched over hundreds of miles, all of which collapsed.

Neither the Russians nor the Chinese arrived in California
until the worst of the quakes subsided. They were able to
salvage food, fuel, tools, vehicles, and ammunition—but the
tools weren't calibrated for their equipment. The ammunition
didn't fit their weapons, nor did the ordnance work in their
artillery or fit their planes. For the short-term, that was fine.
Throughout the first weeks of the war, they sent up makeshift squadrons of Chinese pilots in American planes. They
advanced their infantry in civilian cars and U.S. Army trucks
supported by their own tanks and armor. It had been necessary to press the attack while the Americans were reeling, and
the blitzkrieg was a success.

Peace was more difficult. They were outnumbered. Within
a month of the cease-fire, the Russians began in earnest to
evacuate their people back to their motherland before anyone
else entered its borders, leaving behind only fifteen thousand
airmen and troops as a check and bargaining chip against the
United States. The Chinese themselves drew their occupying
force down to half strength, positioning a hundred and fifty
thousand Heroes of the People's Republic against several million Americans.

Since then, the Americans had reestablished only a few
pockets of heavy industry, but even that outstripped what the
Heroes were able to put together in their battered cities. They
didn't have the power to meet an arms race. Just holding their
ground was difficult enough. They needed water. They needed
housing. The insect swarms were a fine source of protein, but
the bugs made it difficult to grow wheat or rice. They lost as
much food as they gained, fighting the ants. They were also
ordered to tap the invaluable crude in California's many oil
fields, rebuilding the derricks and refineries. In the meantime,
they faced a slow attrition of the pilots and planes lost in every
border skirmish.

Jia had not designed the mind plague himself. He didn't
even know the whereabouts of their labs, yet he had been

among the officers who suggested such a thing even before
their invasion of the United States. The MSS and the Communist Party had nearly a full century of experience with so-
called brainwashing, indoctrination, abnormal psychology,
neurology, and population control. Under the guise of normal
medical research, their weapons programs had also performed
extensive studies with Alzheimer's patients and victims of Par-
kinson's disease.

The mind plague was a bloodless weapon, combining several disciplines into one perfect tool. For years, Jia champi-
oned its potential.

Tonight, he'd become the one who unleashed it.

Jia had hoped to do better. Ideally, he would have finished
his assault before MSS counterintelligence units noticed the
steady number of Chinese planes lifting out of Los Angeles
under new orders, much less before they traced his signals
into the labyrinth of Army bunkers. He'd intended to emerge
from this room with the attack over and done with, allowing a
superior officer to claim responsibility.

His orders never said who that man would be. He'd guessed
it couldn't be Shao Quan, but it wasn't impossible that the
governor, like Jia, also worked for the Sixth Department.
Nearly every officer and politician had been recruited by the
MSS in one capacity or another. Among the Elite Forces, even
the junior officers also held ranks in the intelligence agency,
answering to two masters. Jia had been prepared to obey
Governor Shao if Shao met him with the appropriate codes.
Instead, it looked as if the compartmentalized nature of the
MSS had worked against itself. Jia couldn't be sure when
Shao or Zheng joined the Second Department forces moving
against him, but, after the door was smashed in, the best case
scenario would have been if General Zheng arrived late, trying to stop the governor from interfering. That was why Jia
waited—but Zheng was not part of the conspiracy.

Before the Second Department troops did irreparable damage to his computers, Jia uttered one sentence to the general.
"The autumn rain is cold and sweet," he said.

"Stop!" Zheng yelled.

His troops paused. One of Jia's display screens lay shattered on the floor. Sergeant Bu clutched a laptop in his hands, and another man had grabbed a handful of cables, yet no more harm was done.

Governor Shao's brown face jumped with fear as Jia and Zheng stared at each other. "I represent the Communist Party!" Shao said. The old man recognized Jia's non sequitur as an MSS directive. He knew what was happening, but he fought it anyway. "I am the governor! You will obey my orders!"

Shao's bodyguards lifted their rifles only to find half a dozen submachine guns aimed at them. The Second Department troops had reacted with equal speed, and they outnumbered Shao's bodyguards more than three to one.

"Don't," Dongmei whispered to both sides. Her voice was an odd, lilting counterpoint to the men's voices.

"Hold your fire," Zheng said.

"Obey me!" Shao screamed, stabbing his finger at the bank of electronics again. "Shut it down!"

Zheng said, "The rains give way to winter."

"But winter must always come before the spring," Jia said, completing the protocol.

The crowded room was still. The laptop in Bu's hands beeped once, and, on the floor, Yi brought his palm to his bleeding cheek. Somewhere, a headset murmured.

Zheng turned suddenly on the governor. "Take him alive," Zheng said, indicating Shao—but he dismissed the governor's bodyguards with the same curt, slicing motion of his hand.

Shao's men yelled as the submachine guns blazed. One fired his rifle into the knot of black-uniformed troops, toppling three of them. Then it was over. Zheng's troops restrained Shao as others knelt to tend to the wounded and killed. One soldier screamed and screamed, clutching at the splintered bone shoved through his elbow.

In the swarm of black uniforms, Jia swung on one man in particular. Sergeant Bu had dropped the laptop to bring his own weapon to bear, running forward to shield General Zheng. "Be careful!" Jia shouted. Bu had charged right to the edge of the bodyguard's gunfire, and Jia's feelings turned heartsick at the sight of Bu missing a bullet by inches.

Then he realized the danger in showing his emotions.

"You clumsy bastard, I'll put you in the labor camps if you broke that laptop!" Jia said, finding another reason to berate the other man. Was he overdoing it? No. All of them were shaken, and most of their attention was on the screaming soldier or Governor Shao. "What is your name?" Jia shouted.

"Sir, my duty is to the general," Bu said, stupidly prolonging the exchange.

Jia almost struck him. He even raised his fist. But in Bu's dark eyes, Jia saw unmistakable affection and distress. Bu's heart had also been betrayed by the close-quarters gunfire. In fact, Jia wondered if Bu hadn't run to protect General Zheng but to save *him* instead.

Jia turned from his lover, snapping orders to his squad. "Back to your stations. Confirm all contacts. Lieutenant Cheng, you may need to hand your aircraft off to the others if your station is down."

"Assist them," Zheng said, directing Bu and two more of his soldiers away from the bloody floor. "Colonel, what else can I do? We need to bring our forces to full alert. You must have other signals to send, too."

"Sir. Yes, sir. We'll give those orders now," Jia said. "With your permission, please allow me to reestablish command over our attacks before I explain."

"Yes," Zheng said.

Jia saluted again, admiring Dongmei's self-control as the Second Department troops helped them reorganize their electronics. She had never seen combat before. Her chest rose and fell against her uniform as she laid one slender hand over her breast, trying to calm herself . . . but it was the lines of Bu's shoulders and narrow hips that distracted Jia's gaze from his team.

The other man truly cared for him. Jia was surprised. He'd thought their relationship was merely convenient. As far as he knew, there was no one else like the two of them in Los Angeles. It had been a pleasure to find Bu Xiaowen even though Jia was ashamed of what they did together. Now he was shamed in a different way to think he'd been rejecting the possibility of something more meaningful. Fortunately, there was no time to brood.

"Colonel, I've lost my connection with our UAVs," Yi reported, and Huojin said, "Sir, there are more enemy fighters scrambling out of Wyoming."

"My systems are down, sir," Dongmei said, tapping swiftly at her laptop.

"Have our aircraft hit their targets yet?" Jia asked as he sat down at his own station. It was past time to send new commands to their orbital cameras, and he was worried about Yi's unmanned aerial vehicles. His team wasn't running those UAVs directly. Jia didn't have the manpower. "Call the Air Force units controlling your drones," he said to Yi.

As he spoke, Jia dared another glance at Bu, who lingered nearby, sorting out the last of the cables on the floor. Usually it had been days at a time before the two of them found an opportunity to talk privately, even a few words here and there. These bunkers were overcrowded. They were on duty at different times. Their physical liaisons had been even rarer, and Jia wondered when the chance would come again.

Then he saw General Zheng watching his eyes.

If ever there was a nation that was primed to endure a holocaust and move against its rivals, it was twenty-first-century China. Even before the end of the world, they were a country of desperate young men.

In the late 1970s, the Communist Party initiated their historic population control laws, the so-called One Child policy. Although widely opposed, the laws had prevented more than 420 million births. One couple, one baby. It was the only way to ensure better education and health care and to revolutionize the People's Republic from a rural, peasant state into a technological force. Their population had skyrocketed after World War II, leaving the world's largest nation in danger of collapsing from within. Merely keeping everyone housed and fed became their greatest industry, which was the main reason why they lagged behind other developed countries in the space race, the nuclear race, and in modernizing their armies—but forty years later, the law had changed the People's Republic in unforeseen ways. Forced abortions and sterilizations were not uncommon as local authorities pursued the severe birth quotas set by Beijing. Many families also elected to abort healthy female fetuses, swayed by a preference for male heirs to carry on their name, their businesses, or their place in society. Girls were subject to infanticide and abandonment.

In most areas there had been many, many more young men than women, sometimes by a ratio as steep as five to one. Gay women especially were ostracized because lesbians might rob China of their wombs. Men faced an enormous pressure to avoid failing their ancestors.

Growing up, Jia Yuǎnjun didn't understand there was anything wrong with him. In fact, he noticed he was better than average. He wasn't weakened by a certain anxiety that affected the other boys in their male-only classes. He was comfortable without girls. They were not. So while the others bickered, looking for something they couldn't find, Jia was able to focus instead on his studies and his teachers.

His career in the People's Liberation Army was respectable and covered his basic needs, allowing him to send his small wages home to his parents. A star lieutenant, Jia was approached in his early twenties by the MSS. The intelligence agencies were always looking to recruit overachievers, but by then he'd realized he had a terrible secret. The furtive trysts that so many of his school-age peers engaged in, not only in search of physical relief but also to develop emotional connections, had also been full of dominance games and menace. Boys who were outed were expelled from the military. Perhaps worse, that stain often denied them any high-paying jobs in the cities as word percolated down from the Party of their offense.

There was another risk. Condoms were expensive. Most of his intercourse was unprotected. HIV was rampant in Asia, and if Jia ever tested positive it would be difficult to explain, a death sentence in two ways. There would be no medical care for an officer banished in disgrace.

Nevertheless, he was drawn to his friends despite himself. Was it only luck that kept him from being betrayed? Or was it his true nature that allowed him relationships in which both men became more vulnerable and committed? He was capable of tenderness, which went against their rough, boyish ways. It humiliated Jia that his *yin* was so strong, but the pull he felt was irresistible. The sex was good. The love was better. Jia had also seen that it was often the most reckless affairs that led one man or the other to anonymously report his partner. Jia was safer for committing to his boyfriends. All of them held each other's fates in their hands, and yet it tended to be those who felt the most self-disgust who became the cruelest, destroying their lovers.

In ancient China there had been little or no bias against homosexual relationships. As long as a man fulfilled his duties as a husband and a father, what he did elsewhere was ignored. That attitude changed during the Cultural Revolution. The Communist Party targeted homosexuals as deviants and a threat to their ideal society. Openly gay men were jailed, even executed.

This persecution began to relax again in the twenty-first century. Sodomy was decriminalized, homosexuality removed from a list of mental disorders—but the Party and the military continued to hold onto the conservative views of the Revolution.

The machine plague brought the worst of that era crashing back again. There wasn't enough room in the mountains for everyone. Many of China's minorities were gone. The subtle racism of the Han had become a survival mechanism, blatant and merciless. The Communist Party resurrected all of the old prejudices, cutting away anyone who was suspect.

Jia was not an activist. Even before the apocalypse, he would never have worked against his country. For one thing, it seemed futile. He wasn't a coward. He was smart enough to see how forcefully the river flowed. All he wanted was to belong. He owed them his success. On some level, Jia also knew that the best way to save himself was to become indispensable. The Party overlooked small crimes if a man proved loyal and hardworking. Jia recognized the irony. He was willing to give everything of himself for China precisely because China did not want all of him, only his stamina and cleverness.

He was also aware that a prominent role in coordinating the nanotech would expose him to great scrutiny. The MSS must have interviewed everyone who'd ever served with him.

Many of those men were dead, but what if the MSS uncovered a former lover? What if they spoke to someone who suspected? For weeks, Jia worried at being found out. He did not want to forfeit his chance, and yet it occurred to him that perhaps they did know. They must know.

The mind plague was a gamble. The attack was launched without the knowledge of their own people precisely because it might not work. Jia had been told the nanotech was untested except for a few limited trials, so the job required not only a senior officer but also a man whose obedience was propped up by extreme fear and ambition. He was the ideal fit. If anything went wrong, they could discard him effortlessly, casting him as an over-reaching upstart and a homosexual as well. There would be no defense. Jia would be held up as a failure, and then shot.

General Zheng said, "The governor is not a fool. He's correct that our forces are unready."

"Sir," Jia said, "everything is exactly to plan."

Zheng turned to study their display screens again. "This is nanotech," he said.

"Yes, sir."

"What does it do?"

"Our people taught it to hunt out the basic structure of the human brain, sir. From there, it attacks the frontal lobes of the cerebrum."

"So it kills."

"No, sir. It's a bloodless weapon. I didn't mean to imply that it destroys the tissue. The nanotech simply gloms onto the synaptic clefts in the areas affecting time sense and memory. Right now, the Americans are badly confused."

There was a high failure rate, of course. By clogging millions of the brain's receptors, impeding the electrochemical impulses that normally jumped between the synapses, the mind plague not only left its victims witless and agitated. People varied too much. Sometimes the nanotech caused permanent injury.

Zheng said, "What if the wind changes or if it reaches as far as mainland China?"

"We're immune, sir."

"Your machine is that sensitive to racial genetics?"

"No, sir. We were given a vaccine in our health injections, sir."

There was no difference between Oriental and Occidental brains. The mind plague would have attacked them all without a cousin nanotech to ward it off.

Three weeks ago, Jia had been among the first who received the hypodermic shots of fluid purported to be rich in nutrients. The order to launch the plague had waited only until everyone in the People's Republic quietly received the same shots. The MSS also made certain to allow black marketeers to sell small amounts of it across their borders with the Russians, both in Asia and here in California. Those cases had been altered to have the vaccine to the mind plague removed, of course, because they knew the Russian spy agencies would sell their analysis of the serum to the Europeans as part of their own double-dealings with the enemy. The Russians believed the shots were merely another of China's heavy-handed medical programs, a soup of B vitamins intended to help their malnourished armies.

"I see," Zheng said. "The Americans would have noticed us mobilizing if we were prepared to march in behind the nanotech. Or they might have intercepted our communications if the plan was widespread."

"Yes, sir." Jia was relieved. By reaching the facts himself, Zheng allowed him to say more without costing face. It was a delicate situation. Zheng must feel wildly uneasy receiving orders from a young colonel, which is why he'd sided first with Governor Shao. Jia needed to restore their normal relationship as fast as possible. "You have my loyalty, sir. My role was only to begin the attacks. You reacted more quickly than anyone expected," Jia explained, and that was true. "I'm sure there are confirmations waiting for you even now."

"Who are you reporting to?" Zheng asked.

"I don't know, sir."

"Is it General Qin?"

"I swear I don't know, sir."

"And yet your operation extends through dozens of air and

ground units in addition to our nanotech labs. I want your control codes."

"Yes, sir."

"Who are your contacts? Are they MSS?"

"Yes, sir. Sixth Department, sir. Colonels Feng and Pan have been my go-betweens."

Huojin interrupted. "Colonel? The first transports are in the air, sir."

"Stick to the plan. Take the capital," Jia said.

Their border troops and Elite Forces were always on standby, so Jia had been able to mobilize two companies of paratroopers without being concerned that it might alert the Americans. Soon the entire PLA would be on the move, rolling through the deserts and taking to the sky.

"What about a nuclear response?" Zheng asked. "These bunkers aren't hardened against their missiles."

"No, sir, but we're on American soil, and the plague is spreading like the wind itself. They'll have no time to consider their options."

The Americans would also be in the path of any fallout themselves. If they hit the West Coast, the normal west-to-east flow of the weather would carry the radioactivity over their own homes on the Continental Divide—and the old, implacable power of mutually assured destruction still held true.

"They can be certain our mainland would retaliate with missile launches of our own," Jia said. "The expectation is the Americans will hesitate. Then the plague will have them."

In all of history, had there ever been a war that was decided in a few hours? Jia hadn't accepted this task for the glory. His name was meant to be kept secret, yet he thrilled at the idea that someday he might be remembered among the greatest of Asia's warlords, Khan, Sun Tzu, and China's own heroes like Mao and Chiang Kai-shek.

The war in North America should have been theirs from the start. The Russians had been honed down to a cold-blooded war machine during their long fight in the Middle East, but the all-male invasion of the PLA had a deeper motivation.

They wanted to go home.

They wanted women.

North America could have satisfied both needs, becoming a second China. There had been thousands of prisoners taken in California, Arizona, and Colorado. For every female of age, this was less horrible than for the men. The People's Liberation Army had been too hard-pressed to dedicate any troops to building shelters for their POWs, nor was there water to spare in the desert.

The labor camps killed many of the enemy combatants, but the females were spared. Most of them had been repatriated as part of the cease-fire, except for the *bù lǐ zhì* few who chose to stay with their masters. Victory would have meant a thousand times as many concubines. If the Chinese armies won, they might have been complete, graced with *liēzhide*, low-class wives and a giant work force of slaves to run their farms and factories. Even now, after the stalemate, hundreds of American women must have given birth to Chinese babies. Eventually the People's Republic might claim the world through breeding out the other races. That would take generations and it would create new ethnic minorities, but Jia could see how they might establish their peace one pregnancy at a time.

The new plague was immediate. It was something in which Jia could participate wholeheartedly, and if the attacks went well he should be safer than ever, praised and accepted by the Ministry's highest leaders.

He was unspeakably proud of his inclusion in the Sixth Department, which had only tightened its clutches on the Communist Party. The MSS would use their victory to cement their power, adding momentum to their bid to unify the Party beneath their own generals. With new leadership, they also intended to bring a change in direction. Originally, the People's Republic had planned to evacuate their forces as agreed in the cease-fire. The reality was that much of Asia was eroded down to its bedrock like the American Midwest. Only the coastlines and the mountains were inhabitable. Mainland China was no more able to house and feed another hundred and fifty thousand soldiers than those men were capable of fending for themselves in occupied California.

The mind plague was the only answer for the troops who'd been left behind. They needed to take America or there they would die, because new orders were about to be unveiled along with the announcement of Jia's attack.

They had been told never to come home.

7

Eight hundred miles from Los Angeles, in the town of Jefferson, very little was as it seemed, either. Cam stood at the northern edge of their village with his head ringing, looking inward at the huts when his job was to watch the fences beyond their home. The wind crawled on his jacket hood, sinister and quiet. He tried to ignore it. He'd cinched his mask and goggles tightly across his face. His hands were thickened by old leather gloves. Duct tape sealed his wrists and the cuffs of his pants. Still, he felt exposed. The wind was like a voice at his back. It whispered against his armor, cold and persistent, defining every wrinkle in his sleeves and collar.

The night was absolute. The only light was from the stars—but the darkness was full of technology. Most of Jefferson's homes were wired for electricity, even if they held only a few lightbulbs, and some of the men had brought out floodlamps, too, preparing to light up the perimeter until sunrise. They were far from helpless. The town boasted an M60 machine gun and a Russian Army rocket-propelled grenade launcher in addition to dozens of rifles, carbines, handguns, and military radios.

"This is One," Greg said in Cam's headset, beginning their status checks clockwise around the huts.

"Two," a woman said.

"Three."

The sound-off continued through eleven guard posts until it reached Cam at the northernmost point. "Twelve," he said.

"Thirteen," Bobbi added. Inside the first sealed hut, she continued to monitor their Harris radio as well as the local net on their headsets and walkie-talkies. For nearly an hour, they'd been confirming each other's status every ten minutes. They were afraid they might have to turn on themselves again. Already there had been a burst of flashlights and yelling at Station Eight when David's batteries failed and the people at Seven and Nine thought they'd have to shoot him.

One of their guards wore a painter's dual cartridge respirator. Three others had flak jackets, which were useless against nanotech but might save their lives in combat. It had been decided. Jefferson was under quarantine. Even if outsiders looked like they were okay, even if they needed help, the guards intended to warn off or kill anyone else who walked out of the hills, defending their own families above all else. Cam was ready to take part in a slaughter if necessary, yet he'd convinced them to black out the town instead of powering up their small grid. *What if that old woman came here because she saw the fire?* he'd said. Cam would be a long time forgetting Tony's wide-eyed face. The kid had seemed to *target* them, reeling around to focus on their shouting voices.

There were other ways to watch the darkness. They had two nightscopes in addition to the one they'd lost with Tony when it was contaminated like the boy, and their fences were still a decent early warning system.

Cam believed himself to be an honorable man. Since the war he'd become a public leader much like Allison, supporting her, learning from her, taking charge of Jefferson's economy and politics because he thought he could help. Now a lot of that person was gone. The survivor was back, his instincts and old traumas winning out over the cool, more rational mind of the statesman.

He'd taken the twelve o'clock point in Jefferson's defenses for a reason. Morristown lay just eleven miles north. The nanotech had dropped Allison in seconds and paralyzed Marsha down her left side, but even if the plague crippled or killed

20 percent of its victims, that could leave nine hundred men, women, and children staggering out of the much larger town.

Cam was obsessed with the way the old woman had been heading into the wind, walking out of the southeast where there were no settlements on their maps. Where had she come from? A group of nomads? He was more concerned about what they were going to do if the old woman's direction was not entirely random. He thought she might have been moving into the wind in the same way Tony had responded to their voices—because it was a stimulus. If so, everyone in Morristown might have staggered northwest themselves, chasing the wind. That would lead them farther away from Jefferson. Good. But how long would it be until the first traces of nanotech swept over this village? What if the plague had originated first in Utah or Idaho?

The night must be threaded with poison, and Cam realized he was breathing shallowly, trying to separate himself from one of his most basic instincts. *If you breathe, you die,* he thought, wrestling with the impossible challenge. It had been the same with the machine plague. There was no way to stop nanotech, and he cradled the weight of his M4 instead of pacing. He wanted to save his energy. Even so, it was profoundly unnerving to stand alone in the night with his vision darkened by the bronze lens of his goggles, waiting to die.

The stars were dim points overhead. The buildings around him existed only as square shadows. Then his headset crackled again. "Where is Cam?" a woman asked.

"Ruth?" he said, and there was a burst of chatter from the other guards.

"How are Michael and—"

"—did you—"

"Stay off the radio!" Greg said. "Hey! Stay off the radio so she can talk!"

Cam looked across the village again. He heard more voices in the darkness now. The two men at Station Ten were arguing with each other, and Cam wondered how long they would stay put. It wasn't even midnight.

"Ruth?" he asked, brooding over the tone of her few words. He knew her too well. *Bad news,* he thought. *It's bad news.*

"I need to talk to you," she said.

* * *

Cam stalked through the village without needing a light. The layout was simple, with seventeen huts set in a ring around their four greenhouses, a storage shed, the dining hall, and the showers. Nor did they own enough luxuries to scatter hazards like children's toys or spare engine parts on the ground.

He passed through the leeside of a hut, leaving the wind. Then he moved back into the current. It rushed around his legs and through the spaces between his arms and chest, seeking any gap in his armor. Cold and hungry, it swirled against his face.

Cam was already badly spooked. The transition from that quiet instant back into the wind made him stop at the edge of another protected space. His mind roared with old gunfire and the howl of planes—the stark image of a one-eyed man lifting a shovel like an axe—the feel and smell of an emaciated young woman coughing blood into his face. He could also see Allison's grin, though he tried to suppress that image. The memories inside him were hellish and raw and he didn't want to pollute his favorite things about her.

He turned back into the wind with his M4 swinging beside him in one hand, leaning his weight forward as if walking through deep mud or snow. The truth was that they were already buried in another plague. They lived deep within an invisible ocean, but they all learned to ignore it as best they could. Earth's atmosphere was permeated by the dead. Trillions of people, animals, birds, and insects had been exploded into dust by the machine plague. Replicating without end, the *archos* tech used every available speck of carbon and iron to build more of itself, disintegrating untold megatons of living flesh into microscopic machines—machines that, in their own fashion, still lived on.

The *archos* tech would forever seek new hosts. Thousands of inert nanos covered every short yard of ground, thicker here, thinner there, like unseen membranes and drifts. With each step Cam stirred up great puffs of it. The only reason they could survive below ten thousand feet was because they'd beaten it. Their own bodies had become tiny processing stations, destroying insignificant amounts of the machine

plague every day, after Ruth and her colleagues found a way
to shield them.

Could she do it again?

Protect her, he thought. *Protect her and maybe everything
will be okay again.*

Their only salvation was the vaccine nano. Originally, it
had been an inefficient savior. It could be overwhelmed. In
an ideal scenario it would have killed the machine plague as
soon as the plague touched their skin or lungs. Realistically,
its capacity to target the plague was limited and it functioned
best against live, active infections. That was a problem. The
plague took minutes or even hours to "wake up" after it was
absorbed by a host. In that time, it could travel farther than was
easily understood. Human beings were comprised of miles
upon miles of veins, tissue, organs, and muscle—and once
the machine plague began to replicate, the body's own pulse
became a weakness, distributing the nanotech everywhere.

The first version of the vaccine was not so aggressive. It
couldn't be. It was able to build more of itself only by tearing
apart its rival. Otherwise it would have been another plague.
Ruth had taught it to recognize the unique structure of the
plague's heat engine, which it shared, and she had given it
the ability to sense the fraction of a calorie of waste heat that
the plague generated repeatedly as it constructed more of itself,
but the first vaccine was always behind its brother. Smaller
and faster than the plague, the earliest model of the vaccine
was able to eradicate its prey, but only after the chase.

The final version of the vaccine surpassed all those weaknesses. It suffused their bodies like disease-specific antibod-
ies, attacking the constant absorption of the machine plague
before the plague nanos could activate.

*Maybe the vaccine can be reprogrammed to make us
immune to the new plague, too,* Cam thought.

"I'm here," he said into his headset, reaching up to knock
on the cabin wall. Then he realized he wasn't upwind of her
home. What if it was leaking?

"Cam?" Her voice was muffled, wrapped inside her containment suit. "Where are you?"

"I'm at the wall," he said, although he'd backed away from
the small building. Her place was dark. Even in the daytime,

in fact, it looked no different than the rest of their huts, except that this cabin had even fewer windows than most, just one in the small living room and another in Eric and Bobbi's space. Ruth needed electricity at all hours, so they'd wired her room with more outlets than normal and left it with no openings to betray what was inside.

This hut was the secret heart of their village. Ruth actually slept in the front room, which lacked any privacy, but her bedroom was a clean lab partitioned with plastic sheeting. It was crude and inefficient—and it worked. Eric had been her closest bodyguard, a role that once belonged to Cam. He hadn't been inside for months. There was never a good excuse since they'd upgraded the electrical lines, and he'd promised himself to leave her alone for Allison's sake. Even so, he remembered sharing a cool glass of tea with Ruth and Eric, sitting on the living room floor beside the other man but acutely aware of Ruth's narrow bedroll and the open-faced cupboard she used to store her clothes, her toothbrush, a lipstick, a book. The tidy space had been full of the little personal things he never saw anymore.

"Is there anyone with you?" she asked.

Cam glanced over his shoulder, suddenly uncomfortable with where she was going. "It's just me," he said.

"Can you switch channels? I want to talk alone."

"Greg?" he asked his headset, and the former Army Ranger sergeant said, "This is bullshit. You stay on the line."

Other voices filled the frequency. "He's right!" Owen shouted, as another man said, "We let you *live* here. We took you in when nobody else wanted anything to do with nano-tech and now you're going to hide something from—"

Cam shut off his radio, leaving the headset in place. Then he stepped closer to the cabin and rapped his knuckles against the wood. "Can you hear me? Ruth?"

There was a noise from another part of the hut, a thump, thump like someone convulsing on the floor.

"Ruth!" he yelled, imagining Patrick or Michael loose in the cabin. He jogged alongside the building to the front room before he realized he couldn't fire through the window or break down the door. If he did, the new plague would have him, too. But what if the infected men grabbed Ruth or tore her suit? Cam turned on his flashlight and aimed the beam inside. "Hey!" he yelled. The plastic on the window distorted the light. He couldn't see more than the long shape of the cupboards, so he banged on the glass, hoping to distract anyone at the door to Ruth's lab. "Hey!"

The thumping increased, an uneven drumbeat. It sounded like someone was thrashing back and forth. Cam also heard a woman moan inside. Linda? There were other voices hollering across the village. He saw another flashlight. Then he realized Ruth was shouting in the other end of the hut.

"Cam? Cam, I'm okay! Where are you?"

He ran to the wall of her room again. "I'm here! I thought—"

"They won't stop *moving*. Linda and Patrick especially, they're so restless! I taped their hands and feet, even tied them to the table, but they won't stop *moving*."

Cam grimaced, trying to calm the storm inside his head. It was too easy to picture her inside. Ruth was trapped. Lunatics and corpses blocked the way to the only door . . . and yet she had to stay.

"What can I do?" he called.

"Get me out!"

"I—We can't do that."

Her voice cracked. "Get me out, Cam! I know how to do it. I'm already decontaminating this section of the lab. Then you guys cut open the wall."

The wall? he thought. This hut was wood like all the rest, but they'd lined the inside of the building with bricks and aluminum sheeting, reinforcing it like no other. Cam supposed they could chop out a hole with saws and pry bars, but why?

"You have to stay," he said.

"Please, Cam!"

"Aren't you working in there?"

Ruth only banged on the wall as if echoing the spasms in the other room. Whether she'd done it consciously or not, the sound filled Cam with alarm.

"We can't build you another lab!" he yelled.

The paddle wheels in the creek were a triumph of engineering. They'd hired two guys out of Morristown to install a series of wheels and gears in the strongest part of the current,

trading in corn futures for a five-kilowatt generator to trans-
form that energy into electricity. Then, after those men left,
Cam, Eric, and some others buried most of the power lines to
disguise the real focal point of their grid.

Allison and the mayors of Freedom and New Jackson had
managed to equip Ruth with an atomic force microscope and
basic machining gear. The military had informants everywhere, but Allison trusted her underground.

Cam switched off his flashlight. "It's only been an hour
and a half," he said. "You can fix this."

"I can't."

"If you leave your equipment—"

"Listen to me! I've done what I can here. This AFM is *old*,
Cam. I need better equipment if I'm really going to be able to
understand this nanotech, much less take it apart."

He shut his eyes in the dark. *It was the best we could find,*
he thought, *and you'll never know how much food Allison
gave up just to buy that gear.*

"It doesn't make sense to wait until the helicopters show
up," she said. "I don't think you realize how long it'll take me
to decontaminate or to open the wall! We need to be ready
when they show up."

"I don't think we can count on them, Ruth."

She paused. Then she got loud again. "You said Grand
Lake is sending a chopper!"

"I said I asked for one."

"I can't . . . I . . ."

There was another noise from her side of the wall that
sounded like the infected people, aimless and insane. Was she
pacing? "You can retool the vaccine," he said.

"With what!? Goddammit, with what!? Are you listening
to me? Most of my work here has been *theoretical*, Cam! This
equipment is *junk*!"

He wanted to shout back at her, but the fire went out of him.
For the second time that night, he knew what Ruth intended
to say next, although he shied away from it, hoping he would
hear something else. He had left so many people behind in
other fights.

"What about our friends in there?" he asked.

"My advice is to run for it. We might have some chance at

staying ahead of this thing if we go now. Right now. We need to get away from Morristown."

It was exactly what he'd been thinking, and he hated them both for it. "Not everyone will go," he said. "They'll never go, Ruth. You know they won't. What about Susan or Jen? Their *husbands* are in there."

"There's no other way," she said.

8

Ruth scratched at the wall again. "Please!" she yelled, begging now. Her claustrophobia was alive in her chest, twisting and lashing like the monsters in the other room. More than anything, she wanted *out*.

She wanted to be with him.

"Cam!?" she yelled inside the hot shell of her helmet. Her containment suit was damp with sweat. She was roasting in it. Each breath was an effort and her faceplate had fogged along one edge, creating a blind spot to her right. The lab was a neat white cube and well-lit with four bulbs, but Ruth kept turning her head, thinking she'd seen the shadow of someone who wasn't there.

Her heart jumped each time Patrick lurched against the floor, setting off moans and shuffling from Linda, Michael, and Andrew, too, if he was still alive. Patrick had grown increasingly agitated. Ruth could only imagine the tangled mess of the living and the dead in the next room as Pat dragged himself through his friends. What if she hadn't tied him well enough?

She set her gloves against the plastic sheeting on the wall. How thick was the cabin's exterior? Eight inches? Ruth could nearly feel every layer of wood, brick, aluminum, and wood again, but there was a thinner and more vital barrier between herself and Cam—the plastic itself. Her lab was like a tent inside the white room, and she wondered how long the plastic sheeting would hold if Patrick or Michael burst in. Not long.

"We don't have much time!" she shouted. "Cam!?"

"I'll ask Greg," he said at last.

"Get me out!"

"I'll ask, Ruth."

She could barely hear him, panting inside the muggy air of her helmet. Normally she would have been moving slowly, trying not to overheat, with the knowledge that she could always take the suit off if necessary. Instead, she'd run a marathon. Worse, this work space was filthy with nanotech. Her clean lab had been breached.

The plastic tent in the room consisted of two unequal compartments. The first section was secured to three of the room's four walls, a six-by-six foot area jammed with her small desk, her laptop, the short, stumpy pylons of her microscopes, and other electronics. The second pocket was much smaller, a closet-sized airlock that stood just inside the door to the room. It served as a decon/dressing space, complete with an ordinary vacuum cleaner and storage bags for the blue hospital scrubs she typically wore in the lab. There was also a rack for her containment suit, which was almost impossible for one person to put on alone.

In her hurry to get outside wearing the suit, Ruth must have pulled open one of the seals between the decon chamber and the main tent. The lab was equipped with an emergency kit to resecure the plastic—a low-tech assortment of tape, a box knife, two rolls of plastic sheeting, extension cords, and a soldering gun—but she was uncertain what she could have done about the tear even if she'd seen it before she reentered the tent. There was little chance she could have sterilized her suit in the first place. The vacuum cleaner was only intended to remove dust, lint, and hair from her clothing before she went inside.

They'd installed other emergency measures: a makeshift air exchange system, and powerful UV lamps that should at least hinder an out-of-control nano if not burn it completely. Ruth believed she could reseal the lab from within, then decontaminate it and her suit, but then what? Making a break for the front door wouldn't do her any good. Without the suit, she wouldn't get two steps into the next room, and, wearing it, she would only contaminate herself again with no way left to remove the protective skin before she ran out of air. She needed help. She couldn't cut through the exterior wall herself . . .

What if they said no?

Her sense of déjà vu took her back to the International Space Station. The Leadville government had refused to bring her back to Earth because she was an asset they couldn't replace once she was gone, no matter that she swore there was nothing else she could do in orbit. Now she faced the same dilemma. The terrified people in Jefferson might insist on keeping her in her lab, which was why she'd asked Cam to come alone. Not so long ago, the two of them had been very close, although she could only guess how his grief had changed him.

He sounded as if he'd been about to suggest she had to stay if only to take care of the infected people. No one else could approach them.

But I can give someone else my suit if I'm outside, she thought.

Maybe a better person would have volunteered to tend to their friends. Unfortunately, in her own way Ruth had become as damaged as any survivor, not only because of the bloodshed she'd witnessed but also because of her long months spent in solitude, second-guessing everything she'd done.

Her equipment was not as bad as she'd told Cam. None of the things she'd said were lies, just exaggerations to make her point. The atomic force microscope was an IBM Centipede exactly like the one she'd used in Grand Lake. Instead of the traditional, single probe, it had a tip array of a hundred points working in parallel. Once she'd secured a plague nano to her test surface, Ruth had been able to map its general exterior in less than seventeen minutes, after which she'd begun to probe deeper into the machine, which was covered with wrinkles and furrows, ironically, much like the human brain.

There was no question that she could do better in a real lab with assistants and more computing power—but she could have stayed. She was afraid to remain here alone. She was too full of bad energy, which only compounded her guilt.

These people had put their faith in her. They'd worked so hard, from constructing this lab to selling corn futures to buy the small Ingersoll Rand air compressor they'd modified to recharge her suit's tanks after those rare times she wore it instead of her hospital scrubs. They'd even hauled a washer/dryer unit to the village and installed it in their shower building solely for the use of her scrubs. Everyone else did their laundry in the creek, even the new mothers. All of their precautions, every ounce of determination and grit . . . Would it be enough?

What if she was the weak link?

That's not true, she thought, arguing with herself. *It's not! If nothing else, we need to get moving before more sick people stumble into town. They want to believe it can't happen, but it will.*

Ruth picked up the walkie-talkie. She'd turned it down to hear Cam through the wall, because it was still rattling with other voices. She interrupted them, upping its volume as she hit the SEND button. "This is Goldman." She hadn't planned to speak formally, but the old habit came back easily and she used it like a weapon, covering her remorse with a tone full of steel. "I'm coming out."

"Wait!" Greg said. "Ruth, wait."

"I want to dictate my findings so far."

"What is she talking about?" one woman asked, as another female voice said, "Let me find some paper! Ruth? This is Bobbi. Let me find some paper first."

"You have to stay inside," Greg said. "No one else can do this for you."

"He's right," Cam said.

"I'm coming out!" Ruth said, but this time she heard less conviction in her own voice. Most of her attention was still on the words she couldn't say to Cam.

I'm sorry, she thought. *I miss Allison, too.*

In the next room, Patrick convulsed again, rustling and banging. Ruth wondered if he was dying. Was she honor-bound to go see? What if she could stop him from choking or if he was bleeding again? "I've already done most of what I can with this equipment," she said. "Please believe me. If there was more—"

A different man cut in. "What about Linda and Michael?"

"Someone else can have my suit if they want to go back inside. You should fill the air tanks again, and meanwhile—"

"Ruth, that's a huge waste of time," Greg said.

"Meanwhile, I can run more analysis on my laptop! That's exactly what you want me to do, and it's not safe in here!"

The other man protested. "Linda would never—"

"I'll bring my computer and the AFM, but you need to get me out."

It was Cam who spoke against her next. "You said the lab's contaminated," he said, warning the others.

Oh, Cam, she thought. *I need to be able to count on you.*

"What does that mean?" someone asked, and Greg said, "Ruth, the nanotech's loose in there, too?"

"You're going to need awhile to get some tools together anyway. I'll sterilize things in here, and while I'm doing that I'll tell you what I've learned."

"There's no way to know if you're clean," Cam said.

"There is."

"Ruth, can't it wait?" Bobbi asked. "Pay attention to what you're doing. Tell us what you can after you're outside."

"No, I'll tell you now," she said, struggling again with her claustrophobia, but it filled her voice with emotion. "I'm going to take off my suit before you open the wall," she said, "so there's a good chance I won't make it out of here without being infected myself."

Ruth knew who'd built the mind plague. She recognized the work, even though most of it was based on the same breakthroughs of the machine plague and every other nanotech that followed. The first plague had been a gateway. Once opened, it pointed the way for everything else.

Of course, its design team hadn't meant it as a plague at all. The people behind the *archos* tech, a duo named Kendra Freedman and Al Sawyer, intended their device to be a cancer cure—and they'd succeeded in two of the three major challenges to nano-scale machines. For an energy source, the *archos* tech used the body heat of its host. To create enough nanos to accomplish any significant chore, it contained a wildly efficient replication key, allowing a single nano to become two, which became four, which became sixteen—in seconds.

The vaccine was only the same technology refined. It was no more intelligent than its brother. That was why the early models were imperfect. The vaccine had only the slightest capacity to discriminate between the plague and other molecular structures. That changed when the science teams in Leadville improved the vaccine's ability to think. It was a real chore to bestow the faculties of awareness and decision upon machines this size without crimping their operational speed, but as soon as the vaccine was able to outpace its rival, U.S. forces gained a small advantage over the Russians and Chinese.

Unfortunately, the nanotech was too ethereal for the U.S. to keep to themselves. The final version of the vaccine spread as inexorably as the machine plague itself. Whenever a soldier loaded his weapon, each time ground crews rearmed a jet, their breath, sweat, and blood were thick with microscopic machines—and so another benefit was carried to the enemy, too.

Days before the bombing, Leadville also developed a nanotech called the booster. Again, its core was based on what they already knew. The booster used the same heat engine, and it made more of itself only by disassembling the machine plague, but this nano had the true beginnings of intelligence. The discrimination key that served the vaccine so well was at last becoming something more profound.

The booster was intended to read its host's DNA and to reinforce that information. Ultimately, it would even correct and maintain those codes. A man who received a perfect booster in his twenties would *always* be in his twenties, immune to viruses and infections and protected from the slow deterioration caused by age, poor diet, or genetic miscues like diabetes, heart disease, and cancer. The first model of the booster was light-years short of this magic, but it had given Ruth, Cam, and many others some protection from radiation poisoning on the outskirts of the Leadville crater.

Again, the nanotech had spread. The booster was now

worldwide exactly like the vaccine, available for everyone to use and study. Ruth knew there was also a fourth fully functional nano, because it was hers.

The parasite had no benign features whatsoever. It was a violently simplified model of the booster combined with a new discrimination key, a rough, bare bones machine *designed to attack the vaccine instead of the machine plague*. This was the doomsday weapon she'd created in Grand Lake. It would have left everyone vulnerable to the machine plague again, laying waste to the armies on all sides as they scrambled for elevation.

Ruth couldn't say what avenues were being pursued by other allied researchers. As for herself, she just didn't have the stomach for more killing. She'd set aside her own efforts at weaponized nanotech to develop new spin-offs of the booster, pursuing medical technology that would not only prevent disease—it should also heal wounds such as Cam's old, body-wide injuries. There were hundreds of thousands of people with plague scarring, and thousands more still struggling with radiation sickness or burns. Ruth wanted to help. Now that decision seemed like a criminal error. The other side had pulled far ahead when she might have been the one to destroy them first.

"The nanotech is Chinese," Ruth said, calling to the walkie-talkie. She'd set it on the desktop to free her hands as she worked a UV lamp over her equipment. "The style is too similar to everything else of theirs I've seen. That wasn't much, but Leadville was studying enemy programs as closely as possible."

"You're sure, Ruth?" Greg said.

"Yes. The nanotech is Chinese." She tried to irradiate every nook and seam, which was especially difficult among her paperwork, her laptop, the two microscopes, picoammeter, and power cords. She had to ruffle through her gear with one hand as she held the lamp with the other.

The light seared her eyes even though she kept her face half turned, using her helmet as a shield. The purple-white heat felt like a small sun. It was no accident that she targeted her gear and the desk first, because the lamp might compromise the material of her suit. In fact, it could melt through the plastic sheeting if she wasn't careful.

Ruth heard another thump and lifted her head. Had that noise come from outside? She turned back to her desk. Every drawer was suspect. She opened the first one and shone the light inside, pushing her other hand through a few pencils, file clips, and a voice recorder. The next drawer held her working notes, and the third was empty. She had so little to show for her time in this place.

"I don't know how it's replicating," she said, "but it's closely based on the booster tech. The heat engine is similar, even the general structure, except they've added a lot of bulk. It's bigger. More sophisticated. At a guess, I'd say this thing is made of nearly two billion AMU."

No one questioned the acronym. *Atomic mass units.* Most of them had soaked up as much technical knowledge as possible, and Bobbi said, "If it's using the same heat engine, can't you reprogram the vaccine to attack it, too?"

What had Cam told them?

"We can try," Ruth said. "It's a very different machine. I also subjected it to low air pressure and I don't think it has the hypobaric fuse, so it won't self-destruct above ten thousand feet." She paused over her desk, then aimed the UV lamp at the walkie-talkie, too, uncertain if it would fry the radio.

There was another clunking sound in front of her and this time she was sure it was from outside. *Good.*

"Cam?" she said.

"What is the nanotech doing to us?" he asked, and Ruth smiled with relief that the walkie-talkie was fine. But her smile evaporated in the harsh light. "I don't know," she said. "It goes for the brain, obviously. Maybe the nervous system, too. It's some kind of biological warfare."

"I'll get a work crew together," he said.

"Thank you." *Oh, God, thank you,* she thought. Then she turned the radio over and irradiated its other side.

The UV bath wasn't guaranteed to pulverize the nanotech. At most, it should damage the invisible machines. It would be more effective in combination with X-rays, but they hadn't been able to find what they needed in the small hospital in

Steamboat Springs. Like electrical generators, the most common medical equipment had been scavenged long ago. They hadn't even been able to buy one on the local market.

Trying to scour the light over every millimeter of her suit was infuriating. The tanks on her back nearly threw her on her head when she tried to reach her boots. Once she pressed her knuckles against the plastic on the floor, yanking the lamp away just in time. She knelt against the desk just to keep her balance, working the lamp over every crease in her legs, neck, and sleeves with cold-blooded precision.

Ruth pointed the lamp sideways across her faceplate, too, with her eyes scrunched tight against the purple heat. She twisted to aim the light up and down her air tanks, contorting her upper body. Finally she turned to the tent itself. She was patient, sweeping the light back and forth like a paintbrush.

In the other room, Patrick continued to worm against the floor. *Bam. Scraaatch. Bam. Bam.*

"*Huuh,*" Linda groaned. "*Huuh.*"

"I'm going to turn on the fans," Ruth said. "You guys should back off in case something goes wrong."

"Ruth, wait," Bobbi said, just as Greg said, "No! You have to tell us more."

"That's all I know. Where is Cam?"

"This isn't a good idea!"

"Greg, it would take me days to pull the nano apart with this AFM. What I have is a surface scan. It's in my laptop. I can keep trying to make sense of it, but I'm coming out."

She hoped Cam would say something, too. Anything. She ached for reassurance and a friendly voice. She just wanted to make contact again. Didn't he realize it might be for the last time? But he must have been busy redistributing their guards and finding tools.

"I'll call you when I'm ready," she told Greg. Then she punched the emergency switch bolted to her desktop.

The room jumped. Ruth almost fell. Loose pages ripped up past her face as the plastic snapped tight on all sides. Behind her, it ballooned outward like a sail. The tent was secured to the ceiling, floor, and three of the four walls, where hundreds of carpenter's staples had been shot through reinforced patches, but the airlock and the decon tent were only tied to the floor. That end of the tent wanted to pull free. Her suit leapt in the same way. The chest piece hiked up against her collar and her sleeves trembled in the cyclone.

There were two square metal frames set in the tent, a small one in the ceiling and a larger one beneath her. They'd bolted a heavy-duty exhaust fan into the floor and an air compressor overhead. The fan was nearly four feet wide. Eric and Cam had taken it from a press shop, where it was used to vent bad air away from the shop's employees. Here, it fed clean air into the room through two openings hidden in the cabin's foundation. They hadn't wanted to seat it in the wall where it might raise questions if the military ever came through town.

Ruth rubbed her hands over as much surface area as she could reach in quick, arcing motions, hoping to scrape free any nanotech clinging to the tent.

Suddenly the plastic on her right tore loose from its staples, bumping her shoulder and hip. Ruth screamed. *"Aaaah!"* The plastic itself was intact—only the stapled patches on the outside had torn—but if any more of the plastic came free, the tent might collapse around her like a net—or it might rip.

Either accident would probably kill her.

Don't stop, she thought, clapping her gloves together as she glanced up through the howling channel overhead. Then she began to scrub feverishly at the plastic again.

The A-frame roof of her hut was sturdier than it needed to be. It was designed to bear the weight of snow, but the beams in the ceiling also supported the air compressor and duct work leading to a storage tank about the size of a small car. They'd found the compressor in the garage of a pipeline testing company. It was powered by the huge diesel engine from a Peterbilt truck, which they'd hidden in a cellar beneath the cabin, running a drive belt and an exhaust line into the roof. Ruth couldn't hear the engine because of the fan, but it was probably adding to the dangerous vibrations throughout the building.

The compressor was rated at 2,700 cubic feet per minute. That meant it could swap the air out of her lab in seconds, again and again and again, but it was impossible to ensure that the room was safe. Even if 90 percent of the contamination was sucked away in the first minute, and, in the second minute, 90 percent of the remainder was taken, there would always be a miniscule amount left behind.

Unfortunately, the tent wasn't holding up well, and Ruth worried about the rest of the system, too. If she continued to subject it to full power, the compressor might blow out or the ducts might leak, which was why they'd situated her hut on the southern edge of Jefferson. This cabin was generally downwind. An accidental discharge should be carried away from town.

What if it wasn't?

Shaking from exhaustion, Ruth climbed onto the desk with a fold of plastic from the repair kit. It shook and leapt in her hands like a flag. The vent in the ceiling was already partially blocked by wads of paper and she let go of her patch, clogging the vent completely. Then she kicked her boot into the emergency switch and turned off the system.

The fan died before the diesel engine sputtered and quit. There was no need to hold the patch in place. Most of it had been sucked tight into the grill and Ruth taped the edges as fast as possible, securing it to the ceiling of the tent.

She repeated the process with another, larger square. Then she got down and surveyed her lab. The tent was still secured to the wall behind the desk. That wasn't the wall she'd intended to have them chop open, but it would have to do. Outside the tent, the room itself hadn't been decontaminated. She would need to melt and seal the plastic to the wall before they cut their way in.

She found her walkie-talkie. "I'm okay," she said, leaning over the desk to knock on the wall.

Cam said, "Ruth? Jesus, Ruth, it sounded like the whole place was coming apart."

"Change of plans. I want you to come through this wall instead." She knocked again and was answered by a dull *chak* like a pry bar hitting the wood. There must have been a group of them outside and she yelled, "No, stop! Stop!"

Cam echoed her. "Stop it! Stop! We need to make sure we're in the right place!"

Ruth looked away from the wall, feeling wistful and scared

and glad. He was always so fast to understand her, except when she tried to talk about her feelings—but there was another reason for them to hold off. "I want to hit the entire lab with UV again," she said, reaching for the lamp. "Give me ten minutes."

Twenty minutes later, she realized she was only delaying the inevitable. She had to trust the decontamination. She was out of options. This was it.

"Cam," she said to the walkie-talkie, but everyone else was listening, and Allison's body lay just a few feet away in the other room. It wasn't right to say anything. Still, she wished she could tell him so many things.

"I'm here," he said. "We're ready."

"Wait for my signal," she said lamely. She shut off the lamp and cracked the seal on her collar. The moist heat surrounding her body *woosh*ed out of the suit. Ruth couldn't help but hold her breath even as she closed her eyes, not only to protect them but to savor the soft, cool air on her face.

Did I get all of it? she wondered.

Standing alone in the plastic, separated from him by just a few feet, Ruth waited to see if she'd lose her mind.

9

Cam was uncertain at first when Ruth's face appeared in the gash in the wall. Her curly hair was matted and sweaty. Her skin looked bright red in their flashlights, and her eyes were bloodshot. Some of the men stumbled back. They banged against each other as Greg stiffened with his rifle. "Ruth!?" Greg shouted.

"I'm okay," she said.

There was a sunburned patch across the right side of her face that began as a remarkably square corner on her temple. Cam realized it was the same shape as the faceplate in her helmet. She'd done it to herself with the UV lamp.

He pushed through the others to reach her. "Careful," he said. He was still armored in his goggles and face mask, and yet Ruth tried to meet his gaze in the white beams of the flashlights. Then she smiled and ducked back inside with a noise like a laugh.

"Wait!" he yelled.

Her euphoria seemed out of place. Cam wondered if he had the guts to club her if she popped her face into the gap again. Was she infected? *But she's talking,* he thought.

"Here," she said, filling the hole in the wall with her laptop.

Her hands fluttered once and then vanished. The black Dell would have fallen if Cam hadn't dropped his crowbar and caught the laptop instead.

Through the wall, he saw her lab and the plastic tent. Ruth stood very close to him, yanking at something on her desk with lithe, harried movements. Cam finally realized how eager she was to escape and he thought of other times when she hadn't acted her age, either. Sometimes her intellect was overshadowed by her emotions. In fact, Cam thought that energy was tied directly to her IQ. Part of Ruth's genius was her ability to tap deep into herself, but her moods could be dangerous, too, childish and loud.

"Help me," he said, holding the laptop out to the group. No one took it and he barked, "Help me! There'll be more stuff in a second."

A man named Matthew grabbed the laptop and Cam turned again just as Ruth muscled her AFM into the gap in the wall.

The atomic force microscope wasn't much bigger than his thigh, a white metal cylinder with a stout base and a tapered white cone that rose to a single black eyepiece. Cam had always marveled that something so small could design machines of such consequence, but, by its very definition, nanotech was infinitesimal. The AFM housed a power system and a shovelful of microprocessors, yet most of its bulk was only necessary to provide optics and controls that could be used by human beings. The heart of the machine, its computerized tip array and work surface, filled a space no larger than a dime.

The AFM weighed forty pounds, though, and Ruth shoved it through as hard as she could. Cam slumped beneath the device, catching it at an awkward angle against the wall. "Wait!" he shouted. Owen shouldered in beside him. The two of them lugged the microscope away through the debris on the ground. Cam nearly twisted his ankle when he stepped on a chunk of wood and then some loose bricks.

From the corner of his eye, he saw Matthew go to the hole in time to catch two notebooks and Ruth's containment suit, a yellow wad that spilled its legs and sleeves over Matthew's body. The air tanks tipped out of Matthew's grasp and pulled the suit to the ground.

"Jesus, Ruth!" Cam shouted, but she wasn't listening.

"Cam!" she yelled. "Where is Cam?"

He left the AFM with Owen and another man, running back to the hut. Ruth held a piece of paper. Matthew made as if to grab it, but Ruth shook her head in one violent, sideways motion.

"Cam?" she said, trusting the paper only to him.

He recognized it in a glance. A map. After the war, they'd carried the vial of the parasite nanotech with them. What else could they do? At first they needed it as a goad against the enemy and their own government, forcing both sides to stand down, and then they were caught in another kind of trap. They found a small shockproof case for it, a plastic clamshell meant to hold a pair of glasses, but if the parasite broke loose in an accident—if they were robbed or killed—it would destroy the world again. The vial was too dangerous to leave behind. They wanted to bury it, but what if rain or erosion brought it to the surface? Someone might open it.

They hadn't found a solution until they settled in Jefferson. They bought an iron box in Morristown and stenciled warnings on it in English, Hebrew, and Russian. Now the vial was buried twelve feet down in the foothills west of town. It would have to stay there. They couldn't spare two or three hours to dig the box up again, even if the parasite might be exactly what they needed to threaten the Chinese. Could they still bluff the enemy?

"Cam!" Ruth said.

He was staring. He snatched the paper from her and stuffed it into his jacket pocket, freeing his hands again as he tried to think. "What else do we need?"

Her hands scrabbled at the wall, feeling for places to set herself. Then she tumbled forward. Matthew tried to hold her but Ruth fell against the wall, cracking one arm. "Oh!" she cried.

"Ruth, stop! Is there anything else we need in there?"

She flailed through the hole, hanging upside down until Cam snarled his left hand in the back of her shirt. Matthew took her arm. Together they set her on her feet.

Ruth seemed rejuvenated by the cool night air. In the shifting beams of the flashlights, her burnt, naked face looked both excited and vulnerable. There was sweat in her bangs and her breath came hard, lifting her breasts against her shirt. When she leaned against him, Cam hugged her briefly—but he leaned away before she could put her arms around him, too.

She didn't even turn off the lights in there before she jumped out, he thought, worrying at the illuminated gash in the wall. He realized he hadn't seen her bring her walkie-talkie, either. Should he climb back inside to get it and kill the lights? That seemed crazy.

"Okay, let's go," Ruth said. Her tone was still out of sync with the rest of them, too vibrant, even happy, and Cam sensed the others stirring behind their flashlights.

"Go where?" Owen said.

"East. We can't hold this place against the plague."

Greg shook his head. "We made contact with Grand Lake again. We told them everything you said, and they're sending choppers."

"For everyone? When?"

"If we're not here—"

"Bring the radio," Ruth said. "The helicopters can adjust. But you can't expect everyone to wait for a rescue that doesn't exist. Do you really think Grand Lake's going to send *ten* choppers?"

They stared at her in the dark.

"No," Greg said.

Ruth pressed her advantage. "We don't have the equipment to shelter in place, so we go for Grand Lake. The mountains should stop the infected people! They're clumsy, disoriented. They won't follow us."

How much of that is her claustrophobia talking? Cam wondered. *She just wants to move.* "The nanotech is airborne," he said. "It'll follow us even if they don't."

"It'll be worse where there are carriers! We have to take that chance. Run for high ground."

"Okay." Greg nodded slowly and lifted his walkie-talkie to relay Ruth's demand. "We're going to pack up and drive east," he said to the rest of the village.

* * *

Most of the people in the sealed huts didn't want to leave, nor did several of the men and women at the guard posts. "We don't know what's out there!" Susan yelled on her walkie-talkie from inside.

"At least here we have a chance to protect ourselves," Owen said. "Besides, there's barely any gasoline. How far do you think you can walk after the trucks run dry?"

"You're not taking the radio!" Susan yelled as other villagers filled Cam's headset with noise.

"They can't—"

"—need it as much as—"

He shut off his headset altogether. Most of their voices were still audible in the night, but the decision bought him a little space as he walked to the nearest sealed hut. Greg, Ruth, and Matthew came with him, but Owen went in another direction, probably looking for his buddy Neil. All of them wanted their closest friends.

"Susan!" Cam said, trying to sound calm even hollering through the plastic. "If you're smart, you'll come with us. But the Ranger element is leaving town and that radio is ours."

Greg rapped on the door. "Tricia! Trish! Let's go."

"I don't think we should leave!" Tricia yelled.

Cam tried another name. "Bobbi?" Could she even hear him? People were arguing and the baby was squalling, too. Cam turned to look past the hut. Two flashlights rocked through the darkness on the east side of the village, and a third winked into view from behind the dining hall. There was also someone yelling in that direction. Cam figured they had a minute at most before Owen showed up with Neil.

"We might have to break in," he said.

"She's scared," Greg said, needlessly explaining for his wife. Cam felt a confused pang of envy and his own protective instincts. In some ways things were easier for him with Allison dead. He had less to lose. But he would fight for his friend's wife and infant daughter, Hope.

Greg Estey was as solid as anyone Cam had ever known, smart, if quiet, and unconcerned with bullshit like ego or rank. He'd let go of everything from his previous life to

fit himself into Jefferson, maintaining only his loyalty to
Ruth as he found new ways to define himself. Farmer. Husband. Father. He put his thumb on the SEND button of his
walkie-talkie and said, "Bobbi? It's Greg. Let me talk to
Trish, please."

Cam turned his headset on again as Susan interrupted on
the same frequency. "No way!" she said. "There's no way!"

The door was double-sealed, inside and out. Cam peeled
away the plastic sheeting on the outside, but he didn't want
to tear the layers inside. He wanted them to open up themselves. Then the people who stayed behind would have a better chance of resecuring the hut.

The flashlights were on top of them now. Cam winced as
one of the beams cut across his face. Another light traced over
the front of the hut, lingering on the torn plastic. "You son of a
bitch!" Owen yelled. "They were safe in there! You can't—"

"Bobbi wants out," Cam said softly. Behind his flashlight,
the other man was only a silhouette, faceless and menacing.
"Just let us go," Cam said. "That's all we want."

"The radio stays here," Owen said.

"No."

"Owen, we'll send help if we find it!" Ruth said. "You
know we will."

Greg spoke simultaneously to his walkie-talkie and to the
door of the hut. "My family is coming out! You stay if you
have to. We'll even seal the outside of the door for you."

"Fuck that," Owen said, also transmitting. "We'll do it ourselves. Go on. Go." He jerked his flashlight away from them
into the dark, as if casting them out, but his voice had grown
rigid and controlled like Cam's. Owen was willing to accept
the compromise, giving them the radio to avoid a fight. Cam's
relief was intense. It also gave way to an impulsive sense of
camaraderie, because they were better than their fear. They'd
talked it out instead of using their fists.

"Owen, come with us," he said suddenly.

"Just go," Owen snapped.

The door opened from the inside. The baby's screaming
got louder and lantern light spilled across the ground, full
of shadows. Susan blocked the doorway as Bobbi pushed

through with the Harris radio. Bobbi had already put on her jacket and Cam took the radio so she could don her goggles, gloves, mask, and hood.

"You're making a mistake!" Susan said.

Tricia herself was bare-headed, probably for Hope's sake. Otherwise the little girl might not recognize her mother. Tears spilled down Tricia's cheeks as she desperately shushed and cooed at her baby.

"Sweetheart," Greg said.

Their headsets and walkie-talkies crackled again. "This is Eleven," a woman said in a whisper. "I see people in the fences. This is Ingrid at Eleven and there are at least twenty people in the fences!"

Everyone froze except Hope. The baby's angry sounds continued to lift on the wind.

Oh, no, Cam thought.

They'd done it to themselves. The commotion they'd made had been like a giant beacon in the night, yelling at each other and waving lights all over town. Now they'd attracted more infected people from beyond the village.

"Get inside!" Cam shouted. He tried to force Ruth back through the door, but she resisted.

"Let go of me!"

"I love you! Stay here!" Greg yelled at Tricia as the young woman said, "Greg, no—"

Cam and Ruth stared at each other, locked in each other's grip. The other couple's words might have been their own, and Ruth said, "I—"

Cam broke away from her as there was a second alert on his headset. "This is Eleven!" the radio whispered again. "They're caught up in the fences. Should I open fire?"

The channel filled with noise. "No, wait," Cam said, but Owen and several others were talking on the same frequency.

"—at Two I see them—"

"Light 'em up."

"No!" Cam yelled. "No, shut off every light we've got!"

He and Owen took their first steps toward Station Eleven, but Ruth and Bobbi followed, and Cam whirled to face the two women. "Get back inside!" he said.

In that moment, Owen outpaced him.

"Bobbi," Cam said. "Stop. Ruth, you go with her and—"

"We can't hide in there if—"

"Do it!" Cam bellowed in her face before he shoved the radio against Bobbi, weighing her down. "Go inside! Go!"

People were shouting on the north perimeter as their flashlights jabbed and swayed. "Get back!" a man yelled. "Get back or we'll shoot!"

Two of the villagers stood with their weapons aimed. A third wrestled a floodlight into place. The Bull Dog was a light-weight aluminum tripod with dual five-hundred-watt bulbs. It was the long extension cord that was giving the man trouble. The floods weren't on yet. There were only flashlights.

At the farthest edge of the beams, human shadows moved in the fences. Cam counted nine, and he hoped Ingrid had exaggerated the threat.

I don't see twenty people here, he thought.

The strangers banged through the low obstacles. One was stuck in a line of barbed wire, tugging at her left arm. None of them were fast or graceful. Cam's impression was that of sleepwalkers. Maybe he was too influenced by their clothing. Most of them looked as if they were dressed for bed in loose, warm clothing. One man wore only his underwear. Very few had any shoes. They wore socks or were barefoot. They looked like they'd been taken completely by surprise, rising from their sleep into another kind of dream.

Maybe the ant swarm in Greenhouse 3 had actually saved lives in Jefferson by keeping everyone awake. Otherwise the old woman might have walked among them unchallenged, infecting their guards and then everyone in town.

But why did they come here? Cam wondered. These people had followed the wind southward instead of walking into it. Why? The flashlights couldn't have been visible until they were within a mile or two of Jefferson. Was it possible they remembered this village? Could the nanotech be that sophisticated? Ruth said Patrick and Linda seemed compelled to move no matter how badly hurt or securely tied. What were they looking for? The safety of family and friends? If so, that would be an unstoppable method of spreading the plague.

Everyone in Morristown might be headed this way.

10

The Reverend Timothy Morris had established his settlement directly after the war. As an unexpected reward, he received a full quarter-ton of seeds from Missoula. A few of the United States' seed banks survived the plague year, the seeds held back for their potential rather than being eaten outright. Since then, the government had been paying people to grow specific crops in exchange for a percentage of future harvests and the right to dictate where new seeds and saplings would be sent.

Their wealth steadily attracted more people to the Reverend's influence. The folks in Morristown weren't crazy. They were enthusiastic. The Reverend preached New Evangelism, which taught that man's purpose was to regrow and repopulate. Sometimes it also meant plural marriages, wife swapping, or marriage at a young age. That was one reason why Tony had been so fascinated with Jefferson's neighbors and why his mother despised them.

The crowd on the perimeter was silent. A few of them groaned, but it was their faces that truly spoke for them. Their eyes were huge and afraid. One sandy-haired woman blinked spasmodically, but most of them walked with their eyes wide open as if lost or confused.

"What do we do?" Ingrid asked.

"We can't just kill them!" Cam said.

"Do it! We gotta do it!" another man screamed. The high pitch of his voice made it clear that he was trying to convince himself, too—but what choice did they have? The closest people were about to clear the fences.

Cam wrenched his gaze away from the oncoming shadows as Greg and Neil jogged up behind him. "Where is the hazmat suit!?" Cam yelled, cursing himself. *Did we leave it at Ruth's hut?*

"What if we start a fire?" Ingrid said. "Is there any gasoline?"

"The flamethrowers are back at the greenhouse!"

"Then we'll shoot into the ground at their feet."

Cam glanced at the older woman with respect as her hand clacked against her M16, flicking the fire selector to full auto. Ingrid had volunteered for guard duty when others insisted on taking cover inside the sealed huts, and Cam remembered the handsome, blunt nose and chin behind her face mask. Ingrid Wood was unusual not only for her age—few people in their sixties had survived the plague year—but because of her accent. Ingrid had emigrated from Germany two decades ago after a divorce, and she was friendly, tough, and unfailingly polite.

"We may have to wound them," she said.

"Do it!" Neil screamed.

The first of the infected people staggered out of the fences, a young man in a MICHIGAN T-shirt and a skinny girl with filthy white socks beneath her blue gown. Cam recognized one of them. The young man's thick hair and the plague scarring on his nose were unmistakable. He was a farmer's son and loud in his religion, taking every chance to explain about the Resurrection any time a crew from Jefferson came to trade equipment or food. Jake. The young man's name was Jake and he was a good kid, rightly proud of his family's apple trees.

Cam raised his M4.

The floodlights switched on before anyone fired. David had finally gotten his tripod ready and hit the power, draining electricity away from Ruth's lab. Its dual lights burned into the people in the fences, illuminating the night like stark white glaring suns. Two shadows leapt from each person in a fan of silhouettes. Glass and chrome winked among the car parts on the ground.

Their eyes looked incredibly strange. It was as if none of them had irises. Their pupils were huge, like black pennies, and did not shrink in the light. It was a permanent condition. They shared some uniform injury to their brains.

The floodlights hurt them. The young man reeled away as the skinny girl ducked her head and scuttled sideways. Others raised their arms or moaned. The light stopped them. The Bull Dog was too strong. At first, Cam thought it might work. Then he noticed the second wave of human shapes. The field of light held at least a hundred figures, and there were hundreds more beyond them in the darkness.

Cam felt his blood run cold. The nearest people were repelled by the glare, yet the larger crowd seemed to be attracted to it. It was an eerie sight. Most of the infected people had been headed toward Jefferson, but without purpose. Some had stopped or strayed in other directions. Others were looking at the sky or their feet.

As the Bull Dog lit up the fences, the entire crowd turned as one, their white and brown faces reflecting the light like dishes. Blood gleamed on hands or bare legs where they'd fallen and hurt themselves. Then the crowd began to separate into two halves, circling in toward the brilliant corona from either side.

"Oh my God," Ingrid said.

"Shut 'em off! Shut 'em off!" Cam yelled. Too late. The infected people had a clear goal and began to pick up speed, shambling through the obstacles and barbed wire. Metal clanked, but they were silent, only grunting or heaving for air. Even the young apple farmer seemed to regain his bearings, stalking toward them even though he bent sideways from the light as if it was a physical force.

"Open fire!" Greg shouted, blasting the young man in the head. The boy toppled.

Cam's eyes stung inside his goggles but he repressed the emotion, screaming against his face mask. He welcomed the noise of his M4, too, because it overrode everything else.

The carbine rattled in his arms as he dropped the skinny

girl with a three-round burst. Her blood looked purple in the high-intensity lights. Cam took down the man behind her. Then a woman. Then another man. The range was too close. The M4 and the older model M16 were designed to penetrate Soviet helmets at a hundred yards, not unarmored targets at forty feet. Cam's shots passed through the fourth man's shoulder without knocking him down.

At the same time, Owen and Ingrid blazed at the crowd with their M16s. Two more carbines and a shotgun ripped into action from Cam's left, farther down the perimeter.

The guns were withering. Twenty people twisted and fell. One man lay screeching on a chrome bumper, making noises that sounded almost like words before their Russian grenade launcher coughed somewhere to Cam's right. A small rocket jumped into the field of light, splashing fire and smoke. The men and women of Jefferson had moved to reinforce Cam and the others like a well-schooled platoon, but they were downwind of the infected mob.

The carbines on Cam's left went silent first. He was reloading his own weapon when he noticed the change, yet it wasn't until he set his M4 against his shoulder again that he realized the delay from the other position had lasted too long. Those men weren't reloading. They were infected.

Cam peered at the nearest hut, looking for flashlights or muzzle flashes. There was nothing. Then someone stumbled past the corner of the building. The man was not empty-handed or half clothed like the people in the crowd. In fact, he seemed to be pawing at his jacket hood as he struggled to shake his hand loose from the trigger guard of his shotgun, treating the weapon like a burden rather than a tool.

"Oh shit we gotta move!" Cam yelled at Greg. "Fall back! Fall back!" He slapped at Ingrid's shoulder, but the older woman was too focused on controlling her M16. She fired into the west side of the crowd.

The infected people continued to advance. The guns did not frighten them, nor did the dead and wounded on the ground. They stumbled through their bleeding friends with no more attention than they gave to the fences and car parts. If anything, the muzzle blasts seemed to draw them. It was as if they were so deeply submerged in their trance that they seized on any external sensation. They walked right into the guns, which were much fewer now.

"Hold your position!" Greg shouted, but Cam pointed and yelled, "We lost everyone on our left! Every time you shoot someone—"

The floodlight teetered over and crashed as Neil fell beside them, his body hammering stiffly at the ground. The nanotech was among them.

"Run!" Cam shouted. He dragged Ingrid away from the man. Greg moved with them and suddenly Owen and another villager were there, too, retreating from the floodlight.

Owen and Greg yelled into their headsets for their wives. If the town was overrun, hiding in the sealed huts was pointless. Their air would run out. "Tricia!" Greg yelled. "Tricia!"

"—out of the buildings and run east before—"

Two infected men walked into their path, the village guards who had been on Cam's flank. Even in the half-light, it was obvious they weren't normal. One man had pushed his goggles sideways across his head and was struggling with his hood and mask. The other kept his right arm lifted away from his body, twitching, as his head rocked in the same palsied movements.

It was Matthew. Cam recognized his green jacket. Matthew seemed absorbed with the tremors in his arm and neck, but his face turned at the sound of their voices.

"Watch out!" Ingrid said.

Somehow they needed to get past. Cam dodged left and the others came with him, only to find themselves pinned against a truck and the front of Greenhouse 1. The fifth man, David, raised his rifle, but Cam yelled, "No, you'll make it worse!"

Cam reversed his M4 and took the short barrel in his hands. The muzzle was hot despite his gloves. He clubbed Matthew and then whipped the carbine at the other guy. Someone else threw a pistol, knocking him down. They ducked upwind of the two men and Cam saw it was Owen who'd helped him, emptying his holster. Cam would have said something if there was time. *Thank you.* They were on the same side, no matter if they'd argued.

But their chance was already gone. Forty yards away, the sealed huts were opening up. In the yellow light streaming from both cabins, the other villagers staggered and twitched. Some of them collapsed. Tricia screamed with Hope in her arms before suddenly she jerked, too. The baby's cries shut off at the same time. Tricia fell to one knee and dropped her infant daughter, who rolled halfway out of plastic sheeting her mother had fashioned into a bag around her.

They'd run straight into a drift of the plague.

The baby, Cam thought before his eyes cut left and right through the convulsing shapes. He was looking for Ruth.

"No!" Owen screamed. "No!"

Not all of them had fallen. Several people either tried to break free of the rest or turned to help the infected ones. In many cases it was hard to tell who was sick and who wasn't. Sometimes it was the infected ones who lurched away, bouncing off their neighbors. The healthy people ran from each other or bent and dragged at a lover or a friend only to succumb themselves.

Cam grabbed Owen before the man could run to his wife.

"No! No!" Owen screamed.

His voice turned several heads among the infected. Their faces were horrible. They were *identical*. Dark, white, man, woman—there was only one expression in the group, a numb look that left their mouths sagging. Many of their faces rippled with spasms and tics, but those movements were like whitecaps on an empty, quiet sea, affecting only the surface. That slack expression appeared again and again. It affected their bodies, too, dulling every part of them except their eyes. Their eyes bulged with need.

"We can still make the cars," Cam said. "Go. Run through the greenhouses."

"No," Owen said, no longer shouting. "No."

"Hope," Greg whispered. "Christ, she's—*Hope.*"

They couldn't reach her. There were twenty villagers scattered around the baby. All of them were contagious—and they ignored the little girl. Even her mother was indifferent. Lying against a man who'd dropped dead, Hope pawed weakly at the earth with her tiny hands. The three-month-old girl was too young to crawl on her own. She lacked the motor skills and strength, but, regardless, she was exhibiting the same insistent drive they'd seen in everybody who was infected.

"There's someone behind us," Ingrid said.

The floodlights still shone on the north side of town, a white corona in the dark. Silhouettes walked between the square shapes of the huts.

From the other direction, some of their friends also began to pace toward them—three villagers, then four and five. Tricia joined the disorganized march. She tripped on one of the dead and staggered sideways.

Cam's group backpedaled without a word, even Owen, even Greg. Especially in the dim light, the infected people no longer looked like family. They looked alien and deadly and Cam yanked his 9mm Beretta from his gun belt.

"Run for the cars," he said.

Greg tore his eyes away from his wife. His face was hidden in his goggles and mask, but everything about his posture shrieked of conflict and suffering.

"Greg," Cam said. "Run."

He didn't know what else to do. Without Ruth, they were only a handful of ordinary people, but he would lie to Grand Lake if they reestablished contact. *Get a helicopter,* he thought. *Save who you can. Maybe we can come back for her in hazmat suits—*

A jeep horn startled him. It blared from the other side of the greenhouses. Cam's nerves betrayed him. His hand clenched on his pistol and he put a bullet into the villagers. One of the oncoming shapes fell.

"No!" Owen screamed. He smashed Cam's shoulder with his rifle, knocking Cam into Greg. Then he swung his M16 around and leveled it at Cam's midsection.

The pistol shot must have sounded like an answering signal to whoever was in the jeep. The horn blared again and again. Maybe someone was shouting, too. Cam wasn't sure. The pounding of his heart was too loud and Owen kept screaming.

"No, no, no, no!" Owen yelled.

"Put it down," Ingrid said calmly, although she'd raised her M16 and moved to Owen's left so his rifle couldn't cover her, too. "Owen! Put it down."

"I didn't—" Cam shouted.

"You son of a bitch, no!"

There wasn't time. More and more silhouettes were bobbing through the lights on the north side of town. From the
south, the infected villagers were also closing rapidly. In seconds, they would be overwhelmed.

Cam shoved Greg to one side and jumped the other way,
trying to escape Owen's weapon. He didn't make it. The M16
blazed in his face, deafening and bright. A bullet smashed
into the right side of his chest like an icy ball. Another might
have nipped the inside of his arm. Impact threw Cam onto
his back, but somehow he dragged his arm forward against
that momentum. He shot Owen in the leg—partly because he
didn't want to kill the man. Mostly it was because it was the
quickest shot from the ground.

The wound was devastating. At close range, the 9mm bullet ripped a melon-sized hole through the back of Owen's
thigh. It shattered his femur in a gush of dark arterial blood,
but Ingrid killed him before he dropped. She emptied her clip
into his chest, a burst of five or six shots. Sparks flew from
Owen's M16 as her rounds struck the weapon. Maybe it had
been her real target.

Cam's vision was fading, yet he heard David gasp as the
man turned and fled. David ran into the corridor between the
stripped frameworks of Greenhouses 2 and 3. The jeep horn
was still bleating. Cam tried to get up but his legs wouldn't
work. The best he could do was to squeeze his arm against his
side where his jacket was wet.

Then everything went dark.

He woke between Ingrid and Greg as they hauled him
forward. His feet dragged on the ground, adding to the strain
on his side. It felt like his ribs were being pulled apart and
he tried to run with Greg, who had most of his weight. He
couldn't have been unconscious for more than a few seconds.
They were still five steps from the skeletal wood structure of
Greenhouse 3, moving without flashlights.

The jeep horn had gone quiet, too. Whoever was at the cars
had either been infected or decided to stop making himself a
target.

"Wait," Ingrid said, bumping against Cam.

Greg pulled on his other side and they went two more steps before Greg froze, too. "Oh, God," he said.

David sprawled in the corridor between the greenhouses. Their friend lay on his back, trembling, as if he'd struck a nonexistent wall. But there was nowhere else to go. Behind them, the villagers had walked over Owen's corpse and the flashlights they'd left nearby, filling the few white beams with legs and feet. At the same time, a larger, different group of silhouettes walked into the flashlights from the north.

Jefferson belonged to the infected.

"Run through the greenhouse," Cam said, gesturing with his entire body against Ingrid. Greenhouse 2 was upwind of David, if that mattered. Every breath was a gamble. The air must be streaked with nanotech.

"Go!" Greg said. "Ingrid, go. I got him."

She stepped over the foundation wall, ducking one of the crossbeams that had supported the plastic. Instead of running ahead, though, she turned with her M16. There were more silhouettes to their left, bumbling through the space between Greenhouses 1 and 2. In a moment, they would be cut off.

Cam heaved his legs over the foundation wall as Ingrid took aim. *Chik kik.* She was empty. "Idiot," she said, fumbling a new magazine from her jacket as she backpedaled through the low, broad planters, still soft and green with seedlings.

Greg and Cam outpaced her before she opened fire. Muzzle flashes danced over the posts and crossbeams, throwing shadows like crucifixes on the surface of Greenhouse 1. Someone howled. Most of the others tumbled in silence. Then another gun fired from the jeeps, supporting Ingrid. Cam recognized the chatter of an M4. A pistol barked, too, punctuating the lighter, popping noise of the carbine. At least two other villagers had survived, and Cam lunged forward with Greg, buoyed by a new surge of hope.

"This way!" a woman hollered.

They fell out of the back of the greenhouse. Greg staggered to his feet but Cam's right arm wouldn't work. He could only push himself onto his hurt side. His thoughts were short and confused.

Get up. Get up.

"Cam!" Ruth yelled. She stood over him with her hand

thrust out, squeezing off three rapid shots from her 9mm Beretta. He thought he was dreaming.

Somewhere the M4 blazed again on full auto, running through an entire clip in seconds. Spent cartridges rang against the bumper of a jeep. Cam felt himself dragged against the vehicle's fender, which was alive in a way that the ground was not. The jeep rocked violently as someone climbed in. The engine was idling, too, a low, bass grumble.

"Help me!" Greg shouted, heaving Cam upright. Ruth lowered her pistol and shoved her free hand against Cam's stomach. Together they levered him into the back of the jeep, where Bobbi knelt with the M4, reloading.

"You crazy—" Cam said in admiration before he ran out of breath. *Crazy goddamn females,* he thought. Ruth and Bobbi had disobeyed him, running for the jeeps instead of entering the sealed huts like he'd told them.

It had saved their lives.

"Is there anyone else!?" Ruth yelled.

"No, they're gone," Ingrid said.

"But I saw—"

"They're gone!"

Something was wrong with Bobbi's carbine. Probably it had jammed. The M4 was prone to seizing on full auto, and Bobbi threw it down and lurched into the driver's seat as Ingrid heaved herself in beside Cam. They had almost nothing else besides another carbine and a backpack. Cam didn't see the Harris AN/PRC-117.

"The radio," he gasped.

Bobbi said, "Susan fought us for it—"

"The AFM!" Ruth shouted, firing twice more into the corridor between the greenhouses. "I have my laptop but I think the AFM is still next to my cabin! If we—"

"Leave it!" Greg yelled. "Get in!" Then he stepped away from the vehicle himself.

"What are you doing!?" Bobbi screamed.

"I'll burn the town. The fire should keep them back." His voice was loaded with fear and Cam understood that, more than anything, Greg Estey intended to join his wife and daughter.

"You can't!" Ruth shouted. But their friend had run into

the darkness. He was headed for the toolshed, Cam realized—where the last of their fuel cans were kept—and Ingrid leaned out of the jeep with her rifle and blasted the truck beside them. Bullets slapped and whined from the side of the truck, shredding the rear fender and gas tank. Gasoline spattered on the earth. Ingrid was starting the job Greg intended to fulfill, but then Bobbi accelerated. She nearly threw Ingrid from the jeep. She must have thought the truck would explode and they roared out of the motor pool, speeding between two huts on the east side of town.

Cam might have caught a glimpse of Greg. Would his friend hesitate at the toolshed? Instead of creating a barricade for the infected people, a fire might kill Tricia and Hope and everyone else in Jefferson, asphyxiating them with smoke. Maybe that was Greg's intent even if he couldn't be honest with himself. If he'd been able to get close enough, maybe he would have shot his baby instead of leaving her to suffer in the night and then in the heat of the day, neglected and helpless—or maybe Greg had convinced himself that his love for Hope would survive the mind plague in some form. He might believe he would retain enough of a spark to care for his daughter.

Hurry, Cam thought. He didn't want to say good-bye, so he tried to imagine Greg's success instead. It was the only way he could stay with his friend.

The jeep slammed over a bump in the ground. Bobbi braked hard and swerved through the fences, turning on her headlights at last. Something like a hubcap careened up from the front tire. Then a heavier object smashed against the undercarriage.

"People on your left!" Ingrid shouted.

There were more figures approaching Jefferson in their bare feet and pajamas. The cold made their skin like marble: blue lips, white eyes. One woman had cut her face and her chest was slick with blood.

After that, Bobbi seemed to clear the silent migration. She slowed down and leaned over the wheel to stare into her headlights, weaving constantly. The ground was rough and spotted with rocks. Cam buckled his elbow down against his side, trying to staunch the wound. "Help me," he said to Ingrid, but Ruth turned to him first. "My ribs," he said.

"Oh no," Ruth pleaded, touching his shoulder.

Cam grimaced and sat up. He needed to give her room to inspect his wound and, at the very least, pack something against the side of his chest.

He couldn't let Greg's suicide go for nothing.

Their losses were unimaginable. Allison, Hope, Tricia, Tony, Owen, and the rest . . . the hundreds of people from Morristown . . . How many other survivors must be feeling the same despair? What if the new plague really was everywhere across America? That was how Allison would have looked at things, including herself in the larger whole instead of standing apart, and Cam grasped at the sense of being with her. He nursed the bright embers of his grief, encouraging it. Rage was a defense mechanism he'd learned years ago, burying his pain and taking energy from his hate. At times, it had been the only thing that kept him going.

It gave him direction.

If there was any chance of reversing the mind plague, they had to get Ruth to safety and the equipment in Grand Lake.

11

The soldier at the bunker door stiffened, then relaxed and fell. Beside him, a second Marine began to twitch against the concrete wall. He dropped the medical tape he'd been using to seal the door. Then he collapsed on his friend, bucking all over with short, rigid, stuttering movements. Both men were volunteers, but that didn't make the decision any easier for Major Reece, who stood across the room with her pistol in her small hands.

Dry-eyed, Deborah Reece fired. She had always taken pride in the clarity of her self-discipline, no matter what she was feeling. But she couldn't breathe and her balance was off. She missed her first shot. The round sparked from the concrete floor and banged into the wall.

"Please," she said, like a prayer.

The first soldier was already trying to wrestle free of his buddy, pinned by the other man's weight. Impossibly, he looked straight at her despite his struggle. His pupils were the same enormous holes she'd seen in every other casualty.

She didn't know his name. He was simply one of the J2 specialists who'd been inside the complex when the nanotech swept over the Continental Divide. He looked to be about thirty-five, the same age as Deborah, and very much in his prime. A captain. Lean and sunburnt, he was exactly the sort of man she preferred for her discreet, almost professional affairs, and in that instant Deborah felt a startling intimacy with this stranger.

Kill him, she warned herself.

Grand Lake was buried in the new plague. Even at eleven thousand feet, sealed within the mountain, their superstructures were vulnerable. Everyone up top was infected. Some of them seemed to *remember* what lay beneath, clawing at the tunnels and blast doors. The nanotech was more insidious than fallout or chemical agents. Complex 4 had gone silent within the first minutes of the attack, and 1 and 2 were both compromised.

These warrens had been built by engineers who were limited in equipment and supplies. Most of the subterranean complexes had been designed only to withstand the brutal winters at this elevation. Air strikes had been a secondary concern, and, possibly, the chance of surviving a nuclear near-miss.

Over time, many sections had settled badly, shifting out of plumb. Snowmelt seeped through the mountain and pushed against the bulkheads, eroding the rock alongside or beneath them, creating new pressures and holes. Today, the steel doors would stop people, even fire, but not microscopic machines. Attempts to retrofit the base after the war had been brief. Far more energy had gone into expanding these warrens than into improving the existing, upper levels. Complex 1 had grown to include three entrances to the outside—and from the last reports, the nanotech was cascading inward from all three directions.

It wasn't just the doors. The air systems were also a weak point, as were the thousands of conduits for electrical and communication lines. Once inside, the nanotech was unstoppable. The warrens were too small. Built like honeycombs, even the largest complex barely covered one full acre with its offices, storerooms, and other areas stacked in a tight, vertical puzzle. Deborah had asked for volunteers and the Marine captain turned to his buddy and said, "It's us." Then they gave their lives trying to secure a door with nothing more than medical tape.

He did his best, she thought. *Now do yours.* There was

a terrible symmetry in the idea. Deborah respected their bravery too much not to emulate it, and her next bullet went through the captain's head.

The other Marine's spasms had slowed to a pace that was erratic and weak. He was dying. Her way was quicker. Deborah shot him, too.

She turned and ran past an overturned desk at the back of the room. Her long legs danced easily through the mess as she clapped one hand against the white Navy shirt she'd cinched over her nose and mouth, snarling the knot in her blond hair even though she'd taken to wearing it short.

The mask was still there. So was the team at the rear entrance of the room, which shouldn't have surprised Deborah, but they were less a squad than a hastily picked group without an obvious chain of command. Most of the eleven men and woman were Army, and therefore her subordinates, yet she'd also ended up with an Air Force major and three Navy officers, and their orders were more important than any individual's life.

Seal your exits at any cost.

That duty might have been easier because many of them didn't know each other. Instead, Deborah was saved by the same thing she'd learned to value most in herself—their loyalty to the uniform. They could have slammed the door shut with her locked on the other side, but first they made a hole, lifting their rifles and sidearms so she could pass.

Focused on their weapons, Deborah wasn't light-footed enough to clear their legs. She tripped and sprawled on the hard floor.

"Major!" one of her soldiers cried, Emma Kincaid, a medical corps officer like Deborah.

"I told you to abandon that door!" Mendelson yelled. He was the USAF major, a square-headed man of fifty. His words were directed at the other troops instead of Deborah, challenging her for command.

This short concrete hall was lined with office doors. Several of the men and women held armloads of paperwork and more files lay on the floor. Like most of the complex, these offices served intelligence personnel from all five branches of the military, and yet the low cubicles hadn't only been ransacked for priority files but also for simple, precious desk supplies like Scotch tape. They had no other way to seal the doors. Deborah, Emma, and two nurses had snatched as many medical kits as they could find, breaking out adhesive bandages and tape, but those were almost gone.

Behind her, one soldier had closed the steel door. Three more slapped sheets of paper over the lock and hinges. Half a dozen hands held the sheets in place as others jabbed at the paper with tape or an incongruous tube of toothpaste, anything to create a seal.

"We should give up this door, too!" Mendelson yelled. "We need to get ahead of the nanotech! Don't you see? It's getting deeper into the complex because of us! It needs people!"

Two men had died because of her. That much was true. Still, Deborah said, "No."

She should have volunteered herself, but a CO couldn't afford that luxury. If she'd taken the Marines' place, she would be dead now, too, leaving Mendelson in charge, and either he didn't have the guts or he didn't understand. The air systems had been shut down, so an empty room might serve as a buffer—it might have been best to lock several doors and hope that some dead space between them and the infected soldiers would be enough—but they didn't have any more space to give up. From this hallway, there were barely fifty yards left before they hit the command center. It was critical to protect the operations room. Otherwise they would be deaf and blind to the outside world even if they found their way into a few safe corners inside the complex—and then what?

Without this base, the war was lost. Communications had ceased with nearly every other major installation across North America. Spokane. Calgary. Salt Lake. Flagstaff. Two hours ago, the president was reported safe in Missoula, and there were survivors in Yellowstone and in Albuquerque, but more than 80 percent of U.S. and Canadian forces seemed to have been wiped out. The rest were isolated and in chaos.

"I'm staying!" Deborah said.

"We're with you," an Army man said, as another yelled, "This isn't working! We need to try something else!" His fingers were smeared with blue gel toothpaste, which he'd used like caulk in the doorjamb.

"They were laying insulation in Sector Four," one of the Navy officers said. "What if we—"

"Four is cut off," the Army man said.

"The rest of you get going!" Deborah shouted. "Move!" She turned to the troops at the door and said, "We'll wedge paper into the cracks where you haven't sealed it already. Maybe we can get it wet, too, make some sort of paste."

"We can chew it if we have to," the Navy officer said.

Behind them, there was a rustle of boot steps. Mendelson went with those soldiers, yelling back at Deborah. "Goddammit, leave the door!"

But her orders were straight from General Caruso. Maybe she couldn't walk away from the men she'd shot in the other room, either. She could still see the captain's face and feel her pistol jump in her hands.

What was the plague doing to them? Anything that increased pressure in the skull would push the brain downwards through the foramen magnum, the hole through which the spinal cord exited. The cranial nerves that controlled pupil response were in the brain stem and quit working if they were squashed. Were the infected people hemorrhaging? Maybe the nanotech hit them like a concussion. Deborah wondered if anti-inflammatory drugs could possibly slow or stop the effect.

Then her friend Emma grabbed her arm. Emma's eyes were alive and clean, and Deborah spoke urgently to her. "We need someone to cover us," Deborah said.

"I—No," Emma said.

"I can't do it again!"

"I won't."

"That's a direct order, Lieutenant," Deborah insisted, cradling her friend's waist with her arm when she should have pushed her away.

Emma was a slight, pretty woman much like Deborah herself, although Deborah was taller. A classic blond, Deborah knew she was very pretty, but Emma more than held her own against her. Emma was a carrottop—orange hair, orange freckles—with a shy but ready smile. They complimented each other well, neither outshining the other, and Deborah had been pleased when they became confidants.

"I know I can trust you," Deborah said.

Emma nodded and shook her head in the same uncertain movement. Even her body moved left and right in denial like a fox in a trap.

"Draw your weapon," Deborah said as coolly as if she was working through any checklist. "Get as far back as possible. If you see us fall down or start to twitch, stop it before it gets to you. Shoot us."

"Deborah, please—"

There were shouts at the other end of the hallway. A deep *clang* reverberated from the walls. Deborah pulled Emma aside and raised her gun, protecting her friend.

The far door looked as if it had been thrown open before Mendelson reached it. He'd yelled as the other men and women jumped aside. One of them stumbled to his knees, grasping at the laptop and paper files in his arms.

For an instant, Deborah thought the nanotech had spilled all the way through the complex from the other side. Then a new squad barged through her people. These men were identical in their green containment suits, their heads misshapen by hoods and masks with heavy eyepieces like insects' eyes. Air tanks thickened the lines of their shoulders. The two in front also bristled with carbines and a flashlight, which winked and glared, even though the overhead lights were on. Grand Lake's primary power source was the hydroelectric station in the river much farther down the mountain, but it could be destroyed. There were also diesel generators inside the complex, although their fuel reserves were dismal and would be dedicated entirely to the command center.

My God, Deborah thought. *What are we going to do if the lights go out?*

"Clear a hole! Clear a hole!" someone screamed.

There was nowhere to go. Deborah tried to flatten herself against the wall, only to bump against Emma. By then, the first man had reached them. The hard edge of his M4 caught Deborah in the shoulder—accidentally, she thought—and his weight drove her sideways with exploding force.

"Oh!"

Somehow Emma and another soldier caught her, rucking her uniform up against her neck. Deborah glanced after the suited man, weeping in pain.

Then her eyes stung again from a new emotion. The suited men were combat engineers, sent to burn the door at last. One of them clutched several rods of dark welding metal in his gloves. Behind him, two others wrestled with the pipe-stem nozzle of an acetylene welder and two fuel tanks. One man also carried an oversized helmet with a black-glassed visor.

Deborah's efforts might have delayed the plague just long enough to preserve this hallway and most of her command. But as she regained her feet, she turned her back on Emma's shaken eyes and stared at the blank surface of the door instead. They were safe.

They were safe, and it hurt.

"Deborah?" her friend asked.

Why wasn't there anything on the intercom? she wondered. Then, angrily, *What if I'd listened to Mendelson?*

Her team had lost contact with the command center when they ran for the hallway. Would things have been different if she'd waited five minutes? Her team could have abandoned the other room instead of trying to hold that door, and then the engineers would have arrived before anyone else died.

Deborah's breath returned at last. Her chest loosened and she gasped inside her face mask, hurrying away from the engineers. Their welder hissed to life. Everyone else winced at the incandescent blue light. Deborah did not, striding purposefully through the hallway to turn herself in to General Caruso.

"Let's go! Move!" she said.

A few of her people had gone through the far door, but the others either seemed to be in shock or were collecting papers from the floor. A Navy officer said, "These are the Russian SITREPs from—"

"Move!" Deborah barked, shoving past him.

She hated to cry, but each inhalation was cathartic and sweet even as she shuddered with tears, trying to hide her face with her arm. As a member of the last crew aboard the International Space Station, as a physician and an infantry officer, Deborah Reece had seen more death than she could truly understand, but she had never killed before.

* * *

Deborah had spent the plague year in low Earth orbit, watching from the ISS as the world's cities went dark and stayed dark. The ISS circled the planet every ninety minutes, and, on the nightside of the globe, prehistoric blackness covered every part of the world except for a very few strongholds that burned like weak, fading stars. Leadville. Fuji. Kathmandu.

Her job had been to monitor and maintain the health of the crew. That she became rivals with Ruth Goldman was incidental. For one thing, they were the only two women aboard, and Deborah was the first to find comfort in the arms of their pilot, Derek Mills, whereas Ruth never did resolve her quiet attraction with Commander Ulinov.

The larger challenge was that while Deborah was intelligent, like all of NASA's people, Ruth's genius could make her difficult to reach. Ruth probably had forty IQ points on any of them, and, in her mania to reverse the plague, she exhausted herself and let her moods carry her for days on end. Her jokes were as deft as a scalpel. She cut everyone without trying.

Deborah was unlike Ruth in another way. She lacked Ruth's imagination, which seemed to her to be a good thing. She thought if people were too smart, they lost sight of how to be normal or never understood the basics of social behavior in the first place. As long as she'd known her, Ruth had been a polarizing figure, either drawing people to her or repelling them. Like Deborah, some people had both reactions at once, binding themselves to Ruth but unable to personally identify with her intensity.

Deborah wanted to be friends. They took some steps in that direction. Then Ruth cut her even more deeply. When the ISS crew returned to Earth, it was on a highway too narrow for the shuttle. The *Endeavour* went off the road, killing Derek and injuring most of the rest. Ruth was needed in the nanotech labs—but eight days later she disappeared, joining the conspiracy to hijack the mission into Sacramento, California, where they'd hoped to recover the original designs of the machine plague.

Deborah never expected to see her again. When she did, she was thankful just to find a familiar face. It had taken no less than two miracles to bring them back together. Deborah was not surprised that Ruth had the tenacity to walk all the way from Sacramento to the edges of the Nevada desert, yet somehow she'd also evaded the enemy landings in California. More unlikely, Deborah herself drove out of Leadville only days before the bombing. Ruth's would-be lover, Nikola Ulinov, was also a top Russian diplomat and a friend of Deborah's. Playing upon the authority he'd long held aboard the ISS, he urged Deborah to make something of herself again.

U.S. Command was only too happy to add a physician to their ranks when Deborah volunteered. Even without military training, she had been handed the rank of captain, able to give orders yet equally bound by directives from above. It was a neat trick. Deborah didn't mind. She thought Ulinov was right, and she knew she could handle herself even in a combat zone.

That was exactly where they sent her, even if she was a celebrity. Maybe they did it *because* of the small glamour of being associated with the space station, and if her status was some help to morale, all the better. Deborah was attached to an artillery company on the thin line of Leadville's northern border. She felt some guilt for leaving the other survivors of the ISS crew, but Bill Wallace had been recovering nicely, and Gustavo and Ulinov were both deeply involved with the highest levels of the American government.

Now they were all dead.

Ulinov had saved her even before himself. It was a debt she couldn't reconcile. She hated him for his part in the bombing, and yet she respected his loyalty and his self-sacrifice. He was a good man. He was just on the other side. Ultimately, the bombing had even caused some good. At the edge of the blast zone, beneath a stifling, radioactive haze, Deborah's unit had surrendered to the nearest rebel command. Later, people said there had been thousands of acts of unity everywhere as U.S. and Canadian forces turned to face the invasion together. The truth was that Deborah's company only wanted to run from the fallout without needing to fight through rebel lines. In fact, her people hiked ninety miles north before they learned what was happening in California.

Once more, Deborah's training as a physician brought her straight into the middle echelons of their leadership in Grand Lake. It wasn't what she wanted. She had only been with the men and women of her unit for most of a week, but when the sky ripped open, those soldiers became the only people she knew in the world. Yet she was under orders. Deborah had to believe that Grand Lake knew where she could do the most good—and they were right.

Ruth was rescued from an airfield in Nevada and brought back to the Rockies. Deborah, with Emma, found herself working alongside Ruth again. For the first time, Deborah was glad. Ruth had changed. She was more open. They needed each other.

One of Deborah's tasks had been to organize blood samples from thousands of soldiers and civilian refugees after Ruth discovered a new kind of nanotech inside them, a nanotech that shouldn't exist. Leadville had been testing several prototypes on its own troops, and Deborah chose to serve again when Ruth left Grand Lake, joining an elite military escort meant to aide and protect her. Ruth thought their best chance was to recover every fragment of Leadville's work that the survivors of the bombing must be carrying in their blood.

Unfortunately, many of those refugees were starving and sick and terrified. Chinese aircraft ruled the skies. Soon enough, Chinese armored units rolled into the foothills of the Rockies—and Ruth betrayed her own people again, threatening both sides with the parasite. Deborah still didn't know how to feel about what she'd done. Yes, Ruth's plan had worked, bringing the war to a standstill, but only at the cost of exiling herself. Worse, she'd given the West Coast to the enemy when she might have decimated them instead.

Ruth had even briefly convinced Deborah to help, her crazy goddamned genius shining in her eyes like holy fire, although Deborah's feelings had changed as soon as Ruth left her alone. Holding a vial of the parasite in her bare hand, waiting for Ruth's signal to open the plastic tube, Deborah's heart had soured at the idea of murdering thousands of Americans even if it meant saving millions more. Instead, she'd turned herself in along with the nanotech.

Deborah wasn't proud of being tempted. She had just been very, very tired and hurt and afraid. Nor had she lied to the National Security teams who debriefed her afterward. She was considered a loyalist because of it, which was embarrassing and wrong. That was why she was still in Grand Lake. Deborah was one of the "lucky" people who were hardy enough to survive at this elevation, even if she had sinus trouble, so she'd accepted one of the key personnel slots in Complex 1.

She'd cut her blond hair for the same reason—to make herself a better fit. Deborah was no longer a civilian serving in the Army. She *was* Army.

They carried on a vital peacekeeping mission. Even with the many flaws, the superstructures beneath these mountaintops were a feat of engineering and difficult to replicate. U.S. Command not only needed as many existing bases as possible, they'd always kept one eye toward surviving another plague. The landing strips on the surface were small and congested, but the fuel depot was well protected, and this place had all the advantages of high altitude and geographical isolation.

Grand Lake Air Force Base was a powerful component of the deterrents arrayed against the Chinese and the Russians, not only because of its aircraft but because it served as an Alternate NORTHCOM. Complex 1 housed one of the early warning hubs for NORAD, the organization dedicated to monitoring the world for nuclear launches or initiating a U.S. first strike. They had the eyes, ears, and authority to coordinate with the missile silos in Wyoming and Montana— but even if they achieved 100 percent containment, sealing themselves off from the nanotech, Deborah knew their clean air would only last forty-eight hours.

There was still one final choice to make.

12

"Hold it." Two men in containment suits stood in the next short hallway, blocking Deborah's path. One of them held a submachine gun. The other carried a pistol and a walkie-talkie. Neither weapon was pointed directly at her, but the message was clear. These men were a quarantine point.

Mendelson and three others stood to the side, waiting nervously. "This isn't right," Mendelson said.

Cables lined the bare ceiling behind two fluorescent lights. Deborah's boots scuffed on a rough patch where the concrete had fractured, been repaired, and cracked again. The entire hall had a slight sideways tilt. The air was rank with mold. Originally, these complexes had been sterile places, but there was some moisture leaking through the patch in the floor, and bacteria grew swiftly in the light and heat necessary to make the warrens habitable.

Behind her, the acetylene welder hissed. Its blue light flickered as more of her troops filed in behind her, craning their necks and bumping against each other. Emma said, "Why are we—?"

"Move over there," said the man with the pistol.

It was exactly how Deborah would have organized things herself. Welding the doors wasn't enough. The engineers also needed to be sure that everyone on this side was clean before they were allowed any farther.

What if they weren't? That frightened her, but she covered the feeling with a brisk, impersonal thought. *We did our job.* Deborah holstered her pistol and swiped at her cheeks, embarrassed by the wetness on her face. "We'll be okay," she told her people, trying to help the men in the containment suits. It was important to keep everyone calm.

"You're Reece," the first man said suddenly.

Deborah nodded. "Yes, sir," she said, not knowing his rank. She couldn't even meet his gaze through the Plexiglas eyepieces in his hood.

"Good." The man lifted his walkie-talkie and spoke loudly. It was a clumsy system, but his suit radio must not have been hooked into base communications. "We have Major Reece," he said. "She looks okay."

"Roger that," the 'talkie crackled.

What was happening?

"They think we're infected," Mendelson said.

"They just have to be sure," Deborah said. "That's all. We'll be okay."

She was ready to sacrifice herself if necessary. She had always been ready. There was honor in dying for the greater good, and the past two and a half years had only reinforced that belief in her.

"They need all the help they can get, and they'll want these files," she said, gesturing at the laptops and paperwork in their arms. The command center was too small for the hundreds of staffers necessary to receive and analyze NORTHCOM's data streams, so they worked elsewhere in the warrens. Most of their information was regularly e-mailed inside, but they'd learned redundancy above all things. Paper files could be read even if a virus crashed the system.

The welder shut off. Boot steps sounded in the other hallway and Deborah flinched. Her self-control was eroding. What if the nanotech had sifted through the door before the engineers finished their seal? The plague wouldn't affect those men, but they might be carrying traces of it on their suits. If so, as they walked into this hall, it would jump through Deborah's people like wildfire . . .

One of the Navy officers spoke up. He must have been thinking the same thing, and he wanted to be sure the engineers knew what he was carrying. "I have three years of NSA intercepts on the Chinese LOGSTATs," he said.

"I've got our SATCOM codes," another man said.

"We'll be fine," Deborah told them.

"You're bleeding," Emma said, reaching for her, but she stopped short of taking Deborah's arm, which filled Deborah with regret. They'd learned that touching each other was dangerous.

The engineers pushed into the crowded hall. Deborah heard them talking on their suit radios as they filed past, bearing their M4s and welding gear. "—get started," the first man said, muffled.

Seconds passed.

No one was infected.

The last engineer through the door closed it behind him and the tension went out of the hallway.

"You must have hurt yourself when you fell," Emma said, taking Deborah's elbow at last. They both welcomed the distraction. Emma's hands were skilled and light, gently investigating the bloody tear in Deborah's sleeve.

Her forearm was scraped in two places. Strange. She hadn't felt it. Deborah even smiled at the absurdity of a few cuts. It made her think of Band-Aids and her mother and a song Mom had sung when she was small and hurt herself, something about "oh green grow the rushes, oh."

Emma smiled, too, not understanding but needing the human contact. Then their quiet moment was over.

"What are you doing!?" Mendelson yelled.

The engineers pulled at Deborah's troops, herding them in the direction of the command center. "Down the hall! Down the hall!" one man shouted. They looked like they were preparing to burn the next door, but Deborah realized they were also disarming her soldiers.

"No!" she cried.

"Stay where you are," said an engineer with a Beretta.

"Major Reece," said another man. "You're with me."

"What?"

"Let's go. They need you inside."

"Inside the command center? What about the rest of my team!? These people are fine. You can see everyone's fine!"

"They'll be safe here."

"That's idiotic," Deborah said coldly. "If there's any risk of infection, I have it, too! You'll be taking the same risk when you let me in!"

"I'm sorry, Major. Let's go."

I won't, she thought, glancing back at Emma's blue-green eyes with a thrill of horror and shame. It wasn't right. None of it was right. But she turned and followed the man in the containment suit.

Deborah had come too far to disobey orders now.

The command center stood separate from the rest of the complex. That was one reason why the corridors leading into it were cracking. The command center was a massively reinforced box seated upon forty steel coils, each one as tall as a man and weighing a quarter ton. These shock absorbers were bolted deep into the bedrock, whereas the rest of the complex was simply laid upon the cut, naked stone. They'd never had the resources for better, but the design they'd chosen by necessity also provided the center with an additional, last line of defense. There were only two passageways inside. Both were lined with explosives and could be destroyed to stop invaders or contagion.

A crude decon station had been set up in the main antechamber. Building it might have been what delayed the engineers from reaching Deborah's group any sooner. She barely recognized the small room, which had been a simple, exposed cube with nothing more than an armed guard, a phone to the inside, and security cameras. Now it was crammed full of clear plastic in sheets and channels. The guard on the other side wore a containment suit just like the engineers.

"I'm sorry, ma'am, I need you to strip," said the engineer, pointing for her to walk into the maze of plastic. "There'll be a new uniform for you on the other side."

This was why her entire squad hadn't been allowed to come. In fact, the engineer looked as if he intended to stay outside himself. The maze contained a flimsy shower stall with two tanks alongside it. They must be limited in the amount of water they could run. There were also at least three fans that would blow back into the complex.

It was a pointless effort. If she had nanotech in her blood, they could clean her skin and her hair until Jesus came back in a Ferrari and yet accomplish nothing. Deborah tried not to show her condescension or her disapproval, although she held tightly to these feelings as she removed her gun belt, her boots, and her uniform, wincing at the twinge in her arm. Nor could she stop herself from glancing at the nearest camera in the ceiling. Who was watching? Did it matter? She was mad at herself for reacting at all. People were dying. Taking off her clothes was nothing compared to what she'd already been asked to do, and yet Deborah hated the indignity of it.

She protected herself with her irritation as she removed her bra and underwear. The engineer had the courtesy to turn his head. The guard on the other side of the plastic did not. *Fine.* He was only a distorted shape to her, so he must not be able to see her clearly, either, especially inside his hood, although she expected to be freezing and humiliated when she reached the other side.

"Wash your hair first," the guard called. "Now your body. Scrub your face, please. Now your, um, your front and your behind. Thank you, ma'am. Turn off the water."

Deborah was not allowed a towel. They probably hoped to whisk away any nanotech remaining on her skin as the water evaporated in the blast of the first fan, which the guard operated from his end. Then she walked into a second cell and he hit her again. Each section of the maze was blocked off with long flaps that fluttered backward while the fans were on, then closed again after the guard shut off the power.

When she finally emerged from the plastic, her mind was as cold and tight as her body. She ignored the guard except to nod when he gestured at a rack of uniforms sealed in bags. Deborah took the first Army kit she could find, only to discover it was too big in the waist and too short for her legs. She didn't care. She wasn't undressing again. "I'm ready," she said.

Cradling his M4, the guard lifted the handset on the wall. "We're clear," he said.

The bolts in the door clicked like rifles.

* * *

They'd constructed an opaque white plastic tent on the inside of the door, so Deborah couldn't see anything—but the voices were deafening. She knew the command center was no bigger than a single-family home, and the ceiling, floor, and three walls were bare concrete. Every sound echoed in the box.

"Major Reece?" An Air Force captain intercepted her as soon as the door was sealed by two USAF commandos who wore containment suits of their own, although both men had their hoods open. Their air tanks must be turned off, preserving their air. "This way," the captain said, leading Deborah from the small tent.

The noise was impossible. More than fifty men and women spoke at the same time, few of them to each other. Most wore Air Force blue. There were also people in tan or camouflage or civilian clothes. Nearly everyone was gathered in four rows facing away from her. They stood or sat at overcrowded desks in a forest of display screens. Others shoved through the mob on errands from one station to another.

Larger flatscreens were mounted on the far wall. The smallest flickered and scrolled through aircraft counts. The other two were situation maps. In blue and white, one showed the outlines of the world's continents overlaid with dense, busy symbols wherever there were known populations. The other screen was also a blue field with white lines denoting U.S., Canadian, and enemy borders in North America. Symbols and text blinked on the map in a hundred locations, mostly on the Russian and Chinese side.

Deborah stared as she followed the Air Force captain through the noise. Individual words leapt at her and then an Army officer crashed into her, too, rising from his chair. He didn't stop to apologize or even glance back.

"Roger that," another man said. "Can you confirm—"

"—to coordinates eight seven five—"

If she was reading the situation map correctly, things had grown worse since she'd heard any news. Winking dots showed the remaining elements of the U.S.–Canadian governments and military. There were very few. More than a dozen?

As she watched, one of the dots in New Mexico froze and then dimmed, left on the screen like a gravestone. The map was crowded with static information in faint text. Only the blinking locations were uninfected, and Deborah realized Europe was also crippled. Less than twenty symbols pulsed among a film of dead, gray data, mostly in Britain and Germany. The marks on the rest of the continent were frozen. Gone. Farther east, India was equally silent.

My God, she thought. *It's so fast.*

The whole world was falling to the nanotech. South America. The Middle East. There had never been many survivors in Africa, but even the few repopulated areas along its northern coasts looked to be infected.

The men and women in this box wouldn't quit. They were too well trained. There was order in the noise—unmistakable purpose—and Deborah felt a small prick of defiance and grit. She drew up her chin, sharing their fire. Then she marched after the Air Force captain into the second row of desks, where she'd recognized Jason Caruso in the thick of the chaos.

Army general Caruso was young for his five stars and his role as chairman of the Joint Chiefs. Deborah believed he was still short of fifty. Brown hair, brown eyes, and an average build might have given Caruso a forgettable look, except that his mouth changed everything about him. His mouth was expressive even when he wasn't speaking, creased with worry lines. Caruso had a lifelong habit of pursing his lips or holding a tight smile to one side like a smirk. Deborah supposed he would have been an awful poker player. He telegraphed every thought with his mouth, but among his own troops it was an advantage. Sometimes they reacted even before he spoke.

Caruso was shouting into a phone. Deborah couldn't make out what he was saying. There were too many voices and a bronze-skinned woman at Deborah's side was particularly strident, cupping her hand over the microphone stem of her headset. *"Nà me, nǐ yě shì zài bào gào nǐ de jī dì de wēn yì ma?"* the woman said.

She was Chinese, Deborah realized, though her family might have been in America for generations. What must it have been like to wear an Asian face during the war?

The people in this row were translators or diplomats. Many
of them were in civilian clothes, although this woman wore
Army fatigues. Deborah glanced at her computer screen. It
was an overlapping mess of open windows. From what Deborah could see, she had personnel files on Chinese nationals.

*"Wǒ mén zài wǒ mén de wèi xīng shàng méi yǒu kàn
dào rèn hé jī xiàng,"* the woman continued without inflection. She was loud but very calm, sounding neither angry nor
frightened.

"Commandant, pouvez-vous faire décoller ces avions?" a
man said in French. Deborah also heard Spanish, but the bulk
of the chatter was in Mandarin. Was that significant?

*"Wǒ xiàn zài gào sù nǐ, wǒ mén de wèi xīng tú xiàng xiǎn
shì nǐ de jī dì wèi shòu yǐng xiǎng,"* the woman said as Deborah hesitated. Then she saw the Air Force captain gesture
impatiently.

Deborah pushed into the clusters of people, patting at
their shoulders or backs to make them aware of her. One man
spoke Italian. The lilting flow of it made her think of Gustavo
and his funny grin, but there wasn't time to remember more.
She'd made sense of the clatter of keyboards all around her.
Each of the translators was paired with another person who
transcribed their conversation into English, typing furiously.
Some of the transcribers also muttered into their own headsets. They were collating data from all over the command
center . . . and sending it where?

As she watched, one man stood up and pointed at the next
row as if following an e-mail or a few words, making sure he
gained another soldier's attention. They were funneling information to one station, where other staffers were using that
data to correct and maintain their situation maps. Deborah
looked at the main display again, where occupied California
was still densely packed with blinking symbols. The enemy
seemed unaffected by the plague.

*"Wǒ mén xū yào lián xì zhèng fǔ què rèn shì fǒu xū yào zuò
chū fǎn yìng,"* a man said in Mandarin, as another shouted,
"Still nothing from Two Echo Two, sir!"

Deborah reached the knot surrounding the general. Another
officer touched Caruso's shoulder. He glanced back and forth
among them, settled on Deborah, and said to the phone, "I

will disregard those orders unless the secretary himself tells me otherwise. We've already waited too long."

Her skin crawled with awe and dread at the reptilian focus in Caruso's eyes. He had become one of the few remaining heads of state in allied North America. The weight on his soul must have been crushing, and yet that pressure was exactly what he'd trained for.

He didn't like what he heard. "If your compound has been breached, I am in command," he said. "Is the secretary alive?" Then: "Two minutes." He passed the handset to a Navy officer seated nearby and said, "Keep them on the line. Give me the phone again in ninety seconds."

"Aye, sir."

"Major Reece," he said, his jaw barely moving. Muscles bulged in his cheeks.

"Sir." Deborah's back was ramrod straight.

"Has she seen the photos?" Caruso asked, and another officer said, "I'm sorry, General. No. Over here." He tugged at Deborah's arm and she bent to look at one of the many computer screens.

Behind her, Caruso said, "Who else do we have online at Peterson?"

The other officer clicked through several windows and brought up two still photos. A white man. A dark woman. These pictures were grainy compared to the rest of the images in the room and Deborah thought, distantly, that both stills must have been pulled from security cameras. It was hard to think, because she felt as if she'd been shot.

The faces in the photos were full of the plague's staring confusion. Their pupils were distorted and the man's head hung sideways on his neck, his mouth slanting open.

But they're supposed to be okay! Deborah thought.

All of the complexes in Grand Lake were set apart from each other because they'd been built at different times and because it had been thought best to spread their assets. Complex 3 was also specially retrofitted to make sure it was airtight because they believed it might become dangerous. Three was where Grand Lake maintained their nanotech labs. Those people should have been able to keep the new plague out as perfectly as they kept their own experiments inside.

The woman was Meghna Katechia, an Indian national who became the head of Grand Lake's weapons program after the war. The man was Steve McCown, Katechia's top assistant, who had worked with Ruth Goldman herself for a time.

"Can you confirm—" the officer began.

"Steve McCown and Meghna Katechia," Deborah said. "Where are the others? Did we get out Laury or Aaron?"

"No. We think one of the civilians panicked and tried to run for it. Complex 3 was a total loss."

In the next row, a translator bolted upright from her desk and shouted, "Sir! General Caruso, sir! I have a Russian field general calling on all frequencies for assistance from U.S. forces! He's reporting widespread infections in California and says he's also been cut off from mainland Russia!"

"Jesus Christ," the Navy officer muttered, but Caruso turned to an Army colonel and said, "Get on that, John." He waved to another man and called, "Where are our satellites?"

A double cross? Deborah wondered. *The Chinese are attacking their friends, too. Why?*

"I think he's telling the truth, sir!" the translator shouted as the colonel pressed into the crowd to reach him, calling new orders to the entire group.

"Press the Europeans again," the colonel said. "What do they know?"

Caruso turned back to Deborah. "Can you help us if we get some equipment out of the labs?" he asked.

"Sir?"

"If we can't decontaminate the gear, we'll put you in a suit and bring everything to a safe room. I'm willing to send men out there if you think you have any chance of giving us some information on this nanotech. Anything at all."

Deborah stammered. "I—Sir." She didn't want to fail him, but she couldn't lie. "I'm a physician. My involvement with the nanotech programs was negligible at best."

"You know more than anyone else I've got," Caruso said.

"General, I have the 35 on the phone again!" the Navy officer called, holding out a handset.

Caruso kept his eyes on Deborah. "You know how to operate their microscopes," he said.

"Yes, sir."

"Then I'm sending a team to recover what we can." Caruso gestured to two officers nearby. Both of them nodded. One picked up a phone. Without wasting another moment, Caruso pressed his own handset to his ear and said, "This is A6."

He listened only an instant before his mouth twisted.

"Every minute there is more and more evidence that we know exactly where the nanotech originated," he said. "Goldman was right."

Ruth? Deborah thought. *She's alive!*

More than that, it sounded as though Ruth was working on their side again, which made Deborah happier than she would have expected.

"Where is the secretary?" Caruso asked. "If he cannot personally verify his whereabouts, I am in command." Then: "I am in command." He pointed to an officer seated at the computers and said, "Emergency action message. Authenticate our status as Kaleidoscope."

"This is Wild Fire with an EAM for all units," the man said into his headset. "I repeat, this is Wild Fire with an Emergency Action Message for all units. Prepare to copy message."

Caruso gestured to a different station. "Try to get me a direct line to the Chinese premier or anyone in their civilian government in California," he said. "We'll make one more effort to call them off."

"Juliet Victor Bravo Golf Whiskey Golf November Delta. I repeat, Juliet Victor Bravo Golf Whiskey Golf November Delta," the other man said, and Deborah felt her skin crawl again, because she knew what Caruso was doing.

After the war, they'd dispersed their civilian and military hierarchies as far as they were able. They could have returned to D.C., for example, but it was two thousand miles from the Rockies. The logistics would have been daunting. Even if they'd beefed up local defenses, D.C. would be alone, so the great majority of American and Canadian forces stayed along the Continental Divide, not only to save their strength but to remain massed against the enemy in California.

Fortunately, the Rockies stretched through eight states and one Canadian Province. Only the president, some military staffers, and a few of their irregularly elected congressmen were in Missoula. The rest of the top members of the U.S. leadership were scattered across the Divide to prevent them from ever being killed by one surgical strike. Their command systems were equally redundant.

Peterson AFB, on the east side of the Rockies, had been restored as one of their largest air bases. Years ago, Peterson had served as the new center for NORAD after the famous old tunnels beneath Cheyenne Mountain were mothballed, and the infrastructure at Peterson was too valuable to ignore even if it had taken some fallout. Unfortunately, because Peterson was also home to multiple air wings, it was a surface base. A few of its buildings could be sealed against biological threats or nanotechnology, but Deborah guessed now that Peterson was no better off than the mountaintops above Grand Lake.

If the secretary of defense was in Peterson, he could be lost like the president and the VP, either infected or hurt or cut off. From what she'd heard, the SecDef must have insisted that Caruso stay his hand until they were positive who'd created the new plague, but Caruso was usurping the SecDef in the succession of command for America's nuclear arsenal.

It's come to this, Deborah thought.

A profound sense of reality washed over her. She felt the bagginess of her uniform and breathed in the tense, acrid smell of the men and women who filled this box. Every choice they made now was as large as the world.

"Sir, I'm sorry," she said, trying to interrupt.

There was a new fear coiling in her chest. She knew General Caruso from the war. The American side hadn't had many advantages, and he'd seen little except defeat. He had been an advocate of using Ruth's skills to commit genocide against the Russians and the Chinese, and Deborah wondered if he'd finally seen his chance.

"Sir, you're in contact with Ruth Goldman?" she asked. "We need her—not me. She can tell us what's happening."

"You're all we've got, Major."

"What about Ruth?"

"Sir, I have the assistant secretary of defense on the horn!" called the Navy officer.

"Disconnect that line," Caruso said. His lips pressed together like knives. Then he turned to a woman at another desk and said, "I want an open broadcast to all Chinese forces. They will stop their attack immediately or we'll hit Los Angeles."

What if Ruth is dead? Deborah wondered. *Infected?* She knew she wouldn't be able to provide more than the slightest information about the mind plague herself. Caruso's choice might be the only way. The U.S. had lost control of most of its silos during the plague year, because while those underground holes were well sealed, their oxygen was only meant to last a few days. Only an extremely limited number of crews had managed to wait it out after being equipped with precious supplies and air compressors that allowed them to create the low air densities necessary to destroy the machine plague.

With the vaccine, however, the USAF had retaken those silos, and now they had thousands of Minuteman and Titan missiles on hand—plenty to eradicate mainland China if Caruso gave the order.

You have to believe he's right, Deborah told herself, like she'd always told herself. But her doubt was heavy inside her. She glanced up at the situation maps again, desperate to see some shred of hope. Instead, the dots in Russian-occupied California were turning into ghosts, static and dim, leaving only the Chinese zones in the southern half of the state untouched, like a safe zone or an epicenter.

North America teetered on the brink of nuclear war.

13

The jeep took them thirty miles into the night before the gas tank ran dry. *That's enough,* Ruth thought as Bobbi pumped her boot on the accelerator and tried the ignition again. *That has to be enough.*

"Goddammit!" Bobbi said.

Ruth merely rose into a crouch with her M4 held high, ready to jump down on either side of the vehicle. Ingrid stood taller with her M16. The wind was cold and felt like death. Ruth heard crickets, which surprised her.

Ree. Ree ree.

At first the sound was irregular, but the night quickly filled with it again. The crickets had only stopped because of the intrusion of the jeep. Ruth turned her head to try to get a feel for the size of the hillside beyond the white beams of the headlights and, beside her, she saw Cam with his right arm pressed against his ribs, holding a pistol in his good hand.

She wanted to protect him so much she turned away before he could see it in her eyes. She'd long since removed her goggles to help Bobbi navigate through the dark. Off-road, those thirty miles had taken hours. Several times they'd stopped completely while Ruth or Ingrid paced ahead to inspect a creek or a hillside or groves of dead trees.

"Turn off the lights," Cam said. Bobbi did. Otherwise there were only the stars. The night hinted at a long, slumping ridgeline above them to the southeast.

Far below, looking north, the black valley was marred by a patch of smoldering orange coals. It wasn't Jefferson. Their home was out of sight beyond the foothills. This fire was farther north and much bigger than twenty structures.

Morristown had burned, too.

"We need some recon," Ruth said. Their plan was to stay with the vehicle for a while. Dawn was only a few hours away. No one wanted to break their leg hiking in the dark, and Cam needed stitching. They all needed food and rest. The hot engine would also help them show up on infrared if a chopper flew overhead or if satellites photographed the area. They could use the headlights as a signal, too, at least until the sun came up.

Ruth also wanted to check her laptop. Before the fight in Jefferson, she'd initiated programs to crunch through her surface scan of the mind plague. She didn't expect to have results yet, but she was anxious to confirm that the computer was still functioning. Its battery should be good for another six hours, but she had two extras and she would need to freeze and save her program before switching out.

Once there had been planes in the night. They'd also heard gunshots rolling through the hills up north. There were probably survivors out of Morristown, but even if those people remained free of the plague, the shots would attract more of the infected. Ruth's group faced the same problem with their engine and their lights. They needed to make sure they were alone.

Ingrid slung her rifle. "I'll go."

"Wait. Help me with Cam."

"I'm all right," he said.

"You're still bleeding!" Ruth swung to face him, catching his good arm. He'd leaned forward to climb down from the jeep, which frightened her. "Let me help you," she said.

"All right."

"Let us help," she repeated, correcting herself. *Me. Us.* The words were a small distinction when everyone else they knew was gone, but Ruth was vividly aware of trying to quiet her emotions. The loyalty she felt for him was savage and blind. Ruth wouldn't hesitate to kill for Bobbi or Ingrid, because they were all that was left of her home, but she would die for Cam.

"Here," she said, gesturing toward the downwind side of the jeep. The vehicle offered some protection from the cold. It would do no good if the breeze was threaded with nano-tech, but the alternative was to be completely exposed and she couldn't accept that.

The three of them got Cam out of the jeep without jar-ring the rags she'd cinched under his arm. Then they sat him against the front tire, where Ruth smelled oil and hot metal and the cool scent of the crushed short grass.

She grabbed her backpack. They had almost nothing else except for her laptop—no tent, no blankets, and only the few canteens she'd stuffed into her pack with some cornmeal, potato powder, and dried tomatoes. She was hungry. She ignored it. She flipped open her computer and nodded once in the blue glow of its screen. Her analysis of the nanotech's surface scan was still running. The progress bar stood at 46 percent. She would have liked to use the laptop's screen for a light source, but it was smarter to conserve power.

The screen went dark when she shut its clamshell. Ruth took off her face mask and tried to remove her bloodstained gloves, too, suddenly feeling claustrophobic. It took her a moment to rip away the duct tape sealing her jacket cuffs. Then she knelt in front of Cam. He'd also pushed off his goggles and mask while Bobbi put hers back on. The lack of armor made Ruth and Cam different from the other two.

"Okay, I'll take care of him," Ruth said to them. "You should . . ." She stopped and tried to soften her tone. "Can you set up an LP?"

Ingrid shook her head. "What?"

"Listening post," Ruth said. She'd spent so much time with Cam and Eric, she'd forgotten that not everyone in Jefferson was part of their militia. Ingrid had been an unofficial grand-mother to their babies, a seamstress, a barber, and their den-tist, often working in Morristown and sometimes as far away as New Jackson. The older woman had been an oral hygienist before she retired, years ago, and they'd been lucky to have her as part of their community.

"Maybe we should stick together," Bobbi said unhappily.

"No, she's right," Ingrid said. "If we split up . . . if something happens . . ."

If any of them were hit by the nanotech, the others would have a better chance of stopping the infected one if they weren't too close together. If there was any warning at all in the dark.

Ruth took Ingrid's glove with her bare fingers before the older woman could leave. "Don't go too far," she said. "We just want to make some kind of perimeter. I think on the west side. Downhill. Okay? Find a place where you're out of the wind, but close enough that we can hear you if you shout."

"I don't like it," Bobbi said.

"I'll trade places with you in an hour. Please." Ruth must have let her possessiveness show in her voice or the way she knelt with Cam. Behind her goggles, Bobbi's face was impossible to read, but the small, birdlike movement of her head was full of knowing.

"I can take a shift, too," Cam said.

"You were shot! You need to rest."

Ingrid left them to their quarrel, walking into the darkness. "Let her take care of you," Ingrid said gently. Perhaps her tone was as much for Ruth as it was for Cam.

Bobbi hesitated. She was still in shock and afraid and jealous, too, Ruth thought, but Ruth fixed her attention on Cam, closing her world down to him. She did this without meeting his eyes, studying his torso instead.

"Can you lift your arm?" she asked.

"Yes."

"We need to get your jacket off without moving the bandage, but I don't want to cut it. You need it to stay warm."

Bobbi turned and left with a grunt like impatience.

Everywhere, the crickets sang. The wind curled around either side of the jeep and underneath it. Cam winced as Ruth helped him strip his gloves. She pulled his good arm free of its sleeve, then stood over him to unwrap the jacket from his body. Everything they did felt like a slow dance, moving together. At last, she drew the sleeve from his other arm.

His shirt was damp with blood down to his belt.

"Oh my God," she said.

"I don't think my ribs are broken."

"Shush. Let me clean the wound."

Ruth used her knife to remove his shirt because she needed to save the cleanest parts for a sponge and fresh bandaging. But he was right. The wound wasn't too bad. The bullet had grazed his pectoral muscle just below his armpit, leaving a gash about two inches long, wider in back, like a sideways *V*. In some places he was already clotting, so Ruth was careful not to scrub, pressing delicately at the wound instead.

Cam's body was dark and lean with muscle. His scars were disturbing, though. Most of his chest was peppered with old blister rash, and yet the smooth areas prickled with goose bumps from the cold where his skin was ordinary and perfect.

"Ruth," he said.

She looked up, hoping. But he wasn't watching her. He was gazing at the sky. *You can say anything to me,* she thought.

There was only the crickets. The wind.

He said, "Why is this happening?"

Ruth could barely admit to herself that she'd wanted to hear something else. What was wrong with her? They'd seen so much death. She was crazy to expect him to kiss her.

Kiss me, she thought, even as she rebuked herself. "I don't know," she said. But she knew. Some ideas were too powerful to ignore, forever changing the course of history. The wheel. Agriculture. Industry. The bomb. Today, Earth's population was barely more than five hundred million people. Many of them had dispersed from the mountains, but, for the most part, they were still gathered into a handful of safe zones.

There had never been a better time to attack. One nation or creed could take possession of the entire planet, remaking humankind in its own image. Maybe there would always be one warlord or another returning to the same scheme in different ways, from Senator Kendricks to the Russian generals who'd initiated the war to the men in the Chinese government who must have overseen the development of the new plague.

It's always men, she thought. *Too aggressive. Too afraid. Women would find another way.*

Ruth put all of her concentration into stitching his wound. It was ugly work. The needle was blunt and the heavy thread in her kit was meant for sewing. Nor did they have any anesthetic, not even weed or moonshine. Cam's tolerance for pain was well learned, however, and he said nothing as she fumbled and squinted in the dark.

"Fuck," she said when she lost the needle in the gore. She had to dig for it. "Sorry. Fuck. I'm sorry."

He was bleeding again. She tried to hurry.

She believed the only reason they'd escaped Jefferson was because the plague was its most dangerous in newly infected people. The crowd out of Morristown hadn't been exuding the nanotech as strongly as their own villagers. Somehow it knew not to replicate without end inside any particular host. Otherwise it would flay people alive much like the original machine plague. The amount of soft tissue used from each person was infinitesimal—the merest pinch was enough to create millions of nanobots—but maybe that was why some victims dropped dead. Maybe the problem wasn't that the mind plague experienced glitches when it crossed into the brain. The nanotech multiplied wherever it happened to activate. Being in the blood, sometimes it opened an artery or the muscles inside the heart . . .

Still, Ruth marveled at its capacity to record and verify who was already infected. *There must be a universal marker of some kind,* she thought. *The nanotech communicates with itself. How? Can I use those signals to shut it off or make us immune?*

"I'm done," she said, wiping her hands on her jeans because she wanted to save the last not-so-dirty parts of his shirt to wrap his wound again.

"Thank you," he said.

"Let me get a pressure bandage on there," she said as she washed her hands with the last of one canteen. She was all business. She wanted to maintain her distance in her head, but her fingers shook when she reached for him again.

What must he be feeling? *Pain. Heartache.*

Ruth cut the waist-strap from her pack in order to tie the new bandage in place, and she took a small measure of satisfaction in destroying the pack. She didn't know why, except that she felt angry and helpless. She knew her movements were too rough.

"Ruth," he said.

Don't look at him, she thought, even as another, more persistent voice inside her said, *You could both be dead in seconds.*

"Ruth."

She met his eyes. They were much darker and richer than her own, she knew, sad and frightened and strong. He was the strongest person she'd ever known. Somehow he always knew what to do.

He kissed her. He tipped forward and kissed her with his beard against her cold face and for an instant she was too surprised to react. Then she felt her mouth split open with a smile and a short, happy sound like laughter.

"Oh. Please. Cam, please."

Ruth raised onto her knees without letting herself leave their kiss. She straddled him, spreading her legs to the lean shape of his hips. His hand was inside her jacket. He touched her waist, squeezing as if to make sure she was real. Ruth pulled her shirt out of her pants so he could feel her bare skin.

They broke for air. That was dangerous. When she looked into his face, she thought his expression was even more tortured. The confusion in his eyes made her heart lurch and she almost kissed him again—but she stopped herself, breathing in. She laid her palms on his naked chest and used them like a buttress, keeping her body several inches from his even though they were connected where her open thighs met his hips and groin.

Allison, she thought.

If he wanted to stop, she would stop. She respected Cam too much to mislead him or plead or beg. Then she rocked against him. She didn't intend to. Her body reacted on its own, drawn to the friction and heat against her jeans.

He responded. His hand traced up her neck into her hair, cupping his fingers over the back of her skull. They kissed again and she stopped thinking, caught up in the taste of him and the sweet, maddening pressure of his erection. She pushed down slowly, insistently.

He made her feel young.

They wrestled her out of her jacket. He went to her shirt

next, but he had only one hand, so Ruth began to open her shirt buttons for him and she felt her body flush, nervous and eager. Her face especially radiated heat into the night. She kept the shirt on to cover her back. The fabric rubbed at her breasts and on either side of her stomach, teasing her, teasing him. His hand parted her shirt like a curtain.

Ruth was as lean as Cam after years of hardship and strict rations. She let his fingers wander over her body for a moment. Then she lowered her hands to her jeans and unbuckled her belt.

Everywhere the crickets chirped on the hillside. The short grass rustled in the breeze. Ruth was aware of the stars all around them like a carousel of lights broken by the sliver of moon down in the west, but she refused to let it draw her eyes back toward Jefferson.

She had to move away from Cam to take off her pants. She kicked off one boot. Then she rode her jeans and undies down over her hips, pulling that leg free. She couldn't believe it was happening at last. She crouched beside him with her knees apart, wishing he would touch her. "Let me help you," she said, laying her hand on his jeans. She meant to tug at the button and his zipper, but first she stroked the bulge there.

His good hand lifted underneath her. She was smooth and wet. His fingertip stroked and circled and her pelvis rocked involuntarily, losing that exquisite touch.

"Oh," she said. "Oh, please."

Cam touched her again. Ruth squeezed her hand down on his erection. The feelings coursing through her were bright and delicious even as she closed her eyes against the sting of tears. *This is wrong,* she thought. *Is this wrong?* Her emotions were as bewildered as his own must be, awash in good animal sensations, worry, guilt, and self-hate.

The attraction between them had always been more than a stupid crush. If physical pleasure was all she needed, she would have picked someone who wasn't so badly ruined by the machine plague. That was why they'd managed to be friends all this time. They trusted each other. The affinity she felt for him ran deep enough to overcome any selfishness or even the lonely, painful love she'd tried to forget.

Nevertheless, she'd always wanted to cement their relationship like a woman and man, so she desperately reminded herself again. *The nanotech could infect us both in seconds.*

Cam and Ruth nuzzled together. They rubbed each other. Her orgasm was a quiet thing exactly like her climaxes had been when she was alone in the cabin she'd shared with Eric and Bobbi, sometimes as she listened to them at night or sometimes early in the mornings when she woke from a dream and needed someone, only to find herself with nothing but her memories of Ari and Cam and other fantasies.

Tugging down his pants was another joint effort. She wanted him to make love to her on her back. She wanted him to fuck her on her knees. But his wound left him handicapped, and she knew it would be very, very good just to lower herself onto his lap. "Let me . . ." she said.

Cam nodded. He even helped her, placing his good hand against her side to hold her weight as she straddled him again.

He was damaged here, too. She felt rough old blisters in his hip socket. Was that another reason he'd kept himself apart from her? Because he was embarrassed? He must have known she would keep his secret.

The only thing that mattered was her body working against his in the night.

There was no talk of birth control or protection. No one had seen any pills or condoms for years, except as overpriced commodities on the black market. Most women she knew were either trying to have a baby, using the rhythm method, or having sex in ways that didn't involve intercourse. Ruth was glad she'd had her period eleven days ago, so she didn't have to turn him away. As she got older—the time she'd spent in zero gee might also be to blame—her cycle had shortened until her periods began every twenty-six days, which was annoying as hell, even if she wasn't sleeping with anyone— but the timing also meant that she was ovulating. She could get pregnant. Was that something to worry about?

She was being too cerebral and she knew it. She was recording every moment of their lovemaking. She let it change her. Having him was magnificent. She came again, and she'd nearly worked herself to a third before he reached his own orgasm. Afterwards, she stayed on top of him in a silent embrace, reveling in the sweat trapped between them until her butt was just too cold and she decided she'd better get dressed.

"Cam," she said.

"No. I love you. You know I love you. But let's not talk right now. I . . ."

"It's okay," she said quickly. "It's okay."

Tomorrow, she thought. *We can rest, and tomorrow maybe things will make more sense.*

"I need to find Ingrid," she said.

"No. Don't."

"What?" Ruth would have argued or played dumb for hours just to stay in his lap. In the warm space against his chest, her nipples were still full, and the muscles up and down her belly and spine were tired and relaxed.

"Sleep if you can," he said. "You need to be sharp if you're going to make sense of the nanotech."

"I don't—" *I don't have any gear except my laptop,* she thought, but maybe he was right. Maybe they'd flag down a helicopter or meet up with a convoy, making their way to Grand Lake or any of the other labs scattered throughout the U.S.

Ruth got up at last. Her legs trembled and she smiled at that, flashing her teeth at Cam in the dark before she hid her feelings again. She'd been concealing things from him more and more, which felt especially wrong now that they'd been intimate, but it was the same night he'd lost his wife. She had to be careful.

She got dressed. She helped him back into his pants and his jacket. Then she walked several steps away to pee. She wished she could wash herself but there was no water to spare, and she was girlishly pleased by the evidence of their sex.

When she came back, he shared a little more of a canteen with her. They double-checked that their weapons were at hand. "Rest," he said, staying upright against the jeep.

A large part of her wanted to stay awake. What if they were infected? Maybe it would better if she didn't see the nanotech coming. *Close your eyes,* she thought. Then their time together would be the last thing she experienced.

Ruth curled up on the ground beside him. He set his hand on her side, and she was glad. She shouldn't feel glad—she knew she shouldn't, because she crying, too—but a part of her that had been locked away was now content. She was in love, and, remarkably, she slept. But she dreamed that she lost him.

14

Cam listened to Ruth's breathing change as she fell into a restless doze beside him. Despite her exhaustion, he didn't think she really slept. Her hand closed on his leg, flexing and pulling. Her brain never seemed to stop. He remembered the same habit from their weeks together during the war. Ruth's insomnia had become its own threat, never allowing her to recuperate even when she was staggering from her wounds.

In the darkness, Cam touched her cheek. "*Shh*, Ruth," he said, listening for Bobbi or Ingrid. The crickets might be his only warning if one of them was infected. A person's footsteps would quiet the bugs, so Cam closed his eyes and absorbed the familiar song.

Ree ree ree ree ree.

He was simultaneously elated and suicidal. He felt half insane. Having sex with her had been very good. His body was content where it didn't hurt or where his muscles weren't knotted from stress and grief, but his mind was twisted in the same way. What the hell had they been thinking?

In some ways, the worst part was that he supposed Allison would have understood—even approved. His wife was nothing if not pragmatic. *Fine,* she'd said, like a dare. The offhand remark was the last word she ever spoke to him, and Cam tried to hear it again now. She would forgive him. Wouldn't she?

He could still feel Allison against himself, shorter than Ruth and even stronger, heavier in her breasts, wider in her hips. She liked to be kissed just under her ear.

Christ, he thought. *You betrayed her. Allison died in front of you and hours later you're fucking Ruth.* But he couldn't avoid how right it felt. Touching her was something he'd anticipated for years.

Cam opened his eyes to the stars and darkness. He tried to fight his way toward some kind of peace. Watching the sky made him feel small and lost and yet deeply connected with the earth around him. The grass rustled in the breeze. He smelled spruce or some other pines.

Are you out there? he wondered, but he didn't believe in ghosts or any kind of god, not after so much killing. He knew it was different for Ruth. She'd had an epiphany during the war. They'd never talked about it much. Cam had grown up Spanish Catholic and Ruth as a secular Jew, and he thought she was embarrassed by her new faith because it couldn't be quantified or explained like her research. Before they came to Jefferson, though, there had been times when Ruth said some interesting things. She seemed to need to share, and maybe she still thought she could pry him away from Allison.

On the first occasion, their group had been camped on a hot, dusty plain east of the Rockies with no wood for a cook-fire and only a few stale Army rations in their packs. Cam recalled everything about that evening clearly. Ruth had asked if they thought all of this—their lives, the world—might be some kind of test. "I don't mean between good and evil," she added with a wary look. "I mean like a materials test."

Materials test was an engineering term for methods of determining the limits of any given machine or substance. If there was a Creator, she imagined He was a distant, uninvolved God who was only interested in them in ways they could never comprehend. The notion was typical Ruth. Her ideas were huge and convoluted and, ultimately, also very simple.

"What sort of half-wit God would bother to create quintillions of other star systems if we're the most important thing to him?" she said. "And that's just in this galaxy. There are billions of other galaxies around ours. Why not just one sun and one planet? He doesn't have the whole world in his hands. That's ridiculous."

Earth was a very young planet in the life span of the Milky Way, lost deep in its spiral arms. Their home was just one extremely average ball of rock among an endless sea of others.

"It's laughable to think any of our mythologies have much to do with reality," Ruth said, and yet she obviously tried to conduct herself with goodwill, purpose, and self-restraint. Those were the traits professed by most religions, weren't they? She believed it was what they were made for—to help each other, to cooperate, to show endurance and insight.

Ruth felt like she had something to prove—that her abilities weren't just a randomly generated mistake. She believed there was a divine spark in everyone, something to be found and nurtured.

How did their relationship fit into her sense of destiny? Because he was meant to help her?

Shit, Cam thought. They didn't need to sleep together to be a team, and he knew he was only using rationalizations to justify what they'd done. He wondered what Ruth would say if he asked.

Cam agreed with some parts of her philosophy. He believed everyone was responsible for his or her own life, either trying their best or failing to make the effort. It was so easy to blind yourself with selfishness, fear, or greed. But he still wasn't sure. Had the two of them made a mistake or done something right?

What if the answer was both?

He touched Ruth's cheek again. *Stupid.* She reacted, shifting her weight and her hand on his thigh. This time he didn't say anything to reassure her subconscious. *I love her,* he thought. *I do.* Yet he was afraid to wake her up. He didn't know if he would ever be able to look her in the face again.

The cloudless sky slowly lightened and Cam left Ruth to check on Bobbi and Ingrid, moving through the predawn in full armor—goggles, mask, jacket, gloves. The wind had died. The crickets were silent. The valley below him to the north-west seemed empty and peaceful. Morristown had burned out, and there was only a long, ancient row of electrical lines to indicate that people had ever lived down there.

Bobbi was asleep in a small fighting hole. Cam heard her snoring before his eyes were able to separate her shape from the pile of rocks she'd built. He stopped. Was there any way to be sure she wasn't infected? Sleep was nearly as essential as eating. If the mind plague stopped people from fulfilling those basic needs, none of the infected would last more than a few days. The autumn nights were sharp in the Rockies, and Cam remembered how the crowd out of Morristown had been dressed only in their bed clothes, often barefoot or in socks at best.

They came for us, he thought. *They walked eleven miles to find us even though it was midnight and barely thirty degrees out, so maybe they don't sleep.*

He crept away from Bobbi just the same. If he threw a pebble at her and she stood up and turned on him with that drunken, searching walk . . . He didn't want to kill another friend. Either way, she needed her rest. *Leave her alone,* he thought, searching across the hill for Ingrid. He expected she would be south of Bobbi's position, bracketing either side of the gully they'd driven up. There was a knoll where Ingrid would have a clear field of vision and Cam made for it, cir-cling through the brush and rock in the half-light.

The older woman sat in a hollow in the grass, leaning forward on her M16. It was an uncomfortable position that forced her to stay awake. She'd fall over if she didn't, and Cam smiled to himself. *Good girl,* he thought, pitching his voice at a whisper. "Ingrid."

She turned and nodded.

Cam approached and held out his good arm. "How about breakfast?"

Ingrid took his hand but didn't rise beyond a few inches, trying to work some life back into her legs. The cold had hurt her. "Where is Ruth?" she asked. Maybe she was only trying to cover her infirmity, but Cam owed her an honest answer.

"I let her sleep," he said.

"Good."

Something else went unspoken as she studied him through the yellow lens of her goggles. Ingrid knew they'd made love. She seemed pleased by it. Ingrid lived alone, and Cam supposed she wasn't so old that she hadn't found some enjoyment in the lives and romances of the other women in the village.

They walked down the hill together, Cam sidling in close to support her arthritic frame.

"I'll talk to Bobbi if I can," Ingrid said. Her tone was matter-of-fact, and Cam was glad he didn't have to hide anything from her.

But who's going to talk to Ruth? he worried.

As they neared the jeep, they saw that she was awake. Ruth leaned across the fender with her M4, an unkempt silhouette. Was there some kind of power source behind her like a flashlight? Her jacket was open and her goggles, uselessly, were pushed back into her curly hair.

"It's us, we're okay," Ingrid called.

Ruth lowered her carbine. Cam was glad for his own goggles and mask as her brown eyes shifted from him to Ingrid and back. "Where's Bobbi?" Ruth said, hesitating beside the jeep. Then she laid her hand on Cam's elbow with newfound intimacy. The light he'd seen was her laptop. She'd placed it on the ground. The screen was divided into three windows, a big white one that was full of text and two smaller graphics. Nanotech schematics.

"Bobbi's in a fighting hole, asleep," Cam said. "I think she's okay."

"I can wake her up," Ingrid said.

"I'll get her," Cam said. He was angry with himself for feeling so much like a schoolboy, but a lot of his self-consciousness was brought on by the age of the two women. They weren't old enough to be his grandmother and his mother—Ruth would have been a very young teenager when he was born— but Ingrid especially could have been his mom.

He told himself he wanted to conserve her strength. They were still fifteen or twenty miles from Grand Lake with a lot of rough country in between. Cam estimated the hike at two days if they were lucky, and they'd already done a poor job of protecting Ingrid, keeping her up all night.

"Stay here," he said. "Drink what you can."

Mostly he just wanted to get away from Ruth. Maybe Ingrid could say the right things for him. The anguish he felt was unbearable. He was torn between his memories of Allison and the living woman in front of him, but if Ruth was hurt, his terse attitude didn't mean as much to her as something else she'd learned.

"Cam," she said. "Wait. I have preliminary numbers. This nanotech is much bigger than it needs to be. My guess is that at least 50 percent of its bulk is unused—maybe more."

Her words went through him like another bullet.

"What does that mean?" Ingrid said.

Ruth didn't answer. She was waiting. Cam turned at last and they exchanged a long glance of nervous, wondering horror. "The machine plague had that same handicap," Cam said to Ingrid. "I mean the original *archos* tech."

"It was a prototype," Ruth explained. "Freedman and Sawyer built it with the extra capacity to hold advanced secondary programs. They wanted to be prepared for making it better, and I think the Chinese designed this contagion in the same way. It doesn't look like it's done. It's not ready."

"Maybe they planned to upload new programs after we're all sick. The way this thing affects people right now might only be the first stage of the attack."

"But it's empty coding," Ruth said. "As far as I can tell, it's just bulk."

"You don't know how far they've progressed," Cam said like a challenge. It was heartless, but there was a part of him that believed every implication in his words. *They're smarter than you. Faster. More aggressive.*

Her voice rose to match his. "The new plague would replicate even more rapidly if it was smaller," she said. "It would function more cleanly and be less likely to . . ." Ruth faltered, but then her eyes flashed, responding to his cruelty. "It would be less likely to kill," she said.

"Both of you," Ingrid said. "Stop."

Cam's stomach was clenched like a fist.

"This isn't accomplishing anything." Ingrid stepped between them with her hands on their shoulders, connecting them, but Cam swung away to conceal his rage.

"I'll get Bobbi," he said.

"I'm sorry!" Ruth said. "Wait. I didn't mean—"

They were caught by the sun. Shadows appeared beneath them and Cam's gaze flickered toward the horizon. Across a sprawling, open valley to the north stood the thirteen-thousand-foot wall of the Never Summer Range. Those white peaks glared in the rosy-yellow light. Dawn was spectacular. There were no clouds, but the ever-present haze in the atmosphere acted like a dark prism, refracting and holding the light. Sunsets could be equally gorgeous. Cam and Allison had watched hundreds of these displays together, taking as much solace as they could find in their lives.

Earth was experiencing the first small effects of nuclear winter. It seemed more than possible that global warming had been checked or even reversed. Three years had passed since there were tens of thousands of power plants and factories burning around the world, nor was the total daily traffic any greater than perhaps the equivalent of pre-plague Miami.

At the same time, the atmosphere was dense with smoke and pulverized debris. Some estimates put the bomb in Leadville at sixty megatons. There had also been at least ten detonations on the other side of the planet. The Chinese had been brought to a stalemate in their other war in the Himalayas when India nuked the front lines of their own territory. India had been cautious to announce what they were doing. Nor did they harm the Chinese armies. Their bombings were a defensive maneuver, separating themselves from China with wide swaths of lethal, useless land—and so the Chinese turned their attention elsewhere.

It wasn't unlikely that India's victory in stopping the enemy had led China to accelerate their efforts in North America. If the Chinese had fared better in the East, maybe they wouldn't have felt it necessary to compete directly with the U.S. in the race for weaponized nanotech.

Staring into the light, Cam shook off these thoughts before they paralyzed him. He was exhausted and irritable and he said, "Let me get Bobbi and we'll eat. We need to get moving."

"Cam, I—" Ruth said.

"Sweetheart, he knows," Ingrid said. "Please. Both of you.

Don't fight. You both know you'd never say anything against Allison."

The sunrise fluttered. There were two gigantic strobes beyond the horizon, then a third and a fourth and a fifth. The light was supernatural. It ate the sky, beating against the mountains like a silent wall that jumped up and vanished and jumped up again. Cam had seen it before. He bent and jammed his arm across his eyes—but even then, he was aware of more flashes. *Those are nuclear,* he thought.

"Get down!" Ingrid yelled as Ruth said, "Oh. God. Oh no. Oh no, oh God."

There were planes in the darkness to the southwest. Jets. Cam opened his eyes. The sky sparkled with reflected sunlight and then a phalanx of bright shapes slashed overhead. Only then did the engines' noise hit, dragging over them like a wave. Cam threw himself into the ground, no matter if the fighters had been moving too quickly to spot a few bodies on a hillside.

The shock wave will hit us soon, he thought.

Ruth joined him against the jeep, fidgeting with her M4. "Were those our planes?" she asked.

"I don't think so."

"Where were the nukes? Grand Lake?"

"No. We would have burned."

The sunrise crept over the highest points of the land like yellow paint, touching the earth and the grass with heat. Cam felt the air change as he lifted his head to track a distant howl. The sound reverberated from the mountains in the east. At least one jet was curling back. Or were there more?

Somewhere, Bobbi was yelling, and Ruth shouted, "We're here! We're here!"

Now the sky in the west trembled with new engines—the lower, deeper growl of prop-driven aircraft. Cam waited as Bobbi ran and joined them, shoving her hands against her face to reseat her goggles and mask. "What's happening?" she cried.

Attack at dawn, Cam thought, peering past Bobbi's shoulder. In the east, the sunrise changed again. It began to dim behind the immense, indistinct swelling of mushroom clouds. Then he glanced the other way. To the west, he recognized the stubby fuselage of the first plane to emerge from the night. Another followed close behind. They were Chinese Y-8 cargo planes, very similar to the American C-130 and used for the same purposes—to ferry equipment or troops into tight landing spaces. The fighters were an escort.

Wherever the nukes had landed, it was a long way off. The Chinese aircraft must have a different target. Cam could only think of one place that made sense.

"Those planes are headed for Grand Lake," he said.

15

Deborah Reece looked up from her atomic force microscope when the room trembled with a sharp, hammerlike
boom. "What—" she said, studying the concrete ceiling.
Then her chair rattled as the sound was repeated again and
again. *Boom boom boom. Boom*. The desk shivered, too, and
the faceplate of her containment suit vibrated from the same
onslaught of explosions.

"Air strikes," Bornmann said nearby, muffled in his suit.
"Son of a bitch."

Boom.

"Where the fuck are our planes!?" someone yelled as
another man said, "Rezac, what've you got?"

In her fear, Deborah thought Dirk Walls had called for her.
He was a two-star Marine general and as out of his element in
this tiny squad as Deborah herself. She leaned away from her
equipment, turning her entire torso inside her suit, but Walls
was talking to the communications specialist attached to
their unit, NSA Special Agent Michelle Rezac, a dark-haired
woman with a soft voice and hard gray eyes.

Suddenly the floor went sideways. It shoved Deborah's feet
out from under her. The mountain groaned. Bornmann fell
against her and she screamed—but even in the confusion, it

was the sideways jolt of this quake that caught her attention. The other explosions were clearly downwards. The larger quake felt as if it had come from another direction entirely and it was followed by aftershocks, none of which matched the detonations overhead.

"What was that!?" a man yelled.

Boom boom.

Dust sifted down from a corner of the room where the concrete was under strain. Deborah clambered back to her feet. Somehow her microscope was still on the desk and she grabbed it in case there was another quake.

She wouldn't have believed the pressure on her could increase. Now there were Chinese aircraft in the sky, plastering the surface of Grand Lake with fire. Why? Would they land?

Boom.

She wondered how many people General Caruso could send against enemy soldiers, and if that number included herself. Of course it did. There couldn't be more than a few dozen effective troops outside the command center and she bunched her hand inside her glove, remembering the jolt of her pistol all the way up her arm.

Deborah and four others had left the command center an hour ago, hurrying to a makeshift lab in the upper levels of Complex 1, where they found the hardware retrieved from 3 by a squad of USAF commandos. Those men stayed with her as bodyguards. The other members of the group, like Walls and Rezac, were only here because Caruso had four more suits he hadn't committed elsewhere. Caruso wanted to safeguard Deborah, but he also must have felt like there was no longer any point in holding onto his reserves. They were living on borrowed time.

They were late, so late. Deborah never would have imagined the U.S. arsenal would still be in the ground, and yet she'd been thrilled by Caruso's decision to keep their missiles in check. She had been wrong about him.

Boom boom. Boom.

Across the room, desks and gear clattered against the floor. Deborah looked at the ceiling again. The fluorescent lights gleamed in every scratch in her faceplate. This suit had seen

plenty of action and it smelled of other people despite the nauseating rubber stink. Pulling on the heavy pantlegs, sleeves,
and chest piece had been like wrapping herself in a men's
locker room.

Boom.

"Rezac!" Walls shouted, but Agent Rezac ignored him.
She stood at the intercom with her hand collapsing her bright
yellow rubberized helmet against her ear to secure her headset. At her waist, like all of them, she wore a control box, but
she'd disconnected the short wire that connected her to their
radios and jacked herself into the intercom instead.

The nine of them were a hodgepodge of colors. One man
wore a yellow civilian suit like Rezac, one was Army green,
and the remainder were black as night. Deborah wore black,
too, and she was glad. If they needed to ambush Chinese
storm troopers, she didn't want to do it in an emergency yellow hazmat suit.

Rezac's voice was an unintelligible mumble. Deborah
stared at the other woman, needing information. In fact,
everyone was watching Rezac except Emma.

"I think I have a picture," Emma said.

"Really? Good work." Deborah shuffled to a neighboring
desk, where she'd paired Emma with a magnetic resonance
force microscope and a small plastic tray littered with thin,
square, colorless tabs called substrates. The MRFM was bigger than Deborah's AFM. It had a larger base and internal
arrays. Otherwise it looked much the same—a stout, glossy
white tower with digital controls and a black eyepiece on top.

"This is what we're supposed to be looking at, right?"
Emma said without using the radio, raising her voice to be
heard outside her helmet.

Deborah bent beneath the weight of her air tanks, taking
care not to bang her faceplate against the eyepiece. She saw a
black-and-white topography like the bottom of an egg carton,
a symmetrical row of bumps joined by perfectly identical ribs
and struts—but was she looking at the nano or just the material of the substrate itself?

A speck of dust wouldn't be so uniformly structured. She
was sure of that. But the only way she'd known how to capture
samples of the mind plague was to wave the substrates in the

air, then insert the slides one by one into their microscopes and look for proof of the invisible machines. Unfortunately, holding the tiny squares in her gloves was an exercise in frustration. The substrates were made of sapphire, she remembered, but were just one centimeter across and only one millimeter thick, which made them as substantial as cellophane.

If Emma had zeroed in on a nano at last, this would be only part of it. Was the magnification set too high? They were actually making some progress. It wasn't enough, but at least they'd taken a few steps forward.

Deborah was the most proud of saving Emma. *I need her,* she'd told Caruso. *She worked with me with Goldman,* she said, urging him to bring Emma through their decon tents into the command center, and Caruso agreed. It was the first time she'd deceived a superior in her life. Placing her friend above everyone else was selfish. Something in her had broken, but for Caruso to drop the entire nanotech program on her shoulders was beyond unfair. He expected too much.

Deborah was finally questioning herself and what was most important to her—her country or her life. It was only an incredible bonus that Emma was so smart. Emma had clever hands and a good memory, and Deborah allowed herself to feel a bit of rivalry. *There's no way I'm going to let her show me up,* she thought. "Okay, I see it," she said.

"Now what?"

I don't know, Deborah thought, but Bornmann was watching and she couldn't bring herself to admit her ignorance.

Captain Bornmann was a lion of a man, not because he was especially large but because he had a slow, lazy way of moving that radiated danger and stamina. Bornmann had led the commando team into Complex 3, risking the lives of his men to secure this equipment. Deborah understood why he was hovering. He wanted miracles, but she couldn't give him any.

"Listen up!" Rezac said on the intersuit radio. "They're reporting nuclear strikes across Wyoming and Montana."

"Christ," someone said.

"The Chinese just hit most of our silos. Now they're decapitating our command centers. It sounds like most of our gear topside is gone."

Deborah nearly had to sit down, swooning, as her blood leapt in her veins like a drum. The wildness she felt was unlike her. She wanted to run, but where?

"We just had a coded message out of Salt Lake," Rezac said. "They're getting it, too—fighters, followed by troop carriers."

The attacks were insanely bold and well choreographed. The Chinese had sent their planes toward their own missile strikes, and yet the invasion worked because so many of the U.S.–Canadian radar stations were out of commission. There had also been jamming. During the past two hours, Grand Lake's satellite links had filled with interference or failed completely. The survivors at Peterson AFB and in Missoula reported the same complications. The Chinese had total air superiority. They'd probably set a dozen AWACS planes above the Rockies, creating an electronic umbrella. That was why the missile launches from China went undetected—and now those aircraft must have been sacrificed by their own generals, either burned outright or short-circuited by the electromagnetic pulse.

As for the fighters and troop carriers, no doubt those planes had come in extremely low to the ground, using the Continental Divide as a shield against the nuclear blasts. They must have timed their arrival at their targets just minutes after the ICBMs hit.

This isn't over yet, Deborah thought. It didn't matter that the war was lost. The enemy had beaten them at every turn, but she knew the men and women around her would never give up. Neither would Deborah, not with the guilt she felt for lying to Caruso. That deception had been a small thing, saving Emma, but Deborah had always placed her integrity above her personal feelings.

Now the two of them would pay the price. They were on the front line. If the Chinese wanted this base and high-level prisoners, they would probably succeed, but first a lot of people would die. *Room by room,* Deborah thought like a mantra. *We'll fight them for every goddamn room.*

"General Caruso has ordered us out," Rezac said.

"Out?" Bornmann asked.

Deborah felt the same uncertainty, even dismay. She had made her decision to fight.

"Pack it up," Rezac said. "We can't hold this base against ground troops. That's impossible. All they need to do is bring the roof down on top of us. We're getting out."

"Out where?" another man asked.

"You heard the lady," Walls said. "We'll go for the north tunnel."

"Jesus Christ," the same man said, but the group was already in motion.

This is crazy, Deborah thought, even as she whirled to reevaluate the nanotech gear. The AFM was more versatile, but Emma seemed to have adhered a sample of the mind plague to the test surface of the MRFM.

"We need both of these," Deborah said to Bornmann.

"You got it." He gestured for his men and said, "Sweeney, Pritchard, load 'em up. I'm on point with Lang. General Walls, I need you and everyone else to carry more air tanks, sir."

"Right." Walls accepted the order without protest.

The tanks on their suits were only good for another forty minutes. Deborah didn't want to be a problem, but she wondered how they could have any chance at all if the mountain was covered in enemy troops and nanotech. What if this was another mistake?

Then the power failed and left them in blackness.

Deborah was competitive. She had a hard time understanding anyone's failure, especially her own—and she'd changed her mind about General Caruso. The truth was that he'd misjudged the situation in delaying his launch against the Chinese. He was reluctant to hit U.S. soil. That much was forgivable. They all hoped California would become American territory again someday, and San Diego and Los Angeles were vital cities on the coast.

Before her small group left the command center, Caruso had reversed his diplomatic efforts. He tried to negotiate their surrender. He was willing to lose if he could extract a few conditions from the Chinese before standing down, and it took an

awful kind of bravery to broker a cease-fire. It was the same
sort of courage Ruth must have summoned to end the previous war. Caruso would always be remembered as the man
who capitulated. He'd even fought to take that role, wresting
power away from the secretary of defense because he thought
he could better manage the job.

He should have known better.

The problem was that every word needed to pass through
his translators to the Chinese and back again, sometimes twice
or even three times to be certain. Their failing communication links only intensified these delays as Caruso switched
from satellite phones to radio bands and the very few hard
lines between the Rockies and southern California.

The enemy had strung him along expertly. The Chinese
were masters at stonewalling. They kept promising top-level
contacts even as they claimed that each of these officials were
already engaged with other members of the U.S. military.
Each time, Caruso's teams scrambled to reach those Americans themselves. Too often, they verified that these people
were cut off or infected or dead. Confronting the Chinese with
this information only led to more contradictions and excuses,
all of which needed to be translated as well.

The Chinese had only meant to slow him until their missiles
fell from the sky. Caruso would have been better off with a
limited strike on his own ground, much like India had done in
the Himalayas. If he'd destroyed southern California, mainland
China might have backed off, either suspending their operations
in North America or shutting off the mind plague altogether—
but the enemy must have seen his hesitation as cowardice.

Deborah had been doubly wrong about him, which made
her feel like her loyalty was misplaced.

"Hold it!" Bornmann yelled on the radio.

Pritchard stopped the group. His black suit was the first
Deborah could see in the gloom. They had only two flashlights and a battery-powered lamp. Most of them were only
shadows, except for Rezac and Medrano, whose yellow bodies were brighter in the dark.

Thirty yards in front of Pritchard, a single beam rocked in

another room. Bornmann and Lang had run ahead of them, leaving Pritchard to pace the group. He brought up his M4 as Deborah heard a short, furious scuffle ahead of them. Then it was done.

"Clear," Bornmann said.

"Okay, move," Pritchard said. He carried the AFM in a sling on his side—his air tanks prevented him from carrying the microscope on his back—keeping his M4 and flashlight at the ready. Did he think Bornmann and Lang would miss an infected person in the dark?

Deborah glanced through the doors and offices on either side. Far away, the complex crackled with gunfire. More than once, they'd heard another small *boom*, and there was a dim, irritating whine that rose and fell at the edges of Deborah's hearing depending on the walls and open spaces around her. The Chinese were drilling through blast doors or straight down from the surface. Even a slight hole into the command center would infect it with the plague.

From the fighting, they were sure the main entrance and the south gate had been overrun. If the north tunnel was blocked, too, this would be the shortest escape attempt of all time. Deborah tried not to think about it. She had enough problems jogging in her suit with her arms wrapped around an extra air tank. It weighed twenty pounds. She was embarrassed she couldn't carry more, but the suit alone was like swimming in glue with forty pounds on her back. She just didn't have the upper body strength.

They entered the next room, which had been personnel quarters. It was neat and square with tall bunk beds, low foot-lockers, and two bodies in a heap. They had been bludgeoned by Bornmann and Lang. Both men carried rifles, but gunshots would be another kind of risk.

"Oh, God," Emma mumbled. She looked away. Deborah did not. She thought the two soldiers—their own soldiers—were deserving of her horror. She stopped without intending to. Walls bumped against her and she fell onto one knee, grasping at the aluminum cylinder in her arms. *They'll hear you!* she thought. The tank would hit the concrete like a gong, increasing the likelihood of drawing every infected person in this wing.

Walls caught Deborah's sleeve clumsily. He wore a back-pack sideways over his air tanks, humping two laptops and a sat phone in addition to two spare tanks in another sling.

"I'm okay," she said.

"We're almost there."

He said it like they were going to stop and rest, and Deborah nodded at the lie. "Yes, sir."

Behind him came Rezac. All of them rustled and clanked.

Rezac carried their Harris radio, one spare tank, and an M16. Medrano held two more tanks and their lamp, a white star near his hip, where the light puddled on the floor among the fat, sagging tubes of their legs. Sweeney brought up the rear with an M4, bent nearly in half beneath the MRFM.

As they trotted through the empty rows of beds, Deborah thought again how lucky she was just to be alive. It also occurred to her that General Caruso must have known the risk he'd taken in holding onto his missiles. Maybe he'd been right after all? The composition of this small unit was proof of his intent to fight in any way possible without resorting to a planetwide nuclear holocaust. Caruso hadn't only put them in suits to access the nano-tech gear. With the few people he'd chosen, Caruso had created a backup command group. That was the only explanation for assigning General Walls to a squad of eight people.

Walls was meant to assume Caruso's role as the supreme U.S. commander if Complex 1 was breached. Rezac was his signals intelligence specialist. Medrano, an engineer, served as the team's mechanic, and Bornmann and the other com-mandos were their might. Staff Sergeant Lang doubled as their linguist. Like the other translators she'd seen, Lang was Chinese American and all the more valuable for his heritage and verbal skills. Deborah wouldn't be surprised if others in the group knew some Mandarin, Cantonese, or Russian them-selves. This was a top-level unit, which left only Deborah and Emma as their pathetic science assets . . . And yet what could Caruso honestly hope for them to accomplish? If they escaped and regrouped with other survivors, what use were a few hit-and-run attacks against the Chinese? Even that seemed unlikely. Their air wouldn't last two hours.

"We're there! We're there!" Pritchard shouted, grabbing Emma's shoulder to help her. They'd reached a blast door.

Beyond it was a narrow vertical shaft with a spiral metal staircase. Their boot steps thrummed on the steel.

Stupidly, Deborah looked up. There was no end in sight. The height of it nearly defeated her. She lowered her head, but the climb was endless. Her muscles ached. Then her thighs turned rubbery. Then there was a heavy *clung* above her and suddenly the shaft was in twilight.

Deborah looked up again. Bornmann had thrown open a hatch at the top. Deborah saw a square of light, but it looked like it was another full story above her.

Keep going, she thought. *Keep going.*

Finally, she threw herself through the hatch into the unexpected silence of an Airstream camper. All of their doors to the underground were covered by RVs, huts, and trailers. Other top priority areas were strung with camouflage netting to prevent surveillance by spy planes and satellites. This shaft was no exception. The gutted shell of the Airstream sat above the stairwell. The netting outside was ripped and burned, hanging in brown mats across the shattered windows on one side. The sky was black. It reverberated with the long lines of sound from two jets and somewhere Deborah heard other, deeper engines, but she was shocked by the quiet that otherwise surrounded her.

Bornmann and Lang stood against the wall with their M4s. Bornmann gestured for everyone to get down as they emerged from the stairwell, but Walls joined the two commandos and Deborah continued to peek outside.

She saw fires and dust and the eerie shapes, everywhere, of people staggering through the haze. No one ran for cover. They walked upright. There should have been screaming. One man limped badly. Another's face was blackened by fire and blood except for the jutting white gleam of his cheekbone. He didn't seemed to notice, casting about in the smoke with his only remaining eye.

They were infected. These men and women would never grasp the danger of the Chinese assault—and they provided her group with some cover as Bornmann led them out of the calm space of the Airstream. The mob enveloped them. Lang brought up his M4 when several people turned, but didn't shoot. There was no telling how close Chinese soldiers might be.

Bornmann and Lang clubbed five Americans to the ground
as they ran into a maze of destruction. Some of the buildings
and trucks that coated these mountains hid the antennae and
dishes sprouting above the command complex. Their eyes
and ears had been distributed as widely as possible to mask
their signals, but the enemy must have strived to triangulate
each source of electronic noise ever since the war. It was these
points that had been targeted by the Chinese fighters, not the
people themselves or even the gun emplacements.

Bornmann led their squad past burning campers and an
overturned jeep. Debris lay everywhere, a mix of dark earth
exploded from the hillside and lighter material blasted out of
walls and furniture and people. Camouflage netting sagged
from the structures or twisted on the ground in curls and
lumps. Deborah saw a dismembered arm and a shoe and a
field of broken glass.

She realized her uncertainty was pointless. She was one
of the lucky ones. She reminded herself of it with every step.
Even if she and Emma ran away, where would they go? Agonizing over it was a waste of energy.

Just do your part, she thought.

Deborah resolved her self-doubt as easily as that, and she
was grateful. She felt like the eye of a hurricane, composed
and intact despite the carnage all around her, even because
of it. The chaos was exactly why she needed to remain pure.
That was how she wanted to be remembered—competent and
reliable—and no one would ever know otherwise if she kept
her secret and followed orders to the end.

Suddenly they could see past the sprawl. The mountainside fell away to the northeast, where a familiar trio of peaks
were lost in the filthy sky. Dark clouds crashed against the
land in a billowing conflict of wind and heat.

The fallout will reach us, she thought.

"You're going for Complex 2," Walls said on the suit radio,
breathing hard, and Bornmann answered, "Sir, we have to get
out of the open. Then we'll run for Complex 3 and resupply."

"Rezac," Walls said. "Any contact with 1?"

Rezac had been chanting to herself as they worked through
the ruins, calling for Complex 1 or any allied assets. "No, sir,"

she said. "Even if there are hardened units who survived the blasts, the sky is for shit. I'm getting nothing but static."

"Your call sign is Viper Six," Walls said, undeterred. "Authentication Hotel Golf India Sierra India X-ray. I want—"

"Missiles," Pritchard said.

"Get down!" Bornmann shouted. "Where?"

"They're at two o'clock. Outgoing. I see three. Four. I think they're ours."

Within the turmoil to the northeast, yellow-white sparks raced into the sky. Deborah saw three flecks streaking intermittently through the haze. The rocket trails hurt her eyes, rising, rising . . . "Yeeaaah!" Pritchard cheered. His voice was savage and Deborah felt herself respond the same way, meeting his pride with a keen new predatory feeling of her own.

Smash 'em, she thought.

The blinding white sparks were U.S. missiles intended for enemy targets.

16

Eight hundred miles west of Grand Lake, Colonel Jia Yuanjun walked alone through an empty hallway. The silence was bewitching. Solitude was so unlike his daily life. Part of him welcomed it even as he felt the hair on the back of his neck prickle with anticipation.

You shouldn't be here, Jia thought, but this sublevel was a familiar place. He knew every corner. He went sixty paces into the damp, echoing shadows and moved left out of the corridor. This basement was always quiet. The architect who'd designed these bunkers had overdrawn his plans, no doubt hoping to impress his superiors, and their construction efforts had stopped long before completing the lowest floor. In many areas, the walls showed naked rebar. In others, there were no walls at all. Farther down the corridor, Jia knew there was a great room in which nothing stood except load-bearing pillars and scrawls of white paint to indicate where plumbing and electrical lines were never laid. The lighting consisted of only a few bulbs clipped to the ceiling. Nor was there heating or fresh air.

They'd built this base on the outskirts of Los Angeles, northeast of Pasadena, where the badlands had long since reclaimed the suburban sprawl, raking the streets and abandoned yards with sand. Beneath the sun-baked desert, however, the earth was cold, and the hundreds of people inside the compound were forever exuding moisture. Most of their breath, sweat, and cooking smells evaporated through the exits or dried up in the insufficient circulation of their fans, but Jia believed it was the living vapor of his fellow soldiers that made this sublevel so chilly. It smelled of people and earth, yet not in an evil way, mixed with the tang of concrete and iron. Jia was in the belly of their Army. He supposed that was exactly where he wanted to be. It was peaceful. He felt as if he belonged—and yet he'd risked everything by coming here.

A boot step ticked in the darkness.

What if you were followed? Jia thought. He sidled back against the wall, leaving the dim light entirely as the boot steps moved closer, gritting on the floor. One man? Two?

I was ashamed, he thought, rehearsing the same lies he'd planned for months. Why else would anyone hide themselves down here except to mourn their failures or their lost families? Access to this level was forbidden, but one of its entrances sat directly beside Jia's quarters. The rooms below were used as storage space, giving him a plausible excuse to walk down here, and the crowded barracks were no place to show emotion.

If necessary, Jia would confess one weakness to conceal another. He had often done that to bind another man to him. He'd learned that if he volunteered one candid thought to a colleague or a rival, they felt empowered. Sometimes they would trust him enough to share their own truths. Less often, they reported him. Either way, he gained new relationships, either with the men who opened themselves to him or with the superiors who interrogated him and then saw his drive, his intelligence, and his humanity.

Neither the Communist Party nor the MSS wanted robots if they could have dedicated minds working for them instead. Automatons were easy to find. Men with initiative were not. This was how Jia had survived, but he'd always recognized that it was a double-edged sword.

One day, he would die on the wrong side of the blade. Today?

You shouldn't have come here! he thought. Then he realized the boot steps were in front of him. The walking man had emerged from deeper within the basement. Jia allowed himself a small measure of relief. He had been pressing his shoulder blades against the hard concrete but now he leaned forward into the light, masking his nerves with an alert expression.

"Nǐ hǎo," he said. *Hello.*

The other man jerked in surprise, then glanced left and right before saluting. With anyone else, his poor form would have earned a reprimand, but Jia was touched by the fear in Bu Xiaowen's eyes.

"Colonel," Bu said. "Are you . . . I didn't think . . ."

"I needed a moment to compose myself," Jia said. Then he added, "None of my team have slept since yesterday. General Zheng excused us."

They both listened to the silence. Somewhere, a far-off noise resonated through the concrete. *Pang.* But there was no one else in the basement and Jia stepped forward and grabbed the front of Bu's uniform. He pulled Bu's open mouth against his own for a fierce, exciting kiss.

Jia had not chosen to be the way he was. He certainly did not celebrate his sexuality, but the attraction between himself and men like Bu Xiaowen was undeniable. They never needed words. They just knew. Jia supposed it was the same way in which heterosexual men and women felt a mutual spark. Their bodies were simply calibrated that way, and Jia and Bu had watched each other for weeks before they first discovered a chance to exchange a few words, unheard and unseen, in one of the stairwells.

He lowered his hands to Bu's hips. He could not feel them beneath Bu's gun belt, and yet he enjoyed the frustration of it because undressing each other was usually their only foreplay. Their sexual encounters were always rushed.

He pressed Bu against himself, yearning for more—but his self-control was stronger. He broke their kiss. "I can't stay," he said.

"No," Bu agreed, holding him.

Jia didn't go. In fact, his only movement was to return Bu's embrace, bringing the other man's cheek against his own. His heart continued to beat rapidly and his erection was stiff and eager, but everything else about him softened.

We can never be together, Jia thought. *That only makes*

you more special to me. Your eyes. Your caring. "I didn't think I'd see you," he said.

"You almost didn't," Bu said. "My unit's on standby and then back on duty in another hour."

"I can't stay," Jia said again.

"You shouldn't have come at all," Bu said, fishing for more.

Jia wanted to smile and say exactly what Bu wanted to hear, but after a lifetime of deception, he was too good at shielding himself. He didn't know how to reveal something so honest. *I love you.* The words just wouldn't leave his throat.

"Zheng is watching you," Bu said.

"I know."

Jia had been relieved of his duties as superior officers hurried to involve themselves in the assaults, and Jia hadn't argued. Indeed, he had been most subservient. Their victories would be his success, too, so Jia detached himself from Sergeant Bu and ran his hands over his own shirt, straightening his uniform.

There was regret in Bu's gaze. "I'm glad you came, *zhǎng guān*," he said. It was Bu's pet name for him. *Sir.*

This time Jia did smile. "Me, too," he said, reaching for Bu's hand. Could he actually say what he needed to? Revealing his heart would be insignificant compared to the crimes they'd committed together, and Jia decided he was going to do it.

Tell him, he thought.

Then they were thrown against the ceiling in an upheaval so loud that Jia went blind, too, his senses wiped out by the deafening roar. Slammed up and back, he fractured his left arm. He felt the bones crack within the endless black sound. His chest struck something hard, too. Then his face. He might have been screaming. The sound was too loud to know and he tumbled and crashed inside it.

When it stopped, there was more light than Jia understood. Daylight. Somehow the base had been torn open, leaving him in a pit filled with gray slabs of concrete and smaller debris. The air was choked with dust. It smelled like charred

flesh, and Jia groped to place himself. The sky overhead was
dim and gray. The predawn was much brighter than a few
lightbulbs, but it would still be an hour before morning in
California—if morning ever came.

Voices echoed from the rock. Paperwork spilled everywhere in thin white rectangles. Some of the pages took flight
as the dust lifted and surged in the same hot wind. As he
staggered to his feet, Jia identified the unexpected shapes of
crushed beds and electronics and, incredibly, an entire truck
that must have rolled into the base. The jumble was also full
of bodies. Only some were moving. Not all of them were
whole. Jia saw a dead man pinned beneath a mass of concrete
and another who was missing his jaw and one arm.

He felt as if he was waking from a nightmare. Deep down,
perhaps, he was still screaming, but it was as if he was too
small to absorb what had happened. His surroundings only
came to him in bits and pieces. He saw a shattered door and
an exploded water tank and a desk drawer without a desk.
There was also a blue plastic comb in the rubble and Jia stared
at it without comprehension.

Then he stepped toward the mutilated soldier. The face
wasn't Bu's and the awful, blank feeling in Jia's head lifted
for an instant. Where had they been standing? Was this the
corridor?

The base shuddered again and hundreds of voices reacted
above him, shouting in the wind. A pile of debris crumbled
nearby, burying some of the dead and a wounded man who
thrashed once before he disappeared. *No!* Jia thought. But
the man was gone. A few people were picking themselves up
inside the pit, yet most of the other survivors seemed to be on
the shattered floor above. He couldn't immediately count on
them for help.

"Bu?" he yelled. "Bu, can you hear me!?"

Everywhere the collapsed walls formed barriers and
unstable pockets, any of which could be hiding the other man.
The voices were an obstacle of another kind, making it difficult to hear.

"Bu! Sergeant Bu!" His voice rose. *"Answer me!"*

Later, Jia would learn that a pair of Minuteman ICBMs had
detonated on either side of the Los Angeles sprawl, bracketing

the city on its northeast and southeast borders. The yield of
these warheads was only one megaton each—the Americans
had tried to limit the danger of fallout to themselves—yet that
was several times the strength of the first atomic bomb used
in Hiroshima. Worse, the two blasts slammed together with
gale-force winds.

At the same time, other missiles hit Oahu and Hawaii,
which the Russians and the Chinese both used as staging
grounds. These strikes might also have been a signal, walking
the devastation out into the Pacific, like a feint toward China.
Much closer, more warheads detonated in Santa Barbara,
Oceanside, and San Diego. The Americans also destroyed
the three large military bases far inland among the Mojave
Desert, where the Chinese kept most of their aircraft—but
there were no strikes on mainland China itself. The American launch was precise. Possibly they no longer had enough
operational silos for a larger response.

For now, Jia knew only his private horror. He clawed at a
snarl of wreckage with both hands, ignoring the bolt of agony
through his forearm. There was blood in the gray dust. So
much blood.

"Sergeant!" he yelled.

He found a naked foot. It was crushed and bent, and yet Jia
felt relief. His thoughts were still divorced from him, but he
couldn't imagine how Bu would have lost his boot, much less
his sock. This was someone else, a man who'd been sleeping
in their barracks overhead.

Jia kept moving. The ground was a strange up-and-down
ruin. Most of the dunes gave way beneath his feet. His instinct
was to shy away from the larger slabs, but he ducked his head
beneath them nonetheless, calling for the other man.

"Bu! Sergeant Bu!"

He found a live wire sparking in the rubble. He walked
across a slew of ghosts made of empty clothes. Then he
jumped when another survivor limped out of the dust abruptly
like one of the ghosts come to life.

"You!" Jia shouted. "Help me. We're looking for a Second
Department noncom in—"

The man didn't respond, shambling away. Was he deaf?
There was blood in his hair, so Jia let him go. He'd heard

someone else groan and he followed the sound, pushing his way past a massive hunk of concrete.

Bu Xiaowen lay beyond it. Each breath was a strained rasp. He was bent and gray with dust, but Jia recognized the other man's voice even in this extreme. He ran to him, stumbling once and jamming his fractured arm. "Bu," he said, marveling that they could have been so widely separated by the quake. They were together now. Jia felt himself awaken at last. The emotions in him were terrible—and honest—as he laid his hand on Bu's cheek, assessing his lover's airways. Bu's mouth looked clear of gravel or loose teeth. That was good, but Jia could see that he was seriously injured.

"I can't," Bu groaned. "I can't feel . . ."

"Hold still. I'm here. Just hold still. We'll get you out as soon as we can," Jia said, promising something that he had no right to guarantee. Bu's throat was mashed and swollen. His left arm twisted away from his body like a dead thing. Jia thought he must have been rolled beneath the nearest debris, a tangle of concrete and rebar. One of the steel rods had punctured Bu's leg, spurting blood through the dust.

Jia clamped his good hand down on the calf wound. Mastering the pain in his other arm, he took off his gun belt and wrapped it twice below Bu's knee before cinching the buckle tight. Then he turned and began to open his lover's shirt.

"The roof," Bu groaned. "What . . ."

"Quiet now. Breathe. Listen to me. Just breathe. The base was hit, but we're going to be okay."

Bu's collarbone had come through his skin. His lung was surely punctured, perhaps in several places. That was why he couldn't get enough air, and Jia was unsure if mouth-to-mouth resuscitation would help. *What can I do?* he thought, when really there was a different question he needed to ask himself.

What have I done?

All of his certainty from last night gave way to blame and guilt. He had been so aggressive in lobbying to attack the Americans. Perhaps it wouldn't have happened without him. There were other men with ambition, but his circumstances were unique. Perhaps another officer wouldn't have rushed to prove himself. What if they'd waited until the mind plague was even more virulent? The Americans might never had survived long enough to fight back, and the war would truly have been one-sided.

Jia grimaced through a mask of tears. Then he leaned down to Bu's dazed, pale face. He didn't want this kiss to be farewell, but, more than anything, he didn't want Bu to die without feeling their love again.

Bu was still very confused, but his lips opened to Jia's. They shared this tiny warmth. There was a rattle of someone's boots in the debris and Jia jerked his head up from the other man.

Dongmei stood on the other side of the gray dunes. Her uniform was cleaner than either Jia's or Bu's, and she held a canteen and a small pouch of medical supplies. She was lovely, like an angel. Her readiness was only what Jia would have expected—but while her broad hips were poised to continue forward, the rest of her body seemed unsure. She leaned slightly to one side as if to turn and run.

She gaped at them, open-mouthed.

Jia stared back at her, not believing his bad luck. The women's barracks were set away from the basement. Dongmei had escaped the bombing. Then she'd either climbed into the pit or even jumped down to help. She was a good soldier. She might have run into danger entirely by herself without an officer to direct her.

Jia saw his own choice as other people shouted behind Dongmei. There was no way to silence her without the risk of being discovered, not even if he used his hands instead of his pistol. First he would need to chase her, and Dongmei was thirty meters away. It also sounded as if more troops were entering the pit to look for survivors.

They would need leadership. His role would be even more essential now than ever, especially if the command center was gone. That responsibility was greater to him than anything else and Jia scrubbed at his damp eyes, smearing one cheek with his grime-ridden hand.

"He can't breathe," Jia said, pretending he had been trying to give Bu mouth-to-mouth. "His neck. His ribs."

"I, I," Dongmei stammered.

"Is there a bag and mask in your kit? His leg is cut, too. Are there medics?"

The fear in her round face was disarming, even juvenile. It was the look of a young woman confronted with monsters she'd never believed were real. Could she genuinely be that innocent? Or was she so scared because she admired him and didn't know how to process his homosexuality?

"Lieutenant Cheng!" he barked. "Are there medics?"

Dongmei seemed to grasp at the familiar tone, recovering herself at last. "No, sir," she said. "Not down here. Captain Ge told some of us to help—"

They probably sent only the weakest ones, Jia thought, *the women and the walking wounded. Let the injured take care of the injured.* It was cruel, but he approved. If there were still operational crews overhead, they would be impossibly busy as they tried to meet the American offensive.

Who was in charge? General Zheng? How many officers had been killed when the base collapsed?

"Sir," Bu groaned. "Sir, I can't . . ."

"Come here," Jia called to Dongmei, drowning out his lover's voice. What if Bu Xiaowen said the wrong thing? "Take over," Jia said. "Keep him stabilized. I need to get upstairs, but we never leave one of the People's Heroes behind. This man deserves all the help we can give."

Dongmei nodded, and Jia thought he saw a new uncertainty in her expression. She was beginning to doubt what she'd seen. That was good. But it wasn't enough.

He couldn't leave her alone with Bu.

As she picked her way through the rubble, Jia bent down to the other man again. He'd made his decision. There had always been two of him, the soldier and the man, and it was the soldier who must win over his secret, more gentle self.

"I love you," he murmured.

Bu misunderstood, groggy with pain and shock. "Sir?" he rasped. Then he smiled. "Sir, we shouldn't . . ."

Jia clamped his good hand over Bu's nose and mouth, hiding this action as best he could from Dongmei with his own face. Bu stiffened beneath him. He was too weak to fight. His hips moved but the injuries throughout his chest must have been an agony even worse than smothering. He tried to bite, too. Jia clamped Bu's jaw shut, smashing his lips. Bent close to Bu's face, Jia shut his eyes to block out the sight of his lover's bulging eyes.

Dongmei hesitated again a few paces from them. Jia had forgotten to pretend to be lifting his head for air and exhaling into Bu's mouth. Maybe she'd also seen Bu's face, blotched red from popping capillaries.

Then it was done. Jia didn't look at the body as he stood up. He was afraid he might start crying again if he did.

"He's dead," Jia said, putting too much emphasis on his first word. It might have sounded like an innocent thing to say, except that she'd just seen him commit murder.

"I . . . Yes, sir," Dongmei said. Her eyes were solemn and clear, but was there a quaver in her voice?

Jia could not wait or give her a later opportunity. He needed to trust Dongmei, so he said everything he knew to prove himself to her. "The most important thing is to bring everyone together again and take command. We need to be sure we're protected against more attacks, and our team will be critical in following the nanotech. Show me how you got down here. Is there a ladder?"

"Yes, sir. We used ropes, sir. I think I got down over there," Dongmei said, pointing back to her right. She wouldn't confront him now.

But would she eventually betray him?

Jia strangled her, too, throwing himself on top of the young woman in a grotesque masquerade of intercourse, driving his legs between hers and shoving his arms up through Dongmei's flailing hands to her neck, using his weight to hold her down against the rubble. She was his friend and an excellent soldier, but China needed him. It was the best he could do for his country. It was his duty.

When she was dead, Jia surveyed the wreckage. He dragged Dongmei away from Bu and pulled judiciously at a length of rebar, bringing an avalanche across her face and torso. If there was an autopsy, her neck wounds would be obvious, but Jia knew the survivors were too busy to make time for a criminal investigation.

He stalked away. And when he found his way through the dust and carnage to the rescue teams, no one questioned the bloody slash she'd left on his forehead or the cold, seething fury in his eyes. They helped him up a rope ladder to the second floor. Two medics tried to assess his wounds, abandoning more badly wounded soldiers in favor of him, but Jia brushed them off. "Tend to our Heroes," he said.

"Colonel!" a man called. "Colonel!" It was an Air Force lieutenant whom Jia recognized, although he couldn't remember the man's name.

"Report," Jia said.

"Casualties are overwhelming, sir! Most of the base is gone, sir! I can't raise anyone else on the radio and Captain Ge said it looks like the whole city is gone!"

The young man was hysterical, but his reaction only seemed to increase Jia's self-possession. "Where are Generals Zheng and Shui?" he asked.

"I don't know, sir! You are the most senior officer I've found, sir! We've been trying to organize our rescue efforts—"

"You've done well, but we need to reestablish communications both here and with the mainland. I need to know how badly we were attacked and what assets we have available. Especially our Air Force, lieutenant." Jia clapped him on the arm paternally and saw his own steadiness register in the lieutenant's expression—steadiness and gratitude—and he was glad somewhere beneath his rage.

Jia Yuanjun would hit the Americans with everything left at his command.

17

Cam was no longer sure where to go, but their first priority hadn't changed. Protect Ruth. Survive. He led the women east into a narrow valley because he wanted to get out of the line of sight of any more nuclear flashes. They also needed to stay out of the wind, although he was glad for it. The breeze would be spotted with nanotech, but it might also keep the towering black clouds in the east from collapsing across them with radioactive dust. His most distant landmarks were already gone, the snow-white peaks absorbed by the storm.

"Wait," Ingrid said. "Please."

They were walking single file with Cam in front. He glanced back. Ingrid was favoring her right leg, and he worried that she'd turned her ankle among the immature aspen and crumbling granite shale.

"Keep going," he said to Ruth. "We'll catch up."

"No."

"I'll carry her if I have to—"

"No. We stay together. I need a minute on my computer anyway."

He couldn't see her face because of her goggles and mask, but the stubborn way she'd lifted her chin was enough. What could he do? There wasn't time to argue, and, as Cam wrestled with himself, trying to find some way to outsmart her, Ruth unslung her carbine and her backpack. Then she knelt and opened the pack.

"Goddammit," he said as Bobbi stepped out of his way. He crouched in front of Ingrid, who sat down on a worn nub of rock. The sunrise was gone, lost behind the hideous, roiling clouds, and yet there was enough light that the mica in the granite sparkled and winked. The yellow aspen rattled in the wind.

The land had been scoured by the blast waves. When the ground shook, the four of them tried to hang onto the grass only to be slammed into the sky. Then came swirling winds full of dirt and plant life, but this aspen grove was still beautiful despite everything that had happened. The trees were mostly saplings, reed-thin but strong, growing among the few larger trunks of their parents. Cam hoped this place would always be so vibrant—alone, safe, and forgotten.

"I'm sorry," Ingrid said. "My toe."

"Let's see if we can splint it," he said, yanking at her bootlace as he looked at Ruth. She was gazing at him, too, with her half-open laptop in her arms. They both turned away.

Why does she keep pushing me? he thought.

There was a third reason to move east. They'd heard fighting. It was a distant sound—the snap of outgoing artillery—but it meant someone was alive. Cam knew there were old refugee camps among the upper reaches of these mountains. Some of those camps were still in use as supply depots. They might have been excellent rendezvous points for American units trying to escape the plague.

Who were they firing at? Their own infected people? The artillery might also be aimed at Grand Lake, trying to clear those peaks of enemy troops, if in fact the Chinese had landed. These mountains and Grand Lake were at least twelve miles apart as the crow flies, but that was well within range of their guns.

It was insane to hike *toward* a combat zone and the fallout, yet Cam didn't see any options. If the torn, intermingled bulk of the mushroom clouds was going to drift this far west, hiking a few miles in either direction probably wouldn't matter. They'd eaten the last bits of their food and water. They needed help. More than that, they needed trained soldiers and volunteers.

Ruth saw the Chinese troops as an opportunity, because she thought they must be carrying some immunity to the mind plague in their blood.

However the new plague operated, Ruth continued to believe its core structure was modeled after the booster tech. There was no reason to think the Chinese hadn't also developed a new, contagion-specific vaccine as well. How else could they be operating in the plague zone? Were they all wearing containment suits? It seemed unlikely that the Chinese could have stockpiled or manufactured so many suits, and soon enough the mind plague would reach Asia itself.

If Cam's group could capture or kill an enemy soldier, they might be able to transfer his immunity to themselves as easily as they'd shared the original vaccine.

Was it possible it might even reverse the effects of the plague in people who were already infected? Ruth wouldn't say, which Cam knew meant *no.* At least she didn't think so. It was still worth the chance. If nothing else, they could protect themselves. Then they could begin to hunt out other survivors and protect them, too, creating a small guerrilla force against the Chinese.

Cam frowned as he examined Ingrid's foot for bruises or swelling. She looked okay—but the four of them weren't capable of the last-ditch ambush that Ruth envisioned. *Maybe me and Bobbi,* he thought. *The two of us can try it if there's no one else, but then who's left to protect Ruth? Ingrid? We need more than one old lady to guard her.*

"This vaccine," he said. "Would it interfere with the old one? What if it eats it up, too? Then we'd be vulnerable to the machine plague again."

"No," Ruth said. "They must have reconfigured the heat engine in the new plague and its vaccine. Not a lot. Even reversing its structure as a mirror image would work. Then the different sets of plagues and vaccines wouldn't even notice each other."

"Aren't we going to fill up at some point?" Bobbi asked. "How many kinds of nanotech can anybody have inside them?"

"The vaccines kill everything else, Bobbi."

Arguing with Ruth was pointless. She had an answer for everything, so Cam turned his attention to Ingrid again. Her toe wasn't even sprained that he could see. She was just sixty years old. She probably hurt in other places, too—knees, hips, back—but she'd toughed it out until this one pain was too much.

"Bend your toes for me," he said.

"I can't. I'm sorry."

"Any numbness?"

"Yes."

"Let's do what we can to keep you moving," Cam said, taking a knife to his own sock. He cut off most of the material above his ankle, then did his best to seal his pantleg into his boot again. Next, he used the few inches of spare sock to pad the ball of Ingrid's foot. She didn't have any extra meat on her at all, and her foot was bony and lean.

His thirst was maddening. It made him weak. They needed fluids, especially Cam, after losing so much blood, but running water might be even more dangerous than the air. Ruth had said that if the mind plague only replicated when it found new hosts, the worst of it might have passed. Everyone else in this region was infected, so the thickest clouds of nanotech should have already floated away by now, leaving only trace amounts in random, invisible traps—and yet the plague was less likely to adhere to the earth or rock or plants than it was to be absorbed by water. Moving water would enfold the nanotech in itself, gathering and concentrating the mind plague, lining the banks of rivers and lakes with it, so they didn't know what to do except suffer.

"Are you ready?" he asked, not to Ingrid but to Ruth. The words came out harder than he'd intended, but he couldn't believe she was just sitting there with her computer on her thighs, pecking at the keyboard with two gloved fingers.

"Leave her be," Ingrid said. "She's onto something. You know that."

"Five minutes."

"I need fifteen," Ruth said.

Bobbi found a place against a tree with her M4. Cam didn't sit down himself. He paced away from the three women, dodging through the white trunks and coin-sized yellow leaves of the aspen. There was a low buzzing he couldn't identify, but he knew better than to let his curiosity get the better of him. Was it beetles? "We need more people if we're really going to try to hit the Chinese," he said, circling back toward Ruth. "Let's go."

"Fifteen minutes," Ingrid said.

"There's something in these trees. Bugs."

"Lord God, let me think!" Ruth shouted. "Shut up! Just shut up!" She nearly dropped her laptop as she lurched onto her knees. "What is *wrong* with you? I swear to God, I'm almost done programming this—"

"Move," Cam said.

"I won't!"

"Shh," Bobbi said. "I hear it, too."

"Leave me alone!" Ruth said. "We need to know what we're dealing with even if we steal their vaccine. I'm almost done. Then we can let the computer work through—"

Cam wrenched her to her feet. The pain in his side was bad but his fear went deeper, because he'd finally seen two of the buzzing insects. Yellow jackets. Big, striped yellow jackets. There was no way of knowing how many of the meat-eating insects would swarm from their nests if they smelled him. He could only guess why they were here at all. Yellow jackets, wasps, and bees were believed to be extinct like moths and butterflies. The ants had wiped out everything that relied on hives and cocoons. Flying insects were also vulnerable to the machine plague. They generated too much warmth, absorbing sunlight with their bodies, creating friction with their wings— enough to activate its heat engine. The environment here was cold enough for the yellow jackets to escape disintegration, but something else must have shielded them from the ants.

"Downhill," Cam said. "Fast as you can."

The buzzing grew around them. The fluttering leaves

concealed the smaller, darker movements of the yellow
jackets—but in seconds, there were fifty or more. Then a
hundred.

"Ouch!" Bobbi cried, slapping at her neck.

Ruth quit fighting him. She tucked her laptop into her pack
and grabbed her M4, swinging both objects like unwieldy fly
swatters. Bobbi and Ingrid chopped at the air, too. They drove
some of the yellow jackets away. They enraged the rest. Yellow jackets hummed at Cam's face, swooping and bumping as
he led the group at an angle across the hill. They landed on his
shoulders and pried at his hood.

"Oh!" Ingrid shouted.

Cam looked back. The older woman must have had one
inside her clothing, because she was pounding at her chest.
Then she walked into a tree. She almost fell. Ruth turned to
help and Cam yelled, "No! Ruth! Let me—"

He saw a snake near her feet. Long and thick, it was
creamy brown with dark blotches, a bull snake. It reared its
head back to strike. Bull snakes weren't poisonous, but if it
drew blood it would make her a more desirable target for the
yellow jackets.

Cam jumped forward and kicked, intercepting the bite.
Its fangs grazed his pantleg, stabbing the skin beneath as he
stomped at it.

"Look out!" Bobbi screamed behind him. Her M4 chattered into the ground. She wasn't firing at the yellow jackets.
There were more snakes in front of Bobbi and Cam sank his
good hand into Ruth's sleeve, pulling at her as she pulled at
Ingrid. They staggered away in a chain.

Cam nearly stepped on a writhing nest. Most were shredded and bloody. A dozen more snapped and bit at each other
in a frenzy of pain.

They smashed through the underbrush and the aspen. Cam
punched at as many branches as he could reach, trying to
drive off the insects as Bobbi squeezed off another short burst
at nothing that he could see, sweeping the earth. If there were
more snakes, Cam didn't know if the gunfire would excite
them or drive them off, but he drew his pistol, too, thinking
to reinforce her.

By now, Ingrid was running with more momentum than

intent. She collapsed. Ruth dragged her up and Cam fired six times in front of them, hoping the muzzle flashes and gunsmoke might affect the bugs. Bobbi had the same idea and squeezed off the rest of her magazine, strafing the air. Bullets thunked into the trees. Leaves and bark spun overhead.

Somewhere, far away, Cam thought he heard rifle fire crackling in response to their weapons, like Morse code. They kept running. Bobbi reloaded but held her fire exactly as Cam was hoarding his last shots.

They broke out of the yellow aspen into a green meadow. The insects seemed to be gone. Cam didn't want to stop, but Ruth and Ingrid were staggering and his side felt like it had split open, tearing the stitches.

"Rest," he gasped. "Rest but get ready to move."

"I saw fifty of them! Fifty snakes!" Bobbi said. Heaving for air, she tried to climb onto an old log but slipped and half fell. At the same time, Ingrid, Cam, and Ruth stepped gingerly in the brush, facing outward from each other.

"Water," Ruth said. "There has to be water."

"We'll follow that gully," Cam said. The north side of the meadow dropped away into a pair of ravines. He was sure they'd find a creek eventually . . . but would anything be safe to drink?

Bobbi wept, removing her mask to knead at the welts on her face and neck. Cam distracted himself by listening for more gunfire. The artillery unit must have heard them. Were they trying to signal Cam's group or were they losing the on-and-off battle he'd been following for more than an hour? If they'd left their artillery and were fighting with small arms instead, was that because they were retreating from infected people?

There were no more shots, so Cam glanced back into the trees, wondering at what he'd just seen. Bull snakes were not indigenous to this elevation. Neither were yellow jackets. Cam believed they were at nine thousand feet. There shouldn't be anything here to feed the snakes, who lived mostly on rodents and small lizards. There were no rodents left below the deathline, and not many above it, either—but maybe that was why the bull snakes had migrated this high, finding just enough chipmunks, immature marmots, birds, and eggs to endure all this time. Maybe the snake population was actually *descending* again after surviving the plague year above ten thousand feet, hibernating through the long winters and leaving only the hardiest, most adaptable individuals to reproduce.

The bull snakes could very well be evolving to eat bugs, too, adapting their diet to the only available food source. Maybe they'd kept the ant colonies from expanding into this area, which was why the yellow jackets had survived up here, too, developing a crude symbiosis with the reptiles.

He had more important questions.

"Would the mind plague affect animals?" he asked into the silence. "Ruth? Hey. Would the new plague affect snakes and yellow jackets?"

"How the hell would I know?"

Cam bristled at her tone, but Ingrid spoke first. "We got out of there," Ingrid said. "That's all that matters."

"It's not. We need to know if we're going to have problems with them, too. I mean if they're contagious."

Ruth shrugged. She wouldn't look at him or the other woman. At last, she said, "Animals don't have the same neurological makeup as humans do. Not even close. My guess is the nanotech would misfire or only partially activate, but how would you know if a snake was acting funny?"

"They could be paralyzed," Cam said. "Or go blind or have seizures."

She met his eyes now. "Yes."

"I didn't see any snakes that weren't moving," Bobbi said, and Ingrid said, "Ruth, do you want to finish whatever you were doing with your laptop? Then we'll get moving."

"Yes."

Cam wouldn't let it go. "If they're warm enough, the plague could be breeding in them even if it doesn't affect the way they act," he said. "That means we'd better avoid everything. Kill everything."

None of them spoke. Ingrid worked at her foot. Ruth opened her laptop and Cam glanced over the meadow, watching for yellow jackets.

"Jesus, I'm thirsty," Bobbi said.

He might have had a hand in saving the insects and snakes.

Maybe it was perverse, but the idea made him glad. This world needed every life-form it could find.

Long ago, in Grand Lake, Cam and Allison had participated in a widespread trap-and-release program to share the vaccine with as many animal species as possible. Mostly, they'd succeeded with rats. The elk, marmots, grouse, and birds that were native to this elevation had been hunted to extinction, but the rats thrived in the crowded refugee camps, and, once immunized, the rats did the rest of their work for them.

There were mountaintops where no people had gone. There were others where no one had survived for long. Some animals must have persisted in those lonely peaks. In time, they were attacked by the vaccinated rats. The rats bred uncontrolled beneath ten thousand feet, warring with the insects and invading the new outposts built by men. In the summer, the rats also returned to the mountains, where they took the young of the few remaining marmots and swarmed the old or injured elk. They stole the eggs of the grouse and other birds. But they also passed the vaccine to the animals they attacked but didn't succeed in killing.

Were the yellow jackets now immune after an encounter with the rats? Cam hoped so. *We should come back here if we get the chance,* he thought. *We should come back and do everything we can to protect them, breed them.*

The emotions in him were both lonely and good, because he knew the idea would have made Allison happy. It would have made her feel rich.

Just think what we could do with pollinators again, he thought.

They lost sight of the horizon as they edged into Willow Creek, a high mountain canyon within ten miles of Grand Lake. Cam would have stayed out of this valley altogether if he wasn't sure the artillery unit was stationed inside it. Even so, he kept his group as far up the box canyon's north side as possible, traversing east without losing any more elevation than necessary. He didn't want to have to climb back out if it looked like the gun crews had fled or were infected.

The creek meandered through the canyon floor, running southwest toward the only low point, where eventually it jogged south and fell downslope alongside a small state highway. That road hit Highway 40, which wasn't so far from Interstate 70, Loveland Pass, and roads leading into the Leadville crater. Cam knew the area well. During the war, his Ranger unit had picked their way cross-country from 40 to 70, skirting the fallout zone. Any number of civilian camps and small military garrisons had filled the region since then.

The first body was below them to the south. The man lay on his back, his face and naked chest much lighter than the rock and brush. Only the white skin drew Cam's gaze. Then he realized the ground down there was burned and torn, concealing what had been a rutted dirt road.

"Look," he said.

Ruth and Ingrid both knelt, merely using the opportunity to rest. Bobbi squinted in the direction he'd pointed. Her eyes must have been better than his. "Jesus," she said. "How many people do you think are down there? Thirty?"

Once he understood what he was looking for, his eyes registered at least twenty bodies littered in an area as big as a football field. The mind plague must have driven some of the infected to follow the survivors into these mountains . . . The artillery crews had walked their guns back and forth across the mouth of Willow Creek, dropping everyone who'd chased them. Cam was doubly glad he'd kept them out of the canyon. The battlefield was at least a mile away, but it was surely contagious.

"Bobbi," he said suddenly. "Fire two shots."

"What? Why? I'm almost empty."

He was down to a few rounds himself, but touched his holster. "They'll have spotters looking for anyone like us who comes over the mountains," he said. "Then they'll shell us if they don't think we're okay."

Ruth was already struggling back to her feet. She unslung her carbine while Bobbi stared into the canyon as if looking for FOs, forward observers. Even ragged and dirty and hurt, Ruth processed situations faster than anyone else.

She was a fighter. She was what he needed.

Blam! Blam! Ruth squeezed off two rounds into the air, startling someone above them. There was a clatter of gravel a hundred yards up the slope and Cam whirled, grabbing for his pistol again. *That close?* he thought. Then he caught a glimpse of a slinking little shape. A chipmunk? Rats? Maybe these mountains really were coming back to life. Maybe there would be more snakes or lizards or even wolves or bees in rare places, helping each other in unexpected pairings. *Allison was right,* he thought, feeling that lonely goodness again.

Ruth's shots were still echoing in the canyon when two more answered them. *Crack-ack!*

"One more," Cam said. Ruth obeyed. Within a few seconds, the signal was repeated again exactly, and Cam said, "Okay. They're expecting us."

The survivors were situated on a flat area like a peninsula, surrounded on three sides by a bend in the creek, which they'd used to maximize their defenses. It separated them from Cam's group, even if the water didn't look more than shin-deep, and there were two catwalks built across it.

They had tried to erect barricades on the canyon floor. Cam saw four pickups and a jeep set nose-to-tail across the dirt road. There were no trees available. Everything had been clear-cut for fuel during the long winters, so they'd dug a few pits with shovels and possibly high explosives, too, reducing the canyon to distinct fields of fire. As far as he could tell without binoculars, less than half a dozen infected people had made it anywhere near their encampment. The closest body sprawled two hundred yards away. Their artillery had caught most of the infected at the other end of Willow Creek. Then snipers dropped the rest.

Their base consisted of ten long greenhouses, two smaller barracks, two 155mm howitzer emplacements, and a few trucks and Humvees they'd kept back to avoid contaminating the vehicles. The government had been using this canyon for a major farming operation. It was shielded from the weather and high enough to escape most of the bugs, and they'd already had some of the necessary assets in place. That was why the guns were here—to protect the crops from raiders. Maybe now they were housing people inside the plastic, too. He couldn't tell.

Cam stopped his group within shouting distance of a fighting hole on the canyon's northern slope. He saw at least one soldier. The man's head was obvious. He wore an M40 biochem mask with oval plastic eyes and a shoulder-length hood, but the gear was desert camouflage. Its tan and beige patches were too light for this environment.

"Hands up," Cam said to the women. "Let them see us."

"Identify yourselves!" the man yelled.

"Corporal Najarro with the Seventy-Fifth! I have three civilians with me!"

It probably wouldn't have mattered what he said. They just wanted to verify that he was thinking and talking. The man stood up and waved for them to come forward. "Okay!" he said, lifting a walkie-talkie to his hood.

When they were within a hundred yards, Cam saw two more soldiers with their weapons leveled. Even closer, he helped Ruth and then Ingrid over an uneven wall of earth and rock as Bobbi climbed over herself. The soldiers themselves stayed back.

"We need water," Cam said. "Do you have bottled water?"

None of them directed him to the creek. Either they'd reached the same conclusion about watersheds or they'd seen someone infected by drinking from it. "There are storage tanks," the first man said, pointing back at the greenhouses. "We'll get you inside in a minute. The lieutenant wants to talk to you."

"We've been hiking all night."

"The lieutenant's gonna talk to you first."

Another soldier was already striding across the nearest catwalk. That she was a woman was evident despite her old-fashioned gas mask, jacket, and the rifle slung over one shoulder. She was slim, with no breasts to speak of, but her walk was female and her dark hair fell in a mane very much unlike the rest of her. Her uniform was perfect to the button—dirty, but perfect—whereas her hair suggested a rebellious streak. It spilled from the back of her mask like a flag.

There was something familiar about her, Cam thought, and when she spoke, he knew, even though her voice was distorted inside the rubber mask. "Najarro," she said, glancing from him to Ruth. "I just had to see it myself, you fuckin' traitors."

It was Sarah Foshtomi.

Ingrid went for her M16. Foshtomi's tone was bitter, even hateful, and the older woman wasn't so exhausted that she missed the threat. "No!" Cam shouted, but Ingrid stepped in front of Ruth with her assault rifle, growling, "You can't hurt her!"

Cam grabbed the barrel of Ingrid's weapon and jerked it skyward. At the same time, Foshtomi's men snapped up their own rifles. One of them caught Bobbi's arm. Everyone froze—and then Foshtomi laughed.

"Put 'em down," she said. "Let's talk."

The greenhouse reeked of bell peppers and onions. It was a good smell, and Cam had never been happier to remove his headgear. His bare skin reacted to the warm air as if he'd entered a sauna, soaking in the pungent scent of the crops.

Foshtomi led them through alternating rows of bushy green pepper plants and the onions' short stalks. The hundred-gallon tank in back had been pumped full three days ago, so it was safe. Foshtomi's unit had opened the plumbing at the base of the tank, using a spigot to fill their canteens and cooking pots. The floor was damp with it. Cam only managed to let the women drink first by sheer force of will, shrugging out of his jacket as Ruth and Bobbi splashed water from their hands into their mouths and faces. Ruth coughed but didn't stop. Ingrid drank more slowly from one of the cups left beside the tank.

"You're wounded," Foshtomi said, staring at his bloody side. "Let me see what we can do about that."

"Ingrid's hurt, too. Her foot."

She took her walkie-talkie from her belt. "This is Foshtomi. I need a medic in Building Six."

"Roger that," the 'talkie answered.

"Cam," Ruth said. "Drink." Curly wet bangs hung over her clean face, which was full of contradiction. Her brown eyes were both soft and penetrating. For an instant, she refused to look away from him, even though he could see that she was afraid of what he might say. They hadn't been this close and unguarded since before Allison's death, not even when they made love, hidden in the starlight.

They were bound so deeply together. Cam didn't want to be angry with her and he tried to show it. He touched her arm as he moved past. Then he bent and gulped more water than he should have in five huge uncontrolled swallows. His stomach flip-flopped. He nearly threw up. But it was good. It was so good to be alive and lost in the sensation of the water's cool liquid perfection.

"If you have to pee, just go on the plants," Foshtomi said, as blunt as ever. "They can use the nitrogen. Or there's honeypots in the back. We'll get you some food and stitch you up and then I've got to figure out what the hell we're gonna do with you."

"Thank you," Cam said.

"Yeah, well, I don't have to like it." She looked at Ruth as she said the last part. "Are you responsible for this new shit?"

"She's trying to stop it," Ingrid said, and Ruth shot her a grateful look.

"So it was some other fuckin' genius this time," Foshtomi said. Her dark, oval face was unforgiving. "You're conscripts, all of you. Is that understood?"

"Yes," Cam said.

"You follow orders. You're all privates—even you," she said, pointing at Ruth. "Legally, I have that power under the new Constitution. We're still under martial law."

They used to be squadmates. Sarah Foshtomi had been a member of his Ranger unit, a corporal like himself and the only woman in the group. That was why she talked so tough, overcompensating for her size and gender. Apparently her style had seen some success. Foshtomi must have continued to serve with local forces, that much was clear. She'd even made lieutenant. Had she been stationed here or had she run to Willow Creek with other survivors? It didn't matter. Cam knew she could be a powerful ally.

Suddenly that good feeling gave way to woozy-headed nausea. He slumped to the floor beside the tank. Satisfying his thirst only made him more aware of his tired muscles, his aching feet, and his hunger. He could have slept. He said, "Are you in contact with anyone?"

Foshtomi shook her head. "There are no landlines out of here and the atmosphere's totally fucked. I've got some guys trying to patch into a satellite."

"Okay."

The women settled down around Cam, except Foshtomi, who wasn't good at sitting still. She stayed on her feet, glancing toward the greenhouse door as if that might hurry her medic. In fact, she was probably glad to have Ruth to rally around, because until now her troops had lacked any purpose except to hold on and wait.

"How much fuel do you have?" he asked.

Foshtomi stared at him. "You came on foot out of the mountains, right? So maybe you don't know what it's like in the cities."

"Greg and Eric are dead," he said, meeting her bluntness with his own. The two Rangers had been her squadmates first. "They stayed with us all this time, Sarah. They died last night."

"I . . ." she said.

"Our whole town was infected. There were hundreds of them, Sarah. Greg bought us enough time to get out."

"Eric was my husband," Bobbi said.

"I'm sorry." Foshtomi's gaze went from Cam's face to Bobbi's to Ruth's, but Ruth unzipped her backpack and took out her laptop with that old, stubborn focus.

Cam nodded to himself, admiring the same dedication that had infuriated him in the aspen grove. Ruth would never give up. Not if they gave her time. Her fingers rattled on her keyboard and Cam said, to Foshtomi, "If you have enough fuel, we can try to seal those Humvees. Make a break for it."

"Where you gonna go?"

"Grand Lake."

"You're crazy. There's a million fuckin' zombies between here and there, and we think the Chinese took the base anyway."

Zombies, he thought. In a different life, Cam had loved those corny old movies. Maybe it was strange that his group had never called sick people anything except "the infected." They were zombies in every way that mattered, lethal, stupid, and relentless. But they were family. Cam's group hadn't fought anyone except their own friends and neighbors. Foshtomi's battle had been larger, more impersonal. *Zombies* was a way to make the killing easier, reducing the infected to caricatures instead of real victims.

Cam said, "The Chinese have a vaccine against the new plague. Ruth thinks we can steal it."

"What about the parasite?"

"You . . . What do you mean?" he said, even though he'd imagined the same thing himself. The parasite nanotech would shut off the first vaccine, the one that kept them safe from the machine plague. Anyone who couldn't reach safe elevation would die, and Cam knew how badly that would disrupt the Chinese assault—but at what cost?

Foshtomi's eyes were narrow with hate. "What if we let it go? That'd fuck up the Chinese in a big way."

Ruth's hands stopped on her keyboard but she didn't look up, as if too afraid to let Foshtomi see anything in her expression. Cam worried what Foshtomi might have read in his own face. "Sarah," he said. "The parasite would affect everyone below ten thousand feet, not just the Chinese."

"Our people are already dead, aren't they?"

She lost somebody last night, too, he thought. There was a new, cold edge in Foshtomi's voice, and it made him think she was just barely holding onto her composure, using her reckless tone as more than a front. Her attitude had become a crutch to keep herself sane.

"We don't have the parasite anymore," he said.

"Bullshit. I know it was for real. Deborah Reece gave up her vial. Grand Lake stashed it away somewhere, and everyone says it really would've done what Ruth said. So what could you do? Hide yours somewhere?"

"That's exactly what we did," Ruth said, tapping slowly at her laptop again. "We buried it fifteen feet down in a metal box."

"Where?"

"I can't tell you that."

"I think you still have it," Foshtomi said, and Cam wondered if he was going to have to fight her. Would her troops obey an order to seize and search his group?

Yes, he thought. *They will. For her, they will.*

Cam almost glanced down at his pocket before he caught himself. Even with the map, even knowing where they'd buried the nanotech outside of Jefferson, Foshtomi wouldn't have much chance of retrieving it, but he needed her to stay focused in another direction, toward Grand Lake.

"Sarah, it's not an option," he said.

"They've hit us with nukes."

"Even if we had it, which we don't, the parasite wouldn't be instantaneous. It would take days to spread far enough. It might not reach California for a week. They're up-weather from us. You wouldn't accomplish anything except killing our own people until the wind took it all the way around the world to our coastline."

"So you do have it."

"Sarah, no. My point is that we can't just stay here."

"Driving to Grand Lake is crazy."

"You were glad to see us," Cam said. "You were already restless. Look at you."

Foshtomi sneered even as she turned away. The motion was one of denial, rejecting what he'd said, except that by jumping up she'd proved him right. Yes, she was afraid to leave this canyon. One of her first responsibilities was to preserve her fighting strength—but for what? To sit and wait until Chinese planes attacked them, too?

"We're short on masks," Foshtomi said. "We only put them on our spotters and point men."

"If we get the vaccine, it won't matter."

"You've seen how fast the plague jumps people. How would we get close enough to—"

"Cam?" Ruth said.

Foshtomi turned on her. "He's not in charge here."

"Cam. All of you." Ruth's eyes were stunned. "The extra bulk attached to the nanotech is a message," she said. "It's not meant to do anything. It's just binary code. Someone built it into the machine like a note."

"We don't have anyone who can read Chinese," Foshtomi said, but Ruth shook her head.

"It's in English. Once I isolated the code, the computer translated it in seconds."

"What? What do they want?"

Ruth blinked and wet her lips first, as if testing her words before sharing them out loud. "It says it's from Kendra Freedman," she said.

18

"That's impossible," Cam said, but Ruth thought, *No, it's the only thing that really makes sense.*

She didn't want to fight with him any more, so she tamped down on her excitement. She knew she could be too loud when she was in the grip of inspiration. "Let me show you how it says what it does."

"What do you mean 'how'?" Foshtomi asked. "What's the message?"

Ruth turned her laptop to face them and said, "Look at the coding. It's a spiral of ones and zeroes embedded in the nano. Most of the extra bulk is just nulls, but the binary string is unmistakable."

Foshtomi glanced at Cam, who shook his head.

"Look at it! I highlighted the ones. Here are the zeroes." Ruth touched her keyboard again. "These specific molecular configurations are repeated hundreds of times. That's why my analysis picked it out in the first place."

"All I see is dots and bumps," Foshtomi said.

"Exactly. She chose simple forms to represent her 'ones' and 'zeroes.' They don't need to accomplish anything else. They're static frames. That's why Freedman was able to hide—"

Bobbi interrupted. "My God, Ruth, what does it say?"

" 'My name is Kendra Freedman,' " she said, tipping the laptop back to face herself. " 'I designed the *archos* plague, the nanotech that kills below 9,570 feet. It was a mistake. Maybe it can be stopped. My lab should still be intact at 4411 68th Street, Sacramento, California, along with our design work, software, samples, and machining gear.' "

"That's old news," Cam said. "Years old."

"Please. Just listen."

"You've already been to Sacramento," Bobbi said, echoing Cam. Her eyes were perplexed and, despite the fragrant heat of the greenhouse, Ruth felt cold and off-balance. The message had awakened too many ghosts.

" 'If you can read this, find me. I want I need—' " Ruth glanced up. "There's a break here. Freedman didn't have the chance to rewrite," she said, irritated by the doubt in their eyes. She looked back at her laptop and read, " 'Andrew Dutchess is the man who released the *archos* plague. It was Dutchess. But I'll do anything. I can fix this.' "

She sounds like me, Ruth thought.

The realization was a poignant one. The two of them had never met, except through Freedman's work, but Ruth had spent too much time pursuing Freedman's brilliance to feel anything except admiration. On a personal level, she'd also learned to feel horror and pity for the other woman. Freedman's vision had been one of immortality, wealth, and peace. She'd meant to change the world in a very different way. Without one man's greed, she might have succeeded.

Ruth had never dreamed she would confront Freedman again in a new competition. Cause and effect had come full circle. The science teams in Leadville had designed the booster on the foundation of Freedman's work. Then the booster gave Freedman the insights necessary to accelerate her own designs.

She was alive, and she was the creator of the mind plague.

" 'I reached the mountains in northern California,' " Ruth read, " 'where I survived until the Russian invasion. They traded me to the Chinese.' "

"It has to be a trick," Cam said.

" 'This machine is also mine. It is an unholy mistake, and it is mine. I was deceived. I thought I was working to bring peace in the Himalayas, but they lied to me. I was never in Tibet. There is no snow or Indians and I'm sure now that—' " Ruth frowned. "It breaks again."

"She's rambling," Foshtomi said.

She lapsed, Ruth thought. *She was tired or she was interrupted. She must have been constructing the message letter by letter.*

They don't understand.

Every sentence would have cost Freedman hours, the full message days or weeks, and it sounded like she was in prison. Were there guards? Other scientists? The Chinese must have caged Freedman so tightly it felt like she'd been pinned under a microscope herself, controlling everything about her: when to eat, where to sleep, and, most importantly, what to do and how to think. The idea of that never-ending scrutiny made Ruth claustrophobic.

It was amazing that Freedman had been able to construct her message at all, and yet Foshtomi was right even if she didn't know it. Ruth was also bothered by Freedman's verbosity.

If every letter counted, why so much? Her guilt must be unbearable. That was why she made her excuses, pointing the blame at Dutchess. Still, something in the tone of Freedman's words seemed off. Was there another code hidden within this message? What if she'd used a cipher or some kind of subtle wordplay?

" 'Find me,' " Ruth read. " 'I know I can stop the new plague. As I write this, it is July twelfth, Year Three. I've learned I'm in southern California at sea level, but somehow we're safe. These labs are in the Saint Bernadine Hospital in Los Angeles.' "

"Then we're fucked," Foshtomi said.

"What do you mean?"

"Our guys were hardwired to nuke Los Angeles if the Chinese hit us. That's public knowledge. It had to be if we were gonna keep those bastards from overrunning us. Mutually assured destruction. So one way or the other, she's dead."

"We don't know that!"

"How would you get to L.A. even if it's still there? Flap your arms?"

"The whole thing could just be a trick," Cam said.

Ruth shook her head, imploring him. "Why? What could they possibly gain by faking a message from her? You don't realize how complicated it was, either."

"If you tried to call her . . . Is there more to the message?" he asked. "A specific radio frequency? What if Chinese are waiting?"

"The message ends there."

"It's the perfect trap, like a trip wire," he said. "The only people who could find the message are the ones they'd want to kill the most—the nanotech experts on our side. If it's her, why doesn't she know about the vaccine? 'We're at sea level, but somehow we're safe.' That's what it says."

"She's isolated. They control everything about her life."

"You really think she's alive?"

"Yes. The binary string runs *backward* or even splits in two in thirty places, hidden in the nulls. That's why the Chinese didn't see it. They might not have even realized such a thing was possible."

"And we know Freedman was the best," Cam said as if wanting to convince himself.

He believes me! Ruth thought. He was taking her side against Foshtomi even after playing the devil's advocate, and Ruth flashed him a big, girlish smile. "There's no proof she didn't make it to elevation!" she said. "Sawyer did."

"Sawyer ran for the mountains as soon as possible," Cam said quietly, "but Freedman went downtown to try to find the mayor or the police. That's how he told it. Remember? She stayed behind."

"We need to find her."

Forty minutes later, Foshtomi's unit had done everything possible to seal three Humvees, a Ford Expedition, and a half-ton Army truck. There were only seventeen of them. Foshtomi considered leaving the truck, but they also wanted to carry water, gas, and other supplies. She also hoped they might find other survivors and take them along.

The vehicles were a gamble. Foshtomi's troops didn't have any welding gear, only the plastic sheeting used for the greenhouses and a limited amount of tape. They'd covered most of the doors and seams. Once inside, they planned to finish the job, but if they drove through an invisible fog of nanotech, would the plastic be enough? It was the best they could do.

Ruth wanted to talk to Cam alone, but first he was busy with their medic and then Foshtomi wanted to compare notes with him over her maps. Ruth took her laptop to a spot alongside one of the planters, pursuing a new effort to find secondary codes hidden within the original message.

If Freedman knew how to turn off the mind plague, wouldn't she have recorded that information, too? What if the awkward lapses were on purpose? Ruth tried writing down only the first letters of a dozen words, then only the second letters or the third. Each time, she ended up with nonsense and cursed herself.

Think! You have to think like her.

If there was an additional code, Ruth decided it wouldn't be in word games. Freedman was always direct. Her work was superior exactly because it was so streamlined, which was indicative of a personality that functioned in the same manner. A second message would be carved into the body of the nano just like the first, either in binary or a different physical code like number substitutions for letters. Were there other molecular configurations that should stand out? *What am I missing?*

Cam joined her. "Hey. Change of plans."

Ruth's blood quickened as she glanced past his shoulder, measuring how far they were from anyone else. Fifteen feet. Bobbi was wolfing down a cup of onion soup and Foshtomi had walked away with two sergeants, arguing.

Ruth stepped close and laid her hands on Cam's shoulders. She smiled—and when the motion attracted his gaze to her lips, her smile widened. He was still so cautious with her. He was still afraid. She understood. She'd punished herself for years, too, but she wanted to stop. She wanted to be happy. Would they ever have the chance?

Ruth lifted herself on her tiptoes to match Cam's five-foot-eleven. Her excitement was good. It increased when she peeked sideways and saw Bobbi watching now with an angry face. Let her disapprove. Ruth touched her mouth to his. Their kiss was slow and sweet. It broke her heart.

I'm yours, she thought. *I'm yours if you want me. You know that. Please know that, Cam.*

She didn't want to upset him, so she kept quiet. Maybe the intimacy was too much regardless. Cam squeezed her hand even as he pulled away. "Pack up," he said. "Foshtomi got some of our guys on the radio and we're going to intercept."

"Who? Where?"

"A command group out of Grand Lake. Foshtomi told 'em she has a nanotech expert and they used the same code. It sounds like they've got some scientists, too."

Foshtomi put Ruth in the second Humvee with herself, Sergeant Huff, Bobbi, and Cam. The third vehicle was equally crowded, because Foshtomi deemed those positions to be the safest. The civilian SUV would be fourth, carrying only two men, and last was the Army truck, where Ingrid rode in the cab with two soldiers. Their lead vehicle was the only Humvee that had been outfitted with a FRAG 6 armor kit. All of the High Mobility Multipurpose Wheeled Vehicles were 5,200-pound hardtop jeeps with fat wheels and steel plating, but FRAG 6 added a thousand pounds of metal, so Foshtomi set that Humvee in front with just a driver and a radioman.

As they left, the sky began to sprinkle a few bits of ash like black snow. The wind had failed to push the fallout away, and Ruth worried at that. What if it got worse?

She was grateful for her friends. Squeezed into the rear seat beside Cam, with Bobbi on his other side, Ruth was glad for his warm, firm weight as they rode for two hours on highways that might have taken forty minutes before the plague. Working down from Willow Creek to 40 and then back up toward Grand Lake, they drove south, east, and then north again. Most of the extra time was spent hiding from two Chinese jets. Foshtomi halted their convoy four times as the fighters patrolled overhead, alternately jamming their vehicles together or spreading them apart, parked at odd angles on the road like abandoned wrecks. It helped their little ruse that

the colossal old traffic jams created years ago had been bull-
dozed from these highways, so the roadsides were jammed
with cars and burned out hulks. Their engines would shine
brightly in infrared, but the Chinese must have been wholly
concerned with American missile launches and aircraft. Also,
orbital coverage was hindered by the filthy sky. If the enemy
was monitoring this area via satellite, their capacities were
too strained to care about a few Humvees.

Many of the old cars had skeletons in them. The dead left
by the machine plague had never been cleaned up. The job
was just too big, so the dented cars remained crowded with
screaming ghosts. Skeletons sprawled through broken glass
and doors.

The first time Ruth saw a wreck with living people inside,
she thought she was hallucinating. All of them were on edge,
waiting for the jets to bank toward them and dive. Then she
spotted a white van with three shadows hunched together by
its rear doors. Their lead Humvee had already passed the van,
but the people inside didn't get up. Only one even lifted her
head.

"Look," Ruth said. "What are they doing?"

Foshtomi also drove by without incident, but Sergeant
Huff took the handset of their radio and said, "This is Two.
Heads up. We got zombies on both sides of us."

Ruth glanced the other way. Huff was right. At least one
person was slumped inside a red Toyota across the road. Then
she saw one more in a tan pickup truck. *It's like this spot is a
camp,* she thought.

"Are they okay?" Bobbi asked. "Do you think they don't
have the plague?"

"No. Their faces . . ."

Not all of the infected had chosen their shelters wisely.
Minutes later, Ruth saw two limp, fresh bodies in the front
of a sedan. They were motionless except for a surging black
carpet of ants.

There were zombies on the road, too. Shambling uphill,
arms spread to keep their balance, they turned to meet the
oncoming vehicles with the same dull instinct. *They're so limited,* she thought. *They hear noise, see movement, and they
go toward it.*

Foshtomi tried to avoid them. "Move, you stupid shit," she said. "Move. Move." Then she hit them. Foshtomi braked or weaved if possible and once she ordered the convoy to leave the road entirely, jouncing off the shoulder to get around a dozen people. Ruth knew she was less interested in saving these strangers' lives than in preserving her vehicles. Even in the second position, Foshtomi struck eight people altogether. Ruth wouldn't forget. The harsh *thump* of a body against the Humvee's fender was nauseating.

A naked woman came over the hood in a spatter of blood. Another time the rear axle leapt and clunked and Ruth screamed, sitting just a few inches above someone caught beneath the vehicle with an arm or a leg jammed in the wheelwell. Cam hugged both Ruth and Bobbi after that experience and Ruth rocked against him with her head stuck in a high-speed panic. *Don't think about it. Don't think about it. Don't think about it.*

By then they were driving upslope again, hurrying toward the blue stretch of water that gave Grand Lake its name. Foshtomi's troops broke radio silence again and again to advise each other of more infected people, many of them hunkered down in "camps" alongside the road, either dozing in abandoned cars or snuggled down on the roadside against guardrails or trees. Were the infected communicating with each other? It wouldn't be impossible for them to establish some kind of social order, straining through their limited coherence like cattle or sheep, herding together because it felt safer than being alone. A school of phantoms. How much did they retain? Were they all screaming inside?

Ruth tried to occupy herself with more thoughts of Kendra Freedman. She tried to enjoy Cam's arm on her shoulders.

Too many of the infected are acting differently, she realized.

"Those people taking shelter, that's new," she said without looking up from Cam's embrace. "They barely noticed us. They're docile. They must have walked here last night. Now something's different."

"Move," Foshtomi said up front. "Move."

"Maybe they're just tired and hungry," Ruth said, "but

what if there's a second stage of the mind plague? If the Chinese wanted to kill us—"

"Move."

Wham. The Humvee shook as Foshtomi hit another person and Ruth raised her voice desperately. "If they wanted to kill us, everyone would have seizures or stroke out. That's the only thing the nanotech would do."

Cam tried to quiet her. "*Shh*, Ruth," he said, stroking the back of her neck.

"No one's asked what it's really for! Don't you get it? The first stage is just to spread the plague. They're stunted and afraid. They go after their friends. But then what?"

"Maybe a slow weapon is the best they could make," said Foshtomi's sergeant, Tanya Huff. Tall and thick, Huff was one of the two other females in Foshtomi's unit. Was that why Foshtomi had assigned her to this Humvee?

"I think the Chinese are waiting," Ruth said. "I think everyone who's infected will calm down in another five or six hours!"

"This is One," the radio crackled. "We're nearing position. Over."

"It might make sense to go to ground," Ruth said. "Don't you see? The plague is a first-strike weapon, but it just makes us stupid. Easy to conquer. Then it hits a second stage, and maybe there's a third. Maybe the fog wears off. People regain their coordination, but they're still confused and suggestible. They're slaves. It's self-selecting, too. You're only left with the strongest ones. So maybe we should just hide. If we wait a few hours, we won't have to fight our own people as well as the Chinese—"

"Shut her up," Foshtomi said as she braked and turned to the right. "I want a perimeter but stay in the vehicles."

"Yes, ma'am." Huff picked up the radio again. "This is Two," she said. "Form up in a circle, but stay inside your wheels. Watch for planes. Weapons tight. Remember, we're looking for friendlies on the ground."

"This is Five," the radio said. "I've got zombies two hundred yards behind us."

"Shit." Foshtomi stopped the Humvee. "We probably

need to get uphill if we can, but I don't know if Five will make it. That truck was a bad idea. Call Viper first. Is he still inbound?"

Ruth was barely listening. *Lord God,* she thought. If she was right, the Chinese wouldn't only gain tens of thousands of slaves in victory. There would be concubines, too, and the idea left a cold weight deep in her chest.

"It will be even worse for women," she said. "Remember what happened in the labor camps. There was rape and forced pregnancies—"

"Not now," Foshtomi said. "Christ."

Ruth raised her head at last. She was surprised to find a brick building on one side of the vehicle, an old bank, which Foshtomi was using for cover. Everywhere else, there were only ruins, the square-cornered shapes of foundations lost among brush and weeds. They were in the remains of the original town of Grand Lake, most of which had been dismantled for building material. That meant they were just six miles from the peaks where the military base had been overrun.

Driving here was incredibly dangerous. The Chinese might find them at any minute—and yet they'd come to hunt the Chinese themselves. Rescuing the other Americans was a secondary goal as far as Ruth was concerned. Unfortunately, they could expect heavy casualties when they left their vehicles. After smashing through the infected people, the outsides of their Humvees and trucks would be laced with nanotech.

We'll be lucky if half of us survive, Ruth thought as Huff switched frequencies and said, "Viper Six, this is Gray Fox. Viper Six, this is Gray Fox. Over."

"We have you in sight, Gray Fox," a woman answered. "Stay off the radio. Over."

"Roger that, Viper Six. Be advised there's a crowd of zombies coming up behind us," Huff said. "I see thirty or more."

"We see them, too. Hold your fire. We don't want the Chinese to hear shots. How are your vehicles for space? We want to jump onboard, but we're contaminated."

"What?" Foshtomi barked. "Ask them what the fuck that

means," she said as Huff clicked at her SEND button and said, "Say again, Viper. Your people are infected?"

"We're in suits but we're covered with nanotech," the woman answered. "You can't touch us. Not yet."

"What do we do?" Bobbi asked. "Ruth? What do we do?"

There's nothing we can do, she thought, but it was her job to find a way. "The lake," she said. "They need to wash off in the lake. They'll probably just pick up more nanotech on the shore, but they have to try. Then I'd have them scrub each other with dirt."

"Those zombies will be on top of us in five minutes," Cam said.

19

"We need twenty minutes," the woman on the radio said. "Then we can clear your vehicles, too. Buy us some time."

"Roger that, Viper," Sergeant Huff said.

"I want One and Three to sweep the road," Foshtomi said as she dug for a pair of binoculars. "No guns. Just run 'em down. Is that understood?"

"Yes, ma'am," Huff said without meeting her eyes, and Ruth felt the same squeamish sense of alarm. It was one thing to shoot innocent people from a distance. Intentionally using the Humvees as battering rams was hideous, but Huff began to relay Foshtomi's orders. "This is Two," she said. "Listen up."

Foshtomi turned to Ruth. "How is Viper going to decontaminate?"

"I don't know."

An engine rumbled behind them as one of the Humvees rolled past. The other Humvee appeared from the corner of the bank and followed. Ruth was very, very glad she wasn't in those vehicles, but it had always been that way, hadn't it? Other people did the dirty work while she was safe.

"I think I see them," Foshtomi said. She lowered her binoculars and got up on her seat, twisting in the confines of the

Humvee to find a better angle through the windshield. "Shit. They've got a drape or something like a tent."

"You mean an airtight tent?" Bobbi asked.

"That wouldn't work," Ruth said. "This plague doesn't have the hypobaric fuse."

"It's just some kind of blanket." Foshtomi slid back into her driver's seat and handed the binoculars to Ruth. "Tell me what you see."

Suddenly the radio squawked, full of the sound of a growling motor. "Watch out!" a man yelled. Then the noise shut off. He was gone.

"One and Three," Huff said. "One and Three, are you okay?"

Please be okay, Ruth thought, but the radio answered in the same man's voice. "This is One," he said. "I think Three's infected. They nearly hit us."

Foshtomi punched the ceiling. "Fuck!"

"We're coming back around," the man said. "He's off the road. We—Yeah, I can see Coughlin. He's sick. They're all sick."

Ruth was trembling too hard to see through the binoculars when she finally brought them to her eyes. Then she realized she was crying again. *We just let five soldiers be infected to save a few others,* she thought. *We just lost five people, plus everyone they killed in the street . . .* Maybe that kind of math was necessary, but it felt evil, and she struggled with her helpless guilt and self-reproach.

The hillside beyond the remnants of the town was brown and green. Ruth spotted a yellow figure, someone in a hazmat suit. Other soldiers gathered around him. She was disappointed by the size of the group. *Is that it?* she wondered. Were there more in hiding? Maybe a larger group wouldn't have been able to sneak away, so eight or nine commandos and scientists were all that had escaped Grand Lake.

They wrapped one of their own in a peculiar blanket, an olive green Army-issue blanket that looked like it was pierced with wire. Dimples filled the sheet. Ruth thought they'd attached a great many small things to the other side of the blanket, but what? At eighty yards, from a poor angle, it was difficult to see what they were doing, but they walked the blanket from one person to another, positioning it against their knees, chests, air tanks, and helmets. However the blanket functioned, Ruth supposed it was also how they'd replenished their air tanks, by sterilizing the connections first.

A rain of ash flittered from the sky, then cleared again. Ruth caught several glimpses of the blanket's other side. It was lined with irregular hunks of circuit boards—some barely an inch across, others as much as three—which they'd sewn to the blanket with an odd collection of wire and string. Here and there, a few of the circuit boards were still whole. They were round and set in shallow white plastic caps.

"So what is it?" Foshtomi asked. "Is this gonna work?"

For once, Ruth was a total loss. "They must have rigged some kind of radioactive material," she said. *Those caps look familiar, too,* she thought. *Where have I seen them before?*

Faintly, she heard the screech of tires as the other Humvee continued to cover the road behind her. The commandos hiked down in a group. Two of them were lugging microscopes, which was good, but Ruth was more interested in their blanket, which they immediately spread in front of Foshtomi's vehicle. After thirty seconds, they laid it over the hood.

"Smoke detectors," Foshtomi said. "That thing's got five hundred fucking smoke detectors on it."

They lifted the blanket and brought it to the driver-side fender, then to the door. Ruth shook her head in confusion. The dismantled fragments of plastic and circuitry were mostly unrecognizable, but the few that remained intact were the back halves of ordinary household smoke detectors. Even then, the front casing and some of the innards had been cut away.

"Ruth?" Cam asked.

"Don't open your doors until they take off their suits and prove it's all right," she said, watching the men outside, yet she remembered one of the many calls for material that had gone out since the war. The government paid in ammunition and seeds for items like gasoline, drugs, batteries, and copper. There had also been a bounty for smoke detectors. Morristown had even hosted a collection center for several weeks, where government agents filled three trucks with scavenged goods. At the time, Ruth supposed they were installing fire alarms in a lot of new construction, but there was another reason for this stockpile, something else they wanted.

It took another half an hour before the commandos finished with all four vehicles. "They said twenty minutes," Foshtomi groused even as she made an effort to calm her troops on the radio. "Just hold tight," she told them. "Hold tight." Then she glanced at Huff and said, "Jesus, I gotta pee."

The commandos took turns wrapping themselves in the blanket again. Meanwhile, Foshtomi also spoke with their leader, shouting through the glass as he leaned his helmet close. General Walls was in his fifties, Ruth thought, brown-haired and good-looking without a beard. It was unusual to see a clean-shaven man.

"Sir? What's the plan?" Foshtomi asked.

"There's an Army depot downriver near the hydroelectric plant," he said. "We need to—"

"We just drove through there, sir. It's full of zombies."

"We need to get our science assets out of sight, lieutenant. Every minute we spend in the open is pushing our luck. We need to regroup."

"Goldman thinks we can steal a new vaccine from the Chinese, sir," Foshtomi said. "That's what we'd planned to do—set up a raid."

"How many troops do you have, lieutenant?"

"Eight including me, sir, plus the four civilians."

"She must have balls the size of that Humvee," another man said.

Walls nodded with a grim smile inside his faceplate. "The Chinese put at least two troop carriers on the mountain," he said. "Even if all of us went back, we'd be outnumbered ten to one."

"But then we'd be immune, sir."

"We'd also be dead."

"Wait, that's it!" a woman said behind Walls. "Does he need to be alive? The enemy soldier, I mean. He doesn't need to be alive, does he?"

"What are you thinking?" Walls asked.

Ruth pressed against the plastic on the window with her

fingertips and her cheek, trying to follow their conversation. The woman wore one of the two civilian suits, bright yellow among the others' black.

"The Chinese sacrificed at least a dozen planes when the bombs went off," the woman said. "We tracked an IL-76 Mainstay that crashed not too far from here. That's the only reason we saw it. It cut right in front of our radar."

Walls turned to the Humvee. "Would their pilots have the vaccine, too?"

"Yes!" Ruth shouted.

"What kind of coordinates can you give us?" Walls asked the woman in the yellow suit. She held their radio, but set it by her feet to take one of the laptops Walls carried in a sling with a briefcase.

"Let me see what I can bring up," she said.

"We'll divide into two groups," Walls said. "I need volunteers to go for the plane."

"I know the area," Cam said to Foshtomi.

"No," Ruth said.

"I can scout for them."

"Cam, no!" *He just wants to keep running,* she thought. *From what? Allison's death?* "Let the soldiers handle it. We're already doing our part. We—"

"He wouldn't want you anyway," Foshtomi said. "I don't mean because of what you did. I mean because he can draw on his commandos."

But she was wrong. "Lieutenant," Walls said with impatience, "let's have some volunteers. I need everyone on my team." It was another example of that brutal math. "These men are translators and engineers," he said, indicating his people, whereas Foshtomi's troops were truck drivers, farmers, and artillery crew. Walls could afford to lose them.

"I'll go," Cam said.

"How many suits do I get?" Foshtomi asked through the window. Her tone bordered on insubordination, but Ruth liked her for sticking up for her soldiers.

Walls stared at her. "Two," he said. "Will that be sufficient, lieutenant? I'm going to put my suit on Goldman. The others stay on my nanotech people, my pilot, and my translator."

"Yes, sir. Thank you, sir."

"Let us change out first," Walls said. "Goldman can dress and then we'll mount up."

"Yes, sir." Foshtomi turned to Huff and said, "Get me four volunteers. I need two guys with masks. The other two can have the suits."

"I'll head up this mission, lieutenant," Huff said.

"I didn't ask—Thank you, Tanya."

Another of the commandos sidled up to the Humvee with his head bent to peer inside. But it wasn't a man. The face inside the helmet was female, aristocratic and lean. Ruth gawked at her. "Deborah! Hey! Deborah!" she yelled.

A wan smile was the first reaction from Deborah Reece. Then she set her glove on the outside of the window and Ruth mimicked her old rival exactly, trying to meet Deborah's hand through the glass.

Was there forgiveness in this gesture?

Ruth didn't try to hide her tears. She beamed at Deborah, ecstatic yet also bewildered. Their paths had crossed so many times before. Why? Too many other friends had died or separated themselves from her. Frank Hernandez. James Hollister. Ulinov. Newcombe. Ruth couldn't say if it was fate that had brought her back together with Foshtomi and Deborah, but more and more she believed in providence. Statistics alone couldn't explain this reoccurring destiny. Yes, they'd all made their homes within fifty miles of each other, and she and Deborah were both carefully guarded for their education—but Kendra Freedman was a part of the equation, too, wasn't she?

Four women. They represented darkness and light. Freedman was the most powerful component by far, but Ruth couldn't be sure it wasn't the brash Ranger lieutenant who would bring them to safety. Sarah Foshtomi was here for a reason, too. Ruth believed it.

"I'm sorry," she said, not even knowing why she was apologizing. "I'm so sorry." Maybe the words were a mistake. She didn't want Deborah to assume what Foshtomi had thought—that she was responsible for the new plague.

"It's okay," Deborah said. "I'm glad we found you."

There wasn't time for more. The first commando opened his suit as two others kept the blanket against his face and hands. Deborah stepped away from the Humvee to assist.

Nothing happened. The man was okay.

"What the hell is in those things?" Foshtomi asked, meaning the smoke detectors. Her tone was sarcastic. She wanted to break the tension. Ruth tried to laugh for her, but it was a weak, distracted sound. Everything she did felt forced, a mixture of losing control and keeping herself tightly under wraps.

They decontaminated General Walls next, then the woman in the civilian suit. Moving the commandos into the vehicles was more complicated. Foshtomi's group had to open every Humvee and truck either to let volunteers out or bring the commandos in. They managed it in stages, risking only one vehicle at a time. Ruth hoped Deborah would end up in Two with her, but Walls sent Deborah to Five.

Then it was Ruth's turn to get out. She was helpless to stop the process, but she felt ashamed again as she donned her suit. Walls had decided to risk the plague to save her. What could she possibly say to him?

I won't fail you again, she thought. *I'll find a way. I swear it.*

After she dressed, she told them about Kendra Freedman and the message in the nanotech, but Walls just shook his head. "I don't know if there's anything we can do about that right now," he said.

"Freedman could stop the plague!"

"We'll talk about it. But let's get moving."

Sergeant Huff and three men were left behind with the Ford Expedition to drive north, where Agent Rezac had placed the fallen plane. Ruth wondered at their chances. Walls should have sent a larger force, but Huff expected to go most of the way on foot, hiking into the ravines where the IL-76 had gone down, and Walls couldn't afford to give up more of his few remaining air tanks.

Lieutenant Pritchard was the commando assigned to Huff's empty seat inside Foshtomi's Humvee, probably because Walls wanted to make certain he controlled the vehicle. Foshtomi had challenged him once, if slightly—and Walls must remember how Ruth had betrayed them before. Pritchard was his enforcer.

Like Walls, Pritchard had given up his suit. Ruth was the only one in the vehicle who sat awkwardly, trying to make room for her air tanks, sealed off from everyone else.

Ash swirled up from the road as they drove. Ruth was allowed to call Deborah to quiz her about her equipment, which was good, and the progress she'd made, which was zero. The other woman, Emma, was only another medical officer like Deborah. Neither of them had any nanotech skills. The brief exchange left Ruth disheartened. They were done in two minutes and weren't given the opportunity for more personal words. Walls demanded radio silence.

Ruth turned to Pritchard. "How did you decontaminate these suits?" she asked—anything to divert herself. She was wasting too much energy on recrimination and guilt. She needed to hear that they could keep her friends safe. "How much radiation were you taking?"

"Nothing," Pritchard said. "Millirems."

"So the blanket's no good at a distance."

"Two or three inches. Maybe four."

"I thought we'd made more progress with OECs," Ruth said, but Pritchard only grunted.

"What are you talking about?" Cam said.

"Open environmental countermeasures. During the plague year, we tried everything we could think of to stop nanotech, including beta emitters like Cobalt-60." She saw his confusion and said, "Radioactive material. The idea was that you could carry an OEC with you like a beacon. Anyone within range of it would be safe."

"Except for the radiation," Cam said.

"Right." Ruth hesitated. Radiation sickness had become less of a problem after Leadville's science teams developed the booster nanotech, which provided a low, steady level of protection. The booster would help them against the fallout, and Ruth wondered if it made sense to try a larger radioactive source. "Even a medium dose would be better than dying right away or losing your mind," she said.

Cam nodded. "How does that blanket work?"

"Smoke detectors have a bit of Americium-241 inside," Pritchard said, staring outside as they passed another camp of infected people. "It emits alpha particles into an ionization chamber. If you obstruct it with smoke, the alpha flux drops and the alarm goes off. Complex 3 was full of 'em. Cut away the shielding and you have a very small radiation flashlight."

"Why didn't they tell us? Ruth? Why didn't *you* tell us? We could have had a bunch of these things."

"I didn't know."

"Don't lie to me."

"Cam, I consulted on large-scale OECs, but I never knew how smoke detectors work until Pritchard told us." *And now it's too late,* she thought. *How many stockpiles were never utilized because we've been too busy growing food or arguing politics with ourselves?*

"What do you mean by large-scale?" Foshtomi asked. "Like more bombs?"

"Yes. But what's the point? We talked about laying down huge sterilized areas with nuclear waste, too, but no one could stay there. They tested it in parts of Denver and Phoenix just to give scavenging efforts more time, but then we were losing people and supplies in a different way."

"So the fallout is a good thing as far as we're concerned," Foshtomi said. "It might hurt the plague."

"Yes. That's one reason why we used to be safe in the mountains. The atmosphere's thinner, so we got more UV. A lot of ultraviolet is hard on nanotech."

"The machine plague self-destructed at altitude," Cam said.

He was still angry, so Ruth's tone was cautious. "That's what happened above the barrier," she said, "but sometimes we gained some extra room because nanobots are delicate little fuckers. They burn easily."

People forgot that nanotech was man-made, whereas living things were the result of two billion years of evolution and had learned ways to heal that nanobots couldn't mimic. Not yet. They wouldn't need a great leap from existing replication keys to self-repair mechanisms. It was only one more program to develop—but it would slow both plagues and vaccines.

Self-repairing nanotech would be more durable but less

volatile. That was why it hadn't happened yet, which was fortunate. Otherwise an OEC might not work at all.

"Viruses can be killed by a few hundred radioactive impacts," Ruth said. "Nanobots are probably disabled by no more than five or ten. Imagine a well-made watch being shot by a dozen BB guns. Something inside it'll break."

"So we should be driving up again," Cam said. "Not down."

"It's like nighttime with the smoke," Foshtomi said. "We're not getting any UV today."

"But it'll clear. We could—"

"Hey," Pritchard said. "This isn't open for discussion. General Walls knows where he's going."

"Ruth?"

"Let's see what they've planned," she said. "Okay? If we can get the new vaccine, that's a thousand times better than hoping there'll be enough sun tomorrow to make a difference."

Cam nodded, but she was afraid of his silence. So was Pritchard. The USAF lieutenant turned in his seat and said, "You with me on this, Najarro? We follow orders."

"Yes, sir," Cam said.

Ruth would have touched his leg if she wasn't in the suit, because it wasn't fair that she was safe and he wasn't. She wanted to take it off because she wanted to share his fate, but she knew that would be stupid and disrespectful. Everyone had sacrificed too much for her to reject the thin, temporary luck of her suit.

Then her frustration became something darker. A chill drew up her spine like one slow finger and Ruth tried to ward off the premonition, bowing her head inside her helmet to pray. *Oh please, God, don't,* she thought.

She'd remembered her dream of losing Cam. Was it an omen? Ruth did not believe a higher power was on her side. No one was handpicked for glory or salvation. That was obvious. Their losses were horrific. So were their mistakes. There certainly wasn't a big white Zeus in the sky who favored them over anyone else. To think otherwise was simplistic, even stupid. They made themselves what they were—hero, villain, bystander, linchpin—even as they were influenced by everything around them. The world was always in flux. That was destiny. Ruth had utter faith in the laws of probability, and each step she took was like a promise, leading her in one direction or another. She knew her subconscious often grasped things ahead of her waking mind. Was there a pattern she should have seen? Or was it simply that in a bad situation, she knew Cam would give his life to save hers?

She needed to be ready to stop him.

20

Their convoy decelerated suddenly as they came around a bend in the highway. Ruth looked up, expecting trouble. They'd arrived at the depot and their four vehicles split into pairs to cover the road from both directions.

The depot was larger than she expected. Some of the small base was fresh construction, but the squat new bunkers and fences had also absorbed two preexisting green aluminum warehouses. They were old and weather-streaked. Some sort of company sign had been removed from the face of one warehouse, leaving a less-faded square where the sign had protected the metal for years. The few open areas inside the fence were packed with trucks, an Abrams tank, and several trailers and RVs, which the soldiers would have used for offices and living space. Most of the vehicles were still parked in neat lines. Otherwise the depot was a mess.

To Ruth, it looked as though the mind plague had spared a few people inside the trailers. Then they'd been attacked by the rest. In many places, the windows were blown out by gunfire. Two of the RVs had burned. At least five corpses sprawled on the tarmac, some of them charred.

"This is Bornmann," the radio said. "Hold your positions, but sing out if you see anybody. Over."

Some of the infected would still be alive. Were they hiding? Or had they gotten through the wire and walked away? Ruth's gaze traced along the fence but didn't find any breaks. "You need to call off your general," she said to Pritchard. "We can do better than this."

"Don't worry about it."

"Look at it! This place is crawling with nanotech, and everything's burned. We can do better. Even a regular house—"

"There's a plane inside."

"What? There's a plane in where?"

"We never planned to stay at this location," Pritchard said. "Just relax. We know what we're doing."

Ruth scowled inside her helmet. Then the radio crackled again. "This is Bornmann. We're stepping out. Route to us through Reece's suit if you see anything. Over."

General Walls had put all of his suited personnel in the back of the Army truck with the blanket. It was a decision that allowed him to leave the first Humvee alone, neither removing nor adding people. The suited troops were able to jump out of the covered truckbed freely. They were his strongest force, even if one of them was Deborah, rather than another commando—but only four suited people left the truck, striding quickly to the fence.

"You know how to use that headset?" Pritchard asked, pointing at Ruth's helmet.

"Yes."

"Listen in, okay? Don't say anything."

Ruth fumbled with the control belt at her hip as Cam voiced the same problem that had been bothering her. "I don't see a plane or anywhere to take off."

"Black ops," Pritchard said. "We tried to prepare for as much shit like today as possible. There are aircraft stashed all over the Rockies."

"You mean in the warehouse? Where do you take off?"

"It's a V-22 Osprey. Vertical takeoff and landing. What do you hear, Goldman?"

"They're not saying anything."

"Where are we going?" Cam said.

"Albuquerque. Last I heard, they were still okay. Rezac's trying to confirm. Now shut up. Watch behind us if you can."

They had a bad moment when the Chinese jets roared overhead, unseen in the haze, but the fighters kept going. Bornmann's team cut the fence and ran into the lot. Ruth could just barely see them across the highway. The warehouse had huge rolling bay doors, which they left shut, entering through a man-sized door instead.

"We've got our wings," Bornmann said on his suit radio. Deborah relayed this message to the other vehicles but Ruth had already told her group, raising a small cheer inside their Humvee.

Then the real work began. Bornmann's team had to assume the interior of the warehouse was dusted with the plague, too, even though there was no sign of chaos. Before allowing Bornmann inside to begin his preflight checklist, they decontaminated a wide swath of the fuselage. They also turned the blanket on the air itself as best they could. Meanwhile, Walls asked Ruth to take over as their radio relay. She agreed even though it meant Deborah would be sent into the depot with her friend, Emma Kincaid. They needed the extra hands.

At the same time, eighteen miles north, Sergeant Huff reported that her squad had driven as far as possible to the downed Chinese plane. They were proceeding on foot.

A nasty thought occurred to Ruth. She didn't know what the Osprey looked like and she wondered if there was room onboard for everyone. If Huff's team managed to rejoin the larger group, there were twenty-one of them. Who would stay if their plane was too small?

The wait was excruciating. Ruth was hungry again and her body grew stiff and uncomfortable. Pretty soon Pritchard would have to give her the last air tank in their Humvee. Before then, she was sure she'd need to pee inside her suit. Foshtomi had already crouched under the steering wheel, shucked down her pants and wet the floor. It was unavoidable.

Despite these distractions, Ruth continued to analyze her surface scan of the nano. What she really wanted was a look at

the new vaccine through the magnetic resonance force microscope that the commandos had brought with them. Unfortunately, it sounded as if it would be at least an hour before
Huff's team caught up even if they didn't have any trouble
securing a few samples of the vaccine. Nor was there room for
Ruth to set up the MRFM inside the Humvee in any case.

Cam operated Ruth's laptop for her, since she was too
clumsy in her gloves. His bare hands were scarred and ugly,
but, to her, they were only proof of his incomparable toughness. She was ineffective. Her head was fuzzy. She could have
napped, but no one else had slept, either. All of them kept
going, so Ruth blinked and shook herself and cursed.

No one's going to buy you a goddamned coffee, she
thought.

In the Army truck, Walls and Rezac were also crunching
data, and Rezac came on the Harris radio. "Goldman, are you
sure your translation of Freedman's message is correct?"

"I'm sure," Ruth said.

"There is no Saint Bernadine Hospital in Los Angeles."

"What kind of maps are you using?"

"We've got data files like you wouldn't believe. Google.
State. Fed. That hospital isn't there."

It must be, Ruth thought with new despair. If the message
was wrong—if Freedman didn't really know where she was—
they would never find her. She could be anywhere. That meant
Ruth was alone again.

The suited troops began to clear the tarmac in front of the
warehouse, led by Captain Medrano, their engineer. Some
of the traffic jam was easy to move. The trucks and jeeps in
front were simply driven out onto the highway, but twice they
discovered zombies. These people had been infected long
enough to reach the second stage. Once it was a single man,
apparently dozing. The next time they found four men and
a woman hiding in a truck. The woman jumped Lang and
knocked him down. Sweeney shot them all. Then another
man stumbled out of a bunker into the hammering sound of
Sweeney's M4.

The damage was done. Gunshots echoed up and down the
valley, so Lang killed the fifth man with his pistol—but now
they could expect more zombies and maybe the Chinese, too.

It was hard to gauge how far the sound carried through the fallout.

Medrano urged his team to move the vehicles at double-time, even after Emma nearly ripped her glove after catching it on a belt buckle inside a car. Meanwhile, he sent Deborah into the warehouse with the blanket again to decontaminate as much surface area as possible. More trucks rolled out of the depot. One of the burned RVs was still in the way, but Medrano didn't think it would drive even if he could risk entering it, so they cleared a number of other vehicles just to make room to shove it aside. The half-melted tires peeled away when he nosed a truck into the RV's side, its rims shrieking on the asphalt.

"Two, this is Rezac," the radio said. "I think I have some good news. There's a hospital by the same name in San Bernadino, one of the cities in the Los Angeles sprawl. Saint Bernadine. San Bernadino."

Ruth gestured for Pritchard to give her the handset, which she clunked against her helmet. "This is Goldman, nice work," she said, but Rezac was still talking.

"—makes sense. Most of their people are inside Los Angeles proper or in the desert, using our old military bases. They might have put their nanotech labs away from everything else in case there was an accident."

"I think you're right. Nice work."

"It gets better. Saint Bernadine might have survived the nukes. I mean, it won't be in great shape, but there are some hills and terrain that would have shaded it from the blasts."

"Is there any way you can get a satellite on that area?"

"No. Maybe. I'm still trying to get a signal from anyone else in NORTHCOM."

"Thank you," Ruth said, and Pritchard muttered, "Shit. I hope Albuquerque's okay." Ruth turned to Cam and said, "She's alive. Did you hear? Freedman could still be alive!"

"Yeah." He tried to smile.

Ruth went back to her laptop, but her concentration was shot. It didn't help that she was cramping. Finally she had to pee. Relaxing those muscles was humiliating, even though no one else could feel or smell the trickling puddle. Ruth tried to emulate Foshtomi's tomboy attitude to herself. *Just be glad you only have to pee,* she thought, but she wasn't looking forward to taking off her suit and revealing what had happened. Maybe it was childish, but she wanted to be a giant like Freedman, and legends didn't wet their pants.

Her anger was a spark.

"I might have found a weakness," she said, returning to an earlier idea. "The new vaccine must recognize the same marker that the mind plague uses to identify people who are already infected."

"What does that mean?" Pritchard asked.

"Both nanos are limited by the marker. They communicate with each other. The mind plague only replicates to a certain maximum within any given individual. Otherwise it would tear them apart just like the first plague. The vaccine works almost in the same way. It only protects people in which it finds the mind plague isn't already present. The marker makes all the difference. Without it, the Chinese would lose their advantage. The vaccine would be transmitted to our side, too, the way every other nanotech spread around the world, and Freedman's conceptual work has always been too advanced for that."

"Why would she even build this shit for them in the first place?" Foshtomi asked.

"I don't know. She's a prisoner. Her message sounded like she thought she was somewhere else—that the Chinese were fighting India, not us."

"So you were right," Cam said. "The vaccine won't reverse the plague in anyone who's already sick."

"I don't think so. But if we can isolate that marker, we might be able to exploit it. Theoretically, we could design a parasite that would go after the mind plague and shut it off. We . . ." *Lord God,* she thought. What if Freedman had deliberately constructed the mind plague with the marker available as a kill switch?

"What is it?" Bobbi asked. "Ruth? What?"

"The marker's too obvious," she said, shifting restlessly. "I think Freedman sabotaged the mind plague so people like me could stop it. But I need time. And I need to get out of this fucking car."

"How much time?" Pritchard asked.

"I don't know. Days. Somewhere safe."

"I don't think we have that long."

"I know." Ruth's claustrophobia was squeezing down on her lungs again and she turned away to stare out the window.

The light never changed. There was no sun. The day seemed eternal beneath the black sky, but Ruth guessed it was early afternoon when Medrano came on the suit radio just minutes later. "We're clear, sir," Medrano said.

Walls spoke on their main frequency. "This is Five," he said. "One, you're first. Park to the side of the warehouse door. Two, you drive straight in. Bornmann says there's room behind the plane if you stay to your left. We need space around the forward door, just make sure you don't hit the wing. Is that understood? Take it slow. Over."

"Roger that, sir," Pritchard said. He turned to Foshtomi. "As slow as butter."

"Don't talk dirty to me," Foshtomi said.

That didn't really make sense, but Pritchard laughed and Ruth glanced sideways at Cam. She watched his expression until he noticed her eyes and turned, and she thought again that he was very handsome despite his scars and his beard, which she'd always hated. It was a strong face.

She made a formless sound like a question. *"Mhm."*

I love you, she thought.

"We're going to be okay," he said.

"Yes." Ruth leaned her shoulder against him. Then Foshtomi started their engine and rolled forward.

The first Humvee parked on the side of the warehouse doors, only one of which had been slid open. Foshtomi drove in. As she passed, three of the commandos rolled the door shut again. Foshtomi hit her headlights. One was broken, but the other cut into the gloom.

The Osprey was a sleek, black, medium-sized aircraft that hugged the ground. Its wheels seemed ridiculously small. Thick wings extended out of the top of the fuselage instead of from the bottom or the middle as Ruth had seen on other planes. The propellers were also different, with long, long blades on rectangular engines as big as cars. The plane itself looked large enough to carry everyone, although it would be crowded. An enormous pair of tail fins rose from the back. Foshtomi eased past. In back of the warehouse were a row of white-walled offices and she stopped alongside them.

"Wait for my order," Walls said on the radio. "One, you're out first after Reece decons your vehicle. Move for the plane through the regular door."

"Copy that, sir," a soldier in One answered.

Ruth marveled at their discipline. Walls was using the men in the other Humvee to see if the warehouse was safe. They must know it, and yet they did as they were told.

Five minutes later, Deborah appeared beside Ruth's vehicle with the blanket. As she maneuvered around the Humvee, Ruth's suit radio said, "This is Bornmann. The guys from One are inside the plane and we've sealed up again. Over."

"They're safe," Ruth said to her friends.

"Excellent." Pritchard gestured from side to side. "Make sure we have everything when we go, your laptop, food, water, weapons. I'll grab the radio."

"Move around if you can," Foshtomi said. "Limber up. We've been sitting a long time."

They rustled against each other, and Bobbi fidgeted with her jacket collar. Cam had already donned his goggles and mask. Ruth didn't want to jinx them by saying anything that sounded like farewell—these might be their last words—but it didn't make sense to wait. For what? She wanted to be braver than she really was, so she forced herself to take the chance.

"I love you," she said. "I've always loved you."

The second part wasn't true, but she wanted it to be. She needed that level of connection and support, and she didn't want to lose him without making it real.

"Me, too," Cam said. "I love you, too."

Ruth wept when he kissed the faceplate of her helmet. They were so close, and yet couldn't touch. She also felt like she should say something to Bobbi and the two soldiers. She didn't know what—but just for being alive, they were her sisters and her brother. "Thank you," she said. "Thanks."

"Just get us out of this shit, Ruth," Foshtomi said.

"Okay, clear," Deborah said on the suit radio. Ruth and

Pritchard relayed this information to Walls, and Walls said, "It's your turn. Go."

They stepped out.

There was a man inside one of the office windows. He stood just inches from Ruth, slumping. He must have been asleep until the throaty engine of the Humvee woke him. He'd been hurt. His jaw seemed broken, and blood leaked from his teeth down his chin.

"Oh!" she shouted, flinching back toward the Humvee.

The infected man rattled the glass with both hands. His eyes were huge and disoriented. They didn't match his face, which was aimed directly at her. Instead, he gazed upward and to his right. Almost nothing showed of his eyes except the whites, as if he was staring deep into his own skull. But he was aware of her. He shoved his hands into the window again. A crack split sideways through the glass.

Foshtomi yelled from the driver door as Ruth began to turn. "Run!" Ruth felt Cam grab her air tanks, but his glove slipped off as she bent and shoved him. She was safe in her suit. He was not. She put as much weight into her arm as possible and knocked him past the rear of the Humvee.

I love you.

"Wait—" he shouted.

Foshtomi opened fire. A three-round burst from her M4 punched through the window and the infected man. Debris exploded from the white office wall as he spun away, blood spattering from his chest.

Ruth felt a sting across her wrist, either a ricochet or a shard of glass. Before she could look down, her forearm went rigid. The muscles locked up as if they'd become steel. It nearly tore the flesh from her shoulder. Tendons jumped all the way from her elbow through the side of her chest. She would have screamed if there was time. Then the pain engulfed her heart. The floor sagged up to meet her like a big gray wall and she was only barely aware of slamming her helmet against the Humvee as she fell. She was no longer able to differentiate between the vehicle and the floor at that speed.

Her last thought was a strange sense of déjà vu, as if she

was coming home. She'd been here before. Her agony and confusion were intense, but those feelings were coupled with an impression of longing. Somehow she knew where to go. She would find her way there, and her body jerked with nerve impulses as she tried to stand and walk.

Ruth Goldman had absorbed the mind plague.

21

Cam's choice was the only one. He ran. He rolled onto his feet with the impact of Ruth's hand still aching in his bad side and then he ran from her with his feelings buried in cold screaming terror. He'd left so many other people behind. He was able to submerge his grief, but it destroyed him.

He slapped at Bobbi on the other side of the Humvee, dragging her toward the plane with such maniacal force that he threw her to the ground. "Get up! Go!" he yelled, clutching at her sleeve.

Foshtomi's reaction was more vicious. At first Cam thought she'd killed Ruth. She emptied her carbine on full auto, the gun chattering inside the metal warehouse.

"Noooo!" Cam yelled before looking back. Foshtomi stood in the space between the Humvee and the office wall, but Cam glimpsed just enough details to realize she was firing over Ruth into the far wall of the building. The aluminum popped and rang. Foshtomi was using her weapon to create an airflow away from herself. Maybe it was enough to repel the nanotech.

Men were shouting. "What happened! What happened!"

Pritchard ran past Cam and Bobbi, sprinting in the same

direction as they ducked the Osprey's huge tail fins. Then someone in a containment suit blocked their path. It was Medrano. "Where is Goldman!?" he shouted.

Cam tried to dodge by, but Medrano grabbed him. Cam shoved Bobbi toward the front of the plane even as he yelled, "She's gone—Infected—"

They separated. Medrano and a second man in a black suit charged toward the Humvee. Cam banged alongside the plane. The fuselage was only sixty feet long. There was a loading ramp under its tail, but they'd been using the forward door on its starboard side. Each breath was a searing pain. He staggered, but then Foshtomi appeared beside him. She wrapped her arm around his hips.

Pritchard was holding Bobbi back from the forward door as she kicked and screamed, keeping her from the plane. Cam saw Bornmann on the inside of the small window in the door. Bornmann had taken off his suit, yet still wore his headset. He was shouting, too, but Cam couldn't hear. "Shut up!" Cam yelled. "Shut up!"

"Let us in!" Bobbi screamed.

Ruth was at her most contagious, breathing and sweating out nanotech. Nearly all of it would stay inside her suit, yet there would also be a cloud of it around the dead man in the office. The mind plague would drift through the warehouse. Specks of it had probably wafted in with the Humvee, too. They might have only seconds, but there was no way for Cam to force his way inside. Shoot the lock? Then the plane itself would be open to the plague—but they could seal the holes with something. Cam had nearly convinced himself to fire when he saw Bornmann lift his hand to his ear, listening to his radio.

Bornmann opened the door.

Foshtomi squeezed her temples with both hands and cursed, "Shit! Oh shit! I should have just knocked that guy down, tackled him, anything. He could have had *me*."

Cam didn't blame her for what had happened. They were all making bad decisions, stupid with exhaustion, and Foshtomi's heart had been in the right place. She'd tried to protect Ruth.

The interior of the plane was utilitarian. Except for its snub cockpit, the Osprey was little more than a tube with a flat deck and bare struts on the curved metal walls. The wiring was exposed. There were no seats. It was outfitted for cargo or paratroopers, but Foshtomi found one of the only corners available, sinking down near the long, angled seam of the aircraft's tail end.

"Shit! Oh shit," she said.

So close, Cam thought. *We were so goddamned close. We should've left Ruth in the car until she was immune.*

But they didn't know if Huff would succeed in retrieving the vaccine. The fact of the matter was that getting Ruth into the plane was a necessity. They were down to the last of their air. Very soon, more of the commandos would need to de-suit like Bornmann just to extend the time that one or two were able to remain protected, using the mostly depleted air tanks as a final reserve. Keeping everyone safe had been like juggling time bombs.

Cam stalked away from Foshtomi. There were no windows in the rear of the plane, just a few small portholes along its sides. He bent to gaze through the cockpit but saw only the warehouse doors. All of the action was taking place behind him. Bornmann said the commandos had immobilized Ruth and removed her helmet, watching to make sure she didn't choke or bite her tongue. Deborah checked her vital signs, which were strong except for the poor pupil response they'd come to expect. Her brain was shutting down.

As soon as they had time, they planned to bring Ruth to one of the trailers outside the warehouse. The best of those RVs would become her shelter—but they couldn't just leave her. She might wander away or hurt herself.

Someone else had to stay with her.

First they needed to decontaminate the warehouse again as best they could as well as Ruth's laptop. General Walls, Ingrid, and another man were still in the cab of the Army truck. They also wanted to transfer their other gear, after which the commandos themselves would clean their suits and come aboard.

Cam paced up and down the plane like a man possessed. He would rather have been crucified than see this happen to Ruth. He'd been so cruel, keeping her at a distance. Why? He knew how short life could be. Every second together had been a treasure. Now they were left with one slender hope.

Bornmann was talking on his headset again, communicating with the people outside. Cam put his hand on his shoulder. Bornmann ignored him, so Cam tightened his grip until the other man turned with irritation in his eyes.

"What?" Bornmann snapped.

"We need to get into Los Angeles."

They brought Walls and the others aboard without incident, except for Deborah, who stayed with Ruth, and Sweeney, who continued to stand guard outside the warehouse. Twice, Sweeney's M4 barked, dropping zombies at the fence.

The plane was crowded. Everywhere, men spoke to each other in low tones, relieved to be out of their suits and masks. Cam stood with his arms around Ingrid, comforting the older woman even as he looked past her and shouted into the din.

"It's the only way!" he said. "There's no one else who knows nanotech, and Freedman—"

"This isn't your call," Bornmann said, stepping sideways to physically shield Cam from Walls and Rezac. They knelt on the deck with a radio and the two laptops.

"What else are you going to do?" Cam asked, speaking past Bornmann.

"Leave them alone. Let them work."

"It's too late!" Cam said. "Even if Huff makes it back with the vaccine, so what? You've got a tiny group of people and nowhere left to run."

Minutes ago, Sergeant Huff had reported in again. Her team had found at least ten bodies inside the downed Chinese plane. All of them were hideously burned. Huff said she'd gathered blood and samples. *Samples,* Cam wondered. What did that mean? Had she taken an arm or someone's insides?

The crash site was a trap. The plane must have gathered a high concentration of nanotech on its surfaces as it plunged through the sky. Possibly it had also carried the plague on board, like a bomber. Huff was careful to approach the wreckage herself in her yellow suit, ordering the rest of her team to maintain a distance of a hundred yards—but the wind was against them. Both of her soldiers who wore only biochem masks were infected. They turned on the third man. He broke a seal in his collar. Their courage was wasted. Huff had shot them all. Now she was driving south alone, unable to replace her dwindling air tanks. It was a job that required two people. She thought she could reach them, but Walls had ordered Sweeney into a Humvee to meet her.

In the meantime, Walls and Rezac continued to try to raise anyone on their radios or the satellite phone.

"We can still win this war," Cam said.

"I have a sat overhead in three minutes," Rezac murmured, and Walls said, "Dump it. Everything you've got."

"Kendra Freedman designed both plagues and she probably built the second vaccine, too! What if we had that power on our side?"

"Enough," Bornmann said. "That's an order. Lang. Pritchard. Take him in back."

"We could kill them all," Cam said. "Listen to me! Freedman's our best bet if you want to kill all of those chink motherfuckers."

Something tightened in Lang's face. Cam didn't think he'd upset him with the racial slur. The Chinese American must have endured a thousand slights and bad jokes. In fact, Cam thought Lang approved. The rage in Bill Lang's eyes wasn't directed at Cam but farther outward, at their enemy, as Lang glanced from side to side at the other men in the plane. Their acceptance must be incredibly important to him.

"This is our *home*," Cam said. "This place is *ours*."

"Lang, get him out of here or I'll do it myself," Bornmann said, but Cam wouldn't have stopped even if he was in control of himself.

"Hundreds of thousands of people are dead, and all you want to do is hide?" he shouted.

Lang grabbed his arm. Lang had more to prove than anyone else, which was why he would obey orders to the last.
Cam knew it was the others he needed to convince. "We can
take everything back!" he said. "Colorado. California. What
if Freedman can build a third plague or a new parasite?"

Walls rose to his feet, yet didn't push into the knot of men.
He didn't have to. His presence alone was enough to draw
everyone's attention toward the front of the plane.

"This is personal for all of us," Walls said. "You need to
get your head straight."

"You won't do any good if you just run away!"

"We need the vaccine, and sharing it is our first priority.
Someone has to survive."

"For what? The vaccine won't reverse the effects of the
plague. It'll only protect you if you're inoculated before you
get sick. Even if you save a hundred more people, so what?
Then all you've got is enough of a crowd to watch you get
down on your knees and surrender."

"Sir," Bornmann said, ready to defend Walls, but the general didn't need his help.

"Think what you're asking," Walls said. "The Chinese
hold all the cards. A suicide mission won't change that. We
need time to regroup."

"No. This is the best time to try it, while they're still
shaken up. If you wait, you'll just give them more time to
get organized, too. Let's hit the chinks *now*," Cam said, using
the insult like a knife. He had seen enough discrimination
for the color of his own skin to feel angry and embarrassed
at himself, but he wasn't above using every available tool to
convince them.

Religious hate might be the only option left to sustain these
men. Without blind, unreasoning dogma, they were too battered and worn down to fight. Cam could see it in their faces.
So could Walls. That was why the general wanted to let them
rest and reassess, hoping for the miracle of making contact
with other U.S. forces, but Cam was afraid that if they stopped
moving even for a day they'd never get up again.

If he needed to invoke a race war, so be it. That was the
reality of China's bid for global domination—yellow versus
white, brown, and black. The invaders were despised across

America. No one was unaffected by fury or disgust. Cam only wanted to channel those emotions.

The firestorm in his head must be exactly what Ruth had felt at the end of the last war. He understood her hysteria now. If there was a God, this is what He wanted of Cam. The path was obvious. Once upon a time, men in caves in the Islamic world had motivated themselves against the colossal might of America in the same way, declaring themselves pure and righteous while condemning the West as the Great Satan. Now it had become their turn as the last holdouts against a far superior enemy. There wasn't really any chance of winning. They could only pretend. Hunting for Freedman deep inside enemy lines would have been a madman's scheme even before the missiles landed, reducing Los Angeles to a radioactive hell—but otherwise they were beaten.

Only fanatics would carry on.

"Kendra Freedman may be the last person left who can help us," Cam said. "If she can reverse the infection, she'll give us Ruth back, too. Then the two of them will massacre the fucking Chinese."

"I think you want this for the wrong reasons," Bornmann said. "For her."

"What if he's right?" Emma said softly, surprising them. Emma hadn't spoken for hours, except to acknowledge orders, and Pritchard said, "Sir, we could split up."

"I'll go," Foshtomi said. "I volunteer."

"We will definitely split up," Walls said, "probably into three groups. We need to be sure the vaccine gets out, and the plane will be a very visible target. Some of us will leave in the Humvees in opposite directions. One group will also be tasked with keeping Goldman alive."

"I have a satellite," Rezac said from her laptop.

"Send our files," Walls said.

"Done. We have no other contacts."

"What does that mean?" Bobbi whispered, and Medrano leaned toward her and said, "Exactly what you think. There's no one else on our military nets."

"Our first priority is photos of this area," Walls said to Rezac. "Map it for a hundred miles in every direction."

"Got it."

"Then I want photos of Los Angeles," Walls said, and Cam involuntarily raised both fists, elated and triumphant. He felt more than a little crazy, too, like an animal that had just torn itself from a trap. *We'll find her,* he thought, as Walls said, "How long until we have a bird over the West Coast?"

22

Sweeney returned with Huff forty minutes later. Deborah helped them decontaminate both their suits, and then herself again—but she suggested it was impossible to clean the blood and tissue samples. Huff had splashed two canteens with gore and sealed several pieces of charred flesh in another. Bringing the canteens inside the plane would risk infecting everyone, because irradiating the blood to kill the mind plague would also kill the vaccine. Nor did they have any way to separate the two. That meant it would be a toss-up as to whether anyone without a suit would absorb the vaccine before the plague.

Cam volunteered to be the first to try it, earning another kind word from Emma. "You're very brave," she said, but Walls stopped him. "You know Freedman, don't you?" Walls asked, and it was true that Cam had secondhand knowledge of her, which no one else could match. That put him in Walls's elite with the other untouchables like their pilots, translators, and medics.

One of Foshtomi's Rangers drew the short straw. His name was Ayers. Foshtomi volunteered herself instead, but Ayers refused. "It's all right, Lieutenant," he said.

Ayers walked out wearing his biochem mask and hood. Deborah produced a needle from a med kit. She wet it in the

blood, then stabbed his forearm, repeating the process several
times. Finally, Ayers took off his gear. He went to the warehouse door and walked outside, escorted by Sweeney, who
reported every move on his suit radio.

"He's okay," Sweeney said. "It works."

"What about Ruth?" Ingrid asked. "Cam? What in the
world are we going to do about Ruth?"

They stood beside the plane, breathing in the acrid, dusty
smell of the ash. The immunizations were done. The soldiers were removing their goggles and jackets and chatting in
quiet relief, even laughing. Ingrid's hazel eyes were sad. Cam
hugged her again, but he couldn't allow his heart to soften.
He wanted to keep his rage. So while Ingrid nestled her face
against his neck, he was rigid, with his chin up, which is why
he saw Deborah approaching with a bloody canteen.

Deborah had stripped off her containment suit. She pointed
in the direction of the RVs beyond the warehouse and said,
"Do you two want to come with me?"

"Yes."

"It's good to see you again," Deborah added, briefly
embracing Cam herself. The gesture was uncharacteristic—
but after so much death, all of them were more open and
physical. Every word felt like good-bye.

The three of them walked outside as Bornmann and Pritchard rolled open the tall warehouse doors. Most of the others
were already sorting through their vehicles, food, and other
gear, unencumbered by the fear of infection. Bobbi glanced
after Cam, but she'd gone to help Lang with three cases of
water and didn't break away. Maybe that was smart.

Deborah led them to one of the RVs, a huge, sand-colored
Holiday Rambler. "Brace yourselves," she said. "This isn't
Ruth. Do you understand? This isn't Ruth like you knew her."

Cam heard a repetitive *clunk clunk, clunk clunk* from
inside. What was it? The A/C or the plumbing? He met Deborah's gaze and realized she was gritting her teeth.

"Okay," he said.

Deborah pushed in the folding door and led them up the

steep, narrow steps. Inside, the floor broadened. The luxury vehicle was nine feet wide with long, tinted windows and a lighter windshield. Behind the driver's seat, tan couches and a wood table filled the front space. Cam wasn't watching where he was going. He cracked his head on a low-slung TV, but didn't take his eyes off of Ruth.

She was tied to a cabinet knob behind one couch, her hands drawn up behind her head. *Sweeney did this,* Cam thought. He couldn't imagine Deborah binding her friend so thoroughly. It was an immobilizing position Ruth couldn't outfox without hurting herself. That basic instinct seemed to work. She'd slumped partway off the couch, yet hadn't fought the rope any further, although her ankle beat steadily against the couch's baseboard. *Clunk clunk. Clunk clunk.* The rhythm was unending. Was she trying to signal them? If so, her memory was stunted and pathetic, limited to a few seconds. She was trapped in a loop. *Clunk clunk. Clunk clunk.*

She stank. Her clothes were filthy with ash, sweat, blood, and urine. Worse, she was drooling, and her eyes were twisted in their sockets.

"Oh," Ingrid gasped. "Oh, no. Ruth, no."

Cam didn't move. His thoughts had been compressed into a sharp dark line of disbelief. It rocked him, but he held onto his sense of destiny.

"Try the vaccine," he said. If Ruth was wrong, it would counter the infection. Deborah went to Ruth's side—but Ruth was proved right, as always. They waited several minutes after puncturing her thigh with the bloody needle, yet there was no change in her vacant, animal face.

Ingrid cried. Deborah's smooth, pretty features screwed tight as she battled her own tears. Cam's feelings were strangely muted. This wasn't the end. Ruth was alive, and she'd talked about how there appeared to be different stages of infection. She might wake up on her own tomorrow. Maybe it would take a week. The main thing was to be sure the Chinese weren't in total control, so they couldn't hurt or enslave her.

"Can you hear me?" Deborah asked. At first Cam wasn't sure who she was speaking to. He felt very far away, but then Deborah said, "Ruth? Ruth, honey, please."

"I'll take care of her," Ingrid said, kneeling. She tried to soothe Ruth's jerking leg with one hand. Ruth was oblivious. Ingrid looked back up at them. Her eyes were frightened, but her voice was firm. "I'll stay with her, Cam. You can count on that. I'll feed and bathe her and keep her safe."

"Yes."

It didn't matter if he made it back. As long as they beat the Chinese, that was okay. Even if they failed . . . *It's okay,* he thought. *If there is anything on the other side, I'll find you. If we do go to heaven or anyplace like that, I'll wait for you. We'll be together.*

Allison was in his mind, too, but his love for both women was the same. It hurt him and filled him with resolve at the same time, and it was better than anything else he'd known.

Cam bent and kissed Ruth's sweaty hair, lingering against her scalp as he remembered the good smell of her. *I'll find you,* he thought.

Then he turned and walked away.

General Walls couldn't risk himself on the plane. If they did establish contact with other U.S. forces, he needed to be alive to coordinate them, so Walls intended to remain in Colorado with only Rezac and Ayers in his command, plus Ingrid and Bobbi as nursemaids for Ruth. They would go south. Another small squad would drive east.

Foshtomi herself refused to stay behind. "Sir, I'm responsible for what happened to Goldman," she said. "You have to let me be a part of this."

Walls agreed. He also allowed Sergeant Huff to stay with Foshtomi. He put Pritchard in charge of the second squad, which consisted only of Pritchard, Emma, and the other two survivors from Foshtomi's group. Cam thought it might have made more sense to leave Foshtomi or even Huff in charge, but Walls must have trusted his commandos more. Lieutenant Pritchard would be on his own. In fact, if Walls was captured or killed, Pritchard would become the acting U.S. commander in chief. Captain Bornmann outranked Pritchard, but Bornmann would be radio silent in the plane, thus removing him from the chain of command. Walls also refused to send any of their codes or data on the mission into California. He gave one of his laptops and several files to Pritchard instead.

Rezac had a different sheet of notes for Bornmann. She also passed around her laptop. An hour ago, she'd brought up several file photos of Kendra Freedman—but she had no printer. There was no way to share the pictures, except to commit them to memory.

Freedman had been in her early forties before the machine plague. She was chubby and very black, an African American woman with pitted, rich chocolate skin and even darker lips. Her hair was straightened. She had surprisingly small eyes for her broad face, maybe an illusion caused by her fat cheeks.

While everyone studied the photos, Rezac discussed the Osprey's transponders with Bornmann. "Leave 'em on," she said.

"I can disable the Mode II," he argued, but Rezac said, "That'll flag you as a problem as soon as you're on radar. None of their stolen aircraft run dark."

"Take care of Ruth," Cam said to Bobbi and Ingrid.

Bobbi kissed him. "God bless. Be safe."

Bornmann powered up the plane and trundled out of the warehouse. Cam didn't look for Ruth before he climbed in. He preferred to recall her bright, laughing face instead of the rag doll she'd become. There were no seats. The only restraints were a trio of cargo belts that had been bolted across the struts on the port wall. Cam sat with Foshtomi and Huff against the canvas straps and Deborah joined them, looking grim.

The Osprey heaved into the sky. It lurched out of the narrow space inside the depot's fence, thrumming with its rotors overhead. After a few minutes, Cam heard the wings squeal on either side. The familiar chopping sound of a helicopter's blades intensified into the softer blur of an airplane's propellers. Their speed increased. Somewhere below, General Walls and the others were leaving, too, but their Humvees were already far behind.

Cam had fifty questions for Deborah. She probably wanted at least as many answers from him, but neither felt like talking. They both drowsed. So did Foshtomi, Huff, and

Medrano. The drone of the V-22 lulled them, and everyone
had been pushed beyond endurance. Nor was there anything
to see. The interior of the plane fluttered with shadows and
light, which grew more distinct as they escaped the fallout.
Sunlight gleamed in the windshield. Cam should have slept,
but his thoughts wouldn't quit. His muscles wouldn't relax.
The best he could manage was a light, waking doze.

His view through the front of the aircraft was blocked by
Sweeney, who stood between the two pilots' seats, keeping
his head down with Bornmann and Lang. They expected
trouble. It didn't happen. The Osprey hummed into the west.
Sweeney continued to study Rezac's notes, ruffling through
the few pages with nervous energy. He rearranged and folded
the paper and scribbled in the margins with a blue pencil.

They'd been flying for twenty minutes when Lang began to
chatter in Mandarin. Just as suddenly, he stopped.

They had more than eight hundred miles to go. The Osprey
could push as fast as 315 miles per hour, yet Bornmann said
he'd keep it at cruising speed, which was closer to 275 mph.
He didn't want to look like trouble. Also, he wanted to conserve fuel. With full tanks and a small payload, the Osprey's
range was over 2,400 miles, but someone must have bled off its
fuel for other purposes during the long peace. The tanks were
barely half full. Even so, with nothing on board except eight
people, small arms, and other gear, Bornmann estimated their
max range at 1,500 miles. It wasn't inconceivable that they
could fly into San Bernadino and escape again without needing to refuel. They wouldn't be able to go far, but that extra
margin might make the difference between life or death.

Once they hit a pocket of turbulence. Several times, Bornmann banked through minor course corrections or Cam's
stomach felt the aircraft ease up or down. His impression was
they'd never lifted far from the ground and he wondered at one
big sweeping turn to the left. Were they avoiding mountains?

The flight became mundane. Medrano excused himself to
go to the bathroom by the rear loading ramp. Deborah and
Cam each took their turns. Foshtomi passed around water,
coarse bread, and dried peppers. Cam reveled in the strong
flavor, chewing with his eyes shut. He thought of Ruth. Allison. Everything that could have been.

"Heads up!" Lang shouted, looking back from his copilot seat for Sweeney even he began to jabber into his headset in a much calmer voice. *"Yī yīsì míng hǎi,"* he said. *"Yī yī sì míng hǎi. Wán bì."*

Someone's seen us, Cam thought.

"Here we go," Foshtomi murmured as Lang said, *"Wǒ dān wèi zhēng yòng zhè jià fēi jī yòng yú yì liáo chè tuì. Wǒ mén zài fēi jī shàng yǒu qī míng shāng yuán hé liǎng míng sǐ zhě. Wán bì."*

Beside him, Sweeney said, "You have to give them a name. Here."

Sweeney pointed to his notes and Lang said, *"Wǒ shì shěn yáng měng hǔ duì Běi duì zhǎng. Wǒ zhòng fù yī biàn. Wǒ shì shěn yáng měng hǔ duì Běi duì zhǎng. Yōu xiān yī yī sì míng hǎi. Wán bì."*

Cam didn't think they'd been flying for more than two hours yet. That meant they were still over Arizona or Nevada or just barely inside California's borders. The game was only beginning.

The NSA had caught and decrypted thousands of exchanges between Chinese aircraft and ground control. Some of those signals were very recent, and Rezac had given Bornmann and Lang as much intel as possible. They could only hope their codes worked. In their favor, China had never been as advanced as the U.S. at data sorting or systems integrity. Even better, the Chinese Air Force had been confused even before the missile strikes. U.S. Command estimated that less than 40 percent of the enemy's strength consisted of Chinese aircraft. The rest were captured American planes, both military and civilian.

Cam wasn't sure what Lang was saying, except for what he'd gleaned from hearing the commandos discuss their cover story. They would pretend they were a squad of Shenyang Fierce Tigers, whom Rezac believed were involved in the assault on Grand Lake. Lang would assert that the Osprey had been commandeered to bring the worst of their casualties back to California.

"Què rèn," Lang said. Then, after a moment, *"Bù wǒ zhòng fù yī biàn. Yī yī sì míng hǎi. Wán bì."* His tone was level but he grimaced up at Sweeney.

"This was a mistake," Medrano said.

"Shut up," Foshtomi snapped. "We can outsmart those fuckin' Chinamen any day of the week."

That's right, Cam thought. He gave Foshtomi an admiring look yet didn't say anything, touching her arm and then raising one finger to his lips. It wouldn't help Lang to have Americans chatting in the background.

The silence was anticlimactic. Lang hit two switches above his head. Bornmann continued to fly the aircraft, and, in back, Cam and Foshtomi exhaled at the same time. They were both pleased by the small coincidence. Foshtomi bumped his shoulder with her own in a blunt, sisterly way.

"They bought it," Sweeney said.

Lang nodded. "They're a mess. We're cleared into Bakersfield. Sounds like that's the nearest base they've got operational."

"What about Edwards or Twenty-Nine Palms?" Bornmann asked.

"Blown away," Lang said.

"We need a better story before we divert into Los Angeles," Sweeney said, fidgeting with his notes. "Let's stick with the idea that we're a medevac. There'll be casualties in L.A., too. We can say we have room to evac some of their—"

An alarm sounded in the cockpit. *Bee bee bee bee bee.*

"Oh fuck," Bornmann said. "Strap in."

"Bogies at four o'clock!" Lang yelled.

The Osprey was already rolling to its portside. Cam banged against the curved wall with Deborah and Medrano on top of him.

Through the tangle, looking forward, Cam saw Sweeney hanging onto Bornmann's seat. Then Sweeney opened his arms. He leapt for the same area where the rest of them were piled on the wall, which had almost become the floor. Cam felt the port engine screaming somewhere beneath him. The fuselage shuddered as if buffeted by the wind.

"Strap in!" Sweeney yelled. "Strap in! Strap in!"

The Osprey carried no armament. Nor was its top speed any match for fighters, much less ground-to-air missiles. Their only hope was evasive action, and the plane lifted and spun.

Cam was still pulling free of the others. He grabbed at a cargo belt but swung away from the wall, wrenching something in his wrist and back. Deborah hung beside him from one hand. Everyone else seemed to be roped to the fuselage above. Huff clawed at his jacket. With that slight help, Cam kept his grip, but the accelerating torque was too much for Deborah. Her arm twisted and then her hand sprung free.

"No!" Foshtomi shrieked, snatching at her. Foshtomi had deftly slid behind two straps. They sawed into her waist—but even bent in a horseshoe, Foshtomi didn't have enough reach to catch the other woman.

Deborah tumbled away from them. She smashed into the ceiling and then the far wall. Then the dizzying sideways-and-up motion changed as the Osprey plummeted to the starboard. It threw Deborah back into them. Cam was too off-balance to grab his friend even when her leg thumped him in the chin, but Foshtomi seized Deborah's waist, trusting the straps to hold them both. She'd never lacked for confidence, and Cam felt another glint of admiration for her.

"Here!" Foshtomi yelled. "Here!"

Unbelievably, the aircraft leveled out. The six of them worked to clip themselves down in a furious panic. Cam finished with himself—the canvas belts seemed too thin—and turned to help Foshtomi with Deborah. Somehow they wrestled her in between them. Deborah's forehead was swollen with a fat goose egg that had been cut open on one side, throwing blood through her yellow hair. Her blue eyes were groggy and dim.

Up front, Lang chattered in Mandarin again as his hands danced over the consoles. The Osprey was climbing now and Bornmann hollered back, "Missiles! Two fighters on our tail! We're going to ditch this bitch if we can just—"

The wall exploded. Fire and heat burst through the rear of the plane in a hundred tiny holes. Metal fragments clattered through the fuselage. Then the fire was replaced by smoke and sunlight. Air whistled through the holes at a deafening pitch. Most of the swirling black fog was stripped away, but it was replaced by the red mist streaming from Foshtomi's chest.

"Sarah!" Cam yelled, fumbling past Deborah to help her.

The explosion must have been a near miss, he realized.

Otherwise they'd be gone. But the damage was bad enough. Wind and sunlight howled through the aircraft as he tried to catch the meaty organs spilling from Foshtomi's side. Her intestines were hot. Her face was white and dead. Cam screamed and tried to apply pressure anyway, his arm trembling against the wild force of their descent.

The Osprey was in a tailspin.

No, Cam thought. *No!* He glanced forward again, looking for the sky—for God—for anything other than this horror. Beyond the pilots, he saw a patch of blue. Then the horizon tilted into view.

The hard orange color of the desert filled the windshield. The ground was very close.

It's not supposed to end like this! he thought, but the Osprey caught its starboard wing against the earth and whipsawed into an uneven leaping cartwheel as the fuselage disintegrated.

23

In the cyclone of bodies and metal, Deborah felt a snapping pain through her left shoulder. She breathed hot dust and smoke. Then it was done. The tornado stopped, but the pain stayed with her, crippling that arm.

She was outside the plane. The ground beneath her was tough and dry, and she felt a breeze and daylight. Despite the curtains of dust, she saw most of the fuselage nearby. Then the hazy sun disappeared. When she lifted her head, she'd moved into the shadows beneath the high, broken line of one wing.

There must be other survivors.

"Bornmann!" she shouted, rasping for air. "Cam? Hey!"

Why didn't they answer?

Somehow she staggered up, twisted nearly in half by the dislocated shoulder. Her ribs on that side were hurt, too, and she was covered with grit and blood. Most of it wasn't her own. *Foshtomi,* she thought, trying to calculate how badly the other woman was hurt by how much of her uniform was soaked. *Is there any way she's still alive?*

Gnarled oak trees and scrub brush covered the hillside. The brown plants were peppered with gray and white debris. Fire licked at the brush in several places. The Osprey had flung jagged chunks of aluminum and steel into the hillside along with wiring, glass, and plastic. The wind stank of jet fuel.

Deborah didn't think to run away, not even faced with the rising flames. She was nothing without her squadmates. She barely remembered the self-doubt she'd felt before Walls led them out of Complex 3. Deborah had come a very long way just to find herself back where she'd begun, as a reliable cog in the machine, but she was pleased to be that woman again. It was all she'd ever wanted. Her suffering had reinforced everything that was best in her—her willingness to give of herself. The team needed her, not only as another gun but as a doctor, especially now.

She turned into the wreckage. There was a man crumpled beneath a flat chunk of a propeller blade. She hurried toward him but Sweeney was dead, his neck wrenched backward. His legs were broken, too, and maybe his spine. Looking away, Deborah noticed one of the engines behind her. In one sense, she was still inside the plane. The main bulk of the aircraft surrounded her, forming an uneven barricade.

The sky reverberated with the distant roar of jets. That seemed unimportant. Within two steps, she spotted two more human shapes. Deborah heard someone groan and lurched closer. "Bornmann?" she said. "Hey—"

The first man was Lang. A small area on the left side of his face was unharmed. Otherwise she might not have recognized him. Impact had rubbed most of the skin and muscles from the side of his skull.

Translator, copilot, commando—Lang might have been the most versatile element of their team and Deborah paused over his corpse, feeling demoralized and lost. Then she banished her grief with a bit of gallows humor she'd learned from Derek Mills, the pilot of the shuttle *Endeavour*. "Pilots are always the first to the scene of a crash," he'd said when they were planning their descent from the ISS. She had to honor Lang. Her sense was that their pilots had pulled the Osprey out of a death spiral, bringing the aircraft up at the last minute. If they hadn't, she would have been killed, too, so she moved past him with a firm sense of gratitude.

The next man was Captain Medrano. He groaned again.

"It's me," Deborah said meaninglessly. He was barely conscious. His arm was broken and his face was cut. His pulse was steady, though, and her cursory examination detected no other bleeding or major injuries.

In the short time they'd known each other, Medrano seemed like a badger to her. He was short and roundish and skeptical. Deborah wasn't sure if she liked him, but he was her brother nevertheless. There weren't enough of them left to pick and choose.

As she applied pressure to his face wound, she glanced through the wreckage again. She felt as if she'd failed Ruth for being unable to find Cam. Had Cam and Ruth become a couple at last? What if he was dead like Sweeney and Lang?

Deborah had never approved of Cam. He was dangerous, untrained, and seemed to bring out all the worst in Ruth. He made her so emotional. He was also fiercely loyal. Deborah couldn't help but respect that level of commitment, and, like Medrano, she was also bound to Cam.

"Get up," Medrano said as if to himself.

"Easy," Deborah warned him, but he spoke again, clearly, trying to focus his dazed eyes on her.

"Get up. Run. The fighters—"

The Chinese fighters were coming back.

Deborah had been listening to the distant engines change in volume and pitch without realizing what it meant. The sound galvanized her. "You're coming with me," she said, flush with new strength.

"Can't walk," Medrano said. "My ankle—"

"My shoulder—" she retorted.

A long section of the fuselage rocked toward them. The metal shrieked against smaller chunks of debris. Deborah dragged at Medrano's uniform with her good hand, gaining a few inches as the wreckage teetered overhead.

Someone walked out of the plane like a miracle.

He was filthy, maybe burned. He was also bent much like Deborah, protecting his ribs, and she recognized the shoulder-length black hair. Cam. His luck seemed like something learned—a trait she envied for herself.

"Help me!" she yelled, but Cam stopped and looked up.

The noise in the sky was increasing. It echoed from the

hills. Deborah pulled Medrano upright as Cam raced closer. He grabbed Medrano's other side and the three of them ran downhill into the widely spaced trees. Medrano screamed as his wrist banged against Deborah's back. Her shoulder was agony. Their ragged forward motion carried them past the wreckage and an orange, snarling clump of poison oak.

Cam leaned in front of Medrano, his lips drawn back from his teeth. Two of his incisors were gone. The rest looked like misplaced fangs. "This way!" he yelled, hauling everyone to his side like a human chain.

We're not going to make it, Deborah thought, glancing back as the Chinese fighters screamed overhead. She wanted to face her own death.

Their turbulence washed through the oak trees and her short, dirty hair. In the same heartbeat, one missile slammed into the Osprey's remains. Ordnance was precious. If those pilots knew there were survivors, they must have believed a single missile was enough. The explosion threw the Osprey's belly and starboard wing into the air. There were secondary blasts from the fuel tanks in the wing. Ribbons of fire sprayed over the hillside.

Concussion shoved Deborah into the trees, separating her from Medrano and Cam. Maybe she bounced. The pain in her shoulder was incandescent and she blacked out.

She was brought back by someone pounding on her chest. Cam gasped as he hit her, and she realized this new pain was too sharp to attribute to his fist. She stank of charred skin and cloth. He'd doused a spot of burning fuel on her uniform, scalding his bare hand in the process. They were enveloped in smoke. The forest had ignited.

"Deborah," he said. "Deborah?" He was obviously woozy himself, but she knew he'd had EMT training—nothing like her own schooling, but she was glad just the same.

"My shoulder. Can you reset it?"

"I'll try." He turned and said, "Medrano. Help me."

He bent her arm at the elbow, rotating it outwards as Deborah tried not to twist away from the pain. Then he lifted her elbow even further, wrenching the ball of her humerus back into its socket through the torn ring of cartilage. Deborah grayed out again. But afterwards, the pain was reduced, and she'd even regained some motion.

There wasn't time to make a sling. The smoke was suffocating, and they could see the flames crackling up through the hooked branches of two trees.

"Go," Cam said.

Deborah outranked him—they both outranked him—but she let him take over. She remembered how he'd convinced Walls to send them west. The same characteristics that made him dangerous were exactly what the three of them needed now—decisive, unrelenting nerve. She had to trust his aggression. It was the real basis of Cam's luck. Sometimes the chances he took were the best and only path.

The three of them jogged downhill, groaning, limping. They had nothing but each other. No radio. No water. Where did he think they were going?

The smoke thinned but Cam changed direction suddenly, moving them sideways across the slope when they might have escaped the fire by continuing downhill. Deborah almost spoke up. *What are you doing?* There was a clear area like a meadow below them, empty of brush. Why not run through it? Then she realized those trees were leafless and dead. Worse, something *slithered* on the rotting gray oaks. Ants coated the naked wood.

"Wait," Cam said. "No." He turned with his arms out as if to collect them—to change direction again—but he froze with his hands up.

There were enemy soldiers waiting in the brush.

Deborah saw at least eight men in a skirmish line, their faces hidden by tan biochem hoods or black, older-model gas masks. Their jackets were dark green. Most of them held AK-47 rifles. Others carried submachine guns she'd didn't recognize.

One of them shouted in Mandarin. *"Bié dòng! Xià jiàng!"*

She didn't understand, but the intent was clear. He gestured for them to get down. Within seconds, three more soldiers

appeared uphill. There was no way out except back into the
smoke and the ants, but Medrano was willing. "I'll draw their
fire," he said.

"Hold it," Deborah said. "Don't move."

Neither of them carried any weapons except their sidearms, and Cam's gun belt had been torn away in the crash.

Cam raised his hands even higher and Medrano got one
arm up, keeping his broken limb against his side. Deborah
didn't see any choice except to mimic her friends, although
her disappointment was keen.

The man who'd shouted turned to his men, pointing at two
of them. *"Опустите их на землю,"* he said.

They're Russian! Deborah thought. She should have
known. Chinese troops wouldn't have worn this hodgepodge
collection of masks and gloves—they were immune. These
people were Russian, and they were also on the run from the
plague.

"Займитесь делом!" one said. *"Займитесь делом!"*

Deborah had learned the feel and pacing of their language
during her months in orbit with Commander Ulinov. Nikola
had even taught her several phrases. She tried them now as the
pair of soldiers approached, concealed in their biochem hoods.
"Доброе утро, товарищи!" she said, *Good morning, comrades,* even though the day was well into late afternoon. It was
a game she'd played with Ulinov. *"Как Вы поживаете?"*

How are you living today?

In Russian, the words were ambiguous. The phrase served
as a basic "hello," but could also mean more. It surprised
them. The two soldiers hesitated.

"You're American," the officer called.

They were so grungy and burned, they were unrecognizable. He'd thought they must be Chinese. That was why he'd
shouted first in Mandarin.

"Da," Deborah said. *Yes.* "Where are we?"

"Put yourself on your knees," the officer replied, with a
curt motion for his soldiers to take them.

"Wait!" Cam said. "Stay back. We can protect you from
the Chinese nanotech, but we're probably crawling with it.
We came out of the plague zones. You might be infected if
you touch us."

"You would be sick," the officer said. "Not flying."

"I'm Major Reece with the United States Army," Deborah said, asserting herself, but Cam surprised them all. He was honest.

"We have the new vaccine," he said. "If you help us, we can give it to you, too."

The fire was getting closer. Deborah could hear it licking its way across the hill behind her as the smoke thickened. "We should move," she said, but the officer refused.

"*Nyet.* Give us the vaccine," he said, before barking out a dozen words she didn't understand. The nearest Russians backed off, but none of them lowered their weapons.

"Let me clean myself," Cam said. "I can try to decontaminate, at least a bit."

The officer nodded, but hit the charging handle on his AK-47. Deborah flinched. *One wrong move . . .* she thought, barely allowing herself to breathe as Cam scrubbed himself down with brush and dirt. It was a crude decon procedure but clever as always. Deborah wondered what else Ruth had taught him. Would he have come up with this idea by himself? He was intelligent, just uneducated. That made him unpredictable.

"Major Reece and I are in charge here," Medrano said to him.

"Right."

"Then keep your mouth shut from now on."

"We need them. Look at us." Cam paused with a handful of crumbling brown earth against his sleeve, ignoring the scuffs and gashes beneath his burned uniform. "But they need us, too."

"We should have *negotiated*," Medrano said in a growl. He glanced at Deborah. "Major? It's not too late."

"No, I think he's right," she said.

"These are the same guys who bombed Leadville and started the whole fucking war—"

"They're not. At this point, they're just survivors like us." Deborah turned to Medrano with as much poise as she could muster, watery-eyed in the smoke. "We don't even know where we are, Captain. We're hurt. Unarmed. I think he's right."

"What's to stop them from shooting us as soon as he gives up the vaccine?"

"Information. Tell them, Cam."

Cam aimed a thin smile at her. It was a sign of approval, and, for the first time, Deborah felt some glimpse of Ruth's attraction to him. Beneath the scars, he was lean and dark and competent.

Pulling a jackknife from his belt, he crouched and sank the blade into the ground, trying to clean it of nanotech. Then he stood and held the knife over his left hand. "I need one man," he said to the Russians.

"Sidorov," the officer said.

In response, a soldier gave his rifle to his mates and walked closer.

"Tell him not to take off his hood!" Cam said. "Hold his breath. Give me his arm."

This better work, Deborah thought as the officer translated for Cam. *If he's infected, if he falls down twitching—They'll kill us.*

Cam wet the tip of the blade in his own hand. Next, he worked the soldier's jacket sleeve back from his glove and lightly cut him there. "We were trying to get into Los Angeles," he said as he worked. "My team has information on the original source of the plague. We think we can stop it."

"Крыша поехала?" the officer said. "How?"

"We need to get into Los Angeles," Cam said, taking a hard line with him, but the officer met Cam's stubbornness with a deflection of his own.

"How long is it before our man is safe?" the officer said.

"It's already happened. You know how fast nanotech is."

"But how are we knowing? There is no proof."

"Tell him to take off his gear."

This is it, Deborah thought. She tensed as the officer spoke to his man, ready to draw her pistol, ready to run, making her shoulder throb like a drum.

The soldier removed his biochem hood. He was startlingly young, blond like Deborah and nearly as smooth-faced, no more than a teen, and yet his eyes were like stone. Deborah wanted to say something to him, but he wouldn't understand even if she found the words. *We're your friends,* she thought. *"Доброе утро,"* she blurted.

The boy's veteran gaze flitted up and down her tall, haggard body. Still no emotion showed.

"You can see he's fine," Cam said. "Who's next?"

"We wait," the officer said.

"We need to get into Los Angeles, a place on the far edge of the city. We think it survived the bombs."

"That is not impossible," the officer said.

Deborah felt a thin spark of hope. *Could they have a plane?* she wondered. *Where are we?*

"You come with us," the officer said. "Keep your distance. Sidorov will be your guard. *Обезоружьте их!"*

The boy gestured for Deborah's sidearm. She didn't resist. Medrano might have planned otherwise, but there were half a dozen rifles trained on him, so he let the boy have his weapon, too.

They hiked across the hill. Deborah gained new energy as the sun emerged from the haze, dappling through the tangled oaks. It was a soft, sweet yellow. They reeked of smoke and jet fuel and yet she breathed all the way into her belly from the clean air of the breeze. The earth smelled different here than in Colorado, dustier and less green. She'd never tasted anything so beautiful.

The Russian officer tried to maintain his quarantine, walking the rest of his men several paces from Deborah, Cam, Medrano, and the boy—but Deborah quickly flagged. Medrano tried to support her, but he wasn't much better off. Within minutes, the officer called for a halt and asked Cam to vaccinate two more of his men. He needed someone to carry his prisoners.

A few soldiers had already disappeared, running ahead. Deborah thought two or three of them had also gone back into the smoke. Why? To fight the fire?

Dividing his platoon left the officer with only four men, including himself and the boy. Deborah supposed if there was a time to overpower them, it was now, but she'd slumped to the ground, feeling nauseous. She was only faintly aware of Cam repeating his procedure with the jackknife or of

Medrano removing her gun belt to make a combat sling for her arm.

This is what shock feels like, she thought. *You're in shock.*

"Water," she said. "I—Is there water?"

Medrano got a canteen from the boy. Maybe it helped. When they carried her into the Russian camp fifteen minutes later, Deborah was still conscious. She saw one truck in the rock-strewn gully. There was also camouflage netting strung from a fat gray boulder. They brought Deborah beneath it. Her last memory was of the sunlight in the fabric.

Two hours later, they were slashing over the brown land in a helicopter. Deborah remained numb. She felt hypnotized by the yammering vibration of the rotors and the rolling pattern of shadows in the gullies and foothills below. The sun shone low in the west. Darkness reached away from every ridge and peak.

Enjoy it while you can, she thought.

The air here was clean, but, ahead of them, the southern sky was lost behind gigantic black clouds. Fallout and smoke hovered over the L.A. basin like a mountain range, all of its massive slopes, bulk, and pinnacles leaning inland, blown east by the ocean wind. It was a different world. Not all of them would come out again. Even if there wasn't more shooting— even if Freedman was alive and they found her—there wasn't room in the helicopter. At least one person would need to give up their seat.

The aircraft was an old KTVC News 12 chopper, narrow-bodied and short. It was also bright red. At first, Deborah thought they were dangerously exposed inside its Plexiglas windows, but the color of the helicopter was immaterial. It was their radar signature that mattered, and, more importantly, their transponder and radio codes.

They were a hundred and forty miles from San Bernadino. The Osprey had crashed on the eastern face of the Sierras near Mt. Whitney and Sequoia National Park in the central part of California. Bornmann must have veered north before they were hit, trying to escape the fighters. Even so, they were in

Chinese-occupied territory. The Russians weren't supposed to be here. Their border with the People's Liberation Army had been drawn another fifty miles north, just south of Fresno, and yet they'd maintained Special Forces inside that line. The officer, Lt. Colonel Artem Alekseev, had commanded several covert surveillance units whose isolation saved them. A third of Alekseev's men fell victim to windborne drifts of nano-tech, but there was no one else to fight off. They survived. Now they'd joined with the Americans—or vice versa.

After he decided to risk everyone in his command to Cam's inoculations, Alekseev had rummaged up some spare clothes, putting the three Americans in Russian uniforms. Medrano did what he could to keep them distinct. He insisted on removing the name tapes from his uniform and Deborah's in addition to her Army patch and his own USAF patch, all of which he sewed onto their new uniforms—but there were only four identifiers for the three of them. REECE. MEDRANO. U.S. ARMY. U.S. AIR FORCE. In combat, American soldiers wore nothing else, not even the flag. He put the U.S. ARMY patch on Cam, but the effect was negligible. All of them looked like Russians.

Alekseev proved to be in his forties when he finally took off his biochem mask. His face was dark from sun and weather except along one cheek, where the skin was branded with three white puncture scars Deborah couldn't identify. What could have made those marks? Barbed wire?

Deborah didn't trust him. To convince Medrano to share the vaccine, she'd said the Russians were no longer their enemy. They all wanted to live, and that was true, but Deborah wasn't so forgiving.

Alekseev was a ferret. She planned to watch him closely, even if he didn't seem to have anything to gain by betraying them to the Chinese. Easy prison sentences for his men? His ambitions were larger than that.

Much like General Walls, Alekseev had divided the remainder of his troops into two squads and told them to find other survivors. His assets were too minimal to mount a seri-ous counterattack. Throughout the day he'd waited and lis-tened, raging at his helplessness. By now, the Chinese must have completed their takeover of the top U.S. installations.

Before sunrise tomorrow, if not sooner, they would turn their attention to cleaning up any pockets of resistance in Russian California, so Alekseev chose to support the three Americans in their all-or-nothing gambit to find Kendra Freedman.

First, he owned the helicopter, stashed at an old refugee camp seven miles north of his hiding place. Second, Russian intelligence had been monitoring Chinese radio traffic since the occupation with a great deal of luck. It had been necessary for the allies to coordinate their air missions, which gave the Russians many more opportunities than the U.S.–Canadian side to study, hack, and infiltrate the Chinese system. Colonel Alekseev believed he could fool Chinese air control where the Americans failed. Unfortunately, the KTVC chopper only contained four seats. Alekseev had had far more volunteers than he could send. None of his troops wanted to stay behind. Deborah felt a grudging respect for their courage even as she joined Cam and Medrano in arguing with Alekseev. She didn't want to remain behind, either. What would she do? Nap?

It didn't help that Deborah, Cam, and Medrano were hurt. Alekseev's medic tended their wounds, setting Medrano's arm with a splint and stitching their cuts, but the three of them were a mess. As far as Alekseev was concerned, the only American to fill one of the precious seats would be Cam. They'd explained that Cam knew Freedman and some nano-tech, but Deborah extended this half-truth to herself. *I've been a research assistant,* she said, *and Medrano's studied the Los Angeles area. He's also an engineer. We need him if we're going to be digging through what's left of the city.*

Alekseev believed the chopper's load allowance would permit six people. It would be tight, but they needed everyone they could fit. There must be a large Chinese guard at the labs. Their best hope might be a sudden blitz. When their pilot returned with the chopper, Alekseev's troops loaded it with one person's equivalent weight of rocket-propelled grenades and other weaponry. That left five slots—just four, after the pilot, an unfortunately heavyset man called Obruch.

They were saved from an even tougher decision. In the smoke, Alekseev had sent three men to investigate the plane. These soldiers reported no trace of Tanya Huff or Lewis Bornmann. If they'd survived the crash, which seemed unlikely, they must have been killed in the missile strike.

Like Foshtomi, Huff had been a part of saving Cam and Deborah. Huff's death made her feel small and humble and yet unspeakably proud. She would carry on for them as far as possible.

Deborah expected to die with these strangers. Their entire strike force consisted of herself, Cam, Medrano, Colonel Alekseev, and Sergeant Obruch—and the chopper's tanks were only two-thirds full. That meant their maximum range was 160 miles. They would need to find an airfield and refuel in order to leave L.A.

She was glad she had one friend. Jammed together in back, Cam worked to familiarize himself with a Russian AK-47 as Medrano inspected an RPG. Deborah merely rested her shoulder. She watched the sun and the land below. Impossibly, she was at peace.

Deborah Reece was a good soldier.

They were still a hundred miles from San Bernadino when their chopper hit the ash like a solid membrane. The aircraft rocked. Even the beat of the rotors changed. The *whup whup whup whup* of the blades deepened into a shorter, harsher sound as if everything was closer now.

One thing Deborah didn't worry about was radiation. The booster nanotech would protect them from all but the worst dosage. In any case, she didn't expect to live long enough to get sick.

She stared into the darkness. Dust ticked and clattered against the Plexiglas.

There were layers in the clouds. Sometimes she couldn't see anything but the swirls of gray and black. Other times, the haze opened up and she could see the ground, which was mostly blackened desert. Occasionally there was a road or fences or a line of blown-down telephone poles.

They knew the Chinese had taken over the U.S. military bases in the Mojave. Medrano thought these targets must have been hit, too. The earth was empty and burned, which didn't make their job any easier. They'd lost their maps and electronics in the plane crash. That meant they'd also lost their sporadic satellite connection. They'd memorized the GPS coordinates for Saint Bernadine Hospital, but the News 12 chopper had had its global positioning system torn out long ago to support the Russian war effort.

Working with Medrano, Alekseev thought he'd pinpointed the right spot on a map of his own. By using compass headings, some landmarks in the terrain and dead reckoning, they believed they could find the general neighborhood. Fortunately, San Bernadino lay on Interstate 40 on the south side of a narrow pass between the San Gabriel and San Bernadino Mountains, which formed the eastern border of the Los Angeles sprawl. Those peaks would be tough to miss. A few of the highest nubs actually poked above ten thousand feet, and the Interstate should act like a red carpet, creating a long, distinct ribbon in the terrain.

Four times they saw Chinese aircraft in the murk. The fighters' jetwash cut through the ash like bullets, dragging the soot into straight lines. One plane flew very close, nearly flipping the chopper as Obruch cursed and fought the controls.

Alekseev had already answered two radio challenges in Mandarin. After their near miss, there was a third. Deborah waited for a missile—would they even feel it?—but death never came. Alekseev's codes were MSS, he said, and he posed as a high-level officer, even rebuking Chinese air traffic control for contacting him again. He wanted radio silence.

Eventually they were clattering alongside the San Gabriel Mountains. Obruch also had a railroad track and the dry, broken channel of an aqueduct to follow, both of which led to I-40 and then into the pass.

The land transformed. Gas stations and truck lots appeared first. Warehouses. A car dealership. A quarry. There were homes, too, and freeway billboards and an endless row of great metal trusses supporting electrical lines. Everything looked as if it had been lifted and thrown. The buildings sagged. Even the freeway was buckled and split. Ash covered the world, robbing it of any color.

The destruction grew worse as they thundered through the pass. There were vast residential areas—thousands of homes in neat, boxy patterns on the hills. Street after street had been built on terraces like broad steps down the mountain slope, spotted with larger structures like apartment buildings and shopping centers. From the air, even now, the order that had been imposed was impressive. These roads and foundations might last for eons, although the lighter elements had been torn away. The roofs of the houses were gone. Many of those square little buildings had collapsed. The larger apartments and malls were often missing their tops, too, or had lost one or more walls. Even brick and concrete hadn't survived. Not a single window looked intact. All of that material had avalanched into the streets as it was lifted by the blast waves, creating drifts and dunes that covered earlier disasters. Long before the missiles fell, San Bernadino had been wracked by quakes and flash floods. It didn't rain here often—but when it did, the insect-ravaged yards and hills had melted away, clogging the streets with erosion and debris. Deborah could still see unintended riverways carved through some neighborhoods, spilling down the mountainside.

A small percentage of the debris was bones. Hundreds of thousands of people had died here in the first plague. Their skulls and rib cages mixed with the furniture and other household possessions strewn among the shattered lumber, drywall, doors, shingling, and insulation. Signs were down. Trees and cars had overturned. It didn't seem possible that anyone could have survived, but Deborah did her part, staring into the ruins for any clue. They were about two hundred feet up. Visibility was no more than a few hundred yards. Even the mountains had faded into the gloom. Everything looked the same. All that stood were broken walls—the endless, straight-edged fins of broken walls.

Beside her, Medrano compared notes with Alekseev in the cockpit, trying to make sense of the holocaust. Up front, the two Russians murmured together in their own language until Alekseev turned and said, "We are overshooting our mark. We must turn back north."

"I've been counting streets," Medrano said.

"As have we," Alekseev said. "The hospital is behind us."

"Look," Cam said. "What's that?" He rapped on his window

and Deborah straightened against Medrano, wanting to see past him, which became easier when Obruch banked in a slow glide to Cam's side.

There were people sprawled in the rubble—fresh, whole people, not skeletons. Deborah guessed there were at least ten. They were ash-colored like everything else, but they'd fallen on top of the debris. That meant they'd come after the bombing.

"Не слишком приближайтесь," Alekseev said.

The helicopter had been descending but Obruch adjusted his elevation, rising again and then banking away to keep from passing over the kill zone. Deborah tried to glance back at the corpses through her window. The angle was too sharp.

"What do you think happened to them?" Medrano said, and Deborah thought, *They weren't shot. They looked . . . melted.*

Limbs and heads had come away from some of the bodies.

"It must have been recent," Cam said. "There are no bugs. No ants. The way those people were chewed up—"

"Там!" Alekseev shouted. "On your right."

That was Deborah's side, and she glanced through the broken shapes of the city. She felt both hope and trepidation, because she knew exactly what Cam was thinking.

Those men looked like they'd been killed by nanotech.

"There are more bodies to the north," Alekseev said.

"So we have a trail," Medrano said. "But in which direction? Which group was killed first?"

"There's a chopper on the ground to my side," Cam said.

"Oh, shit," Medrano said. Alekseev barked at Obruch in Russian, but Cam said, "No, it crashed. It's not a problem. I don't see anyone moving there or—"

Deborah gasped.

There was a witch in the rubble below, dark-skinned and wild-haired. She flung one hand up at them as if casting a spell.

"Pull up!" Deborah screamed. "Pull up!"

Obruch obeyed instantly. The engine whined as he lifted the chopper into a hard leftward turn. The additional thrust pulled Medrano against Deborah, squeezing her bad shoulder, but she had never been so glad for a sense of motion.

What was she throwing at us? Did we get away?

"What did you see!" Alekseev said.

"She's below us. She was on my side." Deborah had lost track of the helicopter's direction as they curled into the sky, but Obruch leveled out and brought the nose around. Deborah spotted her again. The witch leapt through the black dunes and fell and bounced up, her coat flapping in the helicopter's downdrafts.

"I see her!" Deborah shouted.

Was it Freedman? Their file photos showed a heavyset woman. This fast-moving spook was wiry and hunchbacked, her shoulders bulging above her waspish frame.

Who else would it be? This woman appeared to have waded through two or three platoons of Chinese soldiers, hurling nanotech, downing helicopters—but it could be anyone, couldn't it? What if the Chinese had captured other American researchers or some of the top scientists in Europe or India?

"Ниже нас," Obruch said.

The witch scampered down the smooth, fallen length of a cinder block wall and limped into the space between a car and a tangle of wire. Then she disappeared like magic.

"Опустите нас на землю," Alekseev said to Obruch, gesturing.

Deborah interrupted. She'd recognized the word *down* and said, "Colonel, wait. You better put us on the ground away from her or she'll kill us, too."

If Alekseev's calculations were correct—if it was really her—Freedman had gone southward as she left the hospital for some other destination. They would have missed her without the fields of dead men to mark her path. Where was she headed?

Obruch powered the chopper down into the wreckage fifty yards from where they'd last seen her. "Cam, you're with me!" Deborah shouted, opening her door to the noise and dust of the rotors. "The rest of you stay here!"

"Nyet!" Alekseev said. "I am also coming!"

"Fine. Don't let her get past you, but don't crowd her,

either! Do you understand?" Deborah squinted through the ash with more dread than excitement. "She's carrying some kind of nanotech!"

"Da." Alekseev drew a walkie-talkie from his belt and yelled back at Obruch, waving him up.

If Freedman kills us, at least Medrano and Obruch can try again, Deborah thought. That was the extent of her plan. Everything hinged on Cam's tenuous link to the woman . . . and if it was someone else, someone who didn't even speak English . . .

We have to take that chance.

The three of them ran into the choking wreckage beneath the helicopter. Deborah only had one hand to grab at the debris. She slipped and banged through a heap of bricks and mortar, bent pipes, a cracked porcelain toilet. Soot burst up from every footstep. She heard Alekseev barking for directions from Obruch, but she was too busy fending her way through a soft, rotting skin of cloth to look back. Then she was startled by two sounds in front of her. Metal banged on wood and Deborah was confronted by the witch, surprisingly close.

She ran toward me! Deborah thought, stunned. Her throat was too dry to get out more than a rasp: "Wait—"

The witch stood above her. She'd climbed over a heap of wooden slats propped up on a fallen street sign. Ash streaked the two bent white panels set in a crisscross on the pole, and yet the black lettering was legible: CRESTVIEW AVE. and EAST 16TH ST. The military officer in Deborah thought that was important. This was ground zero. They'd found their woman.

It had to be Freedman, didn't it? But the witch was faceless. Bodiless. She might have been a walking silhouette. The dark oval where her face should be blended perfectly into her straggly black hair, and her clothes were powdered with ash. The only definition in her thin, hunchbacked frame was her eyes. The white eyes smoldered with power and torment and then her arms spasmed, too.

Deborah stared at those dark hands for one jagged heartbeat, transfixed by the other woman. She wore a knapsack. That was the odd bump on her back. Deborah also saw a thick welt up her left forearm, a failed suicide's mark. At some point she'd cut herself.

"Wait. My name is Major Reece—"

The witch raised both fists.

She'll kill me, Deborah thought, but then Cam shouted, "Kendra! Kendra Freedman!"

The witch turned her head.

"U.S. Army Rangers!" he shouted. "United States Army Rangers! We're here to rescue you!"

24

Every muscle in Freedman's body tensed like a hair trigger. Whatever she was holding, Cam didn't want her hands to snap forward and throw it. "I knew Albert Sawyer!" he shouted. "I'm your friend!"

One problem was that they wore Russian uniforms. Another was that Freedman's face was a wild mask. Her eyes rolled and popped with fear.

"I'll kill you!" she barked. "Stay back!"

"I knew Albert Sawyer," he said.

This time his words seemed to register. Her head ducked and lifted again, not in a gesture like a nod but like a woman double-checking her thoughts. For an instant, Freedman seemed unaware of them. But she didn't lower her arms.

Cam slid into the shallow pit where Deborah stood below Freedman, putting himself at the same disadvantage. He thought it might calm her.

"Sawyer's dead now," he said gently. He hoped this news was something they could share.

Instead, when Freedman's eyes rose, her expression was filled with new terror. "They're all dead," she said, and yet her voice seemed disconnected from the rest of her. It was flat and distant. Was she even talking to them?

Kendra Freedman was insane. At some point, she'd experienced a psychotic break.

Deborah repressed a low sound like a moan, but she didn't try to run. She stood her ground, entrusting her life to him. He wanted to take her hand. He wanted to say *We're going to be all right*, but Freedman needed to be the sole focus of his attention. Her sleeve had shot back from her hand and Cam stared at the scar on her wrist. He had known would-be suicides. Sometimes they were beyond reach.

"We're here to rescue you," he said. "My name is Cam."

She ignored him. The chopper was still hammering over the ruins behind him to his right. Her gaze flickered in that direction, then shifted to his left. At what? Alekseev? Cam would have yelled at the Russian to keep away if he hadn't been afraid to raise his voice.

"I'm your friend," he said.

"Stay back!"

"We're here to—"

"I'll kill you!" Freedman nearly fell when the pile beneath her shifted, her left hand slashing outward for balance. But she stayed up, and they didn't die.

It was the second time she'd reacted violently to that word. *Friend.* Why? The Chinese must have promised her the same thing, and Cam struggled to find a different way to connect with her. *Sawyer.* She'd stopped when he mentioned Sawyer, so he said, "I knew Al. He told me everything. We know it wasn't your fault."

"What was his first patent number?"

"I, uh—"

Freedman's left hand rose away from her body again, threatening. "He loved that number like it was a million dollars," she said. All at once she was in total possession of herself and this change was uniquely frightening, because now Cam saw her true presence and her intellect. Could she really be smarter than Ruth?

If he tried to fool her, she would know.

He said, "Al told me how your sister gave you all of those

old ABBA records on CD for Christmas. You brought them into the lab and played them there. It made him crazy." *Don't say that word!* he warned himself. *Crazy. Friend. Watch your mouth.* His head was racing but he was careful to speak slowly. "Al liked hip-hop, and you made him listen to ancient rock like ABBA and Duran Duran. He laughed about it."

Sawyer had cursed her for a stupid bitch. Sawyer's guilt had turned him cold and mean. He denied that he was even slightly to blame for the end of the world, yet he'd been an integral part of the *archos* tech's design team.

These people were unique. Their rare education set them apart. Ruth had always felt responsible because she *could* do something, just never enough. How much worse would that self-loathing be for the woman who'd been the main force in the creation of the machine plague? A planet had died because of her.

If this doesn't work . . .

Freedman's gaze turned to track the helicopter again, denying Cam the chance to make eye contact. That only increased his nervousness. *We can't shoot her,* he thought, *but we can't leave her here, either. The Chinese have already sent troops to recapture her. They'll send more. Another chopper is probably already on its way.*

"Al," Freedman said, like a robot.

"We're here to rescue you," Cam repeated. "The helicopter is ours. We're American soldiers."

She looked down at her fists. Fear had widened her eyes again, and Cam realized that a lot of her terror was for herself—for the things she'd done to escape. She didn't want to cause any more death.

"Take me to the lab," she said.

"We'll go anywhere you want."

But he'd rattled the words out too quickly, as if speaking to a child. His tone brought her face up again and he saw that she was *there*, inside herself, listening and coherent. Her eyes gleamed with triumph.

"They built a sister lab nearby," she said. "I know it's there."

"You mean in the Saint Bernadine hospital?"

"They built a sister lab nearby. They said no, but they used the same couriers and I saw the same man on the same day. I know it's there."

Couriers, he thought, doubting her. Could she really have discerned the existence of a second lab within walking distance of Saint Bernadine from such a small clue? *She keeps repeating herself exactly,* he thought. She clung to some phrases like a drowning woman tightening her grip on a life ring, as if she questioned or even forgot herself.

This was more than sustained shock and guilt. Had the Chinese tortured her?

"Please." Deborah brushed her good hand through her ash-darkened blond hair, perhaps to reinforce that she wasn't Asian. Then she held her palm up to the woman above them. "Please, Kendra. Come with us."

"We don't have much time," Cam said. "The Chinese will send more men—"

"I'll kill them."

"—and we don't have much fuel."

Freedman began to crouch, settling herself on the loose slats where she paused and stared. "We won't have to go far," she said. "I know it's there."

"Come down," Deborah said. "Please."

"No."

"We can take you back to American lines," Cam said with more certainty than he felt. They would need to refuel even if they weren't blocked by Chinese aircraft.

And if they stop us, he thought, *do I put a bullet in her head? Or do I let them have her because they've won and she might help them succeed in repopulating the planet?*

My God. Is it better if we all die?

Who knows what she could build if the Chinese keep her locked up for the rest of her life. What will they do to us? If they improve the mind plague, they might be able to control everyone on the planet for thousands of years, breeding people like cows or dogs for strength and obedience. Beauty. Sex. It's better to kill her, he realized, wondering if he could draw his pistol before she threw her nanotech.

"I won't go," Freedman said.

"You don't understand," Deborah said. Some of her old

arrogance showed in her voice and posture, and Cam liked her for it. "A lot of good people died just to get us here," she said. "We need you."

"I need to see the other lab," Freedman said. "They built the vaccine there."

"We have the vaccine! You must have it, too," Cam said, but Freedman didn't move on her heap of rubble, squatting on her haunches. He was reminded of a child again. What would she do? Hold her breath?

Abruptly she shoved herself back to her feet, extending her fists to both sides as she looked over Cam's head. Deborah wasn't the only one losing patience. Colonel Alekseev had kept his distance, acting as a lookout, but now he picked his way through the ruins with his AK-47. "We must leave!" he called.

"I won't go."

"It doesn't sound like you even know where this lab is," Cam said, pleading with her, and Deborah said, "We can keep you safe in Colorado. We have some gear. There's an MRFM and—"

"The lab is nearby. I know it's there!"

Freedman's passion reminded him again uncomfortably of Ruth. Maybe that was why he hesitated. They were so intent on getting her out of the Los Angeles sprawl, too tired and rushed to imagine any change in plans. What if it made more sense to stay?

"Why?" he asked, trying not to flinch from a gust of ash. The helicopter thundered closer in response to some signal from Alekseev, whipping the ruins with dust and shreds of paper, but Cam persisted. "Why do you want the vaccine?" he asked. Then: "We'll take you there!"

The worst of the downdrafts shifted away from them as the helicopter landed, making it easier to hear—but Freedman cocked her hands on either side of her body, ready to fight.

Cam bent his body, too, reflexively dropping into a gunslinger's crouch. "We can move a lot faster in the sky," he said.

Beside him, Deborah had also touched her sidearm. "Please!" she said. "Please, Kendra."

"Andrew Dutchess released the *archos* tech," Freedman said. "Not me. It was Dutchess." Her voice was small again, and she fidgeted and blinked.

Jesus, Cam thought. *Jesus Christ, I think she's forgotten where she is.*

He stepped toward her. His legs were stiff. Every movement was reluctant, even as his skin shivered with anticipation. Either he would force her to recognize her surroundings or he would tackle her. If he was lucky, he could disarm her. Her nanotech must be in glass or plastic vials exactly like Ruth had done.

"There's a new plague," he said. "The mind plague."

Snap. Her eyes shifted to him, clear and afraid. "I can stop it," she said.

"How?"

"There's a marker in the vaccine. I helped them build it, but they did as much work as possible without me. I need key components and software if I'm going to design my cat's paw."

"Cat," he said, not understanding.

"I know it's there."

"You saw the same man on the same day," Deborah said, prompting her. She also distracted Freedman. Cam nearly scrambled up the broken wood slats—he could knock her feet out from under her if he lunged—but Freedman smiled and said, "Yes. The other lab is nearby."

"How can you stop the mind plague?"

"I can alter the vaccine and make it a cat's paw. A new kind of nanotech." She was lucid now, speaking rapidly, as if from a memorized speech.

She must have recited those words to herself hundreds of times in captivity, but Cam wondered. Could they trust her? She seemed no more substantial than sunlight caught in a set of window blinds. Snap—open. Snap—closed.

"It will attack the new plague and its vaccine, too," she said. "Anyone who's currently infected will be freed from the plague and it will shut off the vaccine in everyone who's been inoculated."

"Jesus Christ," Cam said.

If they could find the other lab—if Freedman could do

what she said—they would turn the tables on the Chinese.
Millions of people around the world would regain their intelligence even as China's armies became vulnerable to the
mind plague.

Deborah wasn't buying it. "I don't understand," she said.
"Why wouldn't this thing just turn around and leave our side
open to infection again, too?"

"Because I can give it the same self-governing markers we
developed for the plague," Freedman said. "My cat's paw will
know who's immune and who isn't, and it will establish itself
individually in everyone it finds."

"Smart tech," Cam said, looking for Deborah's eyes.
"Remember what a jump they've made. The mind plague and
its vaccine aren't just machines. On some level, they're both
able to *think*, even more so than the booster. They remember
what they've done."

"It still won't work," Deborah said. "None of us are sick.
There's nobody except us and the Chinese for hundreds of
miles, and none of us are carrying the plague. Even if she can
reverse who's immune and who isn't, that doesn't solve anything if the Chinese stop us. Don't you see? They don't even
have to kill us. All they need to do is keep us contained."

"We are carrying the plague," Cam said. "Right? We came
out of Colorado. We must have traces of it in our blood. Our
lungs. Our skin."

Freedman nodded. "Their vaccine is the only thing protecting you. My cat's paw will attack the vaccine."

"That's how it'll spread," Cam said. He touched Deborah's
arm, trying to convey both tenderness and brutal resolve.
"The mind plague will infect the Chinese. Everyone we left
behind will wake up."

"But this includes us," Alekseev said behind him. "My men
and us. What she wants to build will infect us, too, yes?"

"Yes."

Deborah didn't say anything, staring at Cam, but then
Alekseev nodded.

"Okay, let's go," Cam said to Freedman. "You have my
word. We'll find the lab."

He would have done it to save Ruth if nothing else.

* * *

Alekseev bodysearched Freedman with a pistol in his hand, relieving her of four plastic vials that Cam was sure contained nanotech. They also took off her knapsack. Deborah sorted through it gingerly. "There's nothing in here but canteens," she said as Medrano and Alekseev pestered Freedman for more information. "What are we looking for?" Medrano said, but Freedman only cried on Cam's lap once they were aboard, cramming all six of them into the chopper. She turned into his chest and neck and cried like a broken girl, weeping against his ash-black fatigues as she formed words inside her breathless sobs.

"It was Dutchess," she whispered. "Not me. It was Dutchess."

Cam strained to hear. Maybe she needed that secrecy. She'd obviously learned to hide herself during her imprisonment, both from her captors and her own conscience.

"She doesn't know where we're going," Deborah said. "One thing I can tell you, there won't be aircraft or trucks. The Chinese wouldn't have risked constant flights or traffic between the labs. Our satellites would have seen the pattern. That means it's close by."

"There are five thousand buildings close by," Medrano said.

"Look for another hospital," Cam said, "maybe an office complex or a school. They'd need space—clean rooms for labs, storage, barracks. Go south. She was heading south."

"She's out of her mind," Medrano said.

"She's smarter than the rest of us put together. I think she noticed something. There were clues. Kendra?" Cam lowered his voice. "Kendra, where is their other lab?"

"I found the police," she said. "I told them. Nine thousand five hundred and seventy feet. I told them."

She was babbling. She was sick—physically sick. The round face and double chins from Rezac's photos were shrunken down to something more like a living skull. Her cheekbones pressed tightly through her skin, which was why her eyes seemed too large, squeezed out of her face.

She couldn't have weighed more than eighty pounds.

25

Kendra Lelei Freedman survived the plague year only by the strangest karma. As the nanotech ravaged northern California, spreading swiftly, somehow she reached the governor's office in Sacramento. Kendra was still wearing her lab coat, which must have helped. She was also louder than the other people in the crowd outside the capital buildings, using her weight to shove to the front. She convinced a National Guardsman she knew what was behind the confused reports. An officer escorted her through their barricades.

State police put her and the governor aboard a CHP helicopter only to be overwhelmed themselves by the mob, and the pilot's frantic radio calls went unnoticed in the chaos. It didn't help that the March rain turned to snow as they hurried east. Then they were infected, flying beneath ten thousand feet. Their pilot managed to lift the chopper to safe altitude through the storm, but he was bleeding from one eye and semiconscious when they smashed into a mountainside.

Other people reached the same small peak. Too many. They only lasted until summer before they played their first round of Stones. It was a contest Kendra invented herself, a bait-and-switch guessing game that she controlled. The losers were killed and eaten. Kendra knew she would never fail, not with her memory. She talked the majority into supporting it because their first victims were the most traumatized, the less aware, the least helpful. They believed it was fair. They winnowed themselves down with Kendra manipulating the group the whole time.

It split her mind. She wasn't brave enough to commit suicide, so she died in other ways. Nevertheless, Kendra was still alive when the plague war began. The Russians found her. Kendra told them who she was to escape being shot, and they traded her to the Chinese.

The MSS went to work on her brittle soul. They said America had been eradicated by a full-scale nuclear attack and offered proof in satellite photos, some of which must have been real. They took her aboard a plane and flew for nearly a day, then said they'd landed in the Himalayas, where they were desperately fending off India's tanks and infantry.

They gave her a chance to redeem herself: to create new nanotech. Their own people had been working on the mind plague. Kendra was the catalyst in making it operational. They said the new contagion was intended to be a bloodless method of ending the war. They said they only wanted to unite both countries under a single government before another nuclear exchange wiped out these last few safe islands above the machine plague. They didn't tell her Ruth's vaccine was widespread by then, permitting everyone to reclaim the world below ten thousand feet. Nor did Kendra ask to go outside to verify her location. She'd seen enough of snow and wind and desolate rock. She loved her warm prison. The women who tended to her were soft-voiced and kind, completely unlike anything on her mountaintop. She wanted to believe them.

Kendra began to work again. She escaped into the pristine logic of her microscopes, and, when she occasionally stalled on the mind plague, she turned her skills to other projects, daring to reexamine the *archos* tech for weaknesses. There must be some way to destroy it.

Her handlers let her play with different lines of research because it kept her happy. She also came to understand that they hoped her efforts would jump-start new possibilities in their weapons programs. Too late, she discovered Ruth's vaccine in her own blood along with the booster nanotech. Too late, she learned she'd repeated her unholy mistake, providing them with the power to tear the world apart again.

She went on strike. It didn't last. The MSS used sleep deprivation, drugs, and cold to compel her. She quit eating, but they inserted a gastric feeding tube and IVs to sustain her—and when she failed to rouse herself, the pain began. Electricity. Knives. She swore to help again just to make it stop.

She'd become erratic. She knew that. Sometimes she exaggerated her behavior when she was actually in control of herself, creating opportunities to conceal and deceive. It also helped that she'd picked up a good deal of their language by then. She pretended she wanted to be one of them, which she hoped was comforting to her overseers. She refused to speak in anything except Mandarin, deliberately confusing her words and mixing her written notes.

Kendra knew they hoped to improve the mind plague to *introduce* thoughts to infected people, not only disrupting their capacity to think but shaping and encouraging cooperative moods. They were years away from this magic. Merely teaching the nanotech to interrupt higher brain function was impressive enough—but, showing ambition, she convinced them to increase the nano's AMU to allow the space necessary to eventually house those programs. The Chinese didn't realize the extra bulk she built into it also held a coded message.

Unfortunately, she couldn't be sure anyone would ever find her cry for help. Worse, she didn't make the mental leap to using the new self-governing markers to reverse who the mind plague infected until after they'd taken both kinds of nanotech away from her.

Her best chance to stop them was her continued work with the *archos* tech. She crafted a new machine plague, first paring down its size for increased speed. She also replaced its heat engine with a simple protein-based reaction. That was easy. The *archos* tech was nothing if not efficient in disintegrating organic tissue, which she taught it to burn for energy. It would be enough to destroy everyone in their nanotech programs, including herself.

At last she was ready. Too late. More than anything, those bleak, miserable words summed up her life. Too late. She hadn't been able to cut her wrists deeply enough on her mountaintop, and she'd kept eating in small amounts even after she swore an oath to God and the devil to let herself waste away, but the pared-down *archos* tech would kill her exactly as the original model should have done years ago. Kendra never expected to survive beyond opening the first or second vial.

She was wrong.

Saint Bernadine had been retrofitted by the Chinese. Even so, the missiles' shock waves brought most of the building down. Trapped in its dark halls, their research teams and military personnel needed hours to pull each other free. At least a dozen people were hurt or missing. No one else came to help. They kept her away from the windows, and the gloom was everlasting, but Kendra thought it was afternoon before they escorted her to her basement labs to recover her gear. Major Su said they needed to be ready to move.

There weren't enough of them to carry everything, so Kendra filled her pockets with sample cases and flash drives—and eight slim vials of nanotech. Then they brought her outside into the growing beat of a helicopter.

The aircraft flew out of the south as she walked away from the other men and women, staring out across the black, flattened city. They let her keep her distance. They were accustomed to her moods, and there was nowhere for her go.

The helicopter landed in an area cleared by Major Su's men. Kendra didn't know if they intended to ferry her to the sister lab or if they were bringing those teams north. Maybe she should have waited. She didn't have that much self-control. She screamed in anguish and rage as she threw the first vial.

Major Su fell with his cheek eaten away, clawing at his pistol. Others were torn apart through their necks and chests. Like the original *archos* tech, her accelerated machine plague found its quickest entrance through the sinus cavities and lungs.

Watching them die was hellish.

It felt like coming home.

She had killed unimaginable numbers and, more personally, she had directed people to murder and cook eighteen human beings on her little mountaintop. What were a few more? Kendra delighted in feeling anything other than helpless. She became a dark goddess—the destroyer of the worlds.

Laughing, she strode toward the chopper as the pilots powered up again. They began to lift away. She threw another vial, hoping to feel the nanotech across her own body in the blistering wind. But her aim was true. The vial passed through the open side door and the plague never escaped the aircraft, which wheeled onto its side and slammed into the ruins a hundred yards away. Then she was alone except for three wounded and a woman who called herself Jane, one of her caregivers, who had always been respectful and sweet.

Kendra killed them, too.

A second helicopter came as she hiked into the rubble. It buzzed past her only to return, landing in the city ahead of her . . . and she met Chinese soldiers in the ash as the chopper flew back overhead. Her mind disappeared. She must have killed them all, but she had no memory of it. When she gradually returned to herself, she was sobbing against the straight, solid little face of a mailbox. Somehow she'd found one thing that was still upright, although caked with soot. The mailbox remained bolted to the sidewalk and she leaned against it, surrounded by untold miles of flattened buildings and debris.

It was the third helicopter that brought Cam to her.

Alekseev and Obruch argued together in the cockpit until Deborah cut in, hearing something she didn't like. "We need to see this through!" Deborah called forward.

"We are not convinced this hunt is useful," Alekseev said. "Let us try to get her out of here."

Cam shook his head. "For what? The answer is here."

"You are mad," Alekseev said, but then Obruch shouted, *"Туда! В мою сторону!"*

He banked the chopper to the left. They were about hundred feet above the blast-swept neighborhoods. At first, Cam couldn't tell what had drawn Obruch's gaze. There were no variations in the pattern below. The homes were small, eroded squares. The streets formed less-cluttered lines in the wreckage. Then he saw a group of structures with a hint of red in the torn rooftops, which was unusual. There were also the shapes of parking lots in front and a big athletic field on the other side. A school campus?

"Kendra, look," he said. "Kendra?"

Her bulging eyes were locked on something he couldn't see, so Cam swung away from her again. As they flew closer, he noticed two circles in the ash where helicopters had lifted off, scouring the rubble. It was the rotors' force that had revealed what was left of the red tile roofs.

"*Вот именно,*" Alekseev said. Then, in English, "We're putting down. Be ready."

They landed close against the slumping dune of the largest building, which had probably been a gym, leaving Kendra and Obruch in the helicopter. She was catatonic. Obruch drew his sidearm.

Deborah and Alekseev flanked one side of the building as Cam and Medrano took the other. His body clattered with two AK-47s and a submachine gun. Medrano and the others carried the same or more. The chopper's noise meant there was no chance of surprising the enemy. No one expected even enough time to reload, so they would kick in as many doors as possible before they were killed themselves.

Cam's heart rattled like the metal slung across his back, but his head was clear—even disappointed. The campus was empty. Everyone was gone except for four bodies lined up on the floor of one classroom. From their injuries, they'd been hurt when the buildings dropped. The Chinese must have evacuated, first bringing their scientists to Saint Bernadine and then marshalling the remainder of their personnel to find Kendra after an emergency radio call that she was loose.

Cam didn't say it, but his disappointment turned into a new anxiety. What if the data and samples they needed were in the wrecked Chinese helicopters?

They swept the campus more thoroughly, trying to identify which areas had been used for labs and offices. Ten minutes later, Medrano yelled for them to bring Kendra to a building near the athletic field. It had been shielded from the blastwave by other buildings. There was a gaping hole in the roof and one wall was down, but more than a third of its classrooms were intact.

Cam went to help Obruch. Kendra didn't want to leave the chopper. She'd nestled into the back seat and tried to pull free when Cam touched her leg.

"We're here," he said. "We found the sister lab."

It was no use. They were forced to drag her outside—but her mood changed as they half carried her through the fallen buildings. Her giant eyes filled with curiosity. Maybe she'd forgotten her safe little nest in the helicopter.

"What do you think?" Deborah asked when they escorted Kendra inside. There were opaque black plastic tents in two of the rooms, although the plastic was split or sagging, pelted by debris. Clean room suits sprawled on coatracks that had been knocked to the floor. More to the point, there were several desks that had been loaded with microscopy gear. Most of the equipment was on the floor. Another room held rows of laptops and larger computers, file cabinets, and a dry-erase board covered with the deft, boxy symbols of written Mandarin.

Cam felt an unusual flash of optimism. The Chinese had been unable to carry even the beginnings of this stuff in their first flight to Saint Bernadine, and they couldn't possibly have expected American troops this deep into the blast zone. They must have planned to come back for the majority of their equipment. *In fact, we're lucky they were hit so hard,* he thought. *The few planes and helicopters they've been able to make operational have been busy all day with other problems—but that'll change. This luck can't last.*

"We need to hurry," he said.

Kendra was subdued but responsive. She nodded and said, "Let me see. I can see. Let me see."

Was she consciously referring to the sky outside the roof? Cam didn't think so, but it was getting dark. The unending twilight had become something deeper. Beyond the ash clouds, the sun was going down.

Cam left Kendra with Deborah to help the other men. Medrano had located the power room on the collapsed side of the building. All three of the labs' generators were buried.

Worse, most of the fuel cans had ruptured. "I can get one of these running," Medrano said, "but we'd better move it first or this place will ignite."

Cam, Alekseev, and Obruch pulled away the wreckage as Medrano tried to salvage some electrical lines, hampered by his broken arm. Then he identified which generator he wanted. By now, they could barely see. There were no stars or moon beneath the fallout. The night would be absolute.

Obruch produced a small penlight, which he ran to give to the women as Cam and Alekseev dragged the generator into an open spot of concrete. "Give me two minutes," Medrano said, splicing his new line to the classrooms.

Kendra's response was less satisfying when they hurried into the lab. "I need three hours," she told them, rummaging through endless files as Deborah said, "There's a machining atomic force microscope. It looks like it's okay. She thinks she has what she needs."

Alekseev took Cam aside. "This is madness," he said.

"No. We've come too far to quit. Either she can do it or she can't. There's no sense in running away. Where would we go? The chopper's nearly empty."

"They were keeping aircraft," Alekseev said in his odd English. "I will check the fuel."

"Where would we go?" Cam said. "Your side is gone. So is ours. But go ahead—check for fuel. We're going to need every weapon we can make if we're going to hold this place against enemy troops."

Alekseev paused. "You are speaking of something like your Alamo," he said. "Yankee Doodle do or die."

Cam almost smiled. Alekseev had his American history mixed up, but not its spirit. They were a nation created by rebels and underdogs who never did quite figure out how to manage their own success. Cam wanted to see them back on top again. "The Chinese won't expect us here," he said, "so we have surprise on our side. That should work against the first group that shows up."

"What about the next?"

"Best case scenario, we won't have to last that long."

"Do you believe her estimates? Three hours?"

"Yes. You know who she is."

"We know who she *was*," Alekseev corrected him.

"I think she's . . . motivated." Cam chose the word carefully. "She wants to make things right. Do you understand? She wants to do something good."

The generator rumbled outside and the lights sprang on, flooding the building. "Got it!" Medrano called. Kendra screamed, thrashing her arms in the sudden brilliance. Deborah grabbed her, talking fast, as the men scrambled to turn off as many switches as possible. They didn't want to be the only star in the night.

When they were done, Alekseev walked over to Cam again. "We must seal this tent," Alekseev said, indicating the black plastic. "She can work inside it."

Cam met the colonel's hard brown eyes. "So you agree," he said. "We'll stay."

"*Da.*"

Then we have about three hours to live, he thought.

Deborah protested when they asked her to stay with Kendra, but she was hurt and she had some lab experience. It only made sense. They couldn't leave Kendra alone.

Before he went, Cam kissed Deborah's cheek because he knew her better than anyone else. She caught his arm to keep him close, leaning her forehead against his with sudden intimacy. *I wish you were Ruth,* he thought. Who was she wishing for?

"Take care of yourself," Deborah said.

"You, too."

The four men spread through the ruins to dig in against the Chinese. They even hurried despite the knowledge that if they won—if any of them survived—they would be destroying themselves with Kendra's counter-vaccine.

Cam, Deborah, and Medrano must have traces of the mind plague in their systems. All of them had walked outside the warehouse where the V-22 Osprey was stored after they were inoculated, preparing for their flight, and even the slightest whisper of nanotech would be enough. With luck, Kendra would create a new plague zone, a trap for any Chinese who entered it. Cam and the others would be the first to fall, but as more and more Chinese were infected, her counter-vaccine would spread. Their plague zone would grow. It would reach U.S. territory—and from there, the world.

They could still win this war.

26

Colonel Jia Yuanjun snapped to attention and tried to convey in his bearing what could not be seen in his disheveled appearance. Dedication. Fortitude. He'd had only a few minutes' warning to comb his hair and tug uselessly at his foul uniform, trying to straighten it before greeting his visitors. His forearm throbbed in a crude plaster cast.

"Fàng sōng," said General Qin. *At ease.*

"Welcome, sir," Jia responded, also in Mandarin. He was unsure what to make of the general's expressionless face, but Qin's uniform was clean, as were those of his two subordinates and three Elite Forces bodyguards.

MSS General Qin was in his sixties, stout, sunworn, and quivering with strain. Jia saw a tic in Qin's jowls. That was bad. The old man was aware of it, too, patting at the underside of his jaw in a brusque, fussy manner. That his visit was a surprise could also be seen as dangerous. The Z-9 military helicopter that flew up from San Diego had declared itself a medevac, bringing much needed supplies to Jia's base. Instead, it carried the MSS officer who'd become third-in-command of Chinese California after the bombing.

Jia did not believe this subterfuge was intended to fool the enemy. No doubt there were still American satellites overhead, but there was no one left to control those eyes and ears. Jia was fortunate that one of his sergeants had risked a call from their landing field, announcing the real identity of their visitors as General Qin walked into the base.

Jia regretted the look of his makeshift command center even more than his own poor showing. It had been necessary to escape the ash. They'd moved everything they could salvage to a second-level barracks with its ceiling and walls intact, using the bunk beds to hold their electronics, display screens, and paper notes. The place was a madhouse. Forty men knelt or sat on the floor to access their consoles while a dozen more acted as runners, stepping over an unsecured mess of cables and power cords. The noise was staggering. So was the smell. The ash had stolen into the room with them, and everyone was bloodied and sweat-stained and sour with dehydration and fear.

Silence touched the barracks as Jia met Qin at the door. It vanished again in the busy voices, but everyone was aware of the change. The new arrivals looked as if they'd walked straight out of mainland China, unsullied and neat, and their authority was all the greater for their cleanliness. They had been protected while everyone else in California burned.

"Where are your SATCOM personnel?" Qin demanded.

"Here, sir." Jia pointed.

"These officers are now in command," Qin said as his two subordinates moved past him into the barracks, a major and a lieutenant. Each man held a briefcase. The major also carried his own laptop.

Jia felt a flash of resentment. *We've done well,* he thought.

"There is someplace we can speak undisturbed," Qin said, making his words a statement, not a question.

"Yes, sir. Let me leave instructions with—"

"My officers are in charge," Qin said.

"Yes, sir. This way, sir." Jia didn't even glance back into the room to signal the two survivors from his command team, Yi and Renshu. Instead, he walked from the barracks with the first of Qin's bodyguards close at his back. His stride was brisk. It was important to Jia that he wasn't shot within hearing of his troops, and Qin would afford him no more mercy or ceremony than he had given Dongmei.

The corridor stirred with soot and debris, open to the night at one end. Each breath tasted of failure. Then the general emerged from the barracks himself with a second bodyguard. Jia's relief was unfounded, perhaps—would they arrest him?—but he couldn't repress a sense of victory, which made him resentful again. He loathed them for making him afraid.

The door shut and left them in darkness. One of Qin's bodyguards turned on a flashlight. Above, Jia heard shouts from his engineers and the dozens of soldiers pressed into duty as laborers. They had worked all day to secure the base and would continue all night. He was proud of them.

Jia led Qin and his bodyguards past two doors, the second blocked by a hunk of concrete and rebar. Insignificant pieces of grit littered the floor, difficult to see in the ash. Qin moved elegantly in the pool of light cast from his bodyguard's hand. Nevertheless, Jia saw an opportunity to show respect.

"Watch your step, sir," he said.

The third door led to a supply room that had been locked until the wall buckled in the quakes, fracturing the door and its frame. Otherwise Jia would have forced it open. No one had recovered the keys, but the children's boxed juices and the canned goods inside had been all that kept his troops going since sunup.

Jia sidestepped into the doorway and hit the light switch, illuminating the empty concrete. Nothing was left except one garish blue wrapper with a smiling red dog on it. Jia stared at the cardboard. Would it share his tomb?

No, he realized. They weren't even looking at him.

"Sir, I don't like this," the bodyguard said, tracing his flashlight up the exterior of the doorframe.

"A few cracks in a wall are hardly the greatest risk we've seen today," Qin said. "Leave me. Guard the hall. I only require a few minutes."

What does he want?

Jia faced Qin as the older man entered the room alone. Qin hadn't even bothered to have Jia's sidearm confiscated, which spoke of his power and his toughness. Clearly he was also familiar with Jia's MSS files. Qin expected obedience. Jia would give it to him. He only wished he looked the part. He felt conscious again of the blood and filth on his uniform—

yet he also gloried in it. There had never been time to hunt up a new set of clothes. Nor was it likely that there *were* new clothes, certainly not enough for everyone, and Jia was disinterested in making himself more comfortable when his troops could not share the same improvement. His tattered uniform spoke well of his own conduct.

He'd pushed his men harder than ever. It had taken them hours to establish their new command center and reconnect with the few radar stations left in southern California. During all that time, they were helpless, their borders unmonitored and unpatrolled. The majority of their surviving planes had been returning from enemy territory, scattered across North America. A few aircraft were tucked away here and there in California, but lost their runways in the holocaust or their pilots or their ground crews.

Jia's base was among the first to come online again. Until early afternoon, in fact, he had been the senior officer in charge of the People's Liberation Army. Radio was intermittent. Landlines were gone completely. He was able to form up some infantry and several armored units in a dozen locations, but to what point? None of them could reach each other, nor would they have been any use against enemy fighters.

It was even more crucial to watch for missile launches, either China's own or another American attack. He needed to know. Yet he was unable to reconnect with their satellites.

His first useful command had been to redirect their planes into Russian territory, where the air fields were free for the taking. This decision seemed even more farsighted when he learned that a second wave of Chinese ICBMs blasted Montana and the Dakotas, destroying the last of the American silos. He'd preserved their air strength, which otherwise might have suffered further casualties in the missile strikes. Then he set patrols above California again.

There were two counter-attacks. Three F/A-18s flew out of Flagstaff and knocked down five Chinese fighters before falling themselves. A single V-22 Osprey rose out of Colorado and, using Chinese codes, pierced deep into California before it was shot down, too. There were also several American planes that ran for the East Coast or overseas. They were pursued and killed. Perhaps a few escaped.

The fight was won, but the cost had been too steep. Jia was even rightly to blame, not a scapegoat, and honor demanded that the men who'd set the war in motion take responsibility for their losses. Qin would assume command of this base—that much was obvious.

I was glad to serve, Jia thought as he drew his sidearm and presented the weapon to Qin, grip first. With the same motion, he also bowed.

"Twenty minutes ago, our nanotech labs failed to check in on schedule," Qin said, surprising him.

"Sir?"

"Perhaps their radio failed," Qin said. "Their buildings might have fallen in an aftershock. Or there may be a larger problem. We need to be sure."

There may be weaponized nanotech drifting from the site, Jia thought, completing the fear that Qin left unmentioned.

"I considered diverting my helicopter," Qin said, "but my mission here is critical and we were only seven men including our pilot. I believe you've gathered a second helicopter at this base, correct?"

"Yes, sir."

Before the plague year, the PLA had begun a major new initiative to increase their helicopter fleet. Even so, they'd lagged far behind more modern armies. Only a handful of Z-9 and Z-10 birds came with their invasion force, and they lacked enough pilots to fully take advantage of the helicopters they'd gained in the war. A functioning, crewed helicopter was priceless, but earlier today Jia had ordered one of the very few aircraft in the region to himself in hope of salvaging more electronics from other bases. They'd seen limited success, yet this decision also seemed well fated, so he risked a question.

"Are the nanotech labs nearby?"

"They're less than an hour from this base—in San Bernadino, against the mountains," Qin said.

This information had been kept from Jia. He'd only seen reports on the scientists' progress, but he understood why he'd been closer to the program than he'd guessed. There had been quarantine protocols in case of disaster. He was inside those lines. Before the missiles fell, he would have been able to reach the labs if necessary.

"We may bomb the site," Qin said. "I want you to lead a strike team to the labs first. Secure our research and our people there, too. Prove yourself again. There are some who want to strip you of your commission, but you are essential to the MSS and we always take care of our own."

Jia's pulse quickened at the inflection in Qin's words. *We.* Something had been nagging at Jia since they met, but he'd been too upset to realize it. Now the older man grazed the back of Jia's hand with his fingertips. The gesture was fleeting. Qin's hand was already gone, but there was a watchful light in his eyes, and no Chinese officer would have touched another like this in normal conversation.

Qin Cho was homosexual, too.

The realization went through Jia like clean sky breaking through the ash. *He knows my secret,* Jia thought. *He shares it!* Then, even more startlingly, *He could have me if he wanted. He owns me. And I him.*

Jia's pulse quickened. Qin was not unattractive. His authority more than compensated for his stout, older body, as did the experience in his eyes. The danger was its own forbidden thrill. Jia could barely imagine a time or a place to share the other man's bed, but the prospect was unforgettable.

He'd long worried that his superiors knew of his sexuality and were ready to use it against him. What if their plan was even more layered than he'd guessed? If his attacks failed, they could use his deviancy to condemn him—but if he succeeded, they would be certain that the lead officer was one of their own.

There are more of us in hiding! Jia thought. At least, he wanted to believe Qin wasn't the only one like him, because he could barely contain his excitement.

Did their curse supersede their other loyalties? Probably not. But it might create a phantom power bloc within the Ministry of State Security. The most hawkish elements of the MSS had risen to leadership. A few men in key positions could affect the fate of a nation, and homosexuals would be driven by the deepest motivation to succeed as well as the greater goals of China. They were also less likely to be constrained by concern for any wives or children.

What if their shame and their pride were ultimately

responsible for the aggression that led to the war? Or the development of the mind plague itself? Could they hope to use nanotech to rewire themselves and become normal hetero males someday? Was that even possible?

If Jia had been reported when he was young, that information must have been intercepted and suppressed by someone who was always looking for more recruits. Then they'd watched him. Jia couldn't evaluate how high their control might be felt. Qin had been a senior general even before the missiles fell, and he wouldn't have come into the quarantine zone himself if he were the topmost surviving member of their brotherhood.

Jia yearned for more power for himself. Recognition. Acceptance. Even if it was in secret, to be welcomed by people who shared his stigma was irresistible.

This is how he seduces me, Jia thought. They would be like lovers. Whether they literally pleasured each other or not was almost beside the point. It was the hateful truth that committed them.

"I am honored, sir," Jia said. "Thank you, sir."

"Then you understand?"

"I believe I do, sir. Yes, sir."

Qin had studied Jia's face as he worked through his realizations in a flurry, watching every perceivable shock and emotion. *He must have felt the same when they approached him,* Jia thought. How long had the cabal existed? Years? The notion made his head swim. He felt as if he'd found himself on a ladder above a vast pit. One misstep would kill him—but there was also an exhilarating sense of attachment. Some day perhaps he would be looking down at another man, helping him up, too.

Jia grinned, but the older man's face darkened as if rejecting him. Did he think the grin was flirtatious? A ploy?

Did I mean it that way? Jia wondered.

"You know there was an American flight into California four hours ago," Qin said.

"Yes, sir. We shot it down, sir."

"They were using Second Department codes. The timing seems suspicious. The detachment guarding the labs is not unsubstantial. A full platoon of Black Tigers resided with the science teams. They were also equipped with two helicopters of their own. If their radios failed, why haven't either of those helicopters come for help?"

"The American plane was destroyed, sir."

"What if there were more? Could the Americans have slipped another aircraft through your lines?"

"Yes, sir." Jia was formal now. He'd seen his mistake. His relationship with Bu Xiaowen had suffered from the same quandary, which was precisely why homosexuality was outlawed by the PLA. Favoritism was a weakness. So was forced submission and the resentment that might come with rape. If the cabal was as well entrenched as Jia hoped, they must be even stricter in demanding a hands-off policy among themselves. It was a schizophrenic but vital law, denying their very nature. Were there exceptions? Covert liaisons? There must be. But at what penalty?

"I realize you were half-blind," Qin said.

Jia nodded. Their radar net was still only at 40 percent, and, in too many places, orbital surveillance was blocked by fallout.

"We don't expect the impossible," Qin said.

"No, sir. Thank you, sir."

"But all of us will suffer if there are American Special Forces at those labs." Qin emphasized one word again. *Us.* The signal was unmistakable.

If the cabal had started the war, their destinies would be tied to the nanotech. They would live or die with it. The momentum they'd gained from the mind plague and its spin-off technologies would either further their rise to prominence, or, if the research was lost, the sudden lack of potential could leave them susceptible to new bids for power from more conventional elements in the military.

"Don't fail us," Qin said, quieting his voice. Then his fingertips brushed Jia's forearm again as he appraised the younger man.

It was an invitation. Qin could protect Jia from the leaders outside their cabal if he succeeded. Bringing back the scientists and the nanotech would help offset the failures they perceived in Jia's conduct . . . if he really knew what he was getting into.

Jia began to have second thoughts. What if Qin was playing

him? There might not be a cabal after all, only Qin. The general could be running an unsanctioned operation and using Jia for his own purposes. Jia hoped not. If an uncontrolled nano weapon had silenced the labs, he might die as soon as his helicopters flew into the area . . . but if a cabal existed, even his death would serve them by warning them to contain the nanotech by any means necessary, even nuclear, thus limiting the damage to their political strength. He would be a part of their legacy. And if there were enemy soldiers inside California, Jia would welcome a chance to punish the Americans with his own hands.

Either way, Qin owns me, he thought, stiffening into a salute. "I'll have my strike team assembled in five minutes, sir."

Cam tucked the penlight against his uniform when he heard helicopters, smothering its white beam before lifting his head from beneath a Ford pickup truck. "Choppers," he said. "Two, maybe three."

Alekseev didn't climb out from under the vehicle. "I am hearing them," he said. "Let me finish."

"We don't want to get caught in the open."

"They will go to your Saint Bernadine first. Give me the light."

Cam shut his mouth. There was no sense in agitating someone with his fingers in a block of C-4. Alekseev had wedged a fistful of plastic explosive against the Ford's driver-side rear wheel, where it would blow upward through the axle and truckbed. Cam aimed the light below the truck again, keeping his head turned the other way. Unfortunately, his night-vision was awful after watching Alekseev work.

They weren't concerned about anyone sneaking out of the rubble. The Chinese might have garrisoned other troops nearby, or maybe a few men had survived Kendra's attacks, but moving silently through the debris was impossible.

Cam was able to discern most of the ruins immediately surrounding him in the weak halo of the penlight. Within five yards, the ash-colored wreckage faded into the ash-colored gloom. It was silent, too, except for the falling whisper of the dust, which reminded Cam of snowstorms and skiing and better days. He even enjoyed his melancholy, because he knew this small peace couldn't last.

The helicopters pulsed out of the northwest, vibrating across the city. Cam felt the noise in the lumber and glass beneath his boots. Somewhere to his left, he heard the *clink* of bricks as a dune collapsed.

Cam and Alekseev had been hustling through the mayhem on the west side of the school for most of an hour, risking the penlight after Cam opened his cheek on a jutting length of wood. They'd both fallen several times, bruising their hands and knees. Medrano, alone, was on the north. Obruch had the east and southern sides where their defenses would be the weakest. Nor did they expect much chance to reinforce each other if necessary. The perimeter was too big. Cam had accompanied Alekseev less as a guard than as a student. He might need to know how to wire the plastic explosives himself.

"They're down," Cam said as the tremor of the aircraft briefly magnified, then cut off as the helicopters landed at Saint Bernadine. With the change in sound, his pulse deepened, too, finding a familiar calm. Beneath it, he felt a fresh edge of determination that was both welcome and unwanted. The waiting was over.

It won't take them long to realize no one's there, he thought. "We'd better start back. Save whatever you have left."

"*Da.* I'm done."

At each place they'd stopped, first Alekseev had shaped the off-white clay. Then he'd eased a thin cylinder into the explosives and set the tiny digital readout near its top. The cylinders were frequency-specific remote control blasting caps. The initiator was an olive drab clamshell like a small lunchbox. Most of it was nothing but battery, a blunt antenna, and shock-absorbent steel. The bottom face held a digital display and a simple twenty-three button keyboard. The first twenty were square. The next three were rectangular and read ARM, CANCEL, and FIRE. It was American gear that Alekseev's people had scavenged during the first war.

Seeing those words in Alekseev's hands was strange. Just a day ago, they would have been at each other's throats.

Now they were friends. Cam didn't like it, but he needed the other man.

As he worked, Alekseev had keyed each blasting cap to one button at frequencies between 1000 and 3000 megahertz. Medrano used 4000 to 5000, Obruch 6000 to 7000. Each of them would be able to detonate the others' charges if necessary, including Cam, who carried his own initiator. Their best hope of buying time would be to appear as if a significant force had occupied the campus. That meant bombs wherever they couldn't direct their guns. Most of those charges would be small. Alekseev hadn't brought as much C-4 as he would like—but they had other surprises.

They also hoped the Chinese would be hamstrung by the fear of damaging their labs and scientists. The Chinese probably didn't know those people were dead. Alekseev planned to fake a hostage situation. With any luck, they could string out their negotiations until Kendra infected them all.

Deborah flinched but said nothing when the helicopters' beat reverberated through the tent. Instead, she watched Kendra. Then something pattered against the black plastic sheeting above them. The debris slid down two sides of the tent, stroking it like fingers and odd faces. Was the building itself cracking in the new sound? Did Kendra even notice?

The skinny, bedraggled witch had frozen ten minutes ago. She said nothing. She did nothing. She only stared at the machining atomic force microscope. Deborah was afraid to jostle her, but how long could they just stand here?

The black tent held them like a shroud or a veil. It seemed much smaller than fifteen-by-twenty feet. The walls shone in the halogen lamps, crisscrossed with shadows from the equipment and themselves. Maybe it wouldn't have been so bad if the plastic wasn't opaque or if they had a radio or someone to talk to on the outside.

Deborah's shoulder hurt. Her face. Her chest. At least there was water. Medrano had brought two gallon jugs from the labs' kitchen before he taped the plastic shut, and Deborah used one to wash her own face and neck and Kendra's bone-tight skin, too, caring for the dull-eyed witch as if she was a young girl or a doll. It seemed to revive her. For a while, Kendra had been sharp, multitasking like a different person altogether. Their first thirty minutes together had been harried and productive as Kendra skimmed through binders and sample cases, snapping over her shoulder at Deborah as she described the Mandarin characters she sought.

They'd found early models of the vaccine. They inserted one substrate after another into the MAFM, Kendra using Deborah as her hands, talking to her, thinking with her. Deborah was impressed by her momentum. Kendra identified the fifth and eighth samples as ideal. Then she'd sketched on the notepad, solidifying her concepts. Deborah thought the drawing looked like a tadpole. It had one long-necked curl above an oval body, meant to swim and hunt, but first Kendra needed to build it and she'd grimaced when two laptops denied her, lacking the necessary passwords. At last she'd accessed the third, mumbling in Chinese with a laugh. That was the first hint something was going wrong. Her movements became stuttered, even manic. She spoke to Deborah again—in the wrong language.

Kendra had brought up twenty files and discarded fifteen more while Deborah struggled to grasp their significance, recognizing nothing. The other woman's mind simply outprocessed her own, but it was also fragmenting at that speed. "We can program the MAFM to assemble a bastardized nano from preexisting work," she'd said. "We'll save hours. But first I need to . . . What if we . . . No."

Then silence. Kendra stopped. Deborah didn't know where she'd gone. Each breath felt like pressing on eggshells. Deborah thought she could bring Kendra back with a word or a touch, but what if that was a mistake? She might disrupt whatever calculations were taking place. Above all, it was important not to frighten the ugly witch.

They couldn't rely on her, and Deborah wondered what Kendra would do when the shooting started.

27

Jia's Z-9 lifted away from the hospital as he finished his radio call. "Our people at point one were killed by enemy action," he said through heavy static, glancing at the Elite Forces on either side of him. "I say again, our people at point one were killed by enemy action, over," Jia said, inciting his men as much as confirming his report. In the faintest green light reflecting from the cockpit instruments, their eyes were beautiful, feral and bright.

The Z-9 was a small-bodied aircraft. Jia had only five soldiers in addition to the pilot and copilot, both of whom were commandos themselves. The other chopper also held eight men. Jia would have preferred an army, and he'd minimized any risk to his troops after their first pass over Saint Bernadine. The evidence had been grotesque even at a distance. Through night-vision goggles, they'd seen liquefied corpses all over the courtyard and an overturned Z-9 in the rubble nearby.

One of the dead had drawn his sidearm. That was enough for Jia. The corpses looked *melted*, and nobody fought runaway nanotech with a pistol. Qin was right. Impossibly, Qin was right. The Americans had infiltrated far into the Los Angeles basin, surprising the lab personnel. Most likely the

Americans were already gone, fleeing with invaluable data and prisoners.

Where? How?

The anger Jia felt was unseemly, directed as his own people as much as the enemy. He could have protected this place if he'd known it was within reach. The men above General Qin had no right to blame him for this loss, but they would. It made him feel ever more attracted to Qin's cabal.

Jia had ordered both helicopters down only to preserve his fuel, landing in reasonably stable depressions in the wreckage. Then he'd dispatched a three-man team to scout the enormous hospital building. He hated to linger, but they needed to clear this site first. It was the higher priority of the two.

His troops had returned in ten minutes and confirmed his first impression. There were no survivors. Inexplicably, though, there was a significant amount of gear, briefcases, and laptops stacked in the hospital's lobby. Jia turned this information over and over in his head as they droned south. Why would the Americans leave this material behind? Even if their aircraft had been unable to carry it all, why not destroy it?

"Sir, there's another helicopter in the ruins ahead of us," the pilot said, glancing back at Jia.

"Proceed to target."

They could collect their dead later, along with whatever equipment and clues remained. Jia was sure the second site had been attacked, too, but he needed to go through the motions of physically verifying it. A fool's errand. This was how his life would end, cleaning up other men's errors before they condemned him for their own mistakes. His disappointment was sickening, yet he thought, *I'll do my best. Perhaps it will be of some help to Qin if we—*

"Watch out!" the copilot cried.

Two rocket trails lanced through the night. The fiery streaks went wide and cut past Jia's helicopter as the rotors howled, the pilots reacting after the fact. The aircraft banked hard to Jia's left, but the joy he felt wasn't for escaping.

The Americans are still here! he thought.

His retinas burned. Both rockets had come from roughly the same place in the ruins. "There!" Jia yelled, pointing

past the copilot's helmet. The Z-9 had no armaments, but he
wanted to avoid more incoming fire.

"I see them," the pilot said as the copilot chattered into his
headset, "We're pulling left toward—"

A third rocket lifted from the earth directly in front of
them. It slashed across the nose of Jia's aircraft. The pilot
shoved at the collective again, rocking them downwards.
Then the night exploded.

"No!" someone yelled in the glare.

The rocket had struck the other helicopter and puffed away
from its side in a long whipping cloud of fire and smoke.

Got 'em, Cam thought. Three explosions lit the gloom
like fireworks, although two of the RPGs landed in the ruins
beyond the helicopters. Those bright pops of fire were disori-
enting because he expected them overhead. For a moment,
his head reeled, trying to make sense of the distant flashes on
the ground as a third, much closer light etched the shape of a
Chinese bird into the sky.

The third shot was Medrano's, fired from somewhere to
his right. It delivered only a glancing blow. The explosion
seemed to bounce away from the helicopter's side, but it was a
killing strike. With infinite care, Medrano had bolted vials of
the new machine plague to four of their rocket-propelled grenades. His RPG breached the aircraft. The nanotech did the
rest. The helicopter shuddered, then spun away into the rubble
below. The flames went out before it hit. Nor did it explode.
But there was a solid *wham* in the dark.

Cam grabbed for another RPG against the wedge of concrete where he'd chosen to make his stand. They were closer
to the labs than he liked, but they were afraid of being over-
flown, so they also wanted to be able to shoot *at* the campus
in case the enemy got behind them.

The home's foundation was exposed where its walls had
been blasted away, creating a small, open corner for Cam to
lay his arsenal, memorizing each weapon in line. If Alekseev
had lifted a second launcher of his own, the Russian colonel held his fire. Cam couldn't see the other man but he was

fiercely aware of him and the others, too, like echoes of himself. In combat, they were as close as brothers.

"Save your round!" Alekseev called. "Save your round!"

"I hear you!" Cam shouted. This RPG was his last, and they were shooting blind. It was probably only their first shots, like tracer rounds, that had given Medrano an opportunity to zero in on the choppers. Now the surviving bird turned north, the sound of its blades slapping at the rubble.

Cam reached into the night with his ears and his bones, using his entire being as a tuning fork. He could track the vibrations. *There,* he thought. "Eleven o'clock!" he yelled. "They're at eleven o'clock!"

He ducked into the house's foundation.

"Respond, respond!" the copilot screamed, trying to raise their comrades as Jia yelled into his own transceiver. "This is Short Dragon," he said. "We are taking fire. The Americans appear to be dug in around our—"

The city beneath them ripped apart. Jia was still looking for the other helicopter when the black ruins shattered, heaved into the air by four explosions. The fires were distorted. Each sunburst was dirty with wreckage. At least one threw the body of a car spiraling up toward him, its hood and tires leaping away. Something banged off their aircraft with a *crack* like a gunshot and the helicopter lurched.

"We're hit," the pilot said calmly.

I was selfish, Jia thought. *Uncareful.* "Can you fly?" he asked, but the answer was obvious in the accelerating clockwise spin of the helicopter.

"Our tail—" the pilot began.

"Just get us down in one piece," Jia said before shouting at his radio again. "This is Short Dragon at point two! We're hit. We're hit. The Americans appear to have dug in around the target and we're putting down on the northern—"

Two more explosions painted their glass with light. In the false dawn, Jia saw the fins of a hundred broken walls rising from the ground. Poles. Wires. Was there anywhere safe to land? Seconds later they slammed into the mess. The

helicopter bounced, then leaned to one side. "Go, go, go!" the
pilot shouted, powering down as Jia and his men leapt out in a
swift orderly line. He should have been proud of them, but he
couldn't see past his fury at his own failings.

"Split up," he said, pointing Lieutenant Wei's squad toward
his left. The two pilots and another man would form up with
him. "We'll circle to either side. Stay on your radio. Be quick.
We need to pierce their lines as quickly as possible."

First he would advise his old base. Would they send reinforcements? How could more troops reach him if there were
no more helicopters? Jia's loyalty was to China and to General
Qin, but he recognized the danger in what he must say.

Fifty percent of my strike force is dead.

If his superiors felt that he was losing this fight, they would
send Xian heavy bombers over the labs. In fact, Jia wondered
if those planes were already in the air.

Kendra looked up at the first explosions. "Go," she said.
"Help them."

"I'm here to help you," Deborah replied, floundering at the
self-possession in Kendra's face. *My God,* she thought. *Is it
possible she's been totally coherent all this time?*

"I know what to do," Kendra said. "The marker—"

There was another huge detonation outside and their tent
whispered and scratched as debris fell from the ceiling.

"I just need more time," Kendra said.

"I can help."

"You have to trust me."

But I don't, Deborah thought. "Kendra—"

"I'm okay. Look at me. I'm okay. I know what to do."

Deborah stared into the witch's liquid dark eyes. Then she
nodded and grabbed her AK-47 from the desktop, tearing
through the sealed flaps of the tent.

The rubble burned. Fires leapt and crawled through the
ruins in a dozen places, casting orange light and shadows.
Cam waited with his insides crackling in the same way. The

fighting had slowed to nothing for thirty minutes as the Chinese felt their way through the treacherous pitted landscape. Every second that passed was in his favor. Twice he heard people crunching in the dunes, but he held his fire. He was less likely to miss if they were point-blank.

Let them come to you, he thought. *Let them come.*

Suddenly two of Medrano's bombs went off a hundred yards to Cam's right. He heard the heavy stutter of an AK-47. *Medrano?* Another weapon responded. Cam tried to pinpoint either gun's location, but the fight was too far away.

A third weapon joined the second, an unfamiliar *brrp pp pp pp pp.* Were the Chinese carrying submachine guns? Bullets pinged in the rubble. The AK-47 had stopped. Then another bomb tore through one of the standing walls, hurling fire and debris. The submachine guns quit and the AK-47 yammered again, once, twice. Cam realized there were two of the assault rifles. Obruch must have gone to support Medrano. They were holding the line. Cam wanted to help—he wanted to scream and cheer—but he stayed focused on the ruins in front of him, skimming his gaze back and forth through the half-light.

Something moved to his left.

Cam raised his RPG launcher.

Then an object whispered overhead and clanked from a metal surface to his right, bouncing in the wreckage. Maybe there was another impact in front of him. *Grenade,* he thought. He ducked into his foundation again to protect the RPG with his body. If the vial of nanotech on its nose was broken . . .

Three explosions bracketed him harmlessly. Cam was untouched by the nearest bang, though the noise slapped into his ear like a pencil. *They don't know where I am,* he realized, standing again with the RPG on his shoulder.

Alekseev's response was more dangerous. He set off another block of C-4. A boxy commuter car flipped out of the wreckage. Fifty feet away, shrapnel punched into Cam's shoulder and hip. Roughly the same distance from the bomb, the torrent of fire also illuminated a man in a hollow against one of the still-standing walls. The Chinese had used the noise of their grenades to advance. Cam fired but sent his rocket high, shoved off balance by the hot metal in his side. Then the man was obscured by smoke and dust.

Cam flung himself down. Had he seen a second soldier in the dark? Either way, the instinct was correct. Bullets snapped past his position. It was as if the explosions had opened a door. Submachine guns chattered in the haze, stitching through the wreckage. Cam leaned up with his rifle and got a face full of splinters, closing one eye against the pain.

Alekseev's AK-47 roared on his left. Maybe he took some of the heat off of Cam. The submachine guns didn't stop, but most of the noise turned away from Cam. Far to his right, he heard guns at Medrano's position, too.

Cam lifted his rifle again as the firefight tapered off. Without thinking, he hesitated, too. The battle had a life of its own. Every burst of gunfire stimulated more shooting, and each pause did the same. They communicated with friend and enemy in the same way.

"Tíng huǒ!" Alekseev shouted. *"Tíng! Ràng wǒ mén tán tán!"*

There was silence.

Ash fell.

Somewhere, a burning wall peeled apart and clattered on the rubble beneath. Cam listened to the dark. Alekseev's gambit was a risk—trying to engage the Chinese with lies, offering to trade nonexistent hostages for the chance to escape—and Cam wanted to protect his ally. He stood gingerly with his rifle at his shoulder.

Someone called, *"Wǒ mén zài tīng zhe ne."*

"Wǒ mén shǒu lǐ yǒu nǐ mén de rén!" Alekseev shouted. *"Wǒ mén yào hé nǐ mén jiāo huàn tā mén qí zhōng de yī gè, rú guǒ—"*

Two grenades detonated on either side of Alekseev, one of them above his head. The Chinese must have held their weapons as the fuses burned down, only throwing the grenades at the last second.

The concussions shredded Alekseev in a twisting white hurricane. Cam screamed and fired. Another weapon chattered back at him. Bullets thunked into the wood and drywall on his left. He hit someone. There was a yell. Then a round

slammed through his forearm and spun him backward. He
lost his rifle. *Get up!* he thought.

The Chinese were breaking through.

Deborah reloaded quickly, leaning her bad shoulder
against a wall. She'd stayed at the edge of the campus instead
of wading into the ruins. It was a decision that allowed her to
support Medrano and Obruch, sniping at the muzzle flashes
on their flank while keeping the option to run toward Cam
and Alekseev or even to retreat to Kendra's lab.

It was like shooting at sparks. The enemy guns flickered,
faded, and flickered again. Hit or miss, she never saw anyone.
Her frustration helped her concentrate. Every muscle was cen-
tered on her weapon, because firing her AK-47 was agony.
Deborah barely had enough strength to control the weapon
and she probably couldn't have managed it on semi-auto.
Instead, she picked at the Chinese with single shots, jarring
her shoulder with each round.

She knew she'd better move. They would get a bead on her
if she didn't. So far, other guns had distracted them, being
much closer, but now everyone on her side was either hurt
or hiding or dead. The fighting had stopped. *How long has it
been since the chopper landed?* she thought. *Forty minutes.
Maybe less. It's not enough.*

Deborah crept forward in the orange light, torn in two
directions as her body shook with adrenaline and fear. Were
any of her people still alive?

Jia slogged through the rubble on both knees and one
hand, keeping his pistol up. He'd slung his slender-barreled
Type 85 submachine gun in order to climb. The wasteland
was peppered with sharp edges and gaps. It slid. It creaked.
He'd lost count of the bruises on his legs. His left arm ached
inside its cast.

Only Jia and the copilot were still mobile. The other soldier was dead and they'd left their pilot behind after he was
wounded in both thighs.

Jia thought they were very close. In the half-light, past the ragged shapes of the debris and a bent lamppost, he glimpsed a somewhat open field that must have been a parking lot. Several cars were strewn across it in clumps, and the flat ground was covered in soot and trash, but compared to the rest of the city, this clear space was a garden. Beyond it stood larger buildings that might have been the same size and shape before the quakes—the lab site.

The enemy was using AK-47s, not American rifles. Nor was the one man he'd glimpsed wearing a containment suit, so why weren't they sick with the mind plague? Who were they really?

Jia was out of grenades. Otherwise he would have thrown one to mask his approach. It was very quiet. Every movement was painstaking. He crept toward the lamppost through glass and tree branches and the soft cushions of a sofa, testing each bit of junk for noise. He wanted to holster his pistol— he needed both hands—but couldn't bring himself to climb without any weapon at all.

He wondered if he would hear his planes before the bombs fell. How much time was left? Jia was close enough to the site that napalm or high explosives would incinerate him, too, and yet he pressed on, caught between the need for silence and the need to hurry.

Almost there, he thought.

A running shape broke across the field, sprinting out from the buildings. Jia did not hesitate. He leaned up from the wreckage and opened fire.

The pistol barked in Cam's face—but it was not directed at him. It was pointed over his head. *Where?* Someone was racing from the campus. *Deborah?* The figure was too scrawny. Too short. Too crazy. With all the dense clarity of a nightmare, Cam knew Deborah had more sense than the charge into the open.

It was Kendra. What was she doing? He caught one hint of her expression in the fires, huge white eyes, white teeth, black cheeks streaked with sweat or tears.

The gunfire cut her down.

"No!" Cam screamed.

* * *

Jia reeled backward when an AK-47 stuttered in the ruins beneath him, surprisingly close. It chewed through the lamppost, then cut within centimeters above his head. Jia was lucky the copilot was to his left. He heard the copilot's submachine gun chatter.

The two guns dueled, exchanging bursts. In a sudden break, Jia swung himself up and fired, too, emptying his pistol.

His reward was a thrashing body in the night. The enemy soldier collapsed.

Deborah saw the new firefight break out on the perimeter— and just as quickly, she saw the rifle on her side fall silent. Was it Cam or Alekseev? Deborah scrambled to help. She left her corner.

The enemy guns swung toward her. She was spotted against the open face of the building, drawing fire from at least two Chinese.

She leapt into the parking lot, finding safety behind an overturned car. Her shoulder felt like an oven, a hot box of bone and meat. The vehicle rang with bullets. Glass and paint showered her hair, but that didn't stop her from peering through the wheelwell for her friends.

What she found was an even greater surprise. Twenty feet away, Kendra lay dying as she groped at her ruptured chest. *No.* The crazy witch seemed to be making passes at the air above herself, reaching for heaven or hell or something else only she could see.

Where did she come from!? Deborah thought.

Then: *I shouldn't have trusted her! But she said she was okay. The men needed me.* Deborah's conflict of pride and disgust was directed as much at herself as the other woman. *We knew she was unstable. Cam told me to—*

A trick of light changed everything in Deborah. As the fires licked and danced, a tiny square gleamed in Kendra's hand. A substrate. Deborah's low-level training was enough for her to recognize what had happened.

She wanted to celebrate. She needed to cry.

The stupid goddamned witch, she thought. They'd won! Kendra had built her counter-vaccine—but the nanotech needed to be absorbed by a host before it could multiply. It might not have escaped if Kendra inhaled it inside the lab. The mind plague would rob her of her senses. What if she'd become trapped in her tent or if the Chinese sealed her in the building? She needed other people for the new plague zone to expand beyond anyone's control.

Maybe the crazy witch wanted to die. On some level, she must have realized how close the enemy had come. Why hadn't she run to Deborah? Had she been looking for her in the night? The two of them could have infected each other, hiding beside the building or even here among the cars.

Kendra was trying to ingest the substrate, but she couldn't lift her hand to her mouth. Blood dripped from her elbow as she trembled with weak, useless spasms.

This is it, Deborah thought. *All we need to do is get the nanotech inside her. Or me.*

Deborah ran into the open.

Jia fired on the third American, too, grimacing in pleasure as the blond-headed soldier jerked and fell. Then his pistol was empty again. He had no more spare clips, only his submachine gun.

He began to press forward again. He stopped when he realized the American sprawled in the parking lot was still moving. A ruff of yellow hair shone in the guttering light. Jia seated his submachine gun against his shoulder. The weapon was designed for brute power, not accurate shots, but it was critical to stop the Americans from whatever they were doing. Bringing nanotech? Wiring more explosives? Nothing else made sense. They wouldn't have left their fighting holes without good reason, so he would shoot the wounded.

"Kill them!" Jia shouted to the copilot.

Deborah scrunched her eyes shut against the pain, then opened them again in a blur of tears and caustic ash. Her world had shrunk down to a few inches. She clawed at it with one good arm, dragging her body behind her, but the level asphalt seemed like a wall. It felt too steep.

Get to Kendra, she thought. *That's all. Just get to her. There are too many people counting on you.*

Each breath was a struggle. She could feel her stamina oozing away with the blood from her mangled belly. Everything below that was numb. Her nerves were cut somewhere beneath her abdomen except for a single unsteady wire tricking up from her left thigh, where the muscles cramped and bunched.

Kendra lay three feet in front of her—three feet—but it was too far for either of them. Kendra's loose fist hung motionless, propped just above her chest. Her wide eyes stared up. She was dead. Dead, but still warm. The two of them would be enough for the nanotech's gestation if only Deborah could swallow it.

You must be the last one left, she thought. *Cam, Medrano, they're all dead.*

She dragged and fought and got no closer, reaching, reaching . . . She knew she could forget. She could escape this misery if she succeeded. The counter-vaccine would erase her mind, and she yearned for whatever peace the nanotech might bring. It was her duty and her revenge. With one motion she could honor her friends and infect the Chinese, and that was enough. It had to be enough.

Just get to Kendra.

Dust leapt from the earth. At first she didn't make sense of the horizontal rain. The guns were beyond her tunnel vision. Deborah felt two or three tugs in her dead, outstretched legs, but forgot them.

Kendra.

Then a bullet crashed through Deborah's forearm, knocking it aside. The pain was like a cleaver.

She wasn't going to make it.

Jia ceased fire and rolled over the top of the dune, preparing to run for the labs. His moment was now. There were no more Americans in front of him and he didn't have the ammunition or the time to allow the fight to continue.

"Go! Go!" he yelled to the copilot.

Someone rose from the wreckage beside him, a bloody figure as dirty as the night. Jia dragged his submachine gun up. Unfortunately, the man held a firing system between them—a clamshell like a small laptop. The faint light of the fires revealed a beard and old blister rash on his dark face. He was Hispanic.

They stared at each other. Perhaps it was like looking into a mirror. Jia had never put a face on the enemy. They had always been "the Americans." Compassion was not what Jia expected to feel, and yet he'd always been attuned to other men. This soldier was no less human than his own troops. Maybe Jia was the only one who truly grasped how the warriors on both sides were alike, noble and courageous.

Jia would have spoken to the other man if they shared a language. Even so, he tried to communicate. *"Bié dòng! Tíng!"* he shouted. *Don't move! Stop!*

The copilot's feet ticked in the wreckage nearby. His presence added a second gun to Jia's. Jia thought the American might attempt to negotiate, but the man never said a word. Maybe he grinned. A feral expression split his face, yet his hatred and his spite never touched the sadness in his eyes.

He pressed his hand down on his device. The ruins convulsed. Explosions lifted in a broken ring all around the labs, at least ten blinding flashes in the night. Shrapnel crashed against the dunes, but the nearest detonations were behind Jia. He was inside their lines. The bombs threw most of the debris away from him.

It was a final diversion.

Jia shot the American even as they ducked the blasts together. Both men crouched without thinking. Only Jia stayed down. The American flailed upward as Jia's submachine gun blazed into his chest, yet he'd bought his comrades a few more heartbeats of time.

As the explosions lifted through the ash, the blond American lying in the parking lot squirmed once more, scrabbling toward the corpse nearby. Jia took aim again. Beside him, the copilot brought up his Type 85. Their guns raked the fallen Americans—but in that split second, Jia Yuanjun thought he saw both bodies in the parking lot reach for each other. The corpse's arm dropped away from its side, either rocked by the bombs or Jia's own bullets.

The two Americans touched each other.

Then the blond figure jerked one hand to her mouth.

28

Her teeth hurt. Two in front were loose. She was sure she'd crunched through an old filling, and yet she seemed unable to stop pressing her jaws together. In her sleep, the habit was even more severe. She needed some kind of nightguard if it could be fabricated. Otherwise she was going to peel those incisors right out of her head.

The Army doctors said it was PTSD. They'd seen a lot of stress and fear. Ruth believed her neural pathways were permanently altered, because her jitters weren't confined to her grinding. Her left hand tended to make a fist and squeeze like a heart. She glanced constantly to that side. The mind plague had changed her, and she'd noticed the same fidgeting in most of the survivors. The doctors wanted to pass it off as a normal traumatic reflex because a few calm words were all they had to offer. That wasn't true for Ruth. She could build something to fight it.

The worst cases were being treated with weed, alcohol, or restraints. Most people seemed okay. In fact, Ruth was impressed that less than two days had passed since she woke up. The best elements of the U.S. military were quick to regain their feet, staggering up to fight a battle that never came.

The war was over.

Sixteen hours ago, they'd landed her in Sylvan Mountain, ninety miles southwest of Grand Lake. Grand Lake had been abandoned for now, its complexes too damaged by the Chinese assault. Sylvan Mountain was mostly a surface base, a simple garrison lined with armor, artillery, and chopper pads, so it hadn't merited air attacks. The mind plague had been enough to incapacitate this place.

The fallout had also reached these mountains, but the sky was clearing, leaving only a rime of soot. Faint threads of it still curled in the wind, tightening, opening, and tightening again—like her hand.

Ruth watched the horizon, trying to ignore herself. A small part of her basked in the heat of the late yellow sun. Soon it would be dark, and she cherished the light. She also welcomed the bustle of troops around the only helicopter on this broad concrete slab. They were loading the Black Hawk with wire cut from their own fences, shouting in the cold as they wrestled the steel with pliers and gloves. None of it was enough to distract her. She could only watch and wait, pacing, twitching.

A captain with an M4 intercepted her. "You shouldn't be out here," he said. "Dr. Goldman? You shouldn't be out here."

"Beymer," she said, tugging at the white badge on her uniform. *Go ask Colonel Beymer.* The overwhelmed Navy colonel was acting CO, and he hadn't known what to do with her except to give her anything she needed, medical attention, food, rest, and a quiet space for the microscopy gear they'd recovered with her. No one had time to babysit.

The badge was supposed to give her top clearance, which suited Ruth just fine. Speaking was an effort. In addition to hurting her teeth, she'd chewed her tongue and the insides of her cheek while she was infected, possibly because she'd been tied and her body couldn't find any other way to respond to the mind plague's commands to *move*.

"This isn't a good idea," the captain said. "Not without containment suits."

Ruth didn't answer.

"I know what you're feeling," he said, "but we don't know what they might be carrying. What if there are other strains of nanotech?"

Only a few of his words rang through her anxiety. *You don't know what I'm feeling,* she thought. *I should have been there.* But the captain was right, if not the reasons he'd stated. The landing pad was a zoo whenever new birds arrived. After everything that had happened, it would be idiotic for her to be squished by a chopper or run over by their ground crews.

"I'll move out of the way," she said, enunciating slowly through her swollen mouth.

"Thank you, ma'am." The captain hesitated, trying to meet her eyes, but Ruth couldn't look at him. She couldn't look at anyone. They wanted so much from her.

She'd used that need against them. Everyone was afraid of another contagion, something else cooked up in Los Angeles, but Ruth had convinced Colonel Beymer to send a helicopter after her friends nevertheless. Kendra Freedman was the name she'd cited. *We have to find her,* she'd said, and that was true, but she was less interested in saving Freedman than in discovering if Cam and Deborah were alive.

Ruth walked across the landing pad and sat down on a supply crate, picking one fingernail through the splintered edge of the box. It was good to be out of her lab. Even her mouth hurt less outside. The tent was small and dark, and Ruth was more disturbed than ever by small and dark. The waiting was worse. Ten minutes ago, Beymer had sent a man to say that his team was inbound from L.A.

I should have been there.

The thought would always haunt her. How much differently would things have played out if she could have helped them? Would she be dead, too?

Ruth had come back to her senses in a residential home in the flood-ruined old town of Tabernash, twenty miles south of the V-22 hanger. Ingrid was with her in a locked bedroom, but Ingrid was infected and only one of Ruth's hands was partially untied. Ingrid must have seen the others fall sick before running to free Ruth. She wasn't fast enough. Ruth was still tied to the bed. Coaxing Ingrid to her had been impossible. Ruth had screamed and begged in the darkness, hungry, bleeding, and alone except for the senseless ghost of her friend. She watched Ingrid roam back and forth against the walls for hours, never finding the door, until the older woman

finally stumbled close enough for her to grab her belt. Ruth
was weak. Ingrid was clumsy. She fell on Ruth, then rolled
away, but Ruth had already dragged the pistol from Ingrid's
hip. Her wrists were bound too close together to aim the gun
at those ropes, nor did she want to shoot at her feet, but she
was able to use the weapon as a tool to pry herself free. Then
she found her way to their radio.

Earlier today, Ruth had successfully modified the first
vaccine for the mind plague to outpace the counter-vaccine,
thus creating an antidote. Reprogramming the antidote so
it wouldn't replicate except in specific conditions was more
difficult, but they wanted to keep it from spreading to the
Chinese—not until the enemy was gathered into prison
camps. Ruth had devised a governor that limited the antidote
to replicating only in high oxygen atmospheres. This was an
artificial environment within her ability to create, especially
at Sylvan Mountain's altitude, using precious medical supplies. It meant she was able to cultivate the antidote in small
doses. Then she secured it in vials of blood plasma for injection into one person at a time.

Ingrid, Emma, and General Walls were now in a private
tent, recuperating. The rest of these heroes had vanished. From
the data on Walls's laptop, they knew who else had survived,
but Bobbi Goodrich must have wandered away from their safe
house before Ruth got free. Bobbi was missing. Nor had they
been able to locate the other squad of immunized soldiers led
by Lieutenant Pritchard. Wherever the USAF commando had
gone into hiding, his men were infected, maybe starving or
hurt, and Ruth hoped someone would find them before it was
too late. As far as she was concerned, the places they'd earned
in history were paramount even to her own, because it was
these people, not her, who'd struggled on through the end.

Agent Rezac was another complication. Ruth's antidote
carried some of the same risks as the mind plague itself.
Within seconds of her injection, Rezac had stroked out. She
was dead. The same problem had crippled or killed dozens
more just here in Sylvan Mountain as they awoke from the
plague. It wasn't fair.

The first reports out of Los Angeles were even worse. The
recovery team said they'd found Deborah and Kendra dead in

a parking lot outside the Chinese labs. The women's bodies lay side by side, Kendra's arm outstretched, Deborah's hand pressed against her own face with a substrate in her mouth.

They'd done it. Even as they were overrun by Chinese troops, they'd won. From their bodies, the counter-vaccine had drifted to the enemy—and Cam.

He was alive. He was in the second stage of infection when the recovery team found him burrowing in the ruins. His body was in some indefinite form of hibernation. It had saved him. Most likely he hadn't moved more than a few inches during the first, agitated phase of the mind plague. He was nearly dead from blood loss, but they'd done their best to increase his vital signs. They were rushing him back to Sylvan Mountain for surgery. Except for two Chinese prisoners taken on site, Cam was the sole witness to what had happened in L.A. Medrano was dead, too, as were a pair of Russian soldiers in the rubble—allies of the Chinese?

Cam might know something about Kendra's design work or other labs or American survivors, but, in truth, there was no reason for Ruth to stop her own crash programs to wait for his helicopter. He'd never regained consciousness. Even if he opened his eyes, he was a zombie. Cam would have a better chance of pulling through if he was responsive, if he wouldn't fight his restraints, but his body didn't need any more immediate shocks. The doctors wouldn't inject him with the antidote until he'd improved.

Ruth had only come to the landing pad because she needed to see him one more time before they took the chance of killing him like Agent Rezac.

She hoped she was pregnant. It seemed unlikely. They'd only made love once, but she would have been ovulating, so it wasn't impossible. She wanted his child. Some part of him would carry on.

They both deserved that much, didn't they?

Ruth leapt to her feet as two F-35s soared overhead, the recovery team's escort from the West Coast. Where was the

helicopter? Long seconds passed before a black dot material-
ized out of the sunset, *whup whup whup whup*, the drumbeat
of its rotors slapping at the mountainsides.

Their mission had been delayed by the chopper's need to
refuel in Utah, California, and then in Utah again. Its flight
into L.A. had been an exacting game of leapfrog, working
with fighter escorts with far greater range and speed, but there
were no more VTOL planes available. Ruth was grateful just
to have been able to reach into California at all.

She broke her promise to stay off the pad as the Black
Hawk entered its final approach.

"Dr. Goldman, wait!" the captain yelled. He ran to intercept her but Ruth shrugged him off with her head on a swivel,
looking up, looking left, trying to anticipate where the chopper would land. She dodged a jeep loaded with wire. Then
she bumped into two mechanics taking apart an engine and
kicked through the parts spread on the ground.

"Hey!" one man shouted.

"Sorry—" The scattered metal at Ruth's feet seemed like
a bad omen and she wavered, fidgeting. She almost stooped
down to help them sort through the jumble, but medical teams
had emerged from the low buildings beside the field. Ruth
hurried to join them even as the captain grabbed her sleeve.

"Goldman, wait."

She stared at the much larger man. "Get your fucking hands
off me," she said. He hesitated. She pulled away. It wasn't his
fault—he was protecting her—but Ruth was no longer interested in being shielded from anything.

Somehow she controlled herself enough to make room for
the medics and their gurneys as a soldier jumped from the
Black Hawk. At her side, her fist clenched and unclenched.

The first man they lifted from the flight deck was unrecognizable, wrapped in blankets with his face obscured by an
air mask and bandages. The blades overhead were still wind-
ing down. Ruth pressed into the crowd. "Cam!" she yelled.
"Cam!" But the man's dumbstruck eyes were Chinese. A
prisoner.

"Where is Corporal Najarro!?" she yelled.

They were unloading someone else from the other side.
Ruth shoved her way past the Black Hawk's nose, joining

the confusion as they strung IV bags above his gurney. She needed to touch him. She felt the power in her shaking hands. The two of them were a circuit that must be closed again, even if it was only for this instant.

Cam wore an air mask like the other man. One side of his beard had been scorched down to stubble, but she recognized his hair and the muscles along his neck, even though his dark skin was gray and shiny like wax.

"Miss, you can't—" someone said.

Her hand reached Cam's shoulder as she burst into tears. Her grief was a lover's and a friend's, wretched and deep. *Stay with me,* she thought. *Be with me. We haven't had our turn yet. Please.*

There was nothing in his eyes except the slack, uncaring look of the plague, so unlike his anger or his strength. Ruth turned away even before another medic said, "Let us get him inside." She nodded. It didn't matter if they saw her head move or not. She was already retreating and the gesture was as much for herself as anyone else.

The gesture was his, tough-minded and succinct.

She would fight on with him or without him. She owed them that much, but she honestly wasn't sure how far to take the next generation of nanotech. Where did self-defense become something more? Was it possible to draw the line at healing people when she knew how easily new advances would spread to everyone in the world?

As she walked away from the helicopter, the soldiers on board were met by two jeeps and more men. If anyone recognized her, they didn't say. They were following orders, unloading carefully bagged computers, lab gear, and paperwork. Sorting through the material would be a colossal chore. Ruth wasn't looking forward to it. The job would keep her mind off of Cam, but maybe worrying about him would have been better.

I can't go back to that tent right now, she thought. *I should. I have to.* Instead, she walked onto the rutted earth beyond the chopper pads, drinking in the sky and the cold. Her body was as restless as her head.

I can't.

Ruth had considered killing everyone else on Earth. She'd

always thought her role was defensive, but what if it was time for her to launch her own attacks? She could become the planetary warlord that men like Senator Kendricks had envisioned as themselves.

Like earlier technologies, the mind plague and its vaccines were available for anyone to use. Soon enough, there might be yet another plague unless she preempted every enemy. No matter how vigilant they might be, there was no way to know who was becoming a threat. Russia. India. Japan. Brazil. Even on her own side, there would be people who insisted on developing their own weapons without her. Steve McCown was dead, killed in Grand Lake, and Meghna Katechia was missing, possibly taken by the Chinese, but there must be other survivors with at least a rudimentary knowledge of nanotech. Overseas, there would be more.

The same curiosity and ambition that made *Homo sapiens* such an appealing success was also a weakness. Their intelligence was a double-edged sword. Ruth believed the next step in their evolution must be to grow beyond their own suspicion and greed. Maybe they were already too late. The environment was in tatters. War had become a reflex. Her faith was the only thing that had grown stronger.

None of what happened needed to be in vain. All of them had done well, achieving more than anyone had a right to expect. That was also true of their opponents among the Chinese.

Ruth was feeling superstitious. She could almost grasp the pattern that had unfolded. Her premonition of losing Cam had even come true, though differently than she'd expected.

Deborah and Kendra's places in the puzzle were undeniable. Ruth only wished she knew where to find Sarah Foshtomi. In a sense, Foshtomi had saved Ruth by causing the accident that infected her. Maybe the young woman had been instrumental in helping Cam, too? Ruth hoped so. Like so many people, Foshtomi was missing, probably dead, but her life hadn't been without consequence.

Ruth would never have imagined a new mind plague if there hadn't been another war—and without the war, she wouldn't have possessed this next-generation technology.

What if that was why she was still alive?

She had failed the responsibilities that came with her education. Now she had another chance, and even greater tools at hand. Freedman's mind plague offered an intriguing possibility. Ruth did not doubt that some people would argue for doing to the Chinese exactly what had been planned for them, turning their enemies into laborers and slaves.

There was a better way. Ruth could force a lasting peace. She would need to see what sort of progress the Chinese researchers had made, but if the secondary programs they'd developed were as sophisticated as she expected, her idea was to selectively interfere with the brain functions of everyone on the planet. She could release her own mind plague, not only destroying their memories of nanotech but limiting their aggression, their hate, and their imagination. She'd do it to herself as well. Once those traits were curbed, she would have altered the human race, making a change so fundamental that no one knew why or how it had been done.

Ruth couldn't hide their true nature forever. It would persist in books and digital files, even if they were unable to comprehend certain words or concepts. The mental block would be that complete—but eventually, maybe lifetimes from now, someone would unlock the truth. They might begin to teach themselves nanotechnology again. They would experiment with the mysteries concealed in their own DNA, rediscovering the power of fear and rage. In the meantime there would be peace. They would be different, calmer and less selfish. Maybe they could learn new ways of working together. The environment itself would heal.

The paradox she felt was agonizing. Ruth was afraid to cut away a major part of human nature for the same reasons she would never commit genocide outright. She didn't want to become a monster even if her motives were for the best. What if there were side effects? If she inhibited their most basic drives, they might lose the skills they needed to persist in this fractured world. But the fighting had to end. Another war would destroy them.

Go back to your tent, she thought, glancing out across the first stars in the evening sky. *You owe so much to so many people. Go back to your tent and tell Beymer you want the Chinese records now. Tonight.*

Developing a new mind plague would take months, maybe longer, but she couldn't ignore her own urgency. The race had begun. It would be wrong for her to ignore a solution when it was within her abilities, wouldn't it?

Don't be wrong again.

Ruth walked back to her tent.

The light beyond her tiny lab was dim and green in the tent's canvas when a man called outside. "Dr. Goldman? He's awake."

Ruth glanced up from her computer with mixed feelings of joy, relief, and self-doubt. Three days had passed. It was morning. She saved her work and shut the laptop down, hiding what she doing in case Beymer sent anyone into her tent while she was gone. She thought somebody had investigated her equipment before during one of her short breaks.

She pushed through the plastic inside the tent and then a second compartment like an airlock, finding a soldier she recognized from the post-op units. "How is he?" she asked.

"Stabilized. Very weak."

"Thank you."

The soldier led her to a stunted-looking building buried partway in the earth. They went down six stairs into the concrete structure, then to the third door on the left. Ruth had developed a compulsion about numbers. She knew Cam was two more doors down, five total, not six like the stairs. It was a meaningless equation but she worried about it just the same—five, not six—as if trying to fight down her heartbeat.

The third door led to a nurse's station. The narrow space was cluttered with water jugs, a sink, and bloody laundry. Ruth washed up. The soldier gave her a cloth mask and a baggy suit to cover her uniform.

When she approached Cam's room at last, it was with the same piercing uncertainty that had affected her since her decision to improve upon the mind plague. She knew it was better for her to design such a thing than anyone else, but she was afraid of what Cam would think. Why? He would agree with her, wouldn't he?

They'd put him in semi-isolation. They said it was because

of his burns and stomach wounds, both of which carried a high risk of infection. Ruth knew the private room was really because they were still leery of unknown nanotech, even though she'd screened his blood and that of the two prisoners, finding nothing—yet she welcomed their solitude.

His skin had regained most its brown tone. That was the first thing she noticed. His face and hands were the right color again, especially dark against the white sheets. His eyes were closed. She would have left if she hadn't already visited twice before without the chance to talk.

"Cam?" She went to his bed, a thin, handstitched mattress on a low metal frame. There was no chair. "Cam? It's Ruth. Are you . . ."

"Hey." He didn't open his eyes but his hand lifted from the bed an inch or two, groping.

She seized his palm in her own. "It's me. I'm here."

"Your voice."

Ruth smiled through a sting of tears. "I'm okay." Her mouth was healing. "How do you feel?"

"Hurts."

"Yes."

They stayed together for several minutes, just listening to each other live and breathe. Elsewhere, voices sounded in the corridor. Ruth kissed his hand through her gauze mask.

"I need to tell you something," she said.

She tried to explain what she was doing with the Chinese nanotech. His instincts had always been stronger than her own, and she trusted his answer more than herself. She didn't get far. Cam opened his eyes to search her face.

"No," he said. "Don't."

"But if someone else—"

He struggled to sit up and Ruth jumped with her own sense of alarm, pressing at his shoulder to keep him down. "Cam, you'll hurt yourself."

"We'll find another way!" he said. "Don't."

"I won't. I swear it. You're right. I won't." She kissed his hand again to hide her stricken face from his uncompromising gaze.

Don't you see how I need you? she thought.

"Please, Ruth," he said, tiring. He closed his eyes again. "Don't make us fight you, too."

"No. Never."

They stayed together until he slept.

He woke briefly from a nightmare and she was glad she hadn't left. "*Shh*, Cam, I'm here. You're safe. I'm here."

"I love you," he said.

Acknowledgments

My wife Diana has been my greatest supporter. The Plague Year trilogy would not exist without her hard work and sacrifice, so I think everyone owes her a cool drink and some curly fries with a side of ranch,.yes? Our boys are also remarkably understanding of Daddy's strange hours, and I want to thank them, too. I love you, Johnny Six and Bee Ee En.

Some of the usual suspects are also to blame for helping me with this novel: Mike May, Professor of Entomology at Rutgers University; Lt. Colonel "Bear" Lihani, United States Air Force (ret.); Major Brian Woolworth, U.S. Army Special Forces; and my father, Gus Carlson, Ph.D., mechanical engineer and former division leader at the Lawrence Livermore National Laboratory. Anytime I needed to bolt an air compressor to the floor of a single-engine plane or build a clean room out of nothing more than plastic sheeting and duct tape, Dad was there, like Batman, and I appreciate it more than I can say.

I'd also like to express my gratitude to Andreas Heinrich, Ph.D., one of the sharpest minds in nanotechnology today. Andreas fielded any number of weird questions as well as inviting me to step into a lab full of authentic nanotech gear. Wow! Fortunately, he didn't let me turn anything on.

Charles H. Hanson, M.D., and Sumit Sen, M.D., also both took the time to answer morbid questions throughout the genesis of this book.

My friend and evil genius Matthew J. Harrington is responsible for the smoke detectors.

I'd also like to thank Aileen Chung Der and Nissan Jp for their assistance in researching China's culture, languages, and military. The Chinese become the bad guys in the second and third Plague novels, but this turn of events was meant with respect. The story needed a plausible enemy, and China is a major force in the world. Without its strength, I didn't have a plot, so thank you.

My agents, Donald Maass and Cameron McClure, continue to be top-notch. Thank you also to J. L. Stermer, Amy Boggs, and everyone else in the office. I appreciate their hard work as well as the contributions of my team at Ace. Anne Sowards, Cam "The Other Cam" Dufty, and Ginjer Buchanan have all been fantastic, as have Eric Williams and Judith Lagerman, the bright duo behind the cover art for these novels. Meghan Mahler takes credit for the eye-catching maps.

Also a gigantic thanks to Jeremy Tolbert of www.jeremiah tolbert.com for my flashy new Web site at www.jverse.com. Come on by! Jverse offers free fiction, videos, contests, advance news on upcoming projects, and more.

Finally, I'd like to thank Ruth, Cam, and the rest of the gang. They may exist only in my brain, but I really, really enjoyed my time with them. I hope you have, too.